IC3

IC3

*The Penguin Book of
New Black Writing
in Britain*

EDITED BY COURTTIA NEWLAND
AND KADIJA SESAY

HAMISH HAMILTON · LONDON

PR1110·B5I2I   2000t

HAMISH HAMILTON

Published by the Penguin Group
Penguin Books Ltd, 27 Wrights Lane, London w8 5tz, England
Penguin Putnam Inc., 375 Hudson Street, New York, New York 10014, USA
Penguin Books Australia Ltd, Ringwood, Victoria, Australia
Penguin Books Canada Ltd, 10 Alcorn Avenue, Toronto, Ontario, Canada m4v 3b2
Penguin Books (NZ) Ltd, Private Bag 102902, NSMC, Auckland, New Zealand

Penguin Books Ltd, Registered Offices: Harmondsworth, Middlesex, England

First published 2000
2

Filmset in 11/14.75 pt Monotype Dante
Typeset by Rowland Phototypesetting Ltd, Bury St Edmunds, Suffolk
Printed in Great Britain by Clays Ltd, St Ives plc

A CIP catalogue record for this book is available from the British Library

ISBN 0-241-14047-1

Contents

Essays

Stories

Memoirs

CRUSADERS

Poetry

Essays

Stories

Memoirs

COURTTIA NEWLAND

Introduction

It's with a great deal of pleasure and excitement that I write these words. Five years ago, when I began my career as an author, I never envisaged that I would be penning an intro such as this. Six years ago, I wouldn't have believed I could be involved in anything remotely publishable, so I hope you can guess how seriously I take this anthology.

I believe, collectively, that we have put together an amazing amalgamation of all the talents Black British writing has to offer. This was achieved with no regard to the writers' politics, gender, age, or even class – we merely accepted the best each individual had to offer. I found the job of editor time-consuming yet enjoyable, and working on this anthology has only strengthened my belief that, as writers of African descent, we are on the rise. Many of us are moving forwards as a unit, forming a bond as close as the 400-odd pages of this book. People who know me also know that I believe Black writing has been stifled in many ways; but creativity can't be stemmed or halted, even by ourselves.

It only remains for me to answer the question that I'm asked most; why did we call the book *IC3*? To answer that, I'll refer to an e-mail I sent to one of our authors who asked the very same thing. I must take full responsibility for the title. This is more or less my exact reply:

I was searching for a name that defined Black British people as a whole. Lo and behold, there was nothing. I was born here. I've been to the Caribbean once – so I in no way consider myself Afro-Caribbean, or any of the other titles thrown our way. This is what the new generation of kids born here feel, too. Hear us, listen to us, take these things on board.

The fact that IC3, the police identity code for Black, is the only collective term that relates to our situation here as residents ('Black British' is political and refers to Africans, Asians, West Indians, Americans and sometimes even Chinese) is a sad fact of life I could not ignore. The fact that most Black people didn't know it even existed made me more determined to have it out in the open. Street cred wasn't even an option,

I don't care about it, I care about positive dialogue amongst all members of the African diaspora, in this great age of information technology. How about us creating a name for ourselves, describing ourselves? After some talk, including all members of our community, I hope we need never use the term IC3 again . . .

So there you have it. I hope that my intentions are plain to see. I must thank Kadija for her tireless attention, Simon Prosser for offering me this opportunity, Lesley Shaw for her enthusiasm, and all the writers published here or elsewhere who took part in this venture. Let's hope the next century brings even bigger and brighter rewards!

KADIJA SESAY

Introduction

'There can never be too many anthologies detailing our experience – to really give our overview of this presence in Britain,' Jessica Huntley, publisher of Britain's oldest Black press, Bogle L'Ouverture, said to me during October's Black History Month in 1999.

This became apparent as we were compiling *IC3*. Considering the number of writers, the range of themes and experiences covered here, she was right. There was still so much writing and so many writers we could have included, but we are staunch in the belief that with the calibre of writers in this anthology, we have taken concrete steps in recording some of the vast and varied expanse of our history.

Since the demise of the Caribbean Artist Movement in the early seventies there has been no umbrella organization as effective in bringing Black artists – many of them writers – together to support each other. Some of these 'post-colonial' writers who were part of that movement are represented here. They and others who began writing at that time used MAAS (Minority Arts Advisory Service) as a vehicle to write. *Artrage*, MAAS's publication, was the arena in which they met, then they moved on from press and broadcast journalism into literature and academia, using the languages of patois and 'the Queen's English'. The MAAS days of the eighties was also a time when the exponents of dub poetry and other vibrant forms of performance poetry came to the fore, the time when performance poetry really was 'the new rock 'n' roll' and when several poets achieved international status. In the nineties, first- and second-time novelists emerged, forming the 'new wave' of 'Black British' writers. At the start of this new century, we have also welcomed writers currently unheard of, and young writers who are starting out as journalists, writing for national and international publications, making a name for themselves with writing that is not specifically 'Black writing'. They are making their presence known, using the hybridity of the 'English' language, that is, moving off the streets and into dictionaries. *IC3* has effectively brought all of these strands together.

As we were working on this anthology, certain points gradually emerged. Many of the writers overlap under the sections of settlers, explorers and crusaders since these are a reflection of style and content, not just age. From the vast array of cultural backgrounds of people of African descent living in England came the different ways we define ourselves; some see themselves as African, others as Caribbean, Black British, and even solely British; some people see the coming to England *en masse* as immigration, others as migration. Priorities as regards cultural identity and lifestyle change subtly yet distinctly as we move through the generations. Despite the torments and trials that our ancestors went through in reaching the point we are at today, racism continues to be rife, in overt and covert forms, in Britain, amongst individuals and institutions. But that fight goes on – and what this landmark anthology says most of all is that this continued hope is evident in the advances that Black people in England have made and the positive impact we have made on British society, daring and challenging it just as much as our own, by whoever and however we choose to do so.

We are pleased that so many writers of varied experiences and ages (from sixteen to sixty) are here under one title: young and new writers can read and pay respect to established forerunners. Equally, we are confident that the established writers will see the progress that new writers are making and be proud in the knowledge that there are wonderful writers following in their footsteps, and that it is due to their advances that they are able to make their own footprints with surety.

But in saying this, the aim of this anthology has not been to proclaim our 'tigritude'* – our Blackness – or even our 'Black Britishness'; it is not necessary – it's in everything we do and however we choose to live.

'Every human being is artistic and creative by nature. Creativity is a universal human gift and not a distinction confined to any specific group of people or individuals.' *Nawal El Saadawi*

Thanks to the people who helped us to put this together; Dr Ato Quayson for his critical third eye, Susan Yearwood and Emilie Cosna for chasing writers and typing up their work, and Larry Mallory who gave us some vital space in the summer to work in. To the contributors, young and old, new and known, for making this work the landmark that it is and, most of all, to Courttia, who asked me to add to this slice of history by working with him on this project.

* Wole Soyinka's argument against the Nègritude movement was that 'The tiger does not boast of his tigritude.'

SETTLERS

Poetry

suandi

Soho Lunch

I want to squander afternoons in low-slung armchairs next to the fullness of a smile that begins in your eyes suspended between roof-tops and the second floor looking down on traffic moving in sequence to tourists lovers so it is hard to believe that this is London the blaze of the afternoon penetrates the gloomy décor of this surprising retreat that places me within the reach of your hand and I marvel at how the stroke of your fingers on mine reminds me so vividly of love how sad that days end long before they are over afternoon meets evening like rush hour desperate to get home and long nights seem a childhood memory as the hour for demons waking signals its approach to be able to stay on through dawn needs more than this space can allow us so too early for me we rise to walk out into the still day of living and a moment's regret for not being still sixteen which would have allowed me to be swept in a passionate embrace tittering on kerbside indifferent to lumbering passers-by thinking their tutting disapproval to be the stereo level of our lips kiss kiss but we are too cool for that too sophisticated too old to risk much more than the brush lip on lip kiss of farewell did I tell you I missed you miss you will miss you did I see sadness in your final wave goodbye?

FAUSTIN CHARLES

The Boy Who Draws Buildings

(For Stephen Wiltshire)

He dawned upon us
Pencilled into a child's drawing
Of the morning.
His fingers flashed through rooms
With smiling balconies to the sky.
His head danced in decorations
Of a divine light
Fused with the fury of a lover's cry.
Marble marking horizontal
Suspending granite with all his might.
From pillar to post, his pen passions
Palaces towering immortal.
Through steel eyes, windowing stone mansions,
He ignites curves of concrete
Boldly beating blazing gold!
And tender in a baby's soft smile
He rises to the summit in style.
His laugh sparkles the sun,
Firing infinite, but having fun.
The flames framed by the bluest beyond
Surround secrets burning into one.
Iron-willed winging, steps flight to heaven
Shrining his art,
Stephen scaling heights
Unknown and unborn,
Anxious to re-make the world
In the landscape of his heart.

DAVID DABYDEEN

Carnival Boy

not the still sad music of humanity
but a sound – rubber pun
steel, baton beating time to a lynched
nigger head – a sound that bangs out

child – glee

at what death is and what survives
now-now, never mind all that minstrelsy
and white abstraction:
intimations of immortality –
what survives is a sturdy unkillable boy
with a peasant's hard unblinking face
who grazes his sticks in meadows of steel

and plays the rhymes of what you have done
to others, what you will do to him
and he murmurs beforehand
but he knows too that when he shudders
the sticks will move his wrists
to eden fields, to his mother's hymns
which no man can stop when she is in full
brawling flow with Jesu each church
morning – cause Jesu set we freeee
from sTavery
and we go sing clap hands and shake
we glad behinds, for no wand can con-
duct nor whip philosophize we

so he plays to his own blasted
rhythms, relishing his own survival:
the child is father of the pan
fingers that barely scoop from bowl to mouth
will reach for the spiced sticks
to wrench the city's belly
so all along the tinsel tumble-
down streets of George Town or Spanish Town, hungry
people stepping out of line, hungry
people mashing and masking, hungry
people quilling their teeth.

AMRYL JOHNSON

Fear of Knowledge

Knowing as I do the complexity
out of which your passion was forged
I can see how your body became
the temple where every candle was
lit to an altar of fulfilment
positioned with infinite care
Like slow bleeps on the horizon we moved along parallel lines
You were always one move ahead
Why was it so difficult to take
your hand?
Instead of tracing
the outline of your body I
merely brushed the tip
of your fingers
I am by nature guarded,
suspicious of being the victim
reluctant to be led
preferring always to be in control
I could have offered you little gestures
doled out from the bank
of meagre resources
rattling my senses for inspiration
as to the next move
Blind with inexperience
it would have meant manoeuvring in the dark,
sensitive
to every feathery stirring whim
guided only by an instant dulled
through discipline and convention
The chances of burning soles of callous
feet with clumsy steps became a real one

but in the long run
in the final analysis
was it the unknown step
the experience which never
appealed
or simply
the fear of knowledge?

VALERIE BLOOM

Refuelling

Brixton calls with the voice of the Islands,
and I must answer.
Every month must brave the jostling crowds
of Victoria station,
become a subterranean traveller,
for bunches of callaloo, fat yellow yams,
and sugar cane, sold here by the pound.

Yesterday I bought some locusts,
stinking-toe in their shells of flint,
paid two pounds for some childhood memories.

Travelling home on the train,
I fancied my children,
eyes wide with pleasure,
living out my past.
Anticipation brought the ague
to my limbs.

Sparks flew as the cutlass clinked
on the copper shells like chain-gang picks
on prison rocks.
It needed several strokes,
but then the hard shell yielded,
parted to display
the gold dust that I knew so well.
And then the smell!

At the garden centre once,
I chanced across a plant whose leaves
gave off just such an odour.

I let the name cascade across my tongue.
Prostanthera. Prostanthera.
Each day, fingered the leaves to
liberate the aroma.
It died.
I bought another.
It too gave up the ghost.

But now I had the source
of that smell in my hand.
Taste buds would be tantalized some more
before they could be satisfied.

I proffered the powdered seeds,
offered them in their shells
like oysters.

Expectant, searched the faces as I
recalled the legend of the locust.
It's said that John the Baptist lived on these.

Disbelief warred with disgust,
then both succumbed to absolute dismay.
That I, their mother, could ask them to eat that!

And through their eyes I watched the golden powder
dull to dry sawdust.
I dug an index finger into the shell,
determined still to reincarnate the child
who once picked locusts from my uncle's tree.

My son was brave. The taste, he said was bearable,
but could not compensate.
The youngest ventured out her tongue,
now she could see her brother was not dead.

She choked, spluttered and pronounced it vile.
She must be mad, I thought.
The first taste was as I remembered,
honey dust.

The cries of horror I ignored,
but noticed as I ate, the flavour changing,
until it was wood-shavings in my mouth.

In spite of water, soap and brush,
it was some days before my hands
stopped reeking.
Long enough for me to realize,
Time is a bridge that leads in one direction.
We should not try to cross it twice.

JOHN LYONS

Passage Home

As me name is Mabel, I know wen dat black bird fly in me kitchen, I had
to ban meh belly. I so full-up wid meh daughter, Florette, is like a
pregnancy in me head. Den de letters begin to come from dat cole place.
Englan no mudder at all; not a country; milk dry up in she tut-tuts.
Englan is Florette cross to bear. Four letters in one week. She didn' write
home bout missin de cool foreday mornin in de Lavantie hills. She didn'
write home bout missin de eart smell after midday dongpour. She didn'
write home bout longing fuh roti an curry-goat. No she write home bout
how people looks could kill she.

I could feel de sufferin
De way she 'l's crooked,
Not correct on de line
Like in children copy book.
She need meh!
She need meh!
Come hell or high water
I go have to go to Englan.

The Atlantic flexes
Its sinews of water
Dark with an unbearable history.
Mabel's gut heaves:
A sensation more than nau-
Sea. She sees grey shadows
Braving the turbulence
In the ship's wake,
Waiting waiting;
Then the dumping
Of spoilt goods;
A frenzied feasting:

Flesh roukou red
Against glistening ebony.
Screams skim the waters.

Silence.

The Ocean digests.
The Ocean conceals.

Where are the tomes
Weighted
With the agony
Of this history?

But how Florette tin so! Is dis meh one-an-only gurlchile lookin as if she
have marasma? Is dis de gurl who dem jamet limin on street corners use
to call bam-se-lambe? Wey it gorn, de sparkle in she yeye? Eh-eh, ah
never woulda believe dis if ah didn' see it wid meh own two yeye. If she
farda come back now from de grave he gosay, 'didn' ah tell yuh time an
time again, who doh hear go feel. Yuh cahn say ah didn' warn yuh. De
only place fuh a gurlchile is home, lookin after she mudder an farda, not
gallivantin to some place behine God back.'

Doh worry, meh gurl,
Yuh mudder here now,
Yuh mudder here now.

Under voices
Without sun-polish
Piles of eddoes, yams,
Ocroes, earth-textured echoes
Of Port-of-Spain market.
They are tired, tired ground provisions.
They too crossed the Atlantic.

She couldn't find
Soft candle and bay rum
To mix with nutmeg
For Florette's ague;
No zebapique;
No zebafam,
For her menstrual pains;
No soursop bush for flu,
Nor shandilay for fever;

Crapaud is no dark angel
Hopping into drawing room;
Black bird in England
Is no jumbie bird;
They have no secrets to tell.
Mabel has no signs to read.

Am here nine months now,
Florette, meh gurl
Ah have a tie-up kerchief,
In meh bloomers
Wid we passage back home
There is a house waitin fuh yuh
In Sangre Grande.
We cahn stay here;
We cahn stay here.
Lehwe go, chile;
Lehwe go back to Trinidad.

MERLE COLLINS

Tottenham

I walked, one day, into a London place called Tottenham
Tottenham Court Road? the operator once asked
But Tottenham ain't no court, no fenky-fenky road

Avenues, they say, greens, they call them, roads naming
dreams like The Avenue, Broadwater, Lordship, Bruce Grove
Groves that shape a story bigger than the Tottenham space

Dem dere names hinting at past division, present boundary
Dongola, Drayton, Dunloe, Dowsett, Downhills Park
Tottenham ain't just some court, not some fenky-fenky road

Scales, Springfield, Sherringham, Seymour, Station
In that Tottenham mix people claim again a little
sugar-cane, some cocoa juice, some rum. On Tottenham streets

not many faces wonder why you are. They say that
in Tottenham, nineteen-fifties, British butchers gave away
fish head, but then they came to know of broth, of fish

tea. And nowadays Caribbean vendors importing
St Vincent jacks, they tell me. And one day, in that same
Tottenham, I find a mango labelled Grenada.

Yes, oui, sudden so, I sail out and discover this place called
Tottenham. A space a bit like New York's Brooklyn but not quite
And that is another story of islands and of continents

In Tottenham, just the way the tongue taking a word and
lingering long to love it, swing with it and caress it, announcing
Vincentian, Grenadian, Jamaican, Trinidadian, Caribbean

born in Britain. Sit down in the High Road barber-shop
not far from Bruce Grove, tongue curving and cutting a
cadence with a word announcing Dominica, St Lucia, Côte d'Ivoire

names that suggest a story bigger than the Tottenham space
Hear the teteh music of the tongue telling about Ghana
Check that pambere swing to words that speaks of Zimbabwe

And nowadays, you hear the sound of Bosnia
The mix changing again on the green and in the grove

One day, I walk without even knowing into this place called Tottenham
No court, no fenky-fenky road, but a history of islands, continents
Today when people ask, you like England? I cyaan answer quick

Which England? Tottenham Court Road? Tottenham?
The time someone refused to answer when I asked the way?
Or the time some somebody held my hand to lead me?

Cold rainy days or the once-in-a-blue-moon sunshine times?
If I like England? Well, let's take this thing one rainy day at a time
I will just begin by telling you how, one day,

I walked into this London placed called Tottenham

VÉRONIQUE TADJO

The Nature of Things

Every day drags its feet
Time stops
I am suffocating
In a whirlpool of solitude
Tomorrow seems like yesterday
Like nothing
Will be new again
Like I have done it before

The city does not care
Where I am going is far
I hear your voice
In the distance
Sounding like a memory
Knocking at my heart

It is late . . .
Is it time to get up?
I would like the hours
To run like water
High and fast
As the Niagara Falls
Cool and refreshing
As mountain dew
I would like my fingers
To dance on your skin
To the rhythm of your heart

My brother, my friend
I understand no more
The nature of things
And I feel I am at the junction
Of many truths

Long-awaited rains
Fall with a vengeance
And the drenched earth
Loses its taste
Overpowering floods
Disfigure the city

But was it you who said
I must weave days to conquer time?

I shall reduce the map
Of the world
And travel on secondary roads
Comfort my heart
With the knowledge of your love

My brother, my friend
We will meet again
At the frontier of the world
And together
Stone after stone
We will rebuild
The hope
Of our childhood laughter

FOWOKAN GEORGE KELLY

Pay Homage

The spirit of destiny who bore witness to creation,
Came and walked among those whose ancestors
Inhabited the Land of the Gods
In pre-dynastic times.
Beneath the garb of civilization
He wore amulets and charms charged with primal energy.
Bluish-green phosphorescence pulsated beneath his matted hair
As he spoke a mythical language in a garbled tongue.

He had journeyed from the axis of space and time
To bring word to those who had lost knowledge of their ancient ways
Yet were unable to unravel the mysteries of the new,
For foolishly they continue to believe that
'The wolf and the lamb shall feed together,
The lion shall eat straw like the bullock
And dust shall be the serpent's meat.'

He who had journeyed from the place
Where myth mingled with reality,
Spoke to them of their forgotten destiny.
He said that mankind was like a circle
And that Africans had lost knowledge of their centre,
For they no longer know
Where they come from,
Who they are,
Or where they are going.

He said their ancestors were guardians of
A deep knowledge that affirms and aligns
Man's affinity with Mother Earth.
They strove for the perpetuity of the world into eternity,

And the alignment of inner self with the spirit of higher self.
They paid homage to the divine messenger of transformation
Who sits at the crossroads,
And from the hills of creation
Touches the earth with the divine sword of retribution.

He who wore the white cloth of purity said,
You who are the descendants of the first among the initiates
Must respect the mysteries of your ancient land,
And seek reparation for the evils done to those sacrificed
At the altars of alien gods.
He said, you must evoke their memory
For their dying illuminates life, and gives grace.

She who is the spirit of the wind that cannot be seen
Entreats you to take heed of the society of the wise,
For they caution you to be ever watchful of those among you
Who erect altars to alien deities and say
'The written word is the word of the only true god
Who gave man dominion over all things.'
Respect their beliefs but never bow down to it,
For one man's icon is another man's idol,
One man's religion another man's superstition.

He who is the essence of the thunder and lightning
Exhorts you to pay homage to that which extracts
Goodness from the realm of the invisible.
Respect the spirit of health, wealth and good fortune,
For the earth is your feeding ground
Taste in its stores the alimental nature of its spirit,
And know that it is sacred.

Pay homage to the king who does not die
For he is the essence of the knife that clears the path.
He counsels you to be wary of those who say
The god is dead, and all that remains is man's will to power.

For given time there is nothing
That cannot be remade in man's own image.
Understand that science is their religion,
And from its chaotic intelligence flow destructive
Impulses that tempt, and corrupt mankind.

She who is the essence of love, beauty and fecundity,
Implores you to pay homage to the spirit of the seasons,
And know that hatred of that which is created in your own image
Has become your blight.
You must endure the agony of the rites
That will make you whole once more.
She said Africans should never accept their designated
Place in other people's hierarchy,
But must become masters of the totality of their achievements.
For what is two thousand years in the course of your journey
From the Mountains of the Moon,
Down the Blue and White Nile,
To Punt, Kemet and beyond?

For shrouded are the mysteries of Africa
In the course of our diasporan sojourn.
But understand that
This world consists of those who are and those who are not,
And that in time empires all decay,
Like the oak-hulled ships that took us away.

JEAN BUFFONG

My Body, the Landscape

They say my body is marked by time
I say it is the landscape of my people.
Come closer and you will meet
Marcus Garvey on his pilgrimage to Africa.

They say my face is marked by time
I know it is the history of my people
For I stood with Nanny of the Maroons
On the hills of Jamaica
Daring the enemies to 'come'.

Look deeper as I joined Harriet Tubman
The Moses of her people
Ducking and diving around
The Underground Railway
Setting her people free.

They say my face is lined with time
I know it is the voices of my people
For I hear Sojourner Truth
Preaching for our lives
Reminding the 'ismists' that 'she is a woman'.

Yes, my body is the landscape of my people
For I have walked the long road to freedom
From prisoner to president with Nelson Mandela.

I too have a dream
The dream of Martin Luther King.
For while we walk
While we preach
While we duck and dive
And while we dream
We join Bob Marley
As we sing
REDEMPTION SONG.

P. VINCENT MAGOMBE

'Caged . . .'

In many African countries writers and journalists are persecuted by the state
for merely exercising their right to free expression. Quite often, the rulers fear
the writers' PEN and WORD . . . for their great potential to raise the people's
consciousness . . . for their power to transform society's attitudes and minds!
In 1995 Nigerian author Ken Saro-Wiwa was executed by the military for
exactly this reason. The poem is in his honour.

Up and down . . .
I walked in my cage –
Listening to the slowing beat of my heart!
The guards outside had ears . . .
Yet, they couldn't hear –
The clinking sounds of rusting chains!
Chains –
On my neck . . .
Chains –
On my legs . . .
Chains –
On my hands . . .
Chains –
Of death!
Chains . . .
Hooked on me –
For their Master's joy!
Chains –
To humble me –
And make me a human toy!
The guards outside had ears . . .
Yet, they couldn't hear –
The clinking sounds of rusting chains!

I hoped they could, at least –
Smell Something . . .
In the dampness –
Of their stinking mess –
There was –
The Smell of Indifference –
Of those –
Who wouldn't dare to care!

Indifference

[for those who inhabit the Shadows]

They Called Out –
We Couldn't Hear
They Touched Us –
We Couldn't Feel
They Cried –
We Couldn't Care
They Starved –
We Couldn't Feed
They Begged –
We Couldn't Share
They Sung Songs –
We Couldn't Listen
So They Rioted –
We Couldn't Fear
And When They Died –
We Didn't Mourn!
O, O-o-o-h.
What Kind of People are We?

JANE GRELL

Voices on the Wind

There was once a ship, a great big hulking thing
Which dropped anchor
And heaved its massive frame across the Caribbean sea
Carrying a cargo full of dreams to the distant motherland

Passengers and loved ones on the shore
Locked eyes in one last lingering embrace
And as they waved farewell, wistful voices wafted far into the night
Long after the ship had gone

Doudou a' mwem il ka patir
Hélas, hélas, c'est pour toujours
My sweet heart is leaving
Alas, alas, it's forever

For two long weeks the Windrush sailed
Laughter and bravado slowly turning to silence
As the atmosphere chills
And with heavy hearts they land

Well, they endured the cold
Learned to see through the thickest fog
When insults rained, 'blackie,' 'wog,' 'nigger go home!'
Meekly turned the other cheek and grateful for small mercies
They did the menial jobs with fortitude and little pay
For after all, five years and they should have scraped enough
For the journey home

But the years rolled on, children were born and grew
Many restless and resentful
Never quite at home in this, their birthplace, and not understanding
    why
Seeking, searching for their deeper selves and a fairer deal

The years roll on
The passengers of Empire Windrush, now resigned to their new home
Settle down to live their lives
Ever watchful, praying for their children

Then one fateful night at a bus stop in South London
A lone young voice
Too heavy to be carried on the wind
Sank to its knees and, at the altar of Racism, expired

Ever since, a nation united in grief and outrage
Forms a ring around the father as he scoops up the fragments of his
    son
And links arms around the mother as she tries to reconstruct his voice
Hovering over that spot beyond the Thames where a dirge still lingers:

Doudou a' mwem il ka patir
Hélas, hélas, c'est pour toujours

As the collective voice murmurs:

My sweetheart's gone away
Alas, alas, gone forever

The river acquiesces, whispers knowingly
And gushes gallons of tears for Stephen
Weeping yet for the unborn great-grandchildren of Windrush.

Essays

LINDA BELLOS

Age

Late in 1987, I stood before a gathering of people who had invited me to
address them. It was not the first time that I had been invited to speak
to a community group, and I have in the years since spoken to many more.
But what was so memorable about this meeting was that I was faced
with a group of elderly African and Caribbean people, and it was the first
time I had noticed what had previously been missing from my life.

I was born in London in 1950; at that time, though I was not to realize
it for years, I was one of a small number of Black people living in Britain
and one of an even smaller number of Black people to have been born
in Britain. The significance of being in such a small minority does not,
of course, occur to a small child. It is only in later age that one acquires
the perspective of distance to be able to look at the true significance of
events in one's own life. With a shock I realized that my own parents,
plus those of my friends and peers, were by necessity young(ish). At the
time they seemed old, but most of them would have been in their twenties
or thirties when we were born.

When my dad came to England from Nigeria in 1942, his own parents
were dead; even had they been alive, it is doubtful they would have been
allowed to follow him to Liverpool at the height of the war, or afterwards.
When he moved to London in the late 1940s and married my mother,
he socialized with other Nigerian men. Many like him had married
European women and, naturally, they were all of a similar age. As a
consequence I did not come across Black people with grey hair, neither
did I have the opportunity to learn from the experience and maturity of
African elders.

When I finally became aware of what I had missed, it occurred to me
how much this absence symbolized the problematics of racism. In the
mid-1980s, when the campaign for racial equality was most prominent (and
in my view most successful), there were many in both the Conservative and
Labour parties who argued that racism would disappear if we (Black
activists) would stop drawing attention to it; indeed, they positively urged

us to adopt a colour-blind approach. But my revelation had demonstrated to me the weakness of colour-blindness. White people had, and needed, older people. It would be impossible to imagine the British without any grandparents, picture the House of Commons or House of Lords without those over sixty. It is, of course, not merely a matter of how older people look, it is the continuity and experience that they represent which is significant. And yet for the communities from the Caribbean and Africa, we had to establish home and families and, ultimately, communities without elders. The immigration rules meant that only the economically active were accepted, our older 'dependants' were often not. This was the period when we came here in significant numbers, in the 1950s and 1960s. We did so, or at least our parents did, without many of the social support systems which are now rightly considered essential to survival.

And yet, survive they did. In the face of subtle and unsubtle racial discrimination, in a country where it was near impossible to find decent accommodation, or fair wages and working conditions. A generation, my father included, set up shops, churches and sometimes schools, which began to address our cultural needs. In other words, in addition to moving to a new, cold and sometimes hostile environment, our parents met their own cultural needs and those of their children (to some extent) without the support or help of their parents. Indeed, it did not occur to me until recently that they were of course also sending money 'back home', because the legacy of British rule did not run to pensions.

I am myself now in middle-age, so I am naturally sensitive to issues of old age in a way I was not when younger. Maybe it is that I have recently attended a number of funerals or memorials of elderly Black African people. Lord Pitt's memorial service in Westminster Cathedral saw us celebrating the long life of a man who achieved respect and admiration in his lifetime. This was in contrast to the funerals of young people who had died at the hands of the police or street racists. There is, to my mind, something rather good about attending the funerals of old people who lived long, fruitful and varied lives. It offers an opportunity not only to celebrate that particular life but also to gain a tangible sense of our having a history. Grey hair in some ways represents the notion of history as well as age and experience.

One of the things which for me has underpinned racism, and which was most evident during the Windrush Celebration in 1998, is that we are seen as a people without history, just as Africa was seen as a continent without history. Windrush was presented as the point at which we arrived in Britain, having apparently had no history prior to 1948. Grey hair speaks to me of generations, and generations speak to me of ancestors or wisdom – in other words, of history.

My own father, like others of his generation, did not expect to die here. He came to better himself, and he came to serve the motherland at a time of war. Things did not turn out as he would have hoped and expected. He did not, for example, end up a rich man, able to support his family and friends back home. So, in disappointment and shame, he stayed in England; now it looks like he will die here.

While I celebrate those of our elders who are returning, buying or building that long-dreamed-of home, there is also a recognition that the majority of our elders are staying here. This means that there will be Grey Heads for our young people to see and to learn from, a real sense of continuity and history. The other important side of this reality for me is that the services that our parents paid for and worked in now need to be changed to incorporate their particular needs. What I mean here is that our elderly may need 'meals on wheels', and other care, which is sensitive to their needs. In the mid-1980s, when councils such as Lambeth began to provide 'multicultural' meals on wheels, they were attacked as the 'Loony Left'. These days, not even the *Daily Mail* would think it acceptable for Social Services departments to leave elderly Caribbean, African and Asian people hungry, offering only traditional British food.

My own father is the only African man in the nursing home he now lives in. The reason I chose that home was that others had a few Black residents but not as many African staff. As his Alzheimer's has progressed, he has lost control over whether he speaks English or Yoruba, so there being staff who can talk to him in his own tongue is important. The same is true for many other Black people. We hear a lot about new research and campaigning which is being carried out in response to changing demographic patterns, with older people representing a larger percentage of the population; some of these older people are Black and from other ethnic minorities; they may have needs which are specific to their cultural background, whether it be food, religion or bathing. In looking at our elders' needs, an awareness of cultures and ethnicity is essential. It is not merely political correctness that makes me insist that old people's homes, or care and nursing homes, take on board the fact that not all of their residents want meat and two veg, with suet pudding and custard to follow.

I never thought that I would ever allow my parents to be put in a home, and no doubt they would have had some of the same concerns. For both my parents, the idea of a home that is not one's own was too close to the idea of the workhouse. Even though my father had spent the first twenty-five years of his life in Africa, he knew and feared the poor provision for older people in Britain. It was not just the legacy of Poor Laws which made me reticent about old people's homes, it was more that I had grown up with stories of Africa, where older people were venerated, where the idea of putting them out of their homes was utterly alien. My mother too, had similar views about the responsibilities of children towards their aged parents. Nursing homes were no more a part of my view of family relationships than sending my small children away to boarding-schools would have been. And yet when my father's Alzheimer's developed to the extent that he had become a danger to himself, I had no hesitation in finding a nursing home for him. In other words, the reality of the situation made me jettison the rhetoric and deal with the needs of my own father, which I could not, despite my best endeavours, satisfy on my own. I do not feel guilt about my father, and I have long since come to the realization that to try to care for him myself would have been more about me than about him. None the less, there are real difficulties with him being in a nursing home that I would not have anticipated.

It should have come as no surprise that most of the other residents were white, but I had failed to take into account their racism. These were people who, now in their old age, were plagued by the fears and anxieties of Alzheimer's, and some of these fears were triggered by me, my father and the Black staff. Violet, who can be as sweet and charming as one would wish, will in one moment become vile and venomous. It is strange, even surreal, for my father to have to tolerate even such low-level verbal racism.

The nursing home is my father's home, it is a safe place in a world that is otherwise hostile or, at best, confusing to him, and at one level he does cope with the offensive comments made from time to time by the other residents. There is no doubt in my mind that he both hears and understands what is being said. He gives the speaker a careful and thoughtful look and says nothing. It strikes me that his dignity is as intact now as it was over those early years in England of overt and rampant racism. He may have Alzheimer's but that does not mean he is stupid. What bemuses me about his situation, and no doubt that of other isolated Black people, is that when they are old and at their most vulnerable they may be exposed to even more overt racism than they were when they were younger. I do not wish to exaggerate the extent of racism in old people's homes, and from what I have seen firsthand it varies from home to home. In London, where many of the staff are themselves African or African-Caribbean, perhaps that sense of isolation is not as real as in locations where there are few Black residents but no Black staff. Given the nature of Alzheimer's in particular and old age in general, older Black people need to feel safe and protected, yet these are also often tough people, who have survived separation from home, – building new lives amidst blatant racism and discrimination. By retirement age, a bit of offensive language is no big deal.

It is I who feel most offended on my father's behalf but, like him, I say nothing. Partly this is because I know that my father can cope, partly because the old white people who make racist comments cannot be persuaded to change the habits of a lifetime. Ironically, it is the African notion of having respect for one's elders that enables me to cope with the everyday racism in my father's home. I see these old people, white and wrinkled as my father is Black and wrinkled, as people who had histories, indeed, still have them, as people who learned either to hate and fear or to feel superior to people of African origin. Now they are vulnerable, and neither I nor my father feels threatened by their words. I know that many of the Black staff feel the same. They are able to return to their own homes and families after each shift; they have a strong sense both of their own identity and that the old must be respected because of their age.

I have often found a deep irony in the ways in which we Black people were asked to assimilate into British society and culture. This seemed to include the way that British people treat their old folk. Even as a child born in England, I knew enough from my father to know that shutting older people away and treating them with disrespect was not a universal practice, and that maybe Africans and Asians could teach Britain something. Now I have even more reason to believe this to be true. My father's generation may be the first older African, Caribbean and Asian people to die here in numbers, leaving their children and grandchildren probably to remain in Britain. As a consequence, they and we may make a cultural contribution which adds something positive to British life. As we grow older and ourselves reproduce, we may be seen less as immigrants and more as settlers. We will make an impact in pensioners' groups, and in nursing-home management. It is not just about Black faces being seen to be present in more areas of British society than hitherto; more significant may be how African, Caribbean and Asian attitudes to ageing are incorporated or, should I say, assimilated.

I wonder what this society will look like when a generation of Black people born here have parents and grandparents from whom to learn and from whom advice and guidance can be gained. I know that such a sense of continuity did not exist for my father or for many others from Africa and the Caribbean. They made do without Grey Heads, but they retained the memory of them back home. It is we who grew up here in the 1950s, 1960s and 1970s who did not have that benefit and may not have even noticed it was missing. Now, I know what I missed and am pleased and nourished by the sight of old Black people. Ageing for me is like completing a circle.

JOAN ANIM-ADDO

The Colour of Silence

As a historian, I have searched for evidence of the presence of Black women in Britain during the last five hundred years or so. The earliest Black male I found was one who, on these shores, was called 'Cornelius' and was buried in the parish of Lee in Lewisham in March 1593. The precious little information I found about Cornelius is detailed in the book *Longest Journey: A History of Black Lewisham*. Cornelius was not necessarily among the first batch of Africans to be brought to England or even to become resident near the port area in south-east London now known as Deptford. So, while it was exciting to find a record of a named Black male of the period, the question remained: what about Black women? I wanted to find out, and I was only too well aware that a good many people would be interested in knowing. I argued that if, with some certainty, Black men had been living in and contributing to British society for a minimum of four centuries, some trace had to be found of Black women.

Samuel Pepys, a naval man whose work as Secretary to the Admiralty took him with some frequency to Deptford dockyard from 1673, made a few entries referring to Black people in his diary. One such notes:

. . . and for a cookmaid, we have ever since Bridget went used a black-moore of Mr Batelier's (Doll) who dresses our meat mighty well, and we mightily pleased with her.

So, here we have a scrap of information, just enough to titillate the imagination, concerning the Black woman, Doll, whose cooking so impresses her employers. Of course, the term 'employers' is a misnomer here. The cookmaid is described as 'a blackmoore of Mr Batelier's'. In all probability she was his slave. A gift, perhaps? Straight from Africa? Came over from the Caribbean as a child? I doubt we shall ever know. This was the period when the powerful were male and White figures of history. Doll was 'a blackmoore', and that signified chattel or property, so there is little to be found written about her.

Undaunted, my search for Black women took me to Greenwich. During the seventeenth century, Black people were being brought into England in greater numbers, and in the final decades of the century this was becoming evident through the parish registers. Records of births and deaths led to 'a black girl' buried in Greenwich in 1689; just that was mentioned and nothing else. I have written about Greenwich's early Black history in *Sugar, Spices and Human Cargo*, but the shadowy figure of that nameless, voiceless Black girl remains. The evidence is clear that the Black population at that time was a young one. These were, by and large, specially selected young people, chosen to be sold out of their homelands precisely for their physical qualities. The inspections by slave-traders and slave-merchants alike were crude reminders that here was property being purchased. Was the Black girl buried in Greenwich in 1689 very young? This was, after all, the era of the fashionable Black pet.

A few contemporary painters of the period left records of such young boys and girls. Pierre Mignard's 1862 portrait of the Duchess of Portsmouth shows, for example, 'her pet Black'. The young Black girl looks no older than eight. She is probably nearer five or six years old. She has been dressed very richly, and a pale string of pearls lies glistening, in rich contrast to her Black skin. Her hair is closely shaven, an expedient measure, we may guess, in the circumstances. The girl stands holding a bunch of twigs in one hand and a seashell full of pearls in the other, as she gazes fondly up at her mistress. We have no name for the duchess's little pet Black girl. Anonymity characterizes the Black female of the sixteenth to eighteenth centuries. The Black female in Britain rarely had a name, rarely told her story. The same may be said of the nineteenth century, except for the signs that cracks were beginning to appear in the pattern of silence.

Johann Zoffany's eighteenth-century portrait of Dido and Lady Elizabeth Finch Hatton shows a richly textured painting of two young women, one Black and the other White. Each is wearing a beautifully cut gown of expensive fabrics. The Black woman is holding a basket of fruit and her companion is holding an open book. What the audience cannot tell is that the two women are cousins living together. So, Dido has a story. Her cousin can read and, we can guess, given the circumstances, that so can the Black woman. We can conjecture that her White cousin can write, and that Dido also does. Some of Dido's story is to be found in Gretchen Gerzina's *Black London*.

It is not until we come to read *The Letters of Ignatius Sancho* that we find two eighteenth-century Black women with voices in Britain. The first was a visitor, Phillis Wheatley. Phillis's story is remarkable, though it bears some familiar enough features. It is the story of a young Black woman in the most difficult time imaginable, reaching for the stars. Phillis was born in the mid-eighteenth century, during the heyday of British slavery. The year of her birth is possibly 1753, and she is believed to have been born in Senegal. In any event, she disembarked from a ship arriving from Senegal in 1761 and, though it would have made no sense to the young girl, she had landed in Boston.

Benjamin Brawley in his book *Early Negro American Writers* tells us that the eight-year-old African girl was 'a delicate' little girl when she came off the ship. At eight years old, then, the West African child who came to be called Phillis was kidnapped and sold into Atlantic slavery. The wife of a Boston tailor, a Mrs Wheatley, chose the young African girl, who seemed to be just right for training up as a 'special servant'.

Phillis's aptitude for learning was such that her role and status gradually changed in the Wheatley household. Mrs Wheatley and her daughter Mary, already eighteen years old when Phillis arrived, took to instructing the young Black girl in the Scriptures and in Morals, as was suitable for a slave. We are told, though, and this must have surprised everyone around her, that 'within sixteen months' of arriving in Boston Phillis was reading even difficult passages of the Bible fluently. She was taught elements of astronomy, geography and history and her response was found to be just as sharp in these curricular areas. Phillis soon showed a particular interest in poetry, especially writing by classical poets such as Alexander Pope. Before long, the African girl was composing her own verse, and soon Phillis became quite a little Boston celebrity. She also, in due course, had her first poems in print, an important first step for every serious poet.

At a time when enslaved Africans were neither expected nor encouraged to read and write, nor, indeed, generally to develop literary habits, the young Phillis not only grasped the mechanics of literacy, she also mastered the techniques of poetic form, so as to find a literary voice that was her own. Of course, English was not her first language. In all probability it was her third or fourth language; it is likely she would have spoken a couple of African languages in her first eight years of life back in Senegal.

Phillis's health remained 'delicate', and when her master was due to travel to London, in 1773, it was recommended that she try the sea air. As a result, she came to England. The short version of her story is that Phillis became the first Black woman ever to have a book of poetry published in English. And what is more, she was only eighteen years old at the time. Even a couple of hundred years later, for an eighteen-year-old young Black woman to publish her first collection would be stunning. As a female slave, to have published work deemed to be of some literary merit in that period was simply incredible. That Phillis did not stay long enough to be present at her book launch was no doubt a source of disappointment, but her mistress was ill and she returned to Boston. I doubt the young woman knew what an important bid to the claiming of a published voice she was making. Phillis was the second female to be published in America. Yes, only one other American-based woman had been published before her. So, here was one young Black woman achieving what everyone would have thought almost impossible.

Ignatius Sancho, one of the earliest Black British men about whom we have any information, wrote of Phillis Wheatley, lauding her achievements and complaining bitterly on her behalf that in order to get to Britain with her book she first had to be verified as the writer by a whole range of (male) Bostonians. Did Sancho pause to reflect on the fact that in Britain there was no Black woman writer, I wonder? He probably did not. I have come to this conclusion because, reading between the lines of Sancho's letters, one comes across Anne, his wife. If the young West Indian woman ever had any literary pretensions, she probably kept them to herself, since there were all the little Sanchos to be looked after and, of course, her artist husband. We know that Sancho thought highly of Anne, and we know that she, too, could read and write.

Even into the first two decades of the nineteenth century, Black women based in Britain remained with no published voice, despite the rash of Black male writers published: Equiano, Gronniosaw, Sancho, Cugoano and so on. Did any hopeful Black British women try to be published? We shall never know. It was not until the 1820s, when the anti-slavery movement looked set to change the pattern of shackling Black people, body and voice, that Mary Prince's request for publication was granted. At last, in 1831, the story of a British slave woman was published. Why? Not, of course, because Mary Prince thought her story important as a story but because more powerful people had agreed that hers might be useful.

The next Black woman to claim a published voice was Mary Seacole, who, in her distinctive way, took publishing by storm. With her choice of title, *The Wonderful Adventures of Mary Seacole in Many Lands*, the new writer seemed to be on course for a vision somewhere between *The Adventures of Alice in Wonderland* and *The Adventures of Moll Flanders*. And didn't she do well? The book has hardly been out of print since its publication in 1857. The two Marys constituted a rare blip in British publishing history: they were Black women with published voices. Did publishers take stock after this silence-breaking duo and agree that that was it, they had published Black women? The reading public would be forgiven for thinking so, for thereafter silence reigned. The colour of that silence was shades of black.

The end of the nineteenth century arrived amidst millennium excite-ment and a hopeful looking to the future, but in the first two decades of the twentieth century, the Black woman's voice was still hardly seen in print. There were those who were determined. Una Marson came to Britain from Jamaica and learned the joys of living in Peckham, south-east London, in the 1930s. Her story is fully told in Dee Jarrett-Macaulay's *The Life of Una Marson*. What interests us here is that some eighteen months after arriving in Britain, Marson's play *At What Price* enjoyed a West End début which must have thrilled the African-Caribbean writer finding a new audience in Britain. Una Marson was twenty-nine years old.

Una Marson's poetry, much of it bound by the conventions of the period, has not enjoyed extensive appreciation. Marson, however, was undoubtedly a literary foremother of significance to Black women writers in Britain and Caribbean women. Marson's interest in writing included poetry, the short story and theatre-writing. Her writing led her to the BBC, where she was a presenter on *Caribbean Calling*, among other programmes. She would also, like later writers of the fifties and sixties, develop a sense of audience from this platform. For Marson, a pioneer writer, the claiming of a public voice would be aligned to working for the BBC and dramatic writing.

Louise Bennett, a poet, extended her audience like Una Marson, through her stay in Britain. When in 1945 she came to study at RADA, she already had three books published locally in Kingston. But where were the Black women for whom England was home? And were there Black women writing prose at this time? That literary history is yet to be researched and written.

Claudia Jones, who was born in Trinidad, made history in the 1950s by being deported from the USA to Britain. At eighteen years old Claudia was a self-declared Communist activist, and it was this which led to her demise. She arrived in Britain in December 1955 to find a Black presence concentrated in key areas such as Notting Hill Gate in west London. It was in such an area that Claudia was to work. Later, she was also to bear witness to the Notting Hill riots. In 1956 she became editor of the *Caribbean News*, a recent publication aimed at the growing Caribbean population and included in the first issue under her editorship herself being interviewed. In 1958 she launched the *West Indian Gazette*. At this time, it was no ordinary Black woman who wielded the pen or typewriter in public, other than as someone's secretary. Neither did Claudia Jones have a privileged background. Her parents had emigrated in 1924, when Claudia was eight, from Trinidad to the USA. She had been forced to find a job when she was twelve years old, after her mother literally died at her sewing-machine. Claudia Jones undertook the development of the *West Indian Gazette* until her own death in 1964.

Some overlap occurred between the writing career of Claudia Jones and that of Sylvia Wynter, both resident in London in the early 1960s. Like Una Marson before her, Sylvia Wynter also came to be involved in a part-time writing career for the BBC which was to include dramatic writing. Wynter's play *Under the Sun* was accepted for production by the Royal Court Theatre in London and was later dramatized for radio. It was this work which was published in 1962 as the novel *The Hills of Hebron*, the first novel by a West Indian woman of African heritage. Thereafter a steady but important trickle of Black women novelists in Britain have succeeded in claiming a published voice.

Globally, we are told that there are some 519,870,000 Black women on the planet Earth. That is a formidable figure. Black women writers in Britain do not always have a strong sense of this and what it could mean. So far, with history against us, we have not marked our presence indelibly, through publication, on the consciousness of Britain. The published word remains, however, a powerful word in Western society. It is no coincidence that the most detailed records we have of Black people of any period have been left mainly by those who wrote or have had others write about them. Today, of course, we have other powerful ways of recording the present, but has the colour and gender of silence not remained the same in Britain? The nineties was the decade in which the tide really began to turn. The nineties was the decade of the visible Black woman. The new millennium beckons, and here in Britain it must surely be the era of Black women writers, particularly those whose voices resonate with a long silence already hundreds of years old.

Select Bibliography

Joan Anim-Addo, *Longest Journey: A History of Black Lewisham*. London: Deptford Forum Publishing, 1995

— *Sugar, Spices and Human Cargo*. London: Greenwich Leisure, 1996

Benjamin Brawley (ed.), *Early Negro American Writers*. New York: Denver Publications, 1970

Gretchen Gerzina, *Black London*. New Jersey: Rutgers, 1995

The Letters of the Late Ignatius Sancho. London, 1782

Dee Jarrett-Macauley, *The Life of Una Marson*. Manchester: Manchester University Press, 1998

LABI SIFFRE

Choosing the Stick They Beat You With

Geneticists   our modern day shamans   have discovered
that we humans   are so closely related   one to another
that the very idea of race
is a nonsense
a non-starter
a totally artificial construct . . .
'Hello my brother, hello my sister.'

I

SO, WHAT DOES IT MEAN TO BE BLACK?
After four years of age, he knew he was Gay   Way before he knew what sex
or sexuality was
He lacked the FAQ that he was Black   till seven years were at his back
Easy to vid the crack?   No?   Well, let me clear the track . . .

Cast off that self-aggrandizing jive or hetero-think: the view that Hets
are queuing for love, but Gays are just looking for sex.
Have you ever been in love?
The airwaves awash with songs of love, an alien, fresh off the intergalactic
banana boat, and nursing more than a cursory look at human union,
might understandably note that many people, perhaps most, seem unable
to differentiate between love and possession, love and infatuation, love
and the fear of being alone; or the difference between love and obeying
the cultural airline company's rules, stipulating the shape, size and weight,
of your sexo-erotic-romantic hand-luggage.

If you are (and I hope you are) or have ever been in love, or at
least heavily in lust, you may recall what it was like when you first
beheld that person you *really wanted*; that person you hoped would *really
want you*.

It hurts: that helpless, desperate longing. Feels like something unforgiving, uninvited, invading your belly, is twisting your gut with talons of steel and a vicious disregard of your soul.

So there he was, four years old, sitting alone, on the red paisley carpet, by the green velvet sofa, in the cream of the sitting room of Mummy and Daddy's rented maisonette at 18 Pembridge Crescent, London WII.

And he heard a noise and he turned around as his Father walked in with a man the boy had never seen before, and would never see again; a cousin, 'uncle', or friend of his father from Lagos perhaps (the boy never knew). But there and then true life began, with an emphatic and innocent lust. He could see the man from just above the waist to the top of his face (the man was standing behind the sofa). And he saw this man, and felt those feelings; those gut-wrenching feelings of desperate longing.

> And he don't recall what his father said
> Or whether he spoke at all
> And he don't recall what the stranger said
> But he remember it all

And the years flew by and it happened again, and again and again . . . with other men. Different ages, heights, colours, sizes; but most immediate of all, always the same meso-endomorphic build: heavy-set, solid, broad with no visible waist, big hands, thick wrists and prominent features on a square-headed face. Like his father, but different, insofar as the boy detected or wrote on the faces of the men he wanted (needed) a tenderness his father lacked.

Amateur psychologists and lazy professionals would claim the answer is easy to see: and to quote the subject unjournalistically (i.e., with complete accuracy), the man who was the boy says, 'I don't recall my father ever holding me.'

He didn't know he was Black until he was seven, when a White boy called him a Black Bastard, and soon after, a White man called him a Nigger. *Till then, when he'd looked in a mirror, he'd seen himself. Ever after, when he looked in a mirror, he saw something else.*

You taught me to despise
me seen through your eyes
But now I clearly see
the lies you call your 'history'

Imagine:

A world free of atlases or passports. No one has told you that you are British, Nigerian, Chinese, American, Malay, whatever. You have no knowledge of people from another land. Under these circumstances, you wouldn't know what your nationality was. You would have no need of a concept of nationality. On the other hand, considering humankind's desperate need to find someone to feel superior to, perhaps the people in the next village would be used as a group one could look down on as 'other'.

Imagine:

You are Black and live in a country where everyone is Black. You have never seen or heard of Red, Yellow or White people. Under these circumstances, you would never question, never need to question your colour.

But nobody has to tell you who you want to go to bed with.

Imagine:

You have attained that age when, without permission, hormones grow mischievous. The door-bell rings. You open the door. You see a man or a woman standing there with a serious expression and a clipboard, paper and municipal Biro. 'Well,' the official says, 'that time has arrived. You can be a homosexual, a heterosexual, a bisexual or a paedophile. Which would you like to *choose?*'

Now, everyone knows it don't happen that way. So why do so many heterosexuals claim and insist that it happens that way for anyone who doesn't share *their* sexuality.

Nobody has to tell you who you want to go to bed with.

Your sexuality is who or what you are (though not completely). Your colour, your race, is who or what other people *tell you* you are (too often completely). And for many Black, Brown, Red or Yellow people, it is White people who tell us who and what we are; in the same way that the able-bodied have told the disabled, men have told women, and heterosexuals have told homosexuals who and what they are.

A crucial moment, a wondrous moment, is when you find courage and/ or anger, and/or sense enough, to define *yourself* . . . and it ain't easy.

So, with no knowledge of sex or sexuality, the boy wanted the man. And in the language of those who persist that sexuality is subject to choice: at four years of age, according to them, the boy had *chosen* to be a filthy-disgusting-degenerate, a pervert, and in the opinion of many *straights*, *per se*, a paedophile.

Incidentally, if homosexuals are people who have chosen to be Gay, then logically there is no such thing as a homosexual. Homosexuals, using that logic, are merely heterosexuals . . . who are just trying to be difficult.

II

Can you choose your colour? I don't mean the pigmentation of your skin. Regardless of your hue, can you choose to be or not to be Black? What does it mean to be Black?

My mother is 'high yaller': Her father a 'Negro' from Barbados, her mother Caucasian from Europe, she is light-skinned, able to 'pass' as White. She refuses to do so.

Widowed, she moved from London to Amersham, a small town in the home counties. One sunny afternoon, settling in, she was sweeping the path in the front garden. I was indoors moving furniture and boxes, as instructed, to their allotted places. Glancing through the lace-curtain sitting-room window, I noticed her at the garden gate, in conversation with two white women who I gauged to be in their mid-sixties (my mother was in her early seventies). My immediate reaction was to keep out of sight. Yes I know . . . cowardly, prejudgmental, craven. But I wanted my mother to make agreeable acquaintances, find friends, a community she would be happy in, and I didn't want to jeopardize that first impression. 'Let them see what a nice woman she is, before they learn that her four sons are Black.' My subconscious had said something like that.

After ten minutes or so, my mother came into the house. She was angry. The women had been pleasant, welcoming, sympathetic to her recently widowed status. They had offered advice about the local community: the church, the Women's Institute, where to shop, the importance of getting to the baker's early in the morning, and suchlike. And then, everything had gone wrong.

Discussing the joys and benefits of residing in their small town, as opposed to the endurance-test stress of London life, the two had sought to reassure my mother by telling her that Amersham was a respectable place, and that she would be happy to know that there were not many Black people in the area and, as a consequence, there was very little crime.

At this juncture my mother pointed out, with some force, that (despite appearances) *she* was Black, that her children and deceased husband were Black, and that she was sorry to find two such ignorant and prejudiced women living in the town that she intended to make her home; and furthermore, when she met more of the local population, she hoped that they would exhibit a more civilized expression of humanity than that displayed by these two racists. My hiding indoors had been, to say the least, as useful as a pogo-stick in a snowdrift.

My mother does not cook rice and peas. Living with, then married to, the same Nigerian man for more than forty years, she doesn't like and has never cooked Nigerian food. She does not wear 'ethnic' clothes, preferring those with the St Michael brand, and wouldn't be seen dead in a dashiki. She was born in Stratford-upon-Avon, brought up in Moss Side, Manchester (*'It was a very nice area when I was a girl!'*), likes roast beef (well done), makes excellent Yorkshire pudding (the proper flan type, delicious with gravy for starters, meat with main course and syrup for pudding, not that thin, fluffy stuff, as hollow and insubstantial as the mass market it has conquered). She wears subdued colours, sensible shoes, very little jewellery and hardly any make-up. Her little house is homely, uncluttered, and decorated in muted tones of cream, fawn and magnolia. She dislikes loud music, is no fan of reggae and, I suspect (though she would never reveal this opinion to a White person), that she would have considered Bob Marley a finer ambassador for Black people if he'd had his hair cut. I can assure you, however, that my mother is definitely 'Black . . . and Proud'.

*

Oddly enough, many Black people would consider her (and 'high yaller' folk in general) to be not Black enough. Because they are able to 'pass' as White (regardless of whether they do so or not) they are somehow considered to be taking advantage of their genetic foundation-cream in order to avoid the day-to-day problems of racism, thus betraying 'the cause' by not being *completely* Black.

A similar response is to be found in the Gay community, where bisexuals are often considered to be taking advantage of their sexual ambidexterity in order to avoid the day-to-day problems of homophobia, similarly betraying 'the cause' . . . by not being *completely* Gay.

In the art world it seems that Caucasians can work in any genre they wish. White singers can sing country caterwaul, middle-of-the-road mundanity, rock, pop, rap, funk, folk, whatever . . . but with few exceptions, Black popular singers and musicians are expected to '*get down*', '*get funky*', perform '*Black' music*. The wonderful sting in the tail in this (as far as Black people are concerned) is that White people get the Osmond Brothers and we get the Jackson 5. *They* get Take That and Boyzone and *we* get Boyz II Men.

In the plastic arts, if it's from Benin . . . it's *ethnic*; if Picasso does it . . . it's art. In literature, *we* are required to show what it is that makes us different from white writers. White writers are required merely to write.

So what does it mean to be Black? It means whatever White people need it to mean, in order to distance themselves from us as human beings. It means whatever Black people need it to mean, in order to affirm ourselves as equally legitimate members of the human race.

Blame religion and Ham (Noah's second son). Blame religion and the Tower of Babel story (clung to as a justification by religious apologists for apartheid). Blame slavery, blame Empire, blame White people's ability (not exclusive to them) to spout and then ignore or debase philosophical imperatives such as 'We hold these truths to be self-evident, that all men are created equal, that they are endowed by their Creator with certain inalienable Rights, that among these are Life, Liberty, and the pursuit of Happiness.'

★

A Black East-African woman was angry with me for ranking homophobia shoulder to shoulder with racism (and, apparently unnoticed by her, with sexism, and discrimination against the disabled). Attempting to hurt me and, oddly, failing, she said, 'You Black people in the west know nothing. Don't you know what we call you in Africa? Niggers,' she said, 'we call you Niggers.'

Clearly she considered herself to be more 'Black' than I.

On occasion, I have been with White 'friends' or acquaintances when the conversation was turned, with tiresome inevitability, to the problem of immigration. Note that this is an issue of colour and not of race: the election of an antique wickerwork laundry-basket as prime minister of Great Britain would be a more likely occurrence than a conversation with White people centring on the problems inherent in allowing Australians, Greeks, White South Africans, Canadians, or any other pale people unfettered access to British shores.

During those conversations when Whites have been fulminating about the paucity of White-run newsagents, or the inevitable rise in crime (particularly rapes and muggings) which, they maintained, always accompanies an influx of Blacks, I would suddenly be noticed as an apparent representative of those they were attacking. At this awkward moment, the White person holding the floor would say something like, 'Oh no, I don't mean you. You were educated here. You're one of us.' Clearly, these people considered me (at least in my presence) to be less (or, in their terms, more) than 'Black'.

He is thirteen years old. Six years ago, a White boy bruised him *en passant* on the junior school main staircase with a casual 'Black bastard'. That night in the bath he raked his flesh with his mother's scrubbing-brush until he bled.

And now, the school bell having sung, freedom is in the air as he and his White chums flee the bonds of Latin verbs and speed away in the boisterous upstairs fun of a London bus. The liberty game this evening is to make fun of passers-by, who provide, unaware, a focus for childish rudery. We spy, (because of course the boy is me) a particularly appropriate victim. With malicious haste we wind the window down, thrust our noses and mouths through the slim windy gap and scream . . . 'NIGGER!'

He was thirteen years old and had known for some time that he needed a man to love, who would love him and hold him, and make him feel safe. He was thirteen years old, but he didn't *know*, *yet*, that he was Black.

MORGAN DALPHINIS

Lifelong Learning

In the Sahel, the muezzins called the pupils to prayer. After prayers they would continue learning the next suras of the Koran with their wooden writing-boards in order to become gwani *(experts).*

At that time I had done all my duties in the small wooden two rooms on stilts we called home, as well as in a much larger home, an estate running from the river to the sea. I was then ready for my lesson at the home of the St Lucian expert we called teacher. She taught us mathematics and English, as well as what she felt was important for our behaviour, about plants and herbs, how to grow food and how to remain alive on the earth as it is and not as we would like it to be.

I had then not yet gone to formal school, which would start later. Within the family my education continued both before and after formal school. Every evening was an evening for stories: *Konpè Lapen* (Brer Rabbit), *Konpè Tig* (Brer Tiger) . . . *Anansi* was not often talked about.

As children of six years plus, every day was a discovery: of spirits which inhabited rivers and the sea, *Maman Glo* (Mammy Water), the observation of cows, pigs and grass, and the dangerous mounting of horses we had been told not to mount, the fun of milking cows we had been told not to milk. The earth also taught us that it was alive through mild tremors, hurricanes and lightning.

Learning was fun, with songs, stories, proverbs: *Zandoli sav ki pyé bwa i ka monté* – the lizard knows the nature of the tree that it is climbing.

Learning was about experience: my thumb was once hurt and the faith healer (*pansè*) cured it by pulling, with soft-candles and prayer. Learning was about mystery, as some adults listening to a religious talk would suddenly shake and tremble as the spirit seized them.

Learning was imagination, as I stood on the peninsula of the family land and watched the huge blue waves smash against the cliff near my feet and thought, 'This is the best feeling in the best place in all time and in all space, perhaps somewhere else this feeling will be larger and bigger.'

Learning was also experience, its proverbs suddenly added to others. For example, I fell and began to cry, and an adult passed, helped me up and said, 'Don't cry, boy, just get up and go!'

Even the preparation for England was a preparation in other ideas, for example, being shown a coin and told, '*Mi Jab!* (Behold the Devil!)', or being told that if I spat in England it turned immediately into ice. As a newly arrived immigrant at Paddington, I began to climb down to be near a shiny piece of metal called a railtrack in order to spit on it to see if it turned to ice. Luckily, a White adult stopped me.

Somewhere south of the Sahel, the testing for survival and experience continued. Fulani and Hausa boys were tested by being whipped or running the gauntlet, horo (disciplining). They were, however, not to cry as this would imply weakness and not being able to get a wife.

Having arrived in England, I discovered that there was a concept called race in which some others actually felt that they were superior to me, without knowing me. On my first day at school, someone said to his brother, 'You see this wog? Beat him up.' However, I had walked five miles on occasion with baskets of mangoes on my head, not in preparation for this event, but as part of my reality. I was therefore able to do to others what they intended to do to me. I was also confused by the word 'wog'. What did it mean? On asking a schoolmate, I was told that it meant Worthy Oriental Gentleman. I, however, went to the library to check it in the dictionary. It was not there, or I didn't find it. Rage boiled in my head. The next person who insulted me or picked a fight or hit me got my fists. For a while I became purely animal. I leaped up, jumped upon shoulders and let fly. I bent others across my back like the wrestler Mick MacMannus. When they attacked in gangs of five, I discovered that if I took the milk bottles off the steps and threw the bottles at the attackers in the middle of the road, the shopkeepers would come out, and then the racists would run away. On other occasions, someone wanted a one-to-one. On others, I used anything that came to hand.

South of the Sahel, my soulmate was running to compete with his friends or learning to hunt small animals in the bush or swimming against the treacherous

rivers as sport and to learn to make a living from fishing. Nature was our enemy.
The wars with men were less deadly.

In England, our mother country, luckily, I always had a sense of being a
St Lucian and Black, that we were here for the purpose of getting the
best we could out of the education system and the labour market, I had
already been formed, prior to my arrival. Before the next 'slave trade' of
migration to England, I had been grounded deep into Africa; without
seeing Africa, I had already come from Africa, an Africa called St Lucia.
That tradition had given me my stories, language, culture and identity.
Others were added to it, others that had already been added within the
St Lucian heritage, i.e. English, French, Carib and African.

I cannot give other logical explanations for some of the continuities.
They were in a way accidental. My grandfather on my father's side mixed
the herbs and dealt with the spirit world for those who consulted him.
My maternal grandfather was a free thinker, who annoyed the local
church by openly accusing it of hypocrisy, theft and preying upon the
ignorance of most of us. He was right in this perspective, as he had actual
experience of living outside St Lucia in 'White' and other countries. He
spoke German; it was said he understood Latin and an Indian language
and had returned from a prisoner-of-war camp at the end of the Second
World War.

I have always lived in a free environment, in which the thoughts of
my people were as good, if not better than those of anyone else. My
mother was a teacher and my father ran two small businesses, a rum
shop and a taxi firm. We lived our lives accountable only to ourselves,
growing our crops, feeding our animals, building our houses in the
countryside and running our small businesses in the town. However,
having no capital and no ability to create capital we came to England and
America to change aspects of our fortunes.

For my Sahelian soulmate, questions like those I asked myself were always
answered by the name; the name told you everything you needed to
know about the people: *Adémòla* – Crown With Honour; *Okwonkwò* – A
Child Born on Market Day; *Mabrat Ntsenet* – The Lightning of Freedom.
A St Lucian once summarized it in my case: Dalphinis and Isaac. What

a combination (i.e. of landed peasantry and town businesspeople)!

But we are all special, and the accidental nature of human inheritance, genetic, spiritual and psychological, is an area of pride and ambiguity for every human being. And, indeed, the one certainty about African culture everywhere is that it seeks to include everyone. We have taught White people our ways of singing, dancing, greeting . . .

It is not surprising then that African culture in St Lucia belonged to everyone. Our problem then, as today, is that because of the link with poverty, the lack of capital, the paucity of modern technology and the oppressed nature of our circumstances, African-Caribbean culture is the one that many of its peoples wish to distance themselves from, particularly when they believe that they have solved the problem of capital accumulation.

For these reasons, there has always been a respect for skill and knowledge around me. Also, there has always been an artistic streak, with some of my family liking to sing, some wanting to express themselves through religion, some paint, some are engineers, some are doctors and some write poetry. The particular is located in the wider African-Caribbean culture.

African-Caribbean perceptions of learning and education have been centred upon wider inclusion and participation, as well as upon being a lifelong process from its very beginnings. As soon as the first human being, an African, took the historic step to develop language, and through language the basis of reflective thinking, inclusion and wider participation were already stamped within traditional African-Caribbean teaching and learning.

Others had to be included within this new phenomenon of language, to move it from the individual to the social. Language was of itself a collective act seeking to include more than the individual. Language, as a communicative tool, is at its best with the participation of the many. African oral literature, right up to today, seeks to include the many in the repetition of the singer's chorus and at times rhythmic dancing to the tune developed.

Issues important to various African civilizations have been kept in the memory, through language. These for us seem to have to do with survival through an appreciation of what is under the surface, for example, *all skin tiit na laf* – those who smile are not necessarily friends.

The importance of learning to all, at every age, is evident in the need to make learning memorable through fun and enjoyment, for example, as in children's games:

Kwado a koko a k'ogi a k'wanche. 'The frog is lying down and having a cocoa in its hole.' The fun is in pronouncing *k* and *k'* differently and at speed.

Enjoyment can also be enhanced through rhythm:

Dam dam	Moskito one
Damirifa due	Moskito two
Damirifa due	Moskito jump
Due due dam . . .	In the old man's shoe . . .
	– E. K. Brathwaite, 'Masks', 1968

At times learning is enhanced through song and poetry:

Mi say mi kyaaan
Biliv it . . .
– M. Smith, 'Mi Kyan Biliv It'

My own learning through school has been relatively successful, but with underachievement through exam nerves. Luckily, before my retakes some kind individuals outlined to me what the requirements of the exam were and also helped me make a systematic analysis of my errors and thus put me in a position to learn.

Since leaving school, the adult world has been more competitive, and I have had to struggle through with this aspect of my personality. I have found that I do well in situations of research, where there is no guessing about the rules of the examination or test, and where I have been given clear opportunities to understand in detail what the task is about. Other than these opportunities, I have had to lead the double life of knowing more than I am supposed to know in some areas, but not having the associated qualification. My research strength in seeking detailed analysis is at times also my weakness in summing up the same amount of mental detail 'appropriately'.

Underachievement for me, therefore, is always as much part of the system(s) in which I work as it is in myself. I have spent approximately thirty-eight years in Black organizations, working towards the reduction of underachievement. Some of it started long ago in the St Lucian context when pupils were beaten for getting a certain number of sums wrong or promoted and given the opportunity to ask that certain pupils not be punished if they had done very well at their studies. There was a pupil who would always get beaten, simply because he didn't understand how to do the work. How does society construct these understandings or misunderstandings? How do these social realities conflict or converge with the personal competences of the learner?

As a sixth-former (1969), I was invited to provide In-Service Training to teachers on Caribbean issues. I had also joined the Black Supplementary school movement and supported the development of two Black Supplementary schools. Some of the things that remain in my mind from that time are as follows:

i) We went to the African and Caribbean embassies and high commissions collecting money to develop the schools. We got £2.

ii) I went to ask a Black mother whether their child could attend the Supplementary School. She said, '*Im kyan learn. Im too dark*' ('He can't learn. He's too dark').

iii) We asked many organizations for money. Few provided support. One of our teachers was very quiet while we voiced our frustrations with the system. A few weeks later his face was on the news, in the hold-up/robbery/social protest of the 'Spaghetti House'. This involved an attempted robbery, the stated aim of which was to generate money for Black causes.

iv) A black man loaned us his front room to start the school.

v) We received some support from the local council.

vi) Two churches provided us with premises.

vii) Five Black undergraduates worked with us for free.

I am still convinced that underachievement is at least partly socially constructed and that one of the ways out of this endless slave-cycle is to organize at least some of our achievement ourselves. This will mean working with like-minded people everywhere and setting up organizations and behaviour patterns which are world-class, as we have done in the University of the West Indies and in cricket. Other than those areas, in my perhaps presumptuous opinion, we appear not to thrive in proportion to the jewel-box of human talents in Africa, the Caribbean and the rest of the Black diaspora.

Underachievement, however, also has a management context, particularly in class- and race-sensitive societies such as Britain. Consequently, the process of early disillusionment with the education system in boys, particularly working-class White and Black boys, is due to social and educational leadership in Britain, whose hidden 'curriculum' at times excludes them by not offering a cultural or intellectual position, let alone a position of employment, in British society.

These social trends are particularly harsh within an ethic of 'pure' competition in which those whose business skills are sufficient to guarantee their survival thrive, and those who do not are viewed simply as failing. Often, the historical accumulation of initial capital for business through the slave trade and colonialism is forgotten. It also leaves out discussion about the search for self-actualization outside the context of resources alone. Within this vacuum, some young Black boys have argued to me that the only logical outlets are acts of social rebellion, including the criminal. In a sense, their self-regard and self-worth as people have not been developed and neither has their potential net worth in being shown how to start, develop and maintain a business.

These realities underline some of the experiences of many non-managing Black adults in Britain: they are excluded from the option of becoming leaders/managers, as the worldview (*die Weltanschauung*) in which they work does not necessarily include the possibility of Black people as managers.

Black people who have been aware of these constraints have at times opened their own businesses or worked in Black voluntary/community organizations. The most successful models here are, however, Asian, particularly those from East Africa who, in addition to their enterprise, had previously accumulated capital in East Africa before remigration to Britain. Others, however, often fall into the category of Black professionals. Their position is, however, the most tenuous, because of the following:

    i) Society, the organization or the team (and at times other Blacks) does not conceptually accept them in the leadership role.

   ii) Due to the overall social drift of such 'groupthink', Black managers may at times also not fully accept themselves in the role of manager.

  iii) Push-and-pull economic factors have a very pointed effect. For example, years ago, bus driving was viewed as a 'lower level' job, suitable for immigrants. Any job these days is fiercely sought and with this competition, at times resentments about Blacks surface, not only 'taking our women' but 'taking our jobs' becomes part of the context. While I accept that these views may not represent those of the many level-headed people in Britain, bombings, the blatant expression of racism outside the rule of law, the willingness of some to be associated even with murder in the name of racist right-wing groups, leaves a question as to what the economic impact of such extreme actions may be.

The Churchillian or Nye Bevanian inclusion is no longer expressed through action in Britain. Some argue that the right-wing extremists found a home under the Conservative government of the Thatcher years. Others argue that the present Blair government did not include many Black candidates in order to ensure 'electability' within the present cognitive climate.

    This context for management by Black professionals leads to a number of constraints:

    i) Black managers are at times 'punished' for minor misdemeanours or errors where White managers are 'ticked off'. Similarly, Black children are more quickly 'excluded', and sentencing of Black offenders results more often in criminal conviction than community service/probation.

   ii) Management courses do not address the issue of multiethnic workforces or discuss management with Black dimensions. By contrast, there is a wider acceptance of the issues of Women (White?) in management needing attention. Similarly, the national curriculum focuses less on the multicultural than it could.

  iii) Restructuring often 'inadvertently' seems to impact negatively on Black managers, particularly bearing in mind their status as minority within a minority.

  iv) Issues or competences voiced as important by Black professionals may not be considered seriously, for example, the management of racism and levels of competence in articulating their own skills. The issue of institutionalized racism in public services, including schools, universities and colleges, is only becoming a serious one for In-Service Training after the Lawrence case and the MacPherson report.

Ways forward may include the following:

i) Focus groups in workplaces on Black/equality issues. Some of these groups could be Black only, with the agenda of presenting some issues to management.

ii) Management training on the management of racism.

iii) Management development in a multicultural workforce.

iv) Management training courses which actively seek examples from many different cultures and societies.

v) Management training on personal communication.

vi) A serious redefinition of rights and responsibilities for all British people.

In addition to present political debates on devolution and Black sections, there also needs to be the development of an ethics which operates on the basis of collective accountability. I would, one day, 'in my dream' like to defend the right of existence of the Beowulf Adoration Society because of such an ethic of mutual rights and responsibilities, with the sure confidence that the rights of the Marcus Garvey Adoration Society would also be defended, if necessary, in both home and foreign policy.

At this point my Sufi/Muriid brother in Senegal sits contemplating freedom and its nature; everything in the world is part of the universe, therefore the universe is also part of the human, therefore Jama Rèk, Jama Rèk – 'Peace Only, Peace Only' – is the balance that we seek.

ROSALINE NWAGBOSO

African Women in Britain

African women in Britain live in two different but simultaneously oppressive cultures. On the one hand there is the African culture of female oppression that still influences their lives in Britain, and on the other, the culture of British class-oriented society. This essay is based on information gathered for my research paper on *African Women in Britain* in 1989. It explores the basis of the notion that African women in Britain are still subservient as a result of internalized psychological dependence on men rather than being in tune with current ideas of liberation.

I discovered that some African women in Britain are so culture-conscious they seem to have resigned themselves to accepting their traditional roles. According to some of my interviewees, their main concern was not to embarrass relatives back home in Africa by deviating from their traditional roles. (Marriages in Africa involve not only the immediate families on both sides but also extended families.) What came across during my interviews was that, although some of these women are unhappy about their traditional roles, they refuse to instigate any change. They shy away from anything that focuses attention on them and would prefer living in Britain in anonymity. They are distrustful of any action that highlights their plight and would rather endure anything tradition throws at them for the sake of family stability.

The purpose of this research was to add to our knowledge of the experiences of women from other ethnic-minority backgrounds, such as Asians and West Indian women. I had seen some of the materials published and was impressed by the women's courage in giving individual accounts of their lives. One book in particular was the collection of West Indian women's stories, *The Heart of the Race*, edited by Beverley Bryan, Stella Dadzie and Suzanne Scafe (Virago, London, 1985).

Both West Indian and African women shared high expectations of their lives in Britain, with better opportunities to study and develop careers, but both were disappointed at and shocked by the racial discrimination. Asian women share with African women the oppression within the family by male counterparts. My research brought to light the effect of societal problems both in the families and in their working and social lives.

It also emphasized the pressure of tradition exerted on these women, and the inability of the authorities to understand or to help. I searched for similar information from the African woman's point of view, locally and further afield, but failed to find any material of substance which was representative of ordinary working-class African women in Britain. There is, however, fiction and non-fiction, published by intellectuals like Mariama Ba, Buchi Emecheta and Ifi Amadiume, all of whom have stressed the difficulties and sufferings of African women.

When I set out to undertake this research I knew that it would not be easy, knowing how culture-conscious and reticent most Africans are. However, I did not anticipate the extent of the negative reaction I received from some of them. A few of these reactions I will address later.

The idea of putting a collection of their stories together came from various sources. Firstly, as a community worker, I came across some African women who were facing both racial discrimination at work and sexual oppression at home from their partners, and some expressed their fears of racial discrimination for their children at school. Secondly, as a member of an African women's organization, the question of women's experience of oppression and racism were never far from casual conversation. I have also talked to some of the African women in my place of worship, and during these informal chats the focal points were the problems of combining extended African tradition and the British system and the effects it had had on them. Thirdly, at my children's school, which I frequented twice a day for three years, taking and collecting my children, I met many Black women, some of whom were from the African continent, and we got talking to each other. I listened to them talk about their problems and those of their friends and relatives and have participated in their conversations, all of which centred around two major topics, female oppression and racial discrimination. All of this led me to the conclusion that there was overwhelming material to be researched and documented and that it would be a vital contribution to the history of Black women in Britain. I sounded out the opinion of some friends with whom I had been discussing the issue, and there was a general positive consensus – but when I asked whether they would like to contribute to it, some of them declined. Others were enthusiastic, and one woman said she would have to consult her husband first. Of the nine women I consulted, only four were willing to grant me an interview. I prepared a hand-out and distributed it to various African women's organizations, but I got a very poor response: three out of twenty-five. I also approached twelve women I meet regularly at the marketplace and shopping centre in east London, where I live. They were all from West Africa (three from Sierra Leone, one from the Gambia, one from Ghana and seven from Nigeria). I felt this number would be fairly representative if all the materials were adequate as my research was concentrating on women from this region. Some of the women also talked to their friends. I was pleased when I got phonecalls from two women who were very enthusiastic and volunteered to contribute their stories. I tried to sell my idea to some of the African women at my workplace, but I received many negative responses. Perhaps the most surprising was from one particular woman who seemed to take the whole affair very personally. She did not just object to the idea of publishing collective stories by African women; she was incensed by it. She telephoned me the same evening and queried my intention over and over again, refusing to accept any explanation. She totally misconstrued the idea behind the research. She accused me of spying on my people and passing the information on to the British authorities. Our conversation was punctuated with words like 'traitor', 'coconut', 'black sheep' and 'shameful'. The whole episode lasted for about twenty minutes, and I could hear the sound of several coins dropping into a telephone coin-box. When I did manage to end the conversation, I felt as though I had just wrestled with a rhino. My phone rang again a short while later, and this time it was her husband, who continued in the same vein, and then demanded to know who had sent me. The conversation ended when I put the phone down.

When I began to visit the consenting interviewees, I also encountered problems. About a quarter of the women interviewed had a lot to say about their situations and were very co-operative; the rest were reticent. It took some probing questioning to tease out their stories. I realized that, because I was dealing with working-class women, some of whom had little education, I needed to spend time elaborating on the reasons behind the interview, and I had to be tactful while interviewing them. One major thing that emerged was the right of privacy. Most of the women emphasized their need to be anonymous, although not everyone required the same degree of protection. As a result, I decided to reproduce their stories without their names and to acknowledge the contributors on a separate page if they so wished. I also gave them a choice of my tape-recording their stories or making written notes. Even so, it was not easy extracting information, as these women are not used to having anyone making notes for an account of their lives. I had to keep going over their information. In fact, in some cases I got more important information from them when the interview had been officially closed and I was on my feet ready to leave.

Preparing to interview these women was physically and mentally exhausting, considering that at the time I was still studying for my degree with the Open University, had a part-time job to maintain and, of course, my family, but I had an overwhelming wish to put this collection together. However, not all the information collected was used, as some was inadequate. A couple of examples follow.

My interviewees were selected from women residing in north and east London who had been in Britain for at least twenty years and, on average, were about fifty years of age. They were divided into two categories, those who were without partners, (single, divorced, separated or widowed), and those living with partners. The interview consisted of open-ended questions, so as to give the interviewees a chance to talk freely, to be able to describe their background, their expectations on coming to Britain, to match their expectations with reality and how they coped with this.

I looked forward to my first appointment. I was sure that I had everything ready: files, pen, notebook and tape-recorder (most of my interviewees would not give their consent to the use of a tape-recorder). I arrived at my first appointment at the agreed time. After the initial small talk we settled down to business. My interviewee didn't mind me using the tape. Half-way into the interview, at the point when she was about to describe her experience of looking for her first job, her husband returned. He did not disguise the fact that he was not pleased to see me, or the tape-recorder. He promptly took his wife into the kitchen, and I could hear them arguing. He eventually emerged and let me know in no uncertain terms that he 'forbade' me to continue with the interview. I did attempt to explain the purpose of the interview, but he was not interested, so I collected my things and left. Later that night I got a phonecall threatening to do something drastic if I published his wife's story.

My fourth interviewee was a middle-aged primary-school teacher who was on the point of retiring. She didn't mind her husband being present while we chatted. She began by narrating what life was like in her home town, the problems she had encountered being a girl, how she felt when she came over to Britain and her shock at British-born children's behaviour. At this point her husband took over and went on to elaborate on the behaviour of British children and how he blamed the parents; from there he drifted on to single parents and what he perceived to be other societal problems. I was not happy about this intrusion, but I was concerned that if I tried to stop him the interview might end. I tried the tactful approach of turning to my interviewee, who was sitting on my right, and directing the next question, about her experience as an African teacher in a predominantly White school, to her. She began to tell her story but stopped on reaching the point at which she had to make an official complaint about the lack of support from the head teacher. The incident concerned a disruptive seven-year-old boy in her class who was well known in the school. She said that she had reported the problem to the headteacher and other teachers were aware of the problem. One day, as the class was getting ready to go to the library, this boy pushed another boy who pushed him back, and he fell and hit his head on a desk, cutting himself. Medical help was promptly provided, but when the parents complained and accused my interviewee of carelessness, the headteacher gave her an official reprimand.

'When I got that letter,' she said, 'I was furious and went to her to protest.' The headteacher then made an official complaint to the Education Authority, and the next thing the teacher knew was that she was being suspended for a month on the grounds of being aggressive to the head-teacher. Once again her husband intervened: 'Oh, they really sent my wife to Coventry,' he began and continued to the end of that episode. Ironically, whenever he started to talk, she would not speak again until he was quite finished. Sometimes I looked at her for confirmation or to continue when he stopped, but she never did.

After that interview I decided to apply a different strategy and to interview married women away from their homes. I began, whenever possible, to arrange to meet them at their workplaces, tap into their lunchbreaks or to talk straight after work.

Most of these interviews were successful. As I listened to these women recount their lives, I couldn't help sharing their feelings with them, their joys and sadness. For some, the story of their lives was difficult to narrate, and the memories brought tears to their eyes. One of the interviewees who arrived in Britain as a teenager in the late fifties gave a moving account of her life. She recounted, with a sad smile, her aspiration toward marriage: 'Every morning I would hear papa [her landlord] in the kitchen making a cup of tea, which he would take to mama, his wife, in bed to wake her up. I watched this every morning, and I thought that marriage must be a wonderful thing. I couldn't wait to get married, I had high expectations of marriage.' But as it turned out for this interviewee, she had a disastrous and stormy marriage that ended in divorce and left her with four children to bring up. She narrated how, shortly after her marriage, her husband became obsessed with controlling her life, demanded to be waited on hand and foot in line with the traditional role of 'wife', blamed her for having daughters and told her that he was looking for a second wife from Nigeria. Then he lost his job, and things got worse. First, it was frequent arguments, which frightened the children, then his frustration turned to physical violence. The crunch came on the day he went after her with a machete and she ran into the street in her nightdress. She feared for her life.

Another interviewee had been married for over thirty years. She had no problem discussing her experience of life both here and in her home town in Nigeria. She described her life, from her childhood days, in detail: how she met her husband; the humiliation and emotional trauma she suffered at the hands of her mother- and brothers-in-law after her husband left for Britain. She had a miscarriage and was neglected by them. Then, her mother-in-law, who had never approved of her, started to spread a rumour that the child had not been her son's; the gossip nearly ruined her marriage. She said that she came to Britain when landlords used to display signs like 'NO DOGS, NO IRISH, NO BLACKS', and the weather was extremely cold, snow remaining slippery on the ground for days. She expressed how she coped with poverty, scrubbing floors and holding down two jobs while her husband studied and became violent towards her. She went to Nigeria, but after a five-year separation from her husband she returned to England and to him – for the sake of her children, who she said would have better opportunities there, and because her father had persuaded her to continue with her marriage. The physical violence stopped but the emotional and psychological abuse continued; she had learned to deal with it. She described how she regretted not having taken the opportunities available to further her studies but was glad that her three children had learned from it.

This summarizes the results of most of my interviews. Some of the women continued to live in Britain while their husbands retired to their countries of birth. The reason for this, as some of the women explained, was that the women felt that there was nothing for them in their home countries. One of them said, 'I don't have any property to inherit, my life is now here.' But others felt strongly about racism in Britain and had promised themselves to return to their countries. Overall, the women still regretted their failure to take up the opportunity to make good careers for themselves. Some blamed it on African culture, which compels women to conform and to take a subordinate role.

African women seem to be torn between two cultures which oppress them equally but in different ways, the prominent features being male dominance and institutionalized racism. Those women who were still living with their partners were more reticent and seemed to be afraid of their reactions. Although, as some sources, such as Mary Ebun Kolawole in *Womanism in African Consciousness* (Africa World Press, New Jersey, 1997) have emphasized, African women have never been voiceless. But the question of how effective their voices are and have been in matters relating to such things as social status – for example, when women to all intents are barred from inheriting from their fathers – still remains. This view is unapologetically pointed out in Enukora Okoli's *Death in the Family*: 'Every property remains in the family in perpetuity and nothing is inherited by females, who are expected to be married off to another family.' As for marriage, women are the commodity that men negotiate for. It is therefore important that women's voices be used effectively through every available medium. Women should encourage each other to speak out openly and to challenge the tradition of female oppression, both individually and collectively. The attitudes of some African women in Britain towards their culture do seem to be changing. The women do not feel obliged to be subservient to a tradition that offers them nothing but a subordinate role, but there are still those who strive to preserve those aspects of African culture in Britain. How far attitudes have changed is perhaps a matter for further research; there is still a long way to go to achieve liberation.

'There is need for an outright revolution ... Patriarchy should be fought by each woman individually and all the women's organizations ... To be able to fight patriarchy one has to be convinced that men and women are equal' (*Zimbabwe Women's Voices*, Ciru Getecha and Jesimen Chipika, Zimbabwe Women's Resource Centre and Network, Harare, 1995).

Combining the efforts of women both in Africa and abroad and ensuring powerful representation seems to be the way forward. Major issues, such as inheritance, dowry and polygamy need to be addressed, just as Ms Waris Darie, UN Ambassador (UNSPA), is campaigning against female circumcision. Some women, and those men entrenched in tradition, still need to be enlightened.

FLOELLA BENJAMIN

The Three Cs

When kids see me on television, then hear me talking to them in their school assembly or see me in *Hello* magazine, and in newspapers with people who've made it, they see me and think that I've made it, too. So when they see me in their school, dressed down-to-earth, or shopping in Brixton market, doing things which mirror what they are doing in their own lives, they begin to think, if she can do it, I can do it – and even better. The good life looks achievable.

Too many people when they've made it move away, but if you have a social conscience and if you want to do the best for children, then you stay. I don't do this so much for the adults, although adults will benefit, too. I do it for the children as I believe everything we do has to be food for children. We have to focus on our children's lives, to make their lives better.

My mum and all the mums and dads who came to Britain, way back in the fifties and sixties, have paved the way for us. Now we've taken over, we have to try to pave the way for our children, making the path even wider. For my daughter and my son, and all the second and third generations born in this country, I want to make the path so wide, they're going to be spoilt for choice. The opportunities have got to be there for them and we can only do that by giving something back. I got a letter recently from one of the many companies and organizations for which I am on the board, which said:

> Dear Floella,
>   The overall contribution you've made to cultural diversity by showing us and opening our eyes to what we need to do with this company has been tremendous, and we want to talk to you more as we head towards the year 2000 . . .

It's important to communicate on a one-to-one level with people who make decisions. You have to make it personal, you have to present things in a way that shows how people in power can make a difference. If they cannot identify with what you're talking about, you get nowhere. I sit with them round the table and, although it takes a lot of my energy and time, I do it because I know there is a point to everything I'm doing, and I continually see the results on a personal level.

I can go to Tesco's supermarket in Brixton, for example, and someone will come up to me and say, 'Please let me hug you, because you've been an inspiration in my life. You've made me be what I am today.' A total stranger will come up and say that to me. It happens all the time like that.

I'm not doing it for me, I'm doing it for the children, I'm doing it for the future, so that those children will know that there was somebody or something in their lives that motivated them, made them aspire, made them able to think, 'I can do that too.'

But this kind of inspiration has to start in the cradle, from the time they are born. I know it's possible, because that's what my mother did for me every day of my life when I was a kid, and she still does it now. When we came to England, she used to line the six of us up every morning before we went to school and say, 'Listen, I've worked hard to bring you up, now you're in England, you learn. Because education is your passport to life, and no one will be able to hold you back if you have an education and something to offer. Everybody in life knows, if you've got what someone wants, no matter what colour you are, people will want you. If you've got nothing to offer, nobody wants you.'

If you look at my family, my five brothers and sisters have all got important jobs. There are people wanting them, wanting what they've got to offer. I've got a brother, Roy, who is a computer analyst. He's head-hunted by companies all over the world, and whenever there is a crisis in his company, he flies into the area to trouble-shoot. My other brother, Lester, is the over-all maintenance manager, the top man in the House of Commons and the House of Lords. He was there with Black Rod, at the opening of Parliament. My mother felt so proud. My sister Sandra is a trainer and school inspector, and she is on the board of a local health authority. She does so many other things – you name it, she does it. My sister Cynthia works in the City and my other brother, Ellington, is a quantity surveyor. He owns his own company. He builds houses and property for private clients and hotels.

So all of us are successful in our own right; there is nothing special about me. My mother told us that you can get anything you want if you work for it. It doesn't come easy, it doesn't come cheaply. You've got to work, you've got to suffer, you've got to be prepared to do that. That's what I try to teach kids before they get exposed to so many materialistic things – money, and the idea of getting things easily. They might *think* things come easy if no one actually tells them they have to work hard to get what they want to be. They'll be insulted, have to put up with a lot of rubbish, but they have to be focused, know what they're going for and learn from these experiences.

Learn how to play the game. Learn how to play your role in life. And if you learn those things, you'll be well prepared. If you're a cricketer, and you go in to bat without your gloves and pads on, what will happen to you? You end up getting hurt. It's the same thing in life.

You have to be prepared and arm yourself by learning these three things: Contentment – being happy with what you have, and that way more will come to you; Consideration – treating the people the way you want to be treated yourself; and Confidence – loving yourself and having self-esteem. There are other things you can add, like conviction and commitment, but these are the primary ones. You've got to actually learn what to do with them, then nothing will faze you, even when you are disappointed by something. Even in my life, and my work – though I've been working for thirty years in my industry – I still get disappointed, I still have to face adversity.

I feel passionately that we have to focus on all children and see life through their eyes, give them that sense of being able to succeed and cope with success in a positive way. What's the purpose of success if you're flashy and say, 'I've made it. Look at me'? Definitely not! I don't go around that way. I will never turn up somewhere and show off. I find the time to talk to the people who have actually cleaned the room, or prepared the food, or done something that has made the event happen, not the people who are just being flashy or believe in their own importance. I do that because, when I was ten or twelve, I used to go with my mum in the school holidays when she went to clean offices at 5.30 a.m. She did it because she wanted a better life for us and was always home during the day. She worked hard to buy the house that we lived in. We lived in a house in Beckenham when there were no black people living there at all. She wanted us to live somewhere like that, so that we would get the best schooling, the best of everything.

I know that my mother, who is a great woman, had to dirty her hands, washing, cleaning, cooking for other people, so when I see people doing these jobs, I don't think it's menial at all, I think they are very important. You don't know where they've come from, why they are doing it, nothing about their backgrounds, why treat them like dirt? If anyone had treated my mother like dirt, I would be very upset, so if I don't want them to treat my mother like that, then I shouldn't treat anyone else like that either. You see, that's where the big 'C' for consideration comes in, and I try to set an example.

I used to do a lot of visits to Brixton Prison, I'd go in and talk to the prisoners about parenting. I always wore something second-hand, usually I'd wear a nice suit, and I'd go in there looking really sharp. I'd say, 'Hey, what do you think of this suit? Cost me a fiver,' and they'd say, 'It can't be.' So I'd ask them, what makes it look so fantastic? Is it the person inside or is it the suit itself? The suit is not important. I could wear newspaper and you'd think I look fantastic. It's because the person inside is confident in what they are doing. I feel these visits were necessary because a large majority of the people in prison are Black and need guidance.

I'd ask them, 'While you are in prison, what is happening to your children?' A lot of them would say, 'Well, we had to clothe and feed our kids and we didn't have the money so we stole. What else could we do?' Even though I've just shown them what a fiver can buy, they say, 'I couldn't get my kids to wear second-hand clothes,' and I'd say, 'Why, what are you teaching your child then? What are you trying to tell your child? That money and clothes are more important than the person inside? Get the person inside kitted out well first, then they can do anything. There's no point doing it outwardly, it's got to be done inwardly.'

Those in positions of responsibility have to take responsibility as to how they show things to their children. Through our books, through our stamps, our advertising, through television – anything – that is important. The visual aids they see all around them have got to give them the right messages.

People who deal with our children, like teachers, must have our support because, without them, where are our children? I see all these young men standing around on the street, and I want to cry. I feel personally responsible for them, I feel that I have not done my job. I mean, not only Black children but for all children, because if you're going to get all people living together, they've got to understand each other. That's what my books and television programmes try to do. Since I wrote my book, *Coming to England*, I have seen some changes. What has made me really happy is that some schools use my book in teaching modern history – in areas like Devon and Cornwall!

We've all got a story to tell, and my book is simple enough that everyone can identify with what I'm talking about and see that their parents' experiences are similar to my parents' experiences. I feel it is so important that we nurture our children from the cradle. If we don't do it, no one will take their interests into account until it's too late and it becomes a problem. I see long term, and I can see what will happen if we don't do certain things. You only need to do very little at the beginning of a child's life to stop a catastrophe.

I was in Brixton market a few years ago, doing my shopping, buying my green bananas and stuff (I love going there; it gives me a buzz, because it makes me feel like I'm back to my roots, it makes me feel good about myself, it makes me feel proud. I don't go all posh-posh, I'm just Floella) when along came a mother with her little boy of about four. He saw me and said, 'Mummy, Mummy, look, there's that lady on television.' I heard her 'chups' and then say, 'Be quiet, you hear, don't make she feel good about sheself.' And as she pulled the child back, I said, 'My darling, it's not you that makes me feel good about myself, I feel good about myself already. Your son feels good about *himself*. He sees someone who is famous, he sees someone walking down the same street as he does, shopping on the same street as he is. He can be me one day, if not better. Make him feel all that is possible and say, "yes, darling, there she is, go up and say hello, and remember you can be just as good as her." ' If she had done that, I'd have thought we were winning, but for her to give a child negative thoughts about success, negative thoughts about achievement – that's wrong.

We've got to give our children self-esteem, confidence, pride in themselves, but we've also got to teach them how to deal with success, and that being successful doesn't necessarily mean that you've sold your soul.

I know how much I get out of what I do, so it's nothing for me to give back to society. It takes thirty seconds of my life to meet someone, to say hello, to give an autograph, say something nice about them, then they're gone – but that lasts them a lifetime. Every day of my life I have an experience of a young person telling me that I'm their saviour – imagine being told that every day! If I walk up the road now, someone will come up to me and say, 'Gosh, you don't know what you've done for me.'

When you're told that all the time, you can go two ways – you can either get terribly big headed, feel that you're the most wonderful person, or realize that you've got to do more, give to those millions of children out there who haven't got love and security in their lives. Because when you get that sort of positive reaction, you know you're doing the right thing.

I have a mission in life, and that is to show what we as a race have to offer. The only reason that I am what I am and am doing what I do is because I've been given the opportunity. You have to keep a positive mind and even if you get hurt, rejected, kicked in the teeth just meditate, breathe. You have to take time out if you're wounded, because if you don't heal yourself, you can't fight, and you will get hurt again. That's one reason why when people see me I'm always smiling. Part of it is because I don't want people to know what I'm feeling inside. The other reason is, if you smile you have a chemical that goes into your system that's positive.

I will continue to work for what I believe in, the future – children. I do so because I know Britain could be an even greater place if everyone was given an equal opportunity to show what they have to offer. There is such a wealth of culture, talent and diversity among our people, and only when we are accepted on equal terms and allowed to integrate fully into the patchwork of Britain will this country begin to build itself up into a great nation again.

Stories

FERDINAND DENNIS

Sunday Morning Blues

Three days before I was due to attend Lucy Colhern's annual autumn party, I received a letter from the owner of the flat I was living in informing me that he would be back in a month's time. He was in India, had gone there in search of inner peace, and his letter was mostly a panegyric on the soul-enriching experience of living on tenpence a day, saving its most devastating news for the last lines. I'd been living in his Ladbroke Grove flat for over a year, and the prospect of uprooting myself yet again for my sixth move in three years plunged me into depression. None the less, when Saturday night came, I found the energy to attend Lucy Colhern's party.

Lucy Colhern lived near by in an Italianate villa with a floating population of friends. A sybaritic heiress, androgynous in appearance, she was famous for holding parties that went on for days at a time. Her guests that night came from the four corners of the globe, with a liberal sprinkling of Africans. The rich blend of esoteric world-music reflected the cosmopolitan gathering, and provided the *pièce de résistance* of the evening in the only known recording of a musical genius of an obscure island people somewhere between the Antipodes and the Far East. Called 'Symphony of the Dead Souls', it was played on an instrument made from the 300-plus bones in the human body.

The following afternoon, still recovering from my drink and drug excesses in Lucy's house, I received a telephone call. I didn't recognize the voice straight away but once I heard the name, Kawan, I remembered the handsome, bearded African with the barrel-chest and easy laughter I had met at Lucy's party, remembered that we had talked at length about African politics, and parted after swapping telephone numbers. I'd said that I didn't know how long I would be on my number because I was looking for somewhere to live. He was calling to tell me that he had a room to rent in his house.

Following his instructions, I made my way from Ladbroke Grove over to Hackney, to a London that was as strange to me as another city:

narrow streets, countless council housing estates; even the sky seemed somehow lower, as if a permanent depression hung over this part of London. But my journey ended on a pleasant-looking, quiet street of Victorian, artisans' terrace cottages which had obviously been colonized by the lower middle classes. The woman who answered the door of the house I called at was so beautiful that I stumbled to find my opening gambit.

She introduced herself as Olivia, invited me in, and in the kitchen explained that Kawan had been called away on urgent business. (I would soon discover the reason for his frequent and sudden absences from the house.) Her accent evoked images of tea on the village green, encircled by oaks and elms, a summer Sunday afternoon, and men and women dressed in white flannel, blazers and pale floral-patterned dresses, all watching a cricket match in progress. She showed me the room, on the first floor; it was perfectly adequate for my needs. A transit point. The house had a good feel.

She offered me tea after my brief inspection of the room. And as we chatted at the kitchen table, she mentioned that she had seen me at Lucy Colhern's party. I was surprised because I had absolutely no memory of her, yet I was certain that, once seen, Olivia was not easily forgotten. Her thick, shoulder-length, flaxen hair, her pale-blue eyes, a face that made me think of classical paintings and sculptures, her graceful poise, her statuesque figure; and that incredible English accent and fluent speech – those were the memories I took away. Enchanted by Olivia's beauty, I even forgot to ask about the rent. Was she a neighbour? Kawan's girlfriend?

I was out of Ladbroke Grove and in Hackney within a week. The rent was not unreasonably high or charitably low, and had been settled in a discussion in which Kawan participated as if money was a distasteful subject, included in our arrangement only because necessity demanded it.

My curiosity about Olivia was quickly satisfied. She was, to my disappointment but greater relief, Kawan's girlfriend, and she lived in the house. In Kawan's company, Olivia's beauty seemed somehow diminished, less radiant, commonplace even. Before Kawan's lengthy absence, the three of us often went out together – to parties, restaurants – and it never failed to intrigue me how bland, characterless and almost invisible Olivia seemed beside Kawan.

Years later I now recognize Olivia as the sort of woman who, skilled in the art of self-effacement, elects to project and conceal her beauty at will. If she seemed like a pale carnation in Kawan's lapel, a tasteful tie, an adornment that enhanced his natural regality, that was the role she chose for herself. And that was her power.

At the outset, it was Kawan who commanded my attention, loyalty and affection. We often sat up late into the night, discussing politics and women and love. We disagreed with sufficient frequency to sustain many late nights, oiling our conversation with beer, wine or Scotch. It was on one such night that I discovered that his princely bearing was not an affectation; he wasn't just another African in London posing as a prince. He had lived as a prince until his early teens, when a military coup ushered in leaders uncompromisingly committed to Republican rule. The soldiers had sent his entire family into exile, and his father had died in an Earls Court flat after falling out with Kawan's mother. He was attending an English public school at the time. He had not been home to Kanji in twenty years.

Kawan did not seem to feel bitter towards the soldiers, who were themselves ousted a year later in a violent coup. Nor was he without hope of one day returning to the land of his birth, to the land surrounded by seven lakes where flame-red flamingos fed and talapia fish grew in magnificent abundance. But there were days when his hope was wrapped in a cocoon of melancholia and that royal future seemed self-delusional. On such occasions we would talk about our disgust with life, the sense-lessness of suicide; or maybe we would talk about the sweet and wounding loves we had known and lost. The next day, the prince would re-emerge, his belief that he would one day take his rightful place on the throne in the country surrounded by seven lakes restored and implacable.

Olivia sometimes stayed up to play Scrabble with us, but always retired by eleven. I'd begun to notice a subtle unease between Kawan and Olivia but did not attach much importance to it until early one evening, reading in my room, I heard Olivia scream, followed by steps rushing up the stairs, then Kawan shouting angrily, 'Come back here.' I heard her fall, then I heard her scream for Kawan to stop. At this point I opened my room door and saw Olivia on the floor, pressed against the wall, her skirt riding on her thighs, her navy-blue tights torn around her knee, exposing skin several shades lighter than that on her face, her hands raised to protect her face against Kawan's raised fists. 'Kawan, don't,' I shouted.

My voice must have broken some spell, driven his fury away. Olivia scrambled up, sobbing, and ran to her room and locked the door. Kawan did not look at me; he hung his head and walked slowly back downstairs.

Later that evening I took a break from the collection of Somerset Maugham short stories that I'd been reading, left my room and went down the silent stairs to the kitchen. I found Kawan sitting at the table, a half-empty full-size bottle of whisky in front of him, a tall glass in his hand. Remorse and frustrated anger were as palpable as the scent of the whisky. I would not get back to my room until dawn.

Kawan invited me into his study, a ground-floor room lined with books, periodicals, folders and music albums. It also contained a mini-stereo, a small television, an armchair convertible into a single bed, and a leather-bound swivel chair at a desk strewn with papers. We did not talk about the altercation or Olivia but engaged in a rambling conversation which circled the perimeter of that discord without actually touching it. Somewhere in that night, speaking in a tone of apology, Kawan told me this puzzling creation story.

In the beginning God made two holes in the earth, and from one came man, from the other woman. God gave them land to cultivate, a pick, an axe, a pot, plates and millet. He told them to cultivate the land, to sow it with millet, to build a dwelling and to cook their food in it. Instead of carrying out God's instructions, they ate the millet raw, broke the plates, put dirt in their pot and then went and hid in the forest. Seeing that he had been disobeyed, God called up a he-monkey and she-monkey and gave them the same tools and instructions. They worked, cooked and ate the millet. And God was pleased. So he cut off the monkeys' tails and fastened them to the man and the woman, saying to the monkeys, 'Be men,' and to the humans, 'Be monkeys.'

The Hackney night faded, giving way to an overcast dawn visible through the east-facing window, and I decided to go to bed. As I was leaving the room, Kawan stopped me by placing an arm on my shoulder. When I looked at him he said nothing, and for what seemed like a long time he looked deep into my eyes, and I sensed his loneliness and his fear, felt those emotions as sharply as if they were my own; sensed that there was much that he wanted to say, from a heart that had known the remotest corners of pain; sensed that he was inviting me to travel to those territories with him. We parted awkwardly on that grey dawn.

Soon afterwards Kawan began to spend days away from the house. Olivia, who I had seen only once since the fight, became equally scarce. When Kawan was not there, she left for work early in the morning and seldom got back before late evening, by which time I was usually ensconced in my room reading. It was as though our little community had been irreparably shattered. None the less, I was aware that Kawan and Olivia were again on good terms. He would return home late at night, and I often heard his gentle knock on Olivia's door. From my window I saw him leave the house a few times, long after Olivia had gone to work, and noticed how he seemed to steal away, as if departing the home of a mistress.

One Friday evening Kawan invited me out for a drink. I set off expecting to chase the night – a vice we shared – but found myself in a vast apartment in St John's Wood watching dignified elderly men prostrate themselves before Kawan, who accepted these acts of obeisance with calm. On the way there he had explained that a delegation from the court had been negotiating with his country's ruling military junta to restore the monarchy. There had been a major breakthrough, and Kawan would soon be travelling home on an exploratory trip. It was strange to see these old men venerate my friend and landlord in that opulent apartment with its pink-upholstered Victorian wing chairs; stranger still to see the transformation their veneration wrought on him: the almost imperceptible change from being princely to being a prince.

From the moment Kawan took his seat in the giant leather club-chair people began appearing, as if they had been waiting for his arrival. As they rose from the floor after greeting him, Kawan would intone in his language (later he would explain that it was the blessing of the royal house) and hold a brief conversation with the supplicant. Some of the old men went to stand behind Kawan, their grey heads bowed. They were then followed by a younger group. Among them were many beautiful women, whose skins were as smooth and dark as polished black coral.

We remained in that apartment without sleep until the middle of the next morning. Despite having spent over twelve hours greeting people and discussing the state of politics with the elderly men, whom I discovered were his advisers and, at times, I sensed, his prison wardens, Kawan did not seem tired. Indeed, he glowed with an aura of contentment which was no less visible for the intermittent sign of boredom that escaped from him.

There was much that I wanted to ask him in the taxi as we were driven back to Hackney from the salubrious surroundings of St John's Wood. But unable to decide where to start, I held my tongue and wondered instead whether Kawan had always led this double life between tradition and the present, between the sacred and the profane, between the African he was born and the sort of Englishman he had become. Two weeks later Kawan left the country. He would be away for four months.

Olivia and I did not immediately become friends. For some weeks we met each other briefly in the kitchen, exchanged greetings and terse observations about the weather. Then, one rainy Sunday afternoon, we were both in the house, and we spent many hours at the kitchen table talking about the movies we had seen and the countries we had visited. Soon we started meeting for breakfast, and again in the evening, and slowly the gloom that had settled over the house since Kawan's departure began to lift. No matter how late we stayed up, we went to our separate rooms, though I often felt it was an unnatural conclusion to the evening. And the more these evenings happened, the deeper I fell in love with Olivia.

So, when she invited me out for a drink with two of her female friends – Sue and Helen, both white and English – I accepted without hesitation. I had by now made a few friends in Hackney and, not wishing to be alone in the company of Olivia's friends, invited Peter, a friend, along. We met in the White Horse pub on a Friday night. As closing time approached a squat muscular man, his head covered in a woollen hat, came to our table and greeted Olivia. She gave him a broad, easy smile and introduced him as Sylvester, then went off to the bar with him. Jealousy and curiosity swirled inside me. When she came back, Olivia revealed that Sylvester had invited all of us to a blues dance. We had been drinking for hours and had reached that state of intoxication which made any suggestion of extending our drinking irresistibly attractive. The five of us followed Sylvester to a basement several blocks from the pub.

I remember little about the sequence of events in that low-ceilinged basement, only that it filled up swiftly after we arrived, that I saw Olivia dancing a blues dance with Sylvester which revealed that she was no stranger to this subterranean world, saw her elegant-looking body pressed against Sylvester's weightlifter's mass and watched her twist and writhe in sensual erotic movements. I did not see Olivia leave, and when I noticed that she was nowhere to be seen I felt agitated. Her friends were less concerned than me; we all left the blues dance around 3 a.m. and went our separate ways.

When I got home I saw a light under Olivia's door. She was home. I knocked and asked if she was all right, hoping that she would open the door but fearful of what would happen if she did. She simply shouted back that she was fine, and I went to bed.

The following day, as we stood in the kitchen, Olivia asked me to promise not to mention anything about the evening to Kawan. I said I wouldn't and, besides, I hadn't seen anything improper, unless she considered her blues dancing skills an impropriety, which I certainly didn't. So the night at the blues dance became our secret, and this secret our bond. Over the next few weeks my desire for Olivia grew stronger, became a restless beast, and threatened to break free from the platonic bars I had erected between us out of loyalty to Kawan. My nights were a tormented struggle between my conscience and my heart. On two consecutive nights, unable to sleep, I left my room and stealthily approached Olivia's door, intending to knock, to ask her to admit me into her bed. But always, at the last moment, I shrank back at the possibility of rejection, the possibility of betrayal, the possibility of success. When we met in the kitchen or on the stairs, I averted my eyes and feigned business. Finally, I decided that I could not remain in the house with her any longer, and with frenzied resolution set about finding somewhere else to live. Three months after Kawan's departure I moved out, to a squalid room in Finsbury Park. Here I attempted to and eventually succeeded in regaining my equanimity.

I telephoned Kawan's house about a month after his expected return. Kawan answered the phone in a slow, lazy voice. I arranged to visit him, hoping also to see Olivia again. The Kawan I met was plumper and more majestic in appearance. But he was also in the grip of a deep gloom. Olivia had moved out; he had returned to an empty house.

Of course, I was shocked. Olivia had given me no indication that she was planning on moving out. In fact, when I had told her that I was moving, she had said she would be lonely until Kawan got back. But in my conversation with Kawan that night I discovered that he and Olivia had been involved in a long and painful relationship, from which each had been trying to escape. Kawan told me about Sylvester, the dreadlocked weightlifter: two years previously, Olivia had had an affair with him, and she and Kawan had almost parted as a result of that transgression. When Kawan mentioned Sylvester he did so with utter scorn in his voice, which gave me the impression that he objected less to Olivia having had an affair and more to the social status of her chosen lover. She had wounded him by choosing a man who was obviously below his stature. And that had made her action *infra dig.*

He explained that on the night of their fight – not their first – he had been trying once again to explain why her action was wrong, the peculiar and specific way in which she had wounded him. But she had not understood, or had feigned incomprehension. He said that he was the first African Olivia had known, and he had introduced her to the world of the blues dance, the blues dance, which for a brief moment in his life had helped to soothe the pain of his long, long exile. Olivia made no distinction between the West Indian roughnecks in the neighbourhood and somebody like him. A prince.

Yet when I asked him if he had intended to marry Olivia and take her home as his queen, Kawan looked at me aghast. Marrying Olivia had never been an option. His wife would be chosen for him by the royal elders, the old men I had seen prostrate themselves at his feet. His would be a bride from a select family. Not because – he stressed with painful sincerity – because that was the way he wanted it, but because that was how the king of his people married. Olivia had always known that one day his destiny would be fulfilled, that he did not own his life.

We talked until after midnight, and I decided to sleep in Kawan's house rather than make my way back to Finsbury Park. Later that night I was awoken by Kawan shouting, 'Olivia, Olivia, Olivia', as he wandered from one end of the ground floor to another. I went downstairs and met him in the hallway. His face looked pained, his eyes watery. 'She's gone, she's gone,' he said.

But you knew it would always end like this, Kawan,' I said.

He said, 'No. She once promised to stay here, in this house, to be available for me whenever I came back to London. I believed her.'

A violent spasm shook him and the tears he had been holding back flooded out. Involuntarily, I held him, and he rested his head on my shoulder, and we stayed that way for a minute or so, then parted. He went into his study, and I returned to bed. By the following morning he had regained his regal composure. The incident in the night seemed like a dream.

A month later Kawan travelled again to Kanji. I read in the newspaper of the restoration of the monarchy in his country. A year later, having moved to yet another part of London, I read of the coronation of Kawan as King of Kanji.

It is many years since those events, living in Kawan's house, and over the years I have heard from mutual friends that Olivia married a stockbroker and moved to Surrey. I last saw Kawan when he came to London for a medical check-up, something to do with his heart. Somedays, especially on rainy Sunday mornings, I think of them, Olivia and Kawan, of their doomed love, of my own unrequited love for Olivia, and I know then that there are people sadder than rainy Sunday mornings.

VÉRONIQUE TADJO

Images of Exile

I

Here we are in the big city of stone which is so cold. The evening comes fast. At four in the afternoon it is already dark and even the lights come on strangely, throwing a fake brightness. But this darkness which stretches itself to no end is unbearable. Every day it takes you by surprise in the midst of doing something, when you thought you still had time, a little time. And even the night can feel like a betrayal, a compulsory rest despite insomnia.

We have now become small grey creatures, round-shouldered and plump-bellied. I drag my sullen face along, not knowing what breaks my voice and ruins my soul. You see, for days I have been pacing back and forth in my cage, with a thick uneasiness in my throat. What is happening to me?

My energy leaks out of my veins. My heart no longer beats at its own rhythm. Under the blankets, still warm from our sleep, I feel myself suffocating. What is happening to me in this odourless town?

II

Through the window, I see trees swaying. Some children are playing in the square, chirping like sparrows. After all, I never left you.

In the morning, you get up and go to work. I am left alone all day. In a while, I shall go out to get some fresh air and then, maybe, I shall read a book.

We just need coffee and milk. There is still some butter left.

III

In the centre of this great city of stone, the sun sends out a different light and always retains some coolness. It seems that words have a double meaning and that people walk on air-cushions.

Yesterday, I was at home. Today, I find myself here. I am waiting for you, and later, we will go out in the streets.

But sometimes I wonder why I came here. So far away. Your love has led me by the hand. It has brought me to this country which brings confusion to my mind.

It is grey outside. I get up when it rains and I listen to the noise of the drill in the construction site next door. I am freezing under the duvet, even though the window is closed. The radio plays classical music.

I must wake up. Wash. Afterwards, it will be better.

Water touches my body. I feel I am breathing again. Then, at last, time begins to move.

IV

There are no griots here, only poets. You read your work and you think you are living an exceptional experience and people look at you the way you want them to. You wrap yourself round with your writings. They become your identity, your daily bread, your reason for living. You eventually believe what you have been told. You lock yourself in your creation and words bury you, sentences annihilate you and in the solitude of your retreat you forget the blood and the dust of the outside world.

V

I think of my country which is far away, and my eyes open beyond space. In this big city, words travel faster. Ideas assail me. I see myself in this immense conference hall, listening, all ears, to writers from all over Africa: Angola, Ghana, Uganda, Kenya, Nigeria . . .

A speaker stands up and declares, 'It is our duty to understand our place in the history of humankind. We will not have a truly African literature until we free ourselves from the arrogant criticism from the West.'

VI

I want to feel heat and sweat running down my back. I want warm nights and the buzzing of insects, dust and mud. At home, life springs from everywhere. There is no escape. You can never forget that so many things remain to be done.

VII

In the big city of stone, I think of my country. It obsesses me all the time. During the day, I carry it in my inner self. At night, it lies down beside me and makes love to me.

VIII

We must stamp out our bad habits, uproot false theories and look ourselves in the face. Time goes quickly. It has nothing to lose. Our actions become fossilized.

IX

The big city of stone lies under an opaque veil. Outside my window, skeleton-like trees dance the motions of a silent sea.

I don't recognize myself. I am sweating under my coat, and I find my own captive smell unpleasant. The wind keeps striking my face. My skin is drying out. I pass my hand through my hair and it feels like cotton.

X

It is dark. The summer will be a bad one.

My heart skips a beat. In the train which is taking us to the countryside, I have just seen a fox through the window. A red fox. His front legs were perched on a slope and he was watching a farmhouse.

I don't know what is happening to us. It seems that nothing is working out and that everything has become heavy. Our love is sinking.

Life is a trap. I am going mad in this city which revolves around you. In this city where my life has taken on the aspect of a promise. I am becoming short of breath. I have been led here because of love, yet I feel in a comatose state until the sun rises.

XI

His mother has a tumor that is as big as a fist in the middle of her bloated stomach. The mass grows and eats up her cells.

She seems exhausted, shrivelled up in her wicker armchair close to the window. In the garden, the foliage of the trees is gently swaying. A breath of fresh air enters the room and makes the curtains dance like the wings of a morning butterfly. The television set sends out whispering voices and projects furtive pictures. As she looks out of the window to watch the street, she reviews her past in black-and-white snapshots.

Her son has come back after all these years of silence. But it is too late. She knows very well that he believes she is going to die. Otherwise, why would he be here now that this rot has settled in her body? He looks at her, and he tries to be kind. He chooses his words carefully to convince her that she has a son.

She never understood why he went away. Nor does she know why he comes to see her every day. She asks herself if she is happy to see him. His presence is too much for her. She doesn't know what to say to him. She no longer expected him home.

She remembers the way they argued, the words he used to scream in her face: 'You are completely mad, mad!'

Of course she is mad! She has known it for years. But is it her fault if she failed, if nothing worked out as she wanted? She loved her husband. In fact, she loved him so much, she wanted to die when he left for another woman. She remembers the pain and the shame, yes, the shame.

She seems exhausted, shrivelled up in her wicker armchair close to the window.

And the son tells his friends that it doesn't matter to him if she dies or not. He never truly loved her. He left home when he was barely fifteen and, anyway, he felt more comfortable at the neighbour's. They were the ones he really had feelings for.

The way he speaks of his mother, one feels that he holds a lot against her. He claims she had regular fits of hysteria. He also says she was very possessive. But he doesn't want to think about all that any more.

The girl he had been living with for four years has just left him. When he came back from his trip, the other day, she announced that it was finished between them. So he locked himself up in his flat. He cried. He had insomnia. He had migraines. Finally, one morning, he decided to visit his mother.

He doesn't expect anything from the old woman. But he thinks he can help her.

He pictures himself holding her hand. He will wipe her forehead. He will whisper words to her. He will listen closely as she sleeps.

His mother is dying and he wants to be there.

XII

Somewhere, some place, there is a young man lost in his suffering – his wound is deep – he no longer knows the difference between love and destruction. He wants to hurt others in the same way as a warrior wants victory.

He disappears in a desert. As he withdraws from the city, he watches his life fade away.

He is hurt so badly that he wants to punish women. But I say, 'No. Love has the colour of hope. Bitter today, sweet tomorrow. You should not cast away all your tenderness and allow the honey of your caresses to dry up. You do not need to destroy so you can prove who you are, so you can show the sky your open wounds.'

Love is a story that we never stop telling. Allow yourself to be lulled by its soft words. Adorn yourself with its many jewels. But, please, do not wreck your life in the name of true love; denials, sacrifices, disillusions. We have got to survive.

I have seen too many withdrawn women, licking their wounds, stammering words out, suffering from headaches and totally shut off from the rest of the world. I have seen too many women collapsing.

I want women to be sexy, strong and outspoken.

I can be tender to the point of melting. I can undress you and give you all I have. But if because of this, you want to burn my soul and bind my wrists, then I shall leave.

XIII

The postman comes twice: at eight in the morning and at one in the afternoon. He throws a bundle of letters through the slot in the front door. It makes a muffled noise when it falls on the ground. I look for something for me. Stamps from my country. I pick up the newspaper.

XIV

But one day you begin to love the big city of stone when it starts calling forth memories, when one of its streets reminds you of someone you hold dear or when one of its areas awakens a portion of your past.

In an often visited park, you re-create the past.

The big city becomes beautiful under the snow. It looks like a bride, and the joy that fills your heart is equal only to the depths of the sky.

You feel something like peace. You want to laugh about life and its bad humour: the illusion of controlling one's existence.

XV

Maybe, now, you will be able to live your days without hesitation.

Unpublished translation of *À vol d'oiseau*, L'harmattan, Paris, 1992, adapted by the author.

PATRICK WILMOT

The Train to Walthamstow

Ronnie the Rat was feeling on top of the world, though in the cloying grandeur of King's Cross Underground, this was not meant literally. The estate agent who persuaded them to move from Seven Sisters station was right about the Victoria Line platform being 'dark', 'sooty', with 'musty original features' and in 'fotid decorative order': the stale lard-and-onion-scented air was wonderfully damp in its magnificent bouquet of rotting veg and antique pizza crusts, all on a bed of old, lip-smacking nibbles from McDonald's and Burger King. Far out, man.

As he puffed up his chest with lungfuls of air rich in the perfume of old, mint-flavoured condoms, stale deodorant, decaying tabloids and hydrogen sulphide, Ronnie's feeling of well-being was spoilt only by the human infestation. Like all estate agents, his had not been a 24-carat rat, and had shown him the place before dawn, when no humans were around. Although Ronnie thought Finsbury Park was cool, the agent had argued that leftovers from the ethnic minorities, British and Irish working class in the area were not enough to sustain an upwardly mobile rat population. Any wonder the great rat philosopher had accused estate agents of being *human, all-too-human*?

Now Ronnie was worried his grey fur would turn black from the stress of coping with the contrariness of humans, who whinged of rat shit in their sugar, then went out to BUY the *Sun*!

Take the two magnificent blonde beauts watching him with painted, bead-bright eyes from the platform: how could they whine of 'vermin' and a 'plague' of rats, then swarm in such closed spaces, swamping the local rat population and diluting their culture? Didn't they know of the scientific findings of rat experts, which said that overcrowding bred subway rage? Couldn't they hear on the Tannoy, evolved for rat, not human, ears, that the train to Walthamstow was late, due to an 'incident' at Victoria?

Looking at the bleached-blondes near the edge, who were doubtless making invidious remarks about the magnificence of his natural-fibre coat, he marvelled at the colourful paella of polyester draped over haunches of English beef, tomato-ketchup lips, the kebab-chic brown overcoats. What self-respecting rat could stand chattering so idly when a century of soot and grime, embodying an almost Mellor-like debris of English heritage, was there to savour? And Ronnie was sure they were dissing him.

'Rats,' Ena Powell said, 'never had 'em before these immigrants came over.' Although her periods had stopped years ago, there were days every month when she saw an HRT-induced red mist, unlike the bloody Tiber, mind you, not having a double first in classics from Oxbridge, nor having been embraced by Mystic Maggie, and with but a passing, non-Conradian knowledge of the lower reaches of the Thames. She pushed her *News of the World* further down her Asda bag, suspecting the cheeky coloured girl with her in-your-face attitude and head buried in the *Guardian* magazine was looking down at her Bulldog Englishness. But her spine firmed when she contrasted her wholesome British Home Stores florals with the coloured Next pant-suit, Shelley boots, Gucci watch and voodoo jungle bracelet of the aggressive Afro-Caribe. 'Rats followed 'em over here in the Windrush with their big bananas and coconuts.'

Eva Brown nodded, adjusting her blonde wave, the brown roots of which had begun to show. Between studying Ronnie, who refused all eye contact, they admired their dark tans under layers of Avon lard, got from that cut-price trip to Majorca with tokens from the *Sunday Sport*.

'Immigrants,' Ena sighed, 'just like bloomin' rats, smelly, shiftless, on the dole, avoidin' eye contact.'

'Should send 'em back to bloody Africa,' Eva sniffed.

'With their blasted rats.' She curled her nose at the Jap girl with crimson hair blasting African Jungle music from her Sony Walkman.

Ronnie was about to turn away in disgust when the big Black man with locks pushed through the swarm towards the blonde beauts. Though he generally disapproved of humans, his fur always rose for dreadlocks. So cool, man. But what was their *purpose*? Though there was something aesthetically pleasing about the way they swished about – not unlike tails – the evolutionary implications for rats were definite no-nos, totally uncool. How could a rat negotiate small holes, the essence of his identity, with tails on his HEAD?

'Excuse me please,' asked the dread in a strange language, 'where is the train to Walthamstow?'

Ena and Eva were appalled, their English blood boiled, they had never been so insulted: just imagine, this big coloured rapist approaching them on a crowded platform, in broad daylight, making lewd, suggestive remarks, wanting to have it off. Although they hadn't understood a word he said, the body language of these people was obvious, all-too-obvious – sex, crime, government hand-outs – made so clear from the oversexed smell of his thick sweat, his bloodshot eyes, leering, outsized mouth, twitching ears, enormous grabby hands, Lennox Lewis lunchbox, Fatima Whitbread pecs. Not that they looked at the monkey, mind you. God forbid! 'The bloody cheek,' Ena snapped.

'Watch what you say, dear,' Eva hissed, eyes glued to his bulging groin, 'don't overexcite the big coloured baboon.'

The dread's voice almost cracked, desperation in the sweat which cascaded from the crest of his proud brow like scrumptious, melting jellied eels. 'Please, please, ma'am, please tell me where's the train to Walthamstow.'

'Oh, my God, he's becomin' hysterical,' Ena screamed, holding the *Sun* aloft for protection. The crowd was getting tighter as they tried to find someone to look at accusingly, but the coloured girl was still lost in her *Guardian*. Their eyes lit up as they alighted on the Hermès scarf of the daughter of Nigerian general Butt Naked, who tried to buy Chelsea Village from Ken Bates with cash stuffed in Waitrose bags. But the bright, coloured young thing looked at them through her Fashion Fair mascara, as if to say, 'Look, ladies, I'm as civilized as you,' then flashed a look of withering, martial hostility at the dread to let this bushman know it was *ajereke** like him who gave Black people a bad name.

Against his better judgement, Ronnie stayed to watch the unfolding drama.

Ena and Eva were getting desperate, forced to look away from a plump white woman in a Laura Ashley frock whose anxious eyes exclaimed: I'M NO OLD-LABOUR, TRIBUNE-READING SOCIAL WORKER! They also got no satisfaction from Potty Baloony, the coloured girl in a Billy Hague baseball

---

* *Ajereke*: Yoruba for 'sugar-cane eater', derogatory expression for 'West Indian'.

cap, who held up her *Telegraph* like a Gallup poll and out-stared them with a righteous look which said: Don't look at me like that. I was born in Africa but I'm one of you, I pass the Tebbitt test – I cheer when Alan Shearer socks it to the Andorrans, I believe in God, Margaret Thatcher and the Tory Party. What's all the fuss about Stephen Lawrence? All his killers were beer-gutted *Mirror*-reading Old Labour voters, who didn't believe in John Redwood, Michael Ashcroft or Free Enterprise. Without the discipline of racism you wouldn't have such good Black singers, boxers, track stars or footballers. FREEDOM THROUGH RACISM!

Attracted by Ena's scream, two transport-policemen strutted over, and when they saw the big, coloured source of the problem, they shouted for reinforcements.

Only Ronnie the Rat heard the Tannoy announce that the next train wouldn't stop at King's Cross, due to an ongoing 'incident'.

The crush was becoming unbearable as twenty extra transport-police pushed through to sort out the 'incident' by 'teaching the coloured bastard a lesson'.

Hearing the train, the mob pushed to the front to get with it, get it on, and get away from the 'trouble'.

'Is this the train to Walthamstow?' the dread asked of no one in particular, but Ena and Eva screamed, the police charged in, and a skilled worker waving an *Evening Standard* shouted 'Bugger off, you coloured monkey! Fancy trying to get it on with white women with the Bill around!'

The train was coming closer, and Ronnie shook his whiskers as the police raised their batons and their leader used his loud-hailer to tell the suspect to raise his hands. A human forest waved copies of the *Telegraph*, *Mail*, *Express*, *Sun*, *Spectator*, *Sport*, *People*, Norman Tebbitt's letter to Mohammed Al-Fayed and Lord Lamont's autobiography. It really was time Ronnie took himself down his hole to his lusciously moulting pepperoni-and-anchovy Pizza from the Hut, the really smart thing for a cool rat to do. The train was almost upon them, but humans never ceased to fascinate, and Ronnie retreated into a crack over the tracks, not unlike an amphitheatre, to get a rat's-eye view of the action as the Black woman neared the end of her *Guardian* magazine feature. Who needed Alton Towers or the Millennium Eye when the thunder of a ***NEXT TRAIN APPROACHING*** did such wonders for his fur?

The driver, Normo the ASLEF shop steward, who made the trains run on time – no racist; he was a *Mirror*-reader; Old Labour; had Caribbean friends; he was godfather to one of their kids; liked Red Stripe – slowed as he approached, but sped up at the sight of the agitated mass, the ranks of tabloids, waving batons, and FIVE Black faces. He sought the brake as he saw the big, sex-crazed coloured man with the aggressive dreadlocks and angry, contorted face too near the edge, waving and shouting, 'IS THIS THE TRAIN TO WALTHAMSTOW?' His foot found the accelerator instead.

From his sooty-cold concrete-and-steel chorus seat, Ronnie the Rat saw the swarming horde expand to infinity to push the flailing locks into the headlights of the train, whose shadow was like a comet's tail across the *Sun*.

'And he looked like such a nice boy,' Ena wept.

'Even though he was coloured,' Eva blubbed.

'Darcas was right,' the black-pant-suited *Guardian* groupie swore, pointing to the feature on the Stephen Lawrence report, and the horrified Ena and Eva scowled at the picture of the big coloured buck with fat white teeth and bulgy, jungle eyes.

'Institutional Racism!' the Black intellectual shouted, pointing his factory-fresh Sony camcorder above the crowd to get footage for his snazzy millennium pic on the BLACK EXPERIENCE, sponsored by the British National Lottery.

'If only we'd known what he was saying, this wouldn't have happened,' Ena wailed, adjusting her Union Jack scarf.

'Don't blame yourself, love,' Eva consoled, 'we can't know all their coloured dialects.'

'All he wanted was the train to Walthamstow,' the man in the deer-stalker hat said, removing his Sherlock Holmes pipe and fanning himself with the latest issue of the American *Spectator*, featuring the panegyric on Murray's *The Bell Curve*, by Adolf Ovens-Pitchfork.

'How d'you know?' Several voices rang in unison as the crowd recoiled.

'I know all right, I'm Roger Scrotum, Condor Blackamoor Professor of Modern African History at Peterhouse, biographer of my illustrious predecessor J. A. Froude, and author of the *The Noble Arap Moi*. I know more Gikuyu than this late illegal immigrant, who indeed wouldn't have died if he hadn't been here. I advised President Moi on blood sports, human rights, and Michael Portillo. With his dreadlocks and gibberish, the late Gikuyu youth was obviously some leftist disciple of Kimathi or Wa' Thiongo, who didn't believe in the enterprise culture, wealth creation, big-game hunting, or Sir Bernard Ingham –'

'So why didn't you say something, Mr Hitler-had-more-than-one,' the pant-suit shouted, waving her *Guardian* magazine under his English nose.

'We weren't introduced, my dear, maybe in your country, Bongo-Bongo Land –'

'Get the toff!' Eva and Ena chorused. 'String 'im up!'

The *Guardians, New Statesman* and *Societys, Voices, Tribunes, Nations, Marxism Todays, Demos, Jewish Chronicles, Spartacuses, Daily Workers, Progresses,* and *Socialist Reviews* sprouted like the long-lost field of Walthamstow, as the masses converged on the riding crop of the fantastic Café Royale-liveried, Gikuyu-speaking professor. Jolly Roger could have traded his American *Spectator* for a horse, but even in his spanking new W. & H. Gidden riding-boots and jodhpurs he could still outrun these sandwich-eating, beer-gutted, Stuart Hall-reading, Old Labour, leftist poofs with their antiquated beliefs in 'community' and 'society'.

Ronnie the Rat was not human, he was against man traps, poisons, electric prods and other unratlike instruments of torture and extermination. But days like these tested his ratity beyond limits. His nostrils twitched as he worried how he could distil the wisdom of this sad tale for his dear lady wife, who only chewed on mouldy scraps of Marty Amis's simple fables for the valiant, snooker-playing, working men of Hampstead.

As he slid down the crack to his hole, Ronnie felt as if the locks were on his head now, holding him back in a mood of Sophoclean contemplation.

He and his family had discussed a move the first morning after they experienced the rush hour. Now Tony and his cronies had gone to No. 10, perhaps they could relocate to the splendid squalor of Highbury and Islington station, though the creeping scent of polenta, A. A. Gill, extra virgin olive oil, sun-dried tomatoes, truffles, Piers Morgan, dried mushrooms and ciabatta were enough to make any self-respecting rat sick to the tummy.

VERNELLA FULLER

Born For You

She was walking over a bridge. Underneath she could hear the faint trickle of water, as if an idle angel was secretly playing musical notes beneath her. She found herself by the water. It was perfectly limpid, thousands of fish darting here and there. Transfixed by their almost unreal resplendence, she watched for moments before immersing her fingers playfully in the water. Its sharp coldness took her breath away. Gently, she circled her fingers among the fish, creating patterns that lingered momentarily. The fish floated between her fingers, as if she, like them, were at home cavorting aimlessly in shoals.

Carlette was used to vivid dreams, used to being preoccupied with them at least part of her day, and wishing her grandmother, Nana, was around, or even her mother, who had the lesser gift of interpreting them. Carlette had learned the meaning of some of the symbols over the years, but she could not for the life of her remember if she had ever been told what fish inhabiting crystal-clear water meant.

She called Jamaica the following night to ask her mother. Her mother, glad to hear from her, commented only briefly on the waste of money.

'It's a good dream. It means children,' she instructed.

'Not likely with the clips on my Fallopian tubes,' Carlette muttered. Yet she watched for signs throughout the day of spontaneous excessive bleeding, an indication of ectopic pregnancy.

Four days later, other dreams having replaced her frolicking fish, Carlette and her daughter were on the way to see Gerardine for the first time, uncertain how she had let the social worker talk her into meeting her. Carlette's policy had always been to look after teenagers only, allowing a lot of space between them and her daughter. Carlette had no grand psychological theory to support this, only her intuition. A nine-year-old would give only a two-year gap.

Since the divorce Efua had been used to having her mother mainly to herself, or at least being the youngest when the foster-children came. Carlette did not want her to feel insecure or threatened. But social workers have a certain gift for distracting a potential carer from the hastened litany of challenges that a young person presents. This time the litany included 'disinterested', 'rejecting family', 'school-resistant', 'inability to form relationships' and 'four-times-weekly sessions with the psychotherapist'. Inexplicably, all this receded, attention focusing instead on the desperate reasons for the placement; abuse, neglect, rejection, or simply no one else available.

Choosing to have the au pair was one of her better decisions. But Maud came with her problems, too. Sometimes it was like having two children, but the French girl's obvious adoration of Efua, the convenience, and Efua's fast-expanding French vocabulary gave her patience.

When Carlette entered the foster-child's home of three weeks, Gerardine was rolling on the floor, her flimsy dress riding over her head. 'Christ. I won't be able to cope with *this!*' She muttered.

Efua stared from the skinny, boyish-looking girl on the floor to her mother. Carlette was grateful that her daughter was no longer three years old, when she would utter every thought that entered her mind. Carlette took the seat she was offered by Jane, the young girl's present carer, stealing half-smiling looks in the little girl's direction, trying not to focus too directly on her short dry, peppercorn hair, unfamiliar with brush or comb. Flaky white patches on Gerardine's skin tarnished the rich brown fighting to surface. Carlette was not sure that the young girl had noticed them come in, but was told that the floor dance was for their benefit. Jane heard Carlette's sigh.

'I know. Can you imagine having to live with that day in, day out?'

Jane's daughter, Emma, appeared from upstairs, followed shortly by her son, Marcus. Her husband, Mark, was at work in a local supermarket, where he was a deputy manager. The children were not as Carlette had imagined.

She had been told it was a mixed-race family, the mother white, the father black. The children showed no sign of their black genes. Emma, the older of the two, had fair hair and grey eyes like her mother. Marcus shared the grey eyes but had ginger-brown hair.

Jane must have read her eyes. 'Mark is mixed race but his sisters and brothers are all colours of the rainbow, some have come out black, some white, he's black. Our kids are throwbacks I think.'

The two children, who were off to see an aunt who lived locally, kissed their mother, said goodbye to Gerardine and left.

Jane whispered, 'Emma doesn't get on with her at all. She's never met anyone like her before. Her behaviour is completely bizarre. Strange. They share a room. Emma can't take it. She can't be left alone. She's always touching. She sneaks Emma's toys out of the house if you don't keep an eye out. The nightmares are terrible . . . loud.'

The catalogue of troubles presented over the past three weeks made Carlette dizzy. The singing and dancing in the streets, Gerardine's overfamiliarity with strangers, especially men, the violence towards Emma and Marcus and other children, her wilful destruction of property.

Jane lowered her voice '. . . I don't think she's all there really. I think she needs to be in a children's home, I don't think there is a foster-carer who can meet her needs. I have to think of my own children.'

Carlette wondered how much Efua and her would-be foster-daughter were taking in. For her part, she was more confused now than before, more torn. But she had enough experience not to be critical of the foster-carer.

Fleetingly, Carlette saw herself in the child, a frightened and shell-shocked eleven years old, fresh from Jamaica. Entering the cold womb of a house in Clapham for the first time, peered at by her own mother, father and siblings, who she did not know or remember. Thoughts tripping over each other in her head of how to get away, to escape back home to Jamaica and her beloved Nana, to her best friend Sissy, her school, her dogs.

Her longing for the familiar things of life had been so intense, her own skinny body had been racked with pain for a year. She had ached desperately to see, touch and hear the things she knew, the familiar sounds of daylight, the joy of school recesses, rote-learning of tables, reciting poetry, sitting upright in neat wooden bench rows. Cricket. Seville oranges for balls and countless 'How's zats?'. Sharp sound of marbles on polished, red shiny verandas; tired of those quiet games of jacks.

Later, sweetly exhausted, petrified, she gave attention to ghastly *duppy* stories, fast followed by the heart-stopping scary silences of pitch-black nights. She ached for the smell of the earth when it rained after the long spells of drought, of patterns made by black ants labouring together, in red bauxite soil, Jamaica gold. She longed to see the stars, visible every night. She mourned the mountains between which her district was safely nestled, climbing to the top of them, just to prove she could.

Occasionally now, over two decades since that first day in Clapham, the tears still came, for the grandmother she had left in Jamaica and never saw again. And, too, for the parents who, ten years ago, left her. Again. This time retracing their steps, returning to Jamaica, just when she had finally found it in her heart to forgive them for taking *her* away, and even to love them.

Carlette feared a new well of pain would begin now for this young child, taken in the dead of night from her mother. To seek asylum in a land she had not even heard of, with a people and language she had not imagined, even in her dreams.

'Gerardine, Gerardine?' she called gently. The young girl looked briefly at Carlette but did not respond. She turned back to Jane, 'What's her English like? The social worker told me she speaks fluent French and Lingala.'

'She doesn't say much at home. She saves her singing and dancing for the streets,' Jane said without malice.

'Gerardine, quel âge as-tu?'

'J'ai neuf ans.'

'You speak French?' Jane asked Carlette.

'Not really, just half-remembered O-level phrases, learned twenty years ago.'

'I can try speaking to her, Mummy,' Efua offered.

Carlette smiled at her daughter and nodded. Efua sat next to her and began asking her questions in French – name, age, school, best friend, hobbies. Pausing, she looked enquiringly at her mother when no response came. Carlette smiled encouragement. Efua tried again, telling Gerardine about herself in French that sounded wonderfully fluent to her mother and Jane. Gerardine looked at her suspiciously for minutes without answering, then without warning she raised a fist and thumped Efua hard on the back. Instinctively, the child ran to her mother, too startled to cry.

'Did I say something wrong, Mummy?'

'No, sweetheart, you didn't. Don't worry,' Carlette soothed.

'I told you. I don't think it is fair on our children.'

In the car Efua wanted to know what was making Gerardine unhappy. 'Her eyes are beautiful eyes but they are so sad. They don't smile.'

'I know, sweetie, she has had some sad times.'

'Why?'

'Her country was at war and lots of people have hurt her. She has seen her friends and family hurt. She has lost her mum.'

'Will she ever find her?'

'I'm not sure, darling.'

A long silence followed.

'Can we help to make her better?'

'Do you think we should? Do you forgive her for hitting you?'

'I thought it was mean at first. I don't understand why she did it, but I feel sad for her. Her eyes and her hair make me sad. Why do you think they've but her hair so short? Like a boy. Like a boy who doesn't comb his hair.'

Carlette was contacted early the next day by the desperate social worker. They had no other black carer, the next option would be to put Gerardine out of borough or in a children's home again. But Carlette did not have to be persuaded. Her daughter's words had done that the night before.

Gerardine's only relative in the country who could now be found, an uncle, wanted her with an African family. There was none on their books. 'In the end he felt that your having been married to an African was the lesser evil,' the social worker said without irony.

'Kind of an African,' Carlette said. 'Only his mother was African, his father was from Guyana . . .' She thought, but did not say, if denial is what defines a nationality or race, he is a non-colour Englishman, not an African. She said instead, 'How did he know?'

'Your daughter's name?'

Carlette shook her head. The social worker had obviously assumed that she would say yes. It piqued her, but she did not bother to express her annoyance, as the traumatized young girl thrashing about on the floor had not left her mind.

The child was drowning, and Carlette could not get to her. The swimming pool was packed with children screaming enjoyment of their various water games. No one else saw the frantic thrashing or heard the cries. Carlette tried but could not attract the life-guards' attention from her position high on the spectators' balcony. She charged down the stairs, through the door, down more steps, then found herself stuck. Inexplicably she could not move. No sound came from her mouth, screaming help.

The realization that she had been dreaming was evoked by the intense piercing scream that came from downstairs. Carlette, in her half-waking half-sleeping state lay in confusion, trying to move and stay in bed simultaneously. It was the more familiar sound of Efua shouting her mother's name and Maud trying to console her that brought Carlette to her senses.

She charged down the spiral steps that led from her loft room to the next landing, and three bedrooms from which various sounds of confusion and anxiety were coming. Gerardine was still immersed in her nightmare-induced hysterics. In the five months that had elapsed Carlette had not got used to the intensity of Gerardine's soul-wrenching screams, cold sweat bathing her skinny frightened body, the long minutes it took to soothe her, Carlette's fear was that that would be the first of many that night and, even more, that they would come again the following night. Carlette found them more stressful, more difficult, than the strange behaviour patterns that Jane had described. She feared Efua, too, would be traumatized and permanently scarred. She worried that Maud would leave, to au pair for a saner family. Many nights, back in their rooms, everyone finally settled, she lay awake, deep-breathing, trying to coax sleep, turning over in her head the excuses she would make for ending the placement.

In the six-monthly review meeting Carlette tried to focus on the positive. She had to echo some of the previous foster-carer's words but also indicated glimpses of the kind, loving, sweet-tempered child that was often buried underneath the depths of trauma. Afterwards, when most everyone had gone, ambivalent about the next six months which had been agreed, Carlette said to Gerardine's social worker, 'I do find it disconcerting the way she stares at me. She can sit for hours, unblinking almost, just focusing on my face. As if she is trying to bond with me. Yes, exactly that. The way Efua used to stare at me when she was a baby.'

'She *is* trying to bond with you.'

'At nearly ten years old?'

Carlette's parents visited from Jamaica. Although they had vowed that the twenty years in England had been more than sufficient, they returned every two years to visit grandchildren and children.

They were not the first to comment on the resemblance between Carlette's foster-daughter and herself. At first Carlette had been offended, Efua hurt; now she had to admit she could see it too. The high forehead, large dark eyes, even the well-defined lips and perfect white teeth giving the broad ready smile everyone found attractive. The thick rope-like hair, allowed now to flourish, the pure brown velvet-soft skin. Even their body shapes were similar, wasp-like waist and bulbous bottom. And recently Carlette had noticed the birthmark on Gerardine's left shoulderblade, a deeper black than the rest of her body. It looked identical to one on her own chest.

'The girl was surely born for you,' her mother said.

Her father, finding humour in everything he observed, said, 'You sure you didn't have the chil' when you down at that university campus and hide her? The chil' is dead stamp of your Aunt Roberta. Dead stamp, I tell you. I have never seen the like before.'

'I wouldn't be surprised if this child not from some of our long-lost stock in the motherland,' her mother said. 'You could never give that child up, sweetheart. That child was born for you for true.'

That night Carlette went to bed and remembered for the first time in nearly a year her dream of the fish cavorting in clear water and the gift of a child her mother had foretold.

E. A. MARKHAM

Seminar on the Frank Worrell Roundabout, Barbados

She's not going to admit her name just yet. Maybe she'd get cold feet again and just pretend to be somebody else; and crawl away at the end of it all, furious with herself. When is she going to break through this terror? Her name is more likely than not to come up during the proceedings. And she's going to be accused of, well, she doesn't want to think of it. And she would go away without having the courage to come out. She's thinking of a poet called Stapleton, and how that time in Wellingborough he dealt with his other identities, particularly the one who was a woman, can't remember her name – Betty? Sally? – God, the simplest things absolutely refuse to stick.

Anyway, here's this fellow, a bit self-satisfied, hinting at his importance in the university, but interesting nevertheless, white hair and beard – all these Black men with white hair and beards! Glasses, too: as if made up to look like it! The degree show at the art college comes to mind: Black men. White hair. Glasses. Now Go Forth and read the *News at Ten* sort of thing. Though that one doesn't have a beard. Ah, but you're drifting, the woman tells herself, your mind's wandering. So now concentrate, concentrate; where was she?

Oh yes. Stapleton at Wellingborough that night: she (*come on, girl, be serious, the name is Eye See Eye, it's on your book, it's been reprinted*), Eye See Eye, remembers someone in the audience asking Stapleton about his persona who is a woman. One of those names you hear from time to time and never doubt it's a woman. A book of poems under her name. Written by this man. A White woman written by this Black man. The only problem was that feminist magazines had printed some of the work. That was in the seventies. Looking back from the nineties, all that seemed fussy, precious. The nineties were more open, you could play it straight, not that Eye See Eye agreed with that. And how did Stapleton deal with this, how did he get out of that one?

But the taxi-driver is talking to her; she must have said something out loud: she's got to pull herself together, she's in no state to head up the hill to the university: better go round the roundabout one more time.

They were on the Frank Worrell roundabout and the taxi-driver wanted to turn off and head up the hill to the university, to Cave Hill. And she was on the point of telling him to take the next turn-off and head right back to the hotel so she could lock herself in her room till it was time to head home to Wellingborough. Because, really, she couldn't face those people up there, the experts, the writers, international figures, household names, who must see her as an upstart; and unwelcome. Unless she came in really heavy as *Eye See Eye: So bwoy, how yu doin', you arwright?* And maybe she could be carrying a copy of Kamau Brathwaite's *Barabajan Poems* to deflect attention. (Got to get the stress just right): Bara*bajan*. BaraBAJAN. *Bajan.*

'Yes, of course, I'm Bajan.' That was the taxi-driver.

And Eye See Eye is covered in confusion because she had been talking aloud and the taxi-driver is now answering her and asking if she's ready to turn off the roundabout. Or what her intentions are. She had a momentary urge to shock him and say her intentions were to get laid early and often, but who knows if he has a sense of humour?, so she just directs him to go round the roundabout one more time, if he didn't mind. And he says, 'That's your privilege.' She doesn't quite like the way he says that. Patronizing. She'd have him know that in England she is written up as a West Indian writer, whatever her colour, and she can buss bad word with the rest of them: is not only Agard and company who caan mash up language. And she could push up she face and chuppes if any of them man give she grief. But she didn't want to pull rank and get too heavy with the taxi-driver, so she just ignored his tone. (*You talking to me?*) For even coming back at him would be something too intimate. In the end she just said, in her most neutral voice, 'Thank you; thank you very much.' No edge. Just the calmness of the voice to tell the bitch who in charge. And for the first time on the journey, Eye See Eye has a little smile on her face.

And it works, you know, the taxi-driver is apologizing for breaking into her thoughts, and she is conscious that, sitting in the back seat of the car, maybe the relationship between her and the driver isn't as equal as it might be; so the edge in his voice probably came from that sense of uneasiness. But maybe he wasn't thinking any of those things because here he is making a little joke, a joke about having to make a pit-stop. When she understood what he was saying she bent forward, and looking at the petrol gauge and saw that he was very far from being out of petrol, so he was still at it. And, very calmly, she said she'll pay for the extra petrol.

It's not petrol he wants, he wants to go to the loo, and there's a petrol station just along the road next to the supermarket where she bought a heavy cake the day before and a newspaper for the local colour. There was a loo in there. She quite appreciated his delicacy about the loo, and to be honest she too could do with a visit, so she said, 'Yes, why not.' Good idea, she isn't in a hurry.

So they turned off and drove a few yards along the road and pulled in at the petrol station next to the supermarket. And she went to the loo. When she came out the taxi-driver was eating a cake and drinking something from a bottle, and he asked if she wanted something to eat. She wasn't sure whether he was offering her some of what he was already eating or inviting her to buy something from the supermarket. So she said, 'No, thanks', and that seemed to put him out, because here was she, ready to continue the journey, and the driver was caught out eating, and she, the passenger, had to wait. Maybe that's why his tone changed. It was as if he felt the need to atone. And he explained his joke about the pit-stop.

Apparently, on one of the islands, in St Caesare, a small island in the Leewards, they had a famous roundabout race, a race built on the idea of the roundabout. As most races are, come to think of it – apart from those hundred yards, hundred metres sorts of sprints. Anyway, this race was a motor race. Up in St Caesare. And they say it's now spread to Beef Island as well. And Barbardos was the one to thank for it. Apparently, on those little islands the sense of lacking hinterland was even more acute than Barbados, and the idea of the roundabout came about after all sorts of studies of how to relieve *pressure* on the people, giving them a sense of not being hemmed in, giving them a sense of possibilities – a roundabout with lots of signs pointing to places where they could turn off. At the famous St Caesare roundabout just outside Barville, the capital, you could turn off to places like Coderington and Windy Hill and the *soufriere*, which of course blew up some time back. And you could turn off even to Montserrat, which was the next little island. Or you could just go into the capital, Barville. That was Roundabout *one*, an idea that created even greater space for the people of St Caesare, because who's to know that there isn't a Roundabout *two* and a Roundabout *seven* and a Roundabout *twenty-nine*? And this whole idea of a roundabout to solve your problems of space was pioneered right here in Barbados, who had adopted this way of honouring its distinguished citizens without having to take up too much space. Worrell and Walcott were accommodated here on the Cane Gardens highway. Weekes and Sobers were further down the ABC highway on the way to the Grantely Adams airport. Nita Barrow . . .

Eye See Eye was taken by this idea of the roundabout to solve your space problem and thought what a clever way to relieve the pressure on you of feeling trapped in a small space. She couldn't help it, she had to take out her notebook; there was a poem here. There was a book of poems here. Now it was the turn of the driver to wait on her.

Eye See Eye felt better for that little briefing and note-taking at the petrol station. She felt a bit closer to the taxi-driver as a result. Maybe he was the sort of person who might even attend the conference. She could see him now, sitting at the back of the room and saying nothing for a couple of sessions and then stunning everyone at the end of the day with a reference to some obscure Shakespeare play or with a really intimate knowledge of the early novels of Edgar Mittelholtzer and Austin Clarke and Earl Lovelace; so that the prominent writers and scholars and professor would suddenly have to take note and be guarded in their response. *This taxi-driver man will do.*

'So what do you think of Kamau's interview with Nathaniel Mackey?' she asks him.

'Oh, the *conVERSations* . . .' He thought about this for a while and then motioned that he was going to put the empty bottle in the bin outside. Then he wiped his mouth with the back of his hand even though the mouth was already clean, for he had wiped it with a napkin, but she noted the gesture. Then he signalled that she should follow him back to the car.

Should she sit in the back, as before? That film, whatever it was called,

Miss Daisy something something with the White woman in the back of the car and the Black driver doing his Hollywood thing, made her want to sit in the front. But what if *he* didn't want her to sit in front? *Driving Miss Daisy.* What if sitting in front gave him the wrong idea? So in the end she decided to get back into the back seat of the car and let him take the initiative. When they got back to the Frank Worrell Roundabout he seemed to hesitate a little, and instead of turning off to Cave Hill, he decided to go round the roundabout one more time. She liked that.

Third time round he started to talk. She was missing out, you know. On all the hugging and kissing and shaking hands and clapping one another on the back. (*Eye See Eye had a momentary image of Roman senators in the Capitol, and daggers . . .*) These conferences were little United Nations meetings, you know; folk down from Canada and the US and England. And in from the region. Guyana. Belize. Bahamas. All that. Breaking ice. Pulling rank. Liming. She was missing out on the easy entry for those who got there early. By leaving it late she was walking right into the spotlight. *She would be noticed.* She couldn't play shy then, or people would think she was stand-offish. She playing fresh. And another thing – she would miss out on the security of sitting through those early papers which let you pick up the codes and tone of the thing – you know, the sort of reference being made about Kamau and Walcott this year. And whether that boy who took on Lamming at the Warwick conference last year was going to have anyone argue his case about tourism being a good thing for the islands. Or again, Naipaul: was his name still good to guarantee a little ripple of laughter and scorn in the audience? And so on. And she was missing out, during the tea-break and lunch hour, on a little bit of networking. It was a political thing, making out with people you really hate. (Of course, during your paper, you have to look up and see who's who in the audience, and make mention of them, like royalty.) Anyway, the way she was going, by the time she got there, all the invitations to future conferences would have been passed out.

Eye See Eye, in the back of the taxi, had stopped taking notes; clearly this man thought she was a novice: did he know he was talking to someone who only last year got an Eastern Arts Association grant for poems and had invitations for readings galore but declined out of sensitivity to her black sisters and brothers. Anyway, back to the present.

(*Back to the present*: she thought that was a quaint little phrase, but no time to take it further now . . .) She was looking over the conference programme, determined to show the driver who was in charge here, who was on top, sort of thing. *Caribbean Voices: Early Years of Caribbean Writing in Britain*. All about Swanzy and Collymore. Swanzy in London, Collymore in Barbados. Famous BBC radio programme, forties, fifties, coming out of London. Gave space to all those people – Lamming, Naipaul, Salkey, Walcott, Mittelholtzer, etc. – the guys still beating us in we backside to this day. She had a mentor in England (no name mentioned) who had been encouraging her to get rid of the quotation marks from *Caribbean Voices*, opening it out, man, to the wider Caribbean, and not only to include those who live overseas and claim heritage, but to Caribbean people by adoption – Bob Shacochis from America, Stewart Brown from Birmingham. *Eye See Eye* from Wellingborough. She wanted to ask him if he's heard of Eye See Eye. But instead she asked about Kamau's interview with Nathaniel Mackey.

'The man's liming, man; liming.'

'Oh.'

'What them fellow call, them fellow down in Trinidad, call Semilime, man. Liming.'

OK, she could take it. And had he heard of Eye See Eye?

'They run the place, man; all the islands.'

'Eye See Eye. Not CIA.'

But he started telling her about the CIA. Eye See Eye sighed; you couldn't compete. And she wasn't focusing on the thing at hand. She remembered the way in which that fellow, the poet, had justified his female persona that night in Wellingborough. That gave her courage, so she sat back in the seat, closed her eyes and tried to keep cool, emptying her mind as the taxi-driver droned on about *Bim* and Colly and John Wickham, who apparently was alive but a bit shaky. And again, *Bim*, and the other magazines in the region, *Kyk-over-all* in Guyana and Edna Manley's *Focus* in Jamaica. That and more: nationalism and its effect on the literature. Paternalism from the centre. Then he was talking of the race to push the start of West Indian literature to a place further back in time than the last speaker placed it. From *Bim* to the twenties in Trinidad with Albert Gomes and CLR James and those boys round the *Beacon*;

and from there further back to the newspaper stuff at the end of the last century; and of course from there, back to Africa; and beyond Africa to America before Columbus; and then to Noah and the Ark and finally to Eve, who was a West Indian woman come out of the water to find Walcott there again ready to give she language.

'Man, put wey you truncheon, lewme rest.' But she didn't say it. She was thinking of an Andrew Salkey image she might use if she ever got to the conference. There were two she had jotted down. His 'high-rise bottom', describing Caribbean women; she wondered if the driver found it sensuous, but she didn't dare ask. The other image was the one describing the scattered nature of the West Indian family as a 'sea-split marriage'. Maybe that one was safer, if more tame; and she felt strong enough now to interrupt her tutor and order him to head for the university.

They drove into the campus. So far so good. They found the venue. No problem there, it was easy to find because there were important-looking people relaxing outside with drinks and nibbles, as if the drinks and nibbles were beneath them. The writers. The scholars. The professors. Was she dressed right for this? The women looked so cool in the heat. Was her skin conspiring against her: was she *deprived* in this setting? That man. A professor, clearly: how could he keep that line, down to the shoes, crisp and soft, not flabby soft, but soft. And he must be fifty if he's a day. Sixty. Body of a young boy. Even the shirt was cool. Classical and cool. How did his wife let him venture into a place dangerous as this?

And here was he coming forward to shake her hand; it was her knees that needed attention. And her stomach was rumbling, and she needed the loo. Her name was . . . *ackee & salt fish & rice 'n' peas & fried fish & flying fish & fish . . . And plantain & banana and . . . and breadfruit and breadnut and mango. And guava and passion fruit . . . And de Lisser & Mittelholtzer. Just another Mittelholtzer, please. No glass, God, you didn't tell me it was going to be this hard.* And she is half-wondering how she is going to pay off the taxi. And she's missing Wellingborough, missing Wellingborough. And the professor-writer before her has white hair and a white beard. And she can't believe what she hearing because before he shakes her hand and hugs her up and kisses her on both cheeks, he calling her by name, Eye See Eye.

Memoirs

BEN BOUSQUET

The Black Section of the Labour Party

I've been a revolutionary in more ways than one – I was one of the first persons to call a strike in the National Health Service, in 1974, and as a Kensington Labour Party member, I stood against and defeated the leader of the Social Democratic Alliance. However, one of the things that gave me the most satisfaction was founding the Black Section of the Labour Party with Billy Ho Ning Poh and Ray Philbert. For a number of years we'd been trying to create a Black Section movement because we realized that there was a need for Black people to organize themselves within the Labour Party. I was at one of those joint Party meetings when I met Billy and Ray. They said that they had been trying to do something similar to what I was doing in North Kensington. We agreed to work together. For almost two years, we sent out motions to Black Labour councillors and party activists telling them of meetings which we were holding, asking them to attend. They never replied. Consequently, Ray, Billy and myself would meet either at North Kensington or North Westminster Labour Party HQ to set up the principles of the organization.

In 1983 we sent meeting invitations to all the Black people we knew who were members of the Labour Party. We got little response to our invites, yet these were people elected as councillors. We did get a letter from Paul Boateng, saying that he would have loved to attend but was on his way to the US. So we decided to get motions put on the agenda of our local constituencies (Westminster and the Royal Borough of Kensington and Chelsea) and hoped that these would be accepted by the Labour Party at conference. We managed to talk to Iris Slocumb, a Black councillor in Hendon South, and she moved a motion, as we did, asking for Black representation.

So that year at the Labour Party conference for the first time there were three motions, all pertaining to the same subject. We were sent to the Labour Party conference by our constituencies, then we called the first Black fringe meeting, which Keith Vaz, Paul Boateng and Diane Abbott attended. However, some of the Black councillors and others involved in the party didn't support it, believing it to be damaging to the Labour Party.

We had very clear guidelines of what we were going to do. My job was to get the delegates to support our motion. Billy liaised with me and the fringe groups to gain their support. Ray was to monitor the proceedings and come up with clear guidelines so that we were not caught unawares when it was our turn to speak.

But, to our amazement, on the second day of conference, when we tried to get the motion discussed at conference, the Labour Party Executive decided that they weren't going to discuss it at all. That's when we realized we needed the support of more experienced people in the party. Jo Richardson, the MP for Bethnal Green (now Oona King's constituency), and Tony Benn instantly saw what we were trying to do and the necessity of it, realized that it would benefit the Labour Party and gave their immediate and unhesitating support. They worked diligently to get our motion discussed.

When I asked Terry Duffy of the AUEW, he also gave us 100 per cent support, whereas the leader of the miners' union, Arthur Scargill, refused. I told Scargill then that it would be a Black group that would come to his rescue if he ever needed it, and just two years later the miners went on strike. It was the Black people who worked in and supported the TU movement who came to their aid.

The Labour Party conference committee conceded, saying that it might allow a selection of speakers at the end of the day, a short speech. It was surprising – Labour was talking about racism and this was a chance for them to do something positive about it, but they blew it. Eventually, they decided that they would allow us to speak for three minutes. The first person to speak at conference on Black Sections was the councillor from Lewisham; Keith Vaz was the second. I had hoped to speak but I was not called.

Two bodies that Black people have loyalty to are the Labour Party and the Trade Union movement, and neither one had any strong represen-tation for Black people. The Standing Conference of African and Caribbean and Asian Councillors, started by Russell Profitt, was already in existence, but we wanted to do something more than that. We needed an organiza-tion that could do something within the party itself, including looking at racism within the party, the needs of Black elders, of the Black minority, of Black people in the National Health Service.

Our aims and objectives were a) to get the Labour Party to take Black people seriously; by forming our own section it would make Black people more aware of their own needs from the Labour Party and b) to get more Black people in the Trade Union movement to take up representative roles as shop stewards. There were probably a greater percentage of Black people within the movement, but we were only being paid lip-service.

It was at the Brighton conference that the first Black fringe meeting was held. Once we'd established this first fringe meeting, we were on the agenda. Our motion was moved and composited to the Blackpool conference of 1984. By 1986, thousands of Black people had joined the Labour Party and, by 1987 we had our first Black MPs. If it had not been for the Black Section of the Labour Party, there would be no Black MPs today. That's a fact. It empowered Black people by allowing their voices to be heard.

I'm no longer a member of the Labour Party; I left ten years ago. There was a case of racism in Kensington which I was personally involved in, and the Labour Party chose not to pursue it.

I was a councillor in Kensington and Chelsea from 1978 to 1990. Yet in 1987 the Labour Party deselected me. They thought that once I had turned the constituency around, they would automatically win. But they lost by 400 votes, because people in my constituency refused to vote. I don't think the Labour Party understood the pride of a Black man, and I don't think they expected me to react as I did. I won't accept racism anywhere, so I walked out.

The Black Section of the Labour Party had folded by 1990. I still believe in a progressive Black Section organization. But if one was to be set up again, we need to be involved in all political parties and organizations.

BECKY AYEBIA CLARKE

Is Beauty in the Eye of the Beholder?

I have spent the last ten years trying to slim. I have tried the Slimfast juices that promised me all but delivered nothing. No sooner would I have gulped one down one than I'd be hovering by the fridge. On days when the diet is on full steam, I starve myself all day and then binge on all manner of food at dawn, a bit like breaking one's fast to make up for lost time.

At times of utter desperation, I would rush out to the nearest supermarket and stock up on rye bread, cottage cheese and salads. Yes, especially the salads with the accompanying 'oil-free' dressings. I can hear you say, What about cream dressing? What about it? The only oil that sneaks into my system during this oil-free fast is palm oil. You know, it is meant to have real medicinal qualities, is rich in Vitamin A, improves skin texture and aids digestion. No, seriously, palm oil is not part of the diet, but occasionally one gets these urges to eat some proper food. That is not to say that one abandons the diet altogether – far from it! I mean, don't they have half-time during football matches? Tennis players get a few minutes to catch their breath after every two games. And boxers get the odd few minutes to sit down on their tiny stool and work out how to knock their opponent out of the ring. It is in this manner, of giving myself the odd breather, that the rot sets in and I reach out for the *egusi* stew and . . . well, I am sure you would approve of the rest.

When I travelled home to Accra at the height of one of these (stop-start, stop-start) slimming periods, I felt quite good about myself. As I descended the steps of the Boeing 747 into the familiar smells of hot and humid Accra, I could feel the sweat trickling down the back of my figure-hugging Monsoon outfit and felt all was well with the world.

Mama was so pleased to see me, but she was horrified at how 'thin' I looked. For a few days I couldn't quite work out the reason, I kept catching her eye looking me over. Then, one morning as I took breakfast of *koko* and *koose* to her room and sat on the edge of her bed to have our usual tête-à-tête (something we have always done to sort out real problems and share in our joys), she asked if everything was all right between me and my husband. Taken aback by the deep concern Mama had shown, I asked why.

It all came tumbling out – how she had always known me to be big-boned and well-rounded, with child-bearing hips; a real woman and not one of these sticks hiding under *ntama* and *kaba*, parading around as though representing the image of new woman, but really looking quite ill. I tried to tell Mama that in my adopted culture, where I now live and work, it is considered quite beautiful to be thin. Upon which, I was quickly reprimanded and reminded that I might live in that culture, but home is home, and I mustn't forget the good things I was taught about womanhood.

In the early morning sunshine, I noticed Mama's furrowed brow, and the realization came to me that not only are we a generation apart but we live in two different worlds.

Then the lecture started: 'You know, in our culture, at the onset of puberty, a girl is put in a room for a week and fattened for *dipo*. She eats, drinks and does nothing all day, and on the seventh day she is bathed and bedecked in precious beads and expensive gold jewellery and takes her place among her peer group, she's paraded through the town square amid a lot of pomp and ceremony in celebration of her transition from girlhood into womanhood. And that my dear, is our culture.'

Her voice trailed off when she said, 'And I hear the Effiks of Calabar have a similar culture of the fattening-rooms initiation ceremonies for girls before betrothal.' My immediate reaction was to say to her, 'Mama but I don't live in Calabar, Dodowa or Somanya, I live in Oxford.' One never argues with Mama, not if one has any sense.

The final blow came when I excused myself to go jogging. I have found jogging along a sandy beach (something I used to enjoy as a child) a real calorie-burner and I was eager to take advantage of the cool morning sea-breeze. Mama gave me that look, which I know so well and recognized instinctively from my childhood, with its coded message: 'I don't approve.'

Then (casually) she said, 'I was hoping to take you to church on Sunday to offer blessings for your safe return home. The women in the choir (I used to sing in this prestigious Presbyterian choir) have planned a special session and were hoping you would join them for a service billed as a

"Special Sunday". Besides, the Reverend Father is coming especially from our headquarters for this event. But,' she said, 'looking at you, you look so thin and, well, with all the other women looking fresh and womanly, perhaps it's not such a good idea. No offence,' she added, 'but I think you really ought to eat a bit more. Perhaps, you ought to see the doctor, you never know, there may be something wrong and you may not even know it . . .'

On the day I was due to fly back to London, the whole household was up half the night cooking. Mama was determined to pack me off with enough food to ensure that I was well fed until my next trip. I had shrimps, pepper sauce, palaver sauce, gari, yam, a gallon of palm oil, you name it, packed into small and medium-sized plastic containers embossed with people's wedding dates in green, pink, yellow – representing all the colours of the rainbow. My pleas that one could buy most of these foodstuffs in London's Brixton market fell on deaf ears.

As I hugged Mama in a tearful goodbye, she said I should not forget frequently to send home photographs of myself. And (lowering her voice to almost a whisper) she said, 'I would like to know what the doctor says.' Her last words were: 'Don't forget you used to look so nice in *kente!*'

These events compelled me to pen a poem, which may speak to those of us struggling to strike a balance with the time bomb of our 'dual identities'.

So You Think You Are Beautiful

Mama told me how really beautiful
my child-bearing hips are –

She said the colourful beads
would rest majestically on my hips

She said the baby would sit
comfortably on my hips –

She drummed it into me at an early age
that my figure is something to be proud of –

So I grew up believing that a big rounded
woman with a big backside is beautiful –

She said my ebony skin
complemented my dark eyes –

And my tight black curls, softness with firmness
reflected my charm, warmth and strength

What a shock it was
when my plane touched down.

On Oxford Street
the pretty sales maidens
would rush up to me
and ask –
'Can I help you?'
I said, 'I can't find my size
Can you help?'

And their fleeting slim glances
told me what they were thinking
without words,
'Sorry but we only go up to size 14,
what size are you?'

But Mama said I am beautiful –
Silly little girls, don't they respect age?

So I think I am beautiful?
No I don't think I am beautiful
I KNOW I am beautiful, because Mama told me so!

LINDA BELLOS

History

I have noticed with increasing irritation that there is rarely any reference to Black people that draws upon history. Or if it is, it's a history framed and referenced by Europeans. What I mean by this is that it is not often that a historical context is provided for events and achievements by Black people. Newspapers and broadcast journalists are particularly keen on reporting stories about Black people which emphasize our being the first to have done something. Recently, for example, I heard a BBC Radio 4 journalist introduce John Taylor, now Lord Taylor, as 'the first Black lord'. He is not, but the fact that Radio 4 does not know at least of Sir Pitt or Sir Learie Constantine makes the point.

It was even more evident when in 1998 BBC television and subsequently the rest of the media went overboard with the celebration of the arrival of HMS Empire *Windrush* fifty years earlier. Commentators not only referred to Black people as having first arrived in Britain in 1948 but, more worryingly, many people of African origin who had lived, worked and struggled in Britain throughout the previous centuries were excluded. The implication of this omission was that, prior to their arrival in Britain, those 500 'immigrants' had no history. The hype that surrounded *Windrush* created the impression that Black people could be dated from *Windrush*. I know this not to be the case, because my own father came to Britain from Nigeria in 1942, joining many other African and Caribbean men in Liverpool and later in London in the early, mid- and late 1940s.

No journalist seemed to question where these 'immigrants' managed to live, given that pictures of racist housing policies were also included. To have shown Jamaicans staying with African and other Jamaicans or West Indians might have implied that there were others of us here before 1948. Such a view, however accurate, would not suit those who wish to imply that we had neither history nor social networks here. In general, increased use of propaganda, and using events such as the *Windrush* celebrations as a tool, the notion is created that we came into and out of a vacuum and had neither history nor heritage to draw upon.

This brings me to my main concern about the way that Africa and its history are regarded. In recent years the media has covered a number of significant stories about Africa; by 'significant', I mean stories which are covered over days and sometimes weeks. Stories about Rwanda or Sierra Leone are typically about war. Although the coverage made less frequent use of words like 'tribal' or 'ethnic conflict', what each report did, as do so many others about Africa, was to fail to refer to the reasons underlying the war, which, if not known to either reporters or news editors, they did not bother to find out. In referring to the causes of warring Rwanda, a passing reference to Belgium is sometimes made, but I have yet to hear any reference to the creation of Rwanda (as it is now called) by Belgium at the Berlin Congress of 1884, which carved up Africa between the major European powers. It seems improbable to me that one can understand the Rwandan or any other African conflict without understanding the history of Africa over the last 200–300 years. However, if one chooses to limit oneself to looking only at the post-colonial period, one might conclude, as many white supremacists have apparently done, that Africa is incapable of self-government. Media coverage and discussions on Africa and its history are usually more concerned with origins and ancient history on a romantic and emotional level. The hundreds of years in between in which vast kingdoms, well-structured and organized societies existed, before European intervention, are, to a large extent, ignored.

I would not argue that it is possible or desirable to shift all responsibility for difficulties in Africa towards Europeans. African people have agency, many bear personal responsibility for the actions they have taken or failed to take. But it is impossible to consider understanding what is now happening in the former Yugoslavia without an understanding of history. The same, I would suggest applies to Africans and Africa. If nothing else, it will liberate the majority of modern Caribbean people from the dominant supposition that they arrived in the West Indies from Africa on cruise ships.

History may uncover some sad and shameful secrets in all of our closets, but I say, 'Better out than in.'

BONNIE GREER

On Being Half a Hundred Years Old

There are times when you think that maybe you shouldn't admit to that. Being half a hundred years old.

There are times when maybe you should gratefully hide behind the axiom 'Black don't crack.'

Or be coy and slightly apologetic while secretly flattered when some people say, 'Hey, you don't look your age.'

In some cultures, half a hundred years old means that you would be someone's grandmother, maybe even a great-grandmother, full of *gravitas*.

It is strange having been born in the middle of a century that has barely known peace.

A flag made of skull and crossbones flutters over my baby crib. I was born inhaling atomic dust and the smoke from a burning cross.

My father liberated a concentration camp, only to return to one back home.

My mother was a free person, making parachutes in a defence camp. Then the War ended.

But for her, war was just beginning. In the kitchen. In the nursery. Behind the white picket fence of American respectability.

Boys will be boys.

Girls will be girls.

That's what you are taught when you are half a hundred years old.

Yet being half a hundred years old also means:

Seeing Michael Jackson perform when he was a little boy and a genius.

Marching with Martin Luther King, marvelling at how small he was.

Watching Miriam Makeba on prime-time television, short, natural hair like the kind you were told to hide beneath a wig.

Laughing because Malcolm X told great jokes.

Dancing with James Brown for four hours for the price of a candy bar.

Dreaming of a Britain where the Black people were different from the ones you knew back home because Black people in Britain had living roots, and America was just a place like any other to them.

Knowing that masterpieces could come on pieces of vinyl that lasted no more than three minutes.

Liking Black movies that only Black people could understand.

Singing along with singers who sounded better live than on record.

But being half a hundred years old can make you forget things:

Like that old song by that rock group that you used to love:

It went: 'Hope I Die Before I Get Old.'

BUCHI EMECHETA

To Be or not to be British?

When Dr Gwendolyn Mikell of the department of African Post-Colonial Studies in Washington DC asked me to come to Georgetown University and speak about Post-Colonial Studies, I didn't want to go at first, as I don't like travelling much any more. But I was lucky, there were two vacant seats next to each other on the plane, so I could relax and sleep.

Then, an Indian lady came from her seat at the back and sat next to me. She had travelled directly from India. She started chatting; her husband had had a stroke and was really ill. She was going to see her son, who had left Bombay eight years before. He now had a job, she said, a good job. She was going to cook for him as, whenever he wrote home, he always said how much he missed her food. She couldn't wait to escape her husband for a while – he wasn't aware just how much she was sacrificing for him. She took out a photo of her family to show me and so, you know, I took out a photo of mine to show her, and we both talked and chatted about our children. As we arrived in DC she said, 'I'll tell my son, that I met a very nice, intelligent African lady on the plane.' I was flattered.

When we were about to land, she wouldn't open her eyes, I thought she was scared, because we had landed with a bump, so once the plane had stopped throbbing, I said to her, 'You can open your eyes now,' but she still didn't want to open them. She kept her eyes closed; I thought she was praying. In the end, I just got up, and took down my luggage and started moving forward to disembark. Then I noticed that she had just got up. Already there were quite a few people in between us, so she wasn't standing anywhere near me. We got into the satellite bus that takes you from the plane to the terminal. We were still separated. I waved to her, but she didn't respond. When we got to the airport, I turned to see two handsome men meeting her, one of whom must have been her son. I remembered what she had said to me earlier, how she would tell her son that she had met me – a really nice African woman – on the plane, but although she saw me, she pretended that she didn't even recognize me.

She reminded me of another Indian woman, Mrs Sharma, who I had known at a school, Quentin Kynaston, where I had taught many years ago. The same thing had happened, but she at least was sincere.

'If I keep sitting with you at lunch-time,' she had said, 'I'll never get a promotion. I have to go and sit with the others [the 'others' were White colleagues], otherwise they won't promote me.' I talk about that incident in my autobiography, *Head Above Water*.

Yet this lady on the plane didn't even acknowledge me. She had just needed me to keep her company when other passengers could not stand her. Everybody just thinks that Black people are the bottom of the earth. We always bend our backs for others to climb on and reach great heights.

It was raining when I left London, but DC was in blossom, beautiful and sunny. They were having a celebration there, cherry-blossom week. It was so beautiful that despite the incident that had just taken place, it really lifted me.

The next day I gave my talk, on post-colonial literature. I was asked at the end, why it is that I keep saying I'm an African when I've lived in England for over thirty years? Why didn't I call myself British? One woman stood up and said that she was an American – but she didn't look American to me. She said that she had come from Turkey seven years before. I said to her, 'Well, you're not American,' but after six years she could claim to be American, and that makes for stronger communities. In America, the writing community is very strong, it's more like a club. You wouldn't even know that people like Paule Marshall are from the West Indies. It was through her book, *Mama Day*, that I found out that Gloria Naylor was originally from the Caribbean and not from the US. Although many Black writers live in London, we are so scattered, there's no commonality. Maybe, then, to other people and even amongst ourselves we are too Black to be British.

E. A. MARKHAM

Grandmother's Last Will and Testament

Sarah was giving my grandmother her bath and, for once, waiting outside in the drawing-room, I didn't fall asleep over my book. *Robinson Crusoe* was an advance on *The Pilgrim's Progress* in that respect. It was the middle of the week, and we three were alone, as before, in the big house in Harris', now that my grandmother's crisis had passed. My mother had gone back to the old routine, staying in town during the week with my elder brothers and sister, who were at grammar school. Then we'd all be together for the weekend, from Friday evening, when they came with news and presents.

The wick wasn't burning well in the lamp, darkening the shade on one side, but I could see to read. I had been trying, now, to feel the pain of Crusoe hitting his leg on the sand as he was washed ashore, and to figure out why he had two surnames, Robinson and Crusoe, at the expense of a Christian name. I had three Christian names: I was ahead of him there! (The only other person I could think of with no Christian name was my friend RR – Russell Riley. Russell was the son of Professor Croissant down in the village. Professor Croissant was an ignorant man who didn't believe in God. On top of that he had a drink problem – two things which meant that he would never become our headmaster.)

During all this, Sarah came out to say that my grandmother – her bath over – wanted to see me. A quick check. No panic. She had called me a heathen just this morning, but that was because I hadn't cried at a funeral: it was just her way of speaking. She often called teacher Riley a heathen because he wouldn't say 'D.V.', which was the Latin for 'God willing' when he made plans for his or his children's future. So the fact that I was now a Heathen, a member of my cousin Horace's gang, dedicated to the worship of Satan both in the pulpit at the Methodist church in Bethel and at the Anglican church in Harris', was something she couldn't know about.

I checked for more obvious things: yes, I'd washed my hands and feet. Hadn't cleaned my teeth yet, but I wasn't ready for bed; I hadn't forgotten: I was ready for grandmother.

But as I entered the room I found her not under the mosquito net but sitting on her commode in nightdress and dressing-gown. She had an expression as if she was up to something. I liked the smell of bay rum in the room, so much better than the Canadian Healing Oil which she sometimes used and which got everywhere. I thought about the joke we'd been doing to death since last weekend, about my grandmother's new servant. She had got a letter from the governor, in connection with registering some land at Mulcares, and he had signed it 'Your Humble Servant'. We liked the idea of the plump, well-dressed fellow, all superior and fat-cheeked, descending from his official car to fetch my grandmother's ewer of water or to feed the pigs in the animal pound last thing at night. My grandmother herself, protesting, had been tickled by the idea. This was a bayrummy sort of joke that her present aspect seemed to invite, not a Canadian Healing Oil explanation for wrongdoing.

'Yes Mammie.'

'The teeth still hurt?' she asked me. I was tempted to correct her: you got the same treatment for one tooth as for three, so there was no benefit in having more than one go bad at a time; but I let it pass in case she thought I was checking up on her grammar. Anyway, that was all in the past; that was this morning, when I thought there might be a chance of missing school.

'You too small to always have teeth hurting. Get the glass.'

'The glass?'

'The glass, the glass.'

The glass was on top of the dressing-table. At the same time she reached towards the press – she didn't have to move from the commode to do this; she had a bad leg, she was lame – for the hidden bottle. The press also contained books to do with magic I was not allowed to read, so I was already thinking of its new name – wardrobe – to see if that would help to open it up to me.

And then she handed me the bottle.

'Here, here. Open it, open it. Your teeth wearing out and you don't even grow up yet. The Lord works in mysterious ways. Judge not His ways.'

I braced myself for the sermon; but she had finished.

'Pour, pour.'

So I poured brandy into the glass; and looked around for the water that she diluted it with when she had to take 'medicine' for her asthma.

'Now you must gargle.'

The brandy was for me. This was a trap. I had to be careful. There was already talk in the village about two or three of my friends at school – particularly Russell, 'not even at grammar school yet' – who were addicted to toothaches. It was well known that when you had toothache in the middle of the night – or at a time inconvenient to go to the dentist in town, the only thing to do to relieve the pain was to gargle with brandy. Because he was now so far gone, Russell had long been taken off brandy and put on rum – 'and white rum at that', which no one but a heathen like his father would let get past his throat. But Russell, writhing and moaning (with his parents rowing over it), always ended up *drinking* the medicine and having either to miss school or Sunday school because of the state of his breath. So there was talk, and I had to be careful, because it was hinted that if neither brandy nor white rum worked for us, we would have to go back to taking the traditional castor, cod-liver and Canadian healing oils.

I sipped the brandy and made a face, a face intended to indicate that the brandy was unpleasant, not that the toothache was unbearable. So it wasn't an extravagantly ugly face, just a moderately ugly face; and that seemed to satisfy my grandmother, a shrewd judge in these matters. She chuckled a little. And as I gargled I felt the full force of the medicine which, as medicine, didn't have to be diluted with water.

'I'm going down, you know,' she said, as if I was an adult. So I had to pretend not to understand. 'Going right down.' The only thing to do was to take another sip of the brandy and pretend to be in pain.

'Then you children will be without me . . . Baby and the rest of you.' ('Baby' was my mother. It embarrassed me to have her referred to in this way.) But then my grandmother grew philosophical. 'The Lord will provide,' she said.

To which I felt obliged to counter, 'The tooth's really getting better.'

'Things turn upside-down.' She wasn't listening to me, but her mood was lightening. 'Bright ones turn out bad. Your great-uncle turn out bad. And your father.'

I didn't say anything.

'You know?'

'Yes, Mammie.'

'Who tell you?'

'Don't know.' I lied.

'Your father was one of the bright ones.'

'Sorry, Mammie.'

'And you just as stubborn. When I hear that you refuse to cry at Bess Chamber's funeral . . .'

'I forget. Forgot.' I said. But of course, I hadn't forgotten. Our gang, the Heathens, decided not to cry at funerals because we hated to see the adults in our family cry. Horace, our leader, went one further, and vowed he would laugh at them; and sure enough he managed to laugh at Bess Chamber's funeral, which was the first one that had come up after the vow. But Horace was clever. (That's why he was elected leader. Or rather, that's why he wasn't challenged when he elected himself our leader). He had a way of laughing that those adult mourners who weren't in the know could confuse with crying. That's why you always had to be careful with Horace: he got away with things that the rest of us couldn't.

'A funeral is a funeral,' my grandmother was saying. 'You have a hard heart. To forget.' Then she sighed and changed the subject. 'Why that child taking so long with the hot-water bottle? Go and see what Sarah doing with the hot-water bottle. And tell her, bring a glass.'

It was a relief to be doing something, so I went for the glass myself. I had to open up the trapdoor between the corridor and the 'boys' room to the dining-room downstairs. Sarah must have used one of the outside steps to get round to the kitchen or breadroom underneath my grand-mother's room. From the dining-room, I called to tell her that my grandmother was waiting for the hot-water bottle; and she answered by sucking her teeth, saying something about the fire in the coal-pot going out.

Back upstairs, we settled down to our new drink. My grandmother's consisted of very little brandy drowned in water, and mine was, as before, undiluted. I now gave up the pretence of gargling.

She was daring me, testing me, pouring more brandy into the glass each time I finished. Now I was emboldened to smack my lips in the way Professor Croissant and the men in the rum shops did. I calculated that my grandmother had already made up her mind not to beat me. And if I had a hangover in the morning she would have to explain it away. So I continued to drink, silently, 'To the Heathens!'

'Your grandfather never touched a drop,' she said simply. 'But God take him nevertheless.' And now she was direct, dropping the roundabout approach: she wanted to die in peace. Many of the best didn't die in peace. There had been a doctor in the family. And a lawyer. And many parsons, one of them ordained, even. But these things didn't hide godlessness. She was frightened for me. I was even beginning to look like my father. There was talk in the house that I should be a doctor or a lawyer or a priest. She was frightened of such talk, for such a position, when you were stubborn, could lead to harm. Her brother Ned managed to remain a Christian even though he was a doctor. But he wasn't stubborn and wilful. Unlike me.

In the end I assured my grandmother, as she demanded – and as an eleven-year-old, I didn't see what I had to lose – that I would not become a doctor or a lawyer or a priest.

'You swear?'

I swore and raised my glass.

Finally, Sarah came with the hot-water bottle and took away the glasses to wash them; and I got myself ready for bed.

That Sunday evening, Parson McPherson preached in Harris' and visited our house to eat and to pray with my grandmother. This time when I was called in after her bath there was no promise of brandy, my grandmother was lying under her mosquito net, and the room smelt of Canadian Healing Oil.

I would be given a chance, she said, her voice registering a new distance between us; for no one was so far gone that he didn't deserve a chance.

What sort of chance?

I learnt that a heathen among heathens might still find the Lord merciful. If they were all heathens and didn't know better, the Lord might not punish them.

I wanted to own up that Horace and I were *knowing* heathens, that we went into the pulpit at the empty church and opened the Bible at Deuteronomy and loudly preached a sermon to the many breasts of Fatima, to the gold in her nose and the bracelet on her ankle; but I know that was not what my grandmother was referring to. No, she had spoken to Parson McPherson and would alter her will to put a little money aside to send me to a heathen country where God might not notice me in the crowd. But the choice had to be mine; they couldn't banish me. I had to choose my heathen country. I had to kneel down and ask God for advice. What heathen country would I go to?

'Russia,' I said, without thinking, it being the only heathen country I knew about.

'You stupid or crazy?'

To my discomfort she insisted on an answer to the question, so eventually I said that I was stupid, as craziness was not allowed in the family. Then her breathing changed; she was asleep.

During the week, I naturally consulted Horace on my choice of heathen country, and he said there were many countries, like America, that were heathen, but the best of the lot was China: what *they'd* forgotten about heathenness, Russia didn't even begin to know. In a roundabout way, I sounded out Professor Croissant, and he confirmed that the Chinese were seriously heathen people. So China it was.

It was difficult, though, to get back to my grandmother; she was worse, and until my mother could arrange to come from town, a woman from the village was now living permanently in our house and trying to keep me from the sick room. But I still managed to convey to her that China is where I would go to, and become a good heathen.

'They have coloured there?'

'Don't know.' I didn't trust Horace's advice enough to say yes.

And she seemed to lose interest. She talked from time to time about her passing on, of not being able to take things with you: 'the Lord taketh away. We are just instruments, after all. Poor vessels at that.' But she returned to our pact.

'And what will you do in that place?'

'Don't know. Study.'

'You determined to study their heathen ways?'

'No, no. Not study, work.'

'What work you could do?'

'I could look after the goats and . . . Or I could weigh the cotton.'

'No one sending you anyplace to become labourer.'

'No, I mean . . . something really big like . . . flying an aeroplane.'

'Like father like son.'

'Not preaching or anything like that.'

'Don't bring more disgrace on your poor family,' she said at last. 'They suffer enough.'

And that was the last time I heard her speak.

MARGARET BUSBY

Who's Afraid of Notting Hill?

For years, Notting Hill was where I lived because it was where I could afford to live, but it scared me witless. The 1960s, when as a student of London University I first became a resident of the capital, were too perilously close to 1958 for the so-called Notting Hill race riots yet to have receded into folk memory. That Kelso Cochrane, a young Black man on his way home, was stabbed to death by White youths in the wake of those troubles became an unforgettable nightmare, recurring as much in the glare of daylight as in the anonymity of dark, played out in countless reports from metropolises the world over, made reality once again in London with the death at the hands of White racist thugs of another innocent Black man named Stephen Lawrence.

So don't believe the old hippie maxim that if you can remember the sixties you weren't there. I can, and I was. It was a heady enough mix without having to resort to mind-blowing drugs. A time of mixed emotion and transition: from formal education to life, from expectation to realization, from theory to practice.

Above all, that decade for me was a time of daily racial consciousness, crystallized in West London but encompassing all the twentieth-century struggles of Black people internationally. African and Caribbean countries might be gaining independence, civil-rights battles might have been won in the USA, but I could find nowhere to live. 'SORRY, NO COLOUREDS' remained the mantra of many landlords, and I waged a weekly campaign to find suitable lodgings, any lodgings, from which to study the finer points of genteel nineteenth-century English Literature for my degree.

I sampled the charms of the YWCA for a while. At one time, all I could find was a seedy private hotel in Earls Court, and though I was somewhat reassured by the presence in the next-door room of a kindly West African gentleman called Mr Jupiter, my meagre funds meant that for the several days I was there I had an invidious choice: either to buy a sandwich and walk to college, or to take a bus and starve. My extracurricular education was furthered when I found temporary haven in the flat of an eccentric vaudeville actress who pranced about rehearsing her showpiece, the words ricocheting off the kitchen walls and indelibly into my memory:

> I'm Gilbert the filbert, the nut with the k,
> The pride of Piccadilly, the blasé roué,
> O Hades, the ladies who'd leave their wooden huts
> For Gilbert the filbert, the colonel of the knuts

I would have settled for any kind of a hut, but eventually I found sanctuary in Shepherd's Bush, my landlord an enlightened Englishman who relished the company of Caribbean and African tenants. Then finally I graduated to the bargain of a Notting Hill flat that was to become my base for the next two decades. My street seemed to epitomize everything about the area, past and present. The mixture of lifestyles and aspirations made some of my neighbours insist that they lived in Bayswater, while others admitted to nothing less than being residents of Kensington. In reality, we all lived in Notting Hill, though each of our imaginations fashioned it differently. It seems to lend itself to fiction, to fantasy, to faction. G. K. Chesterton in 1904 placed the area centre-stage in his futuristic novel *The Napoleon of Notting Hill*, while acknowledging that 'Notting Hill is Notting Hill; it is not the world.' Trinidadian novelist Sam Selvon unforgettably chronicled the peopling of the area by the Windrush-generation of Black immigrants in *The Lonely Londoners* (I felt a *frisson* of belonging the first time I came across the name of my street on those pages), published in 1956 and presaging both the racial highs and the lows of the district.

Yes, there was fear in Notting Hill when I first knew it. Fear lurked in the shadowy exits from the Underground station, making me shoot looks over my shoulder at every turn. But I also saw the reclamation of the streets by my people, the coming of joy to the neighbourhood as the Notting Hill Carnival burgeoned, determined to survive the phalanxes of police that tried to contain it.

So does it matter if Notting Hill is now the home of trustafarians, that the eponymous film has, by all accounts (I have yet to see it) performed a magic feat of ethnic cleansing by eliminating the Black presence? On one level, Notting Hill – the Notting Hill I knew and feared and loved:

enduring symbol of the presence of Black Britons – has betrayed me by becoming so fashionable that I can no longer envisage ever living there again. Then again, perhaps I have betrayed Notting Hill by becoming a North Londoner. Maybe Chesterton was right all those years ago: 'Notting Hill has fallen; Notting Hill has died. But that is not the tremendous issue. Notting Hill has lived.'

EXPLORERS

Poetry

HEATHER IMANI

Xaymaca

The rush of heat at the 'plane door is
a wave of memory –
more than mine alone.
I smell thick heat:
oppression I like.

Paradise is hell –
overloaded textures, smells,
reds too red, greens too green,
fruit too ripe, too sweet.
Face on face mirrors mine; smile.

My senses explode and I
succumb to the absolute dark
and silence of night
that amplifies the most still sigh,
magnifies the tiniest flicker of light.

I see a panorama,
hear an age of music and moans in
that pitch hush,
and I begin to know how
such abundance can yield such lack.

Souls here are elsewhere
in this second home, where pain
mis-remembered is not understood.
Its blood blurs the eyes;
Paradise is displaced.

But I,
I see the bounty
of this second home;
feast on its yielding seas,
gorge my self on overgenerous land.

I protect my bloated belly
this very first time;
don't know when I
will quench such hunger
and thirst again . . .

I feel the soothing salve of
herbs on my mosquito leftovers –
marvel at how
they read my strangeness, when
I am not a stranger.

I drench myself in hibiscus, orange blossom,
without sneezing or sniffing – fuse it to my core.
I imbibe turbulent rivers,
the languid Sargasso, flat as glass;
bright bauxite earth fills my mouth,
while intense fertile greens of a million trees
shield me from the hyperbole sun,

and I hear my cousin say:
'Sometimes, all I can do is pick aloe vera –
send me shampoo.'

Do I not,
with my belonging to this,
my second-but-third home,
by my drenching, my gorging, say:

It is here, it is here, it is here?

Xaymaca: Arawak name for Jamaica.

BENJAMIN ZEPHANIAH

The One Minutes of Silence

I have stood for so many minutes of silence in my time
I have stood many one minutes for
Blair Peach,
Colin Roach
And
Akhtar Ali Baig,
And every time I stand for them
The silence kills me.
I have performed on stage for
Alton Manning
Now I stand in silence for
Alton Manning
One minutes at a time, and every minute counts.
When I am standing still in the still silence
I always wonder if there is something
About the deaths of
Marcia Laws
Oscar Okoye
Or
Joy Gardner
That can wake this sleepy nation.
Are they too hot for cool Britannia?

When I stand in silence for
Michael Menson
Manish Patel
Or
Ricky Reel
I am overwhelmed with honest militancy,
I've listened to the life stories of
Stephen Lawrence

Kenneth Severin
And
Shiji Lapite
And now I hear them crying for all of us,
I hear so much when I stand
For a minute of silence.

The truth is,
Being the person that I am
I would rather shout for hours,
I wanna make a big noise for my sisters,
Mothers and brothers,
I want to bear a million love children
To overrun the culture of cruelty,
I want babies that will live for a lifetime,
I don't want to silence their souls
I don't want them to be seen and not heard,
I want them to be heard
I want them loud and proud.

My athletic feet are tired
Of standing for one minutes of silence for
Christopher Alder,
I should be dancing with him,
Ricky Reel
Stephen Lawrence
And
Brian Douglas
Make silence very difficult for me.
I know they did not go silently,
I know that we have come to this
Because too many people are staying silent.

The silences are painful,
They make me nervous,
I fear falling over

Or being captured and made a slave
So I will not close my eyes.
I look at the floor for ten seconds
I look at my left for ten seconds
I look at my right for ten seconds,
I spend ten seconds scanning the room
Looking for someone that looks like my mother,
I spend ten seconds looking for spies
And ten seconds are spent looking at the person
Who called the one minute of silence,
And I wonder how do they count their minutes?
I always spend the extra seconds
Looking for people I know,
Wondering how long they will live.
I spend hours considering our trials and
Tribulations,
I seem to have spent a lifetime
Thinking about death;
Rolan Adams
Will not leave me.
I've tried to look at this scientifically
I've tried to look at this religiously,
But I don't want to limit myself either way.
I've spent so much time standing in silence,
It reminds me of being in trouble
In the headmaster's office,
Waiting for the judgement.
I've spent hours
Standing for minutes
Pondering the meaning of life,
The reason for death
And considering my time and space.

JOY RUSSELL

I Don't Do

windows
barbecue chicken watermelon
jerri-curl sta-sof-fro
quivering lower lip
head forward and back pulse on Ricki Lake
hand on hip slap child at bus
Sainsbury's or Tesco
pink green yellow sponge curlers
crack addict noisy snort
dissin on reglar basis
Thunderbird Frascati Pink Lady
mm mm mm girl
after every sentence
booty bounce ragga at 4am
while fucking
riding
my man's dick
to inform my neighbours
of the fine
insatiable quality
of my brown pussy

Don't do
clean musk smell
Marks and Sparks sock shirt and tie
ladies first
upright law-abiding
business management computer studies
New Testament in hand
Sunday church without fail
obeying strict mama's boy

never curse never swear
voice as sweet as soft as a lamb
never disagree
to each their own
work hard to get ahead to make a better life
marriage to raise the children to have the wife to get the sex
the carnal sin of fold-up crease clothes place by bed
quick grope in dark in shame
you on bottom me on top
minimal sweat
never never go down *there*
never partake
always good always nice

Don't do
wise woman
no pain no fears
ever strong boulder unheard of grief
fifteen children single parent breeder hips
I don't know nuthin' 'bout birthin' no babies
rag head wrap
tacky tacky nappy bit exposed
cheap weave blue contact lens
only date white
only date black
don't trust my own
won't trust the other
emotional range of rage rage rage
and more rage
cook eat and breathe rice 'n' peas
live in a house built
of rice 'n' peas doily bless this home
de rum come out
for de special occasion
from de dark wood cabinet

Don't do
grunt man
nuf respect word up
rap instead of read
sport Kangol Hilfiger Armani Nike
Versace Adidas Reebok Fubu only pleeease
shake shoulder dip
curl finger clutch pull away release handshake
don't vote cuss suck teeth
gangsta batty man queer bash
at any given opportunity
check my lunchbox
on every other
down step
of my cool walk
mug on the upbeat
cruise loud bad mean and hard
in stolen Mercedes
wear gold teeth
gold shoes
gold underwear
gold mobile phone
gold rings on every finger
gold rings on every toe
and five hundred gold necklaces 'round my neck
heavy enough
to do a serious
DIY lynching

No
I don't do
don't do

Well uh . . .
maybe
sometimes

The Waitress and the Nights of the Round Table

Each immaculate table a near perfect reflection of the next,
A 40s' Hollywood formation dance captured in time
In black and white.
On the mahogany, polished as a morning pond,
Each table-cloth flapped as swan's wings
And each landing perfect.
She made pieces of butter intricate
As the hand-woven curls in a judge's wig
And if not so legal and final
They'd be a crest of waves
Caught in yellow sunshine.

Each serviette a silent smiling cygnet born in her hands,
Each flower arranged as if grown for this evening
Sucks water slowly through the stem and raises its neck.
They bathe in the light flitting from cut-crystal vase
And standing assertive in centre tables, waiting.
She picks a speck of dust from a spotless unspeckled carpet,
Her reflection buckles in the neck of a mercurial fork
While the solemn red candles wait too,
To weep their red tears.

She pauses as a mother would for a moment
In the front room, before the visitors arrive,
In admiration and slight concern
And bathes in the symmetry and silence
And the oddness of order –
Even the tables seemed to brace themselves as she left.

The picture was distorted when she returned from the kitchens,
A hungry horde of steak-sawing, wine-guzzling,
Spirit-sapping, double-breasted suits had grabbed their places.
They dug their spiked elbows into the wilting backs of the tables.
The table-cloth dripped congealed red wine from its quiet hanging
    corners
And the sounds of their grunts, growls, their slurping.
Their gulping and tearing crept in and invaded the hall.
But a black swan amongst a sea of serrated cutlery, she soared just
    above
And wove a delicate determined ballet in between and invisible.
She walked for miles that evening, balancing platters,
Pinafore-perfect hair clipped so not to slip.
The wine warmed and the candles cried.

In the background of the laughter of their greed –
The guttural sound of wolves.
She retrieved a carcass of lamb, poured red,
And didn't notice the bloodshot eyes slide over her
Nor the claws stretching and puncturing leather brogue,
Scratching the wooden floor, nor their irritation at her.
One mauled a mobile phone with a clumsy paw.
The alcohol-fuelled change was taking hold
And together they could be and become who they really were.
Wolves. Wolves in their pride. Wolves in their pack.
Their lower jaws had stretch and eyes slitted –
Some even bayed as wolves, heads flicking side to side,
Tongues slipping low, slow and deliberately from their mouths
And curling sensually to their snouts. The wolf has a permanent
    smile.
It grew, first half-cough half-bark. One paw banged on the table,
Another banged and another and another and another
Until the whole hall echoed with the unified clatter
Of the guttural phlegm-flicked word that brought them together.
'Gerni gerni gerni gerni,' they chanted. 'Ggerni ggerni,' they chanted
    faster

'Ggerni ggerni ggerni ggerni,' faster and faster and faster and faster

'Ggerniggerniggerniggerniggerniggerni

She turned to her colleagues by the kitchen entrance,

But their eyes! Their eyes slipped sideways away from her.

They too were wolves! Her lips parted for her voice and the room
    hushed itself

But for the slipping of saliva from their jaws and the flickering candles

And the dripping of the red wine from the tablecloth.

As instructed by her manager, she smiling politely,

Asked a wolf, 'More coffee, sir?'

PATIENCE AGBABI

The Excoriation

I

For my twelfth birthday I asked for a snake,
green, white and green. I fed it raw whitebait

and named it Hope after my best friend Hope
who sends me thin blue letters from Lagos.

That night my father dined on raw silence
but my dreams were embossed with his curses

translated through rose-pink anaglypta.
That grave morning after, my stepmother,

tired and white, whispered me the bad news
as I smirked behind striped, brushed-cotton sheets.

Hope was donated to the local zoo
and I was expelled from home to boarding school.

II

I am getting too big for my body.
Tiny fists for breasts. Bomb-black thighs. Silence
plucks each brazen swelling. I'm a ripe bruise

smarting under double-barrelled asides.
I bleed letters to Queen's College, Lagos,
stilted in pidgin English, and I bleed

pink-black humiliation as Miss strips
my vowels, clips my consonants until
my voice breaks in Queen's English. The puce scar

is bleached blond on stiff, white cotton gusset,
an invisible message for mummy
who forgives me at half-term, pink and smiling.

III

For my thirteenth birthday I've asked for a horse.

MAUREEN ROBERTS

The Way We Were

They thought we did not speak English.
Our words lilted up to grey skies
Fell in sweet cadences to our ears only.
We learned that a bloomer was bread.
We learned to count shillings and pence
Not dollars and cents.

The woman in the bread shop
Stole my silver three-penny piece
Told me it was not six pence
Sent me home to get another three pennies
Before she would hand over
My large, white, sliced, loaf
Small, brown, Hovis
Unsliced of course.

Stood waiting in the greengrocers
To buy Irish potatoes for West Indian soup.
They thought I was too young to understand them
They did not understand us.
Stood waiting, while the greengrocer
And his headscarfed customer discussed us.
Listened to a whole conversation on how
Ugly we were, but then
They looked at me standing
Patiently waiting for
My turn to buy Irish potatoes,
'At least she's pretty,' they,
the ugly ones said

and lo and behold
they were talking about me
assuming still that I did not speak English.

Got my potatoes.
Went to the butchers.
Joined another queue.
Local butcher and customer
'When they come in they
always reject the first thing
I put my hands on.
So, I always pick up the good meat first.'
Told my mammy what I had heard
Got good meat from that butcher from then on.

Mother sent us to dancing school
Learned tap, ballet and modern
She sewed elastic in my dancing shoes
In the late evenings, while listening to the radio
Sitting in the big armchair
With the rose-patterned stretch covers.
She bought me the little yellow, pleated, dancing skirt
The purple, hand-knitted, crossover cardigan
The leotard, the tights
And I danced
But crippled by shyness
Never showed my freestyle pieces
To the rest of the class, when asked.
Watched theirs
Did not mind demonstrating
My perfect, natural turn-out
Or particularly high grand jeté.

At our annual party, won a prize
Went to get it,
Was not allowed to choose what I wanted
Like everyone else had.
Ballet mistress thrust into my hand
The cheapest thing on the table
A plastic make-up bag
Looked into her face, looked into her eyes
Learned
The meaning of prejudice
Learned
A smile can tell lies.

My father would arrive each month
To pay for our lessons.
His children
Never counted out shillings and pennies each week
Like the other kids.
He was always proud, smiling,
Magnanimous, wealthy-seeming.
The ballet mistress, hated us, my sisters and me
Especially when, precisely because
He took crisp pound notes from his pocket and paid her
She made us take extra ballet lessons
To prepare us for exams which we never took
For which we were never entered.

Took piano lessons from an elderly
Smooth-cheeked, old, English lady
Who loved music, *ergo* life.
The piano teacher pushed silver, grey, angel's hair
From her face and talked to me
Prepared me for exams, which I took.
Knew that I understood English, better than most
Gave me warm Ribena before I entered cold exam rooms

Fingers stiff with fear, vocal cords contracted with the curse of
   shyness
Made me skip grade I, go straight to grade II
She always knew what I could do
Taught me new ways to look at life.

But, I realized when she gave my sister and me
A lift home one day
She checked out our house
The size, the type, the street.

This saddened me
Because I knew then
That even if you beat race
That still leaves class.

MARIE GUISE WILLIAMS

Of Love and Settling

(for FG)

And *what*
of love
and settling down?

True. You and I
were meant to
share kisses
but only
the contents
of old tin cans
settle.

Listen:
When fields of wild flowers
no longer bring me joy

and solitary hours
no longer bring me peace

and fantasy and freedom
no longer bring me
anything

I'll stop
what I'm doing
and settle.

Then you can
cut my skull of metal

put my dreams
on to your plate

and pick at
my brains
for supper.

The Flood

Held the tears in
case the well
spilled out of
my control, but
couldn't help it
when the car hit
the grid in the
road just before
the shopping precinct,
the shaking of the
car broke the seal
and out they came;
not one by one
like children are
told to queue for
ice-cream and
not two by two
like the animals did
in the ark, but
in floods which
threatened not just
to rock the boat
but to

      sink it.

VANESSA RICHARDS

Maybelline Ruby Ice/Stakis Hotel

You stroll into the lobby.
Arms wide as a smile
wrap my stiff back.
It's been too long.

I make a line of my lips every time you press me into your chest.

You enfold
memories
intimately

unintentionally
perhaps.

I am the lady in the yellow dress
skirting assumption and a rubine smear.
Offering a cheek when you seek my hibiscus pout
that would kiss
but not
here,
standing,
people checking
in.

My left hand a starfish
swimming between your shoulderblades.
Behind your back
my right palm quick as police wipes the luring shade away.

A woman too familiar with Saturday nights alone
may prefer a private
pre-storm-silent,
when-stillness-swallows-time
kind of kiss.
I think she would.

A man too long on the road
could strip lips of their gloss and favour.
Deliver a down-home, body-locking, hips-rocking kind of kiss.
I think he would.

I want to hold you.
Leaving no stain.
Making no mistakes.
Fearing nothing,
naked.
So your vanishing lips could find mine
across miles and years,
open and unembarrassed
at how long and well you have
known my heart.

BERNARDINE EVARISTO

Heart of Exile: Looking for Kwaku

London: *'A market for many peoples coming by land and sea'*
  – Bede, AD 730

Satellite the worlde of cartographers,
betraying land mass so the nerve centre
is grander than the subject body, yer Majesty;
earth's sphere made one-dimension
on my injured map, new borders of Sellotape.

How can I trust the ghostly blue-veined hand?
Grey threads of my mother's clan,
palette translucent in a slanting attic light,
goose-feather quill in precise calligraphy,
apex and stem on Standard European Paper?

You are not the stuff of our legends.
I finger the routes in my palm, dark
with my father's carbon, lifelines span Good
Hope, Mogadishu, Carthage, footprints
tracked prey, traders bartered up

rivers not then charted by Dr Livingstone –
blank spaces all. Clans not yet severed
by the intricate jigsaw of this continent; a web
of veins clutch my aching neck. What becomes
of fractured hearts? Sickness in the family.

Somewhere on the skulled coastline, your sad
profile, Kwaku, unconquered kilometres
of 900 AD now shrunk into a 1:9 million

projection, at the tip, Gibraltar's two-way trail,
fleeing the throne of old Ghana, Uncle's poison,

via lamp-lit boulevards of the moor's Spain,
now on a barge on the Thames, deathly
the white forest at Gravesend, the vicious
bitterness of this thing called snow –
you cannot believe you have come to this.

Crouched behind trees, men, alert as eagles
watch, iron spearheads glint, the boat creeks
on iced water and sinking inside a cotton robe,
your lips are petrified, *I cannot turn back*. Not
seaman but wanderer, in this Age of Darkness.

PANYA BANJOKO

Brain Drain
Brain Drain

Do you

feel

less

Privileged

Subordinate

Peripheral

. . . a minority?

Does

Class

Race

Gender

Age

. . . matter to

you?

you?

Would you

Like to

Fight away

Frustration

Anger

Futility

. . . despair?

We

can

offer

you

you

the

best

in Brain Care

Brain Care

Don't

worry

about

the state

of world

affairs

YOU

YOU

too

can be

Less dark

Younger

Male

Rich

even have

Bigger tits

Remember

Whatever

desires

wanted

can be

implanted

so try

Brain Drain

Brain Drain

The

New

microchip

666 CALL 666
666 **666**

JUDITH BRYAN

Llandovery Mountain

Arthritis in Hendon:
Mother arches her spine, hands on hips.
She shifts from side to side
to shake away the pain.
She shuts her eyes,
moans between pursed lips
as if enraptured.

Bunions in Caterham:
Mother carries sandals, wears shoes,
winces all the way to where her friend lies, dying.
And while cancer takes Vicky's firm flesh,
Mother talks about her own poor health:
her feet, her joints
and how her breath is short, these days.

Angina in Kingston:
She can't keep up with sister.
They march around the market,
heat running rivulets down her dusty face.
Light years ago she walked
two miles for the morning water.
Nearly ten on market day.

So – up through bush-land, back-a-yard, Country!
Llandovery Mountain looms;
cool breeze, clean air, space.
Mother strides the steep path,
past family graves, to the painted house in the hillside.

She cuts cane to suck sugar,
draws water from the well,
wanders the wide land . . .

And she is broad in accent,
deep in spirit.
Overflowing, dancing, laughing.
Her face is smooth and soft,
her eyes shine,
her hands fly like birds above her head.
And she sings, and sings, and sings.

CYRIL HUSBANDS

An Urban Lynching

Out of Africa, to the Land of the Free
But the price of freedom was too high
Forty-one pieces of silver
Spat with murderous contempt
From the uniform barrels of those
Supposed to serve and protect
But treat people like Amadou Diallo
with deadly disrespect

No one is to blame, it seems
He asked for it, standing at his dark Bronx doorway:
How were they to know he was unarmed?
And forty-one pieces of silver
is a price worth paying
When the thin blue line sees red
So another joins the thick Black lines
of the needlessly, cruelly dead

I travelled to New York from my native London
Spoke to my African-American friend on return
Sharon asked me how it was
I told her I loved it, but
the cops and a group of young white men seemed menacing
'So,' she said, 'it's just like being here . . .'
I hadn't thought of it that way
But she's right, it's painfully clear

Amadou got lucky
Went to the land where millions of dreams reside
But his luck and his life ran out
Leaving grief-stricken family, friends, community in Guinea

Haven't we been this way before?
Isn't history repeating itself?
The first time as slavery
Now as legal, lethal stealth

I never knew you, Amadou
and I will never get the chance
But I mourn you, and share in the pain
of all those who love you.
And I dream of the day
I'll no longer have to qualify
That old cliché, I love New York
Because Black lives are cheap as talk

DOROTHEA SMARTT

c. 1950 *Bubble 'n' Squeak*

In post-war days
market barrows bubble
and squeak under King Edward's
potatoes and cabbage. Heads
in flat-caps, with sack aprons,
old men trundle. Handling,
sure and swift, filled baskets
of turnips and swedes
fresh from the Counties,
4d a pound. Savoy cabbage
complexions, transport loads.
With cauliflower ears
and parsnip noses even
in rain and smog,
their market boots
carry their feet,
over charcoal silver cobbles.

c. 1967 *Sweet Potato 'n' Callaloo*

After Parkes Drugstores came
Timothy Whites and, now
by Boots, on the corner
of Electric Avenue,
they're selling soul food.

Strange at first, but
slowly came a liking for
Jamaica's patties.
Opened the way, to foreign roots
formed into 'Back Home Foods'
eddoes and ackees
sweet potatoes and callaloo.

Faces reach from scarves,
head tied against the cold.
In days ahead bustling,
for cow-feet and pig-tail
the women offer open bags
for warmer foods to tumble into.

JACKIE KAY

Piano 4 p.m.

The music lifts – up and up and up –
my son's scales,
trails his long brown fingers.

It is so particular. *Doh ray me.*
He sits like time held still
on the red piano stool.

Fah soh la. The scales linger on his shoulders,
circle his childhood, *Te Doh*,
and saunter down the hall,

to float above me
in the kitchen cooking his dinner.
The music mingles with the smells.

Biding time; holding the moment well.
In the interval, the stranger space
between notes,

I chop onions. I stir and wait.
Taste and pause. I grind some pepper.
Sprinkle some sea salt. He plays *Friday*.

And in they come, the children
from another time; lifting their skirts, running
by the dark river.

And the bells of the past, they ring and ring;
an old woman remembers how she used to dance,
waltzing, waltzing into the night air.

And the night waves rise and crash and falter,
And the rocks are always bare and glistening,
My son plays *Arioso in F*

away into the future.
I can hear him grow up,
up and off, off and up

I can see us
in the space between the bars:
mother and son.

Here we come and go,
My boy will become a man.
The light will seek the dark.

The music, majestic,
sweeps and turns,
rising and falling, innocent and knowing.

Pushing out its long limbs,
The dance of the bones.
It yearns and swings,

through the heart of our home.
I hold my wooden spoon mid-air,
like a proud conductor.

Tears fall down my face like notes.

LINTON KWESI JOHNSON

If I woz a Tap-Natch Poet

'Dub poetry has been described as . . . "over-compensation for deprivation"'
  – *Oxford Companion to Twentieth-Century Poetry*

'mostofthestraighteningisinthetongue'
  – Bongo Jerry

if I woz a tap-natch poet
like Chris Okigbo
Derek Walcott
ar T. S. Eliot

ah woodah write a poem
soh dam deep
dat it bittah-sweet
like a precious
memory
whe mek yu weep
whe mek yu feel incomplete

like wen yu lovah leave
an dow defeat yu kanseed
still yu beg an yu plead
till yu win a repreve
an yu ready fi rack steady
but di muzik done aready

still
inna di meantime
wid mi riddim
wid mi rime
wid mi ruff bass line

Linton Kwesi Johnson

wid mi own sense a time

goon poet haffi step in line
caw Bootahlazy mite a gat couple touzan
but Mandela fi im
touzans a touzans a touzans a touzans

if I woz a tap-natch poet
like Kamau Brathwaite
Martin Carter
Jayne Cortez ar Amiri Baraka

ah woodah write a poem
soh rude
an rootsy
an subversive
dat it mek di goon poet
tun white wid envy

like a candhumble/voodoo/kumina chant
a ole time calypso ar a slave song
dat get ban
but fram granny

       rite

       dung

       to

       gran

       pickney
each an evry wan
can recite dat-dey wan

still
inna di meantime
wid mi riddim
wid mi rime
wid mi ruff bass line

wid mi own sense a time

goon poet haffi step in line
caw Bootahlazy mite a gat couple touzan
but Mandela fi im
touzans a touzans a touzans a touzans

if I woz a tap-natch poet
like Tchikaya U'tamsi
Nicholas Guillen
ar Lorna Goodison

ah woodah write a poem
soh beautiful dat it simple
like a plain girl
wid good brains
an nice ways
wid a sexy dispozishan
an plenty compahshan
wid a sweet smile
an a suttle style

still
mi naw goh bow an scrape
an gwan like a ape
peddlin noh puerile parchment af etnicity
wid ongle a vain fleetin hint af hawtenticity
like a black Lance Percival in reverse
ar even worse
a babbling bafoon whe looze im tongue

no sah
nat atall
mi gat mi riddim
mi gat mi rime
mi gat mi ruff bass line
mi gat mi own sense a time

goon poet bettah step in line
caw Bootahlazy mite a gat couple touzan
but Mandela fi im
touzans a touzans a touzans a touzans

Essays

COLIN BABB

Cricket, Lovely Cricket: London sw16 to Guyana and Back

My love affair with cricket began during the spring of 1973 in a south London flat. As a nine-year-old, Sunday was the ultimate television day. I could monitor the latest escapades of Barnaby the Bear, the animated antics of The Jackson 5, the further adventures of Catweazle, gawp at *University Challenge* and feel elated if I actually understood a couple of the questions. These events preceded the main business of the afternoon. This was to tune in to the *Big Match*, which featured football highlights from the previous day's action and was presented by Brian 'The Voice of Football' Moore.

While preparing for the start of the *Big Match* I took up my usual spot between the coffee-table and the television set. Without any warning, a figure approached from a darkened corner of the room and calmly switched the television over to BBC2. My dad was home on British Army leave, and therefore my usual Sunday television viewing was cruelly disturbed. 'We're going to watch the cricket,' was his command and despite my bitter protests the decision was not to be overturned.

It was clear that after the first ten or so overs had been bowled, I was beginning slowly to appreciate my dad's judgement. I found myself spellbound by John Arlott's observant and humorous commentary, gift for language and that distinctive Hampshire accent. I thus began keenly to follow the John Player League one-day games every Sunday with increasing enthusiasm. 'Run-rates' and 'maiden overs' became part of my ever-expanding cricket vocabulary.

I briefly supported Sussex in all of the main county cricket competitions. I can't remember why I made this decision. Perhaps I felt sorry for them when they were defeated in the 1973 Gillette Cup Final. However, when it came to supporting a national cricket team there was no choice. It had to be the West Indies.

I was born in east London and brought up mainly in south London, but it never occurred to me to support the England cricket team. My parents were from Guyana and Barbados, and I had often heard talk of Charlie Griffiths, Wes Hall, Everton Weekes, Ramadhin, Valentine and other 'greats' during high-spirited, nostalgia-driven and occasionally drunken cricket debates. Cricket always appeared as a key element of conversation in which the grown-up men would participate when we had any kind of gathering in our flat.

The first colour television to arrive in our flat was purchased to coincide with the 1973 England v. West Indies series. Therefore, I was able to watch the third test match – including the spectacle and tension of a bombscare at Lord's, with spectators gathered in bewilderment in the outfield, and umpire Dickie Bird perched in the middle of the ground on the pitch-covers; and followed by Gary Sobers from Barbados and Rohan Kanhai from Guyana each scoring a century, live in magnificent colour.

I rifled through books in nearby public libraries to enhance my knowledge of the game. I indulged in regular banter with my classmates at primary school who supported England during any England v. West Indian test series. Whether I played for the primary-school cricket team or spent hours at a time during school holidays playing with my friends in local public parks or in various back gardens, I always took huge run-ups to mimic the smooth, cultured but fiery bowling style of Michael Holding.

During school summer holidays in England, I eagerly awaited the beginning of any cricket test series. I would settle into position in front of the television at five to eleven, just before the start of the day's play. My pulse-rate would increase as the first notes of the Booker T and the MGs' theme-tune piped up. Therefore, if play was interrupted by rain, irritating news and weather broadcasts and unnecessary golf or tennis tournaments, I would storm around the flat in frustration. Thankfully, I could rely on uninterrupted ball-by-ball BBC Radio 4 commentary, or at least radio cricket conversation if play was delayed or interrupted. I began to develop a habit, which I still have, of listening to the radio commentary and watching the television coverage with the volume turned down.

During summer months spent with relatives in Barbados, I would spend virtually every day playing cricket with assorted relatives, friends and friends of friends. I was keen to prove that as 'an Englishman' I was good enough to hold my own during any beach, street or yard cricket session I was involved in.

As a Black lad growing up in south London, the West Indian cricket team provided me with an enormous source of pride, and they regularly triumphed in test matches against England. In Andy Roberts, Michael Holding and Malcolm Marshall, they had the most fearsome fast bowlers in the world. Viv Richards, Gordon Greenidge and Clive Lloyd were arguably the most exciting stroke-playing batsmen around.

The cricket team was filled with sportsmen, who appeared to me as superstars. I was being presented with the opportunity to idolize people who came from countries where my parents came from. Clive Lloyd had attended the same secondary school as my mother in Georgetown, Guyana. As a teenager I was privileged enough to be shown around the pavilion at the Bourda cricket ground in Georgetown. Rohan Kanhai and Alvin Kallicharran were from Port Mourant, Berbice.

Cricket was something that 'we' were good at. Beating England at cricket gave me and other first- and second-generation Caribbean cricket enthusiasts a chance to assume temporary superiority over our white British friends, colleagues and enemies. Before the 1988 test series, Viv Richards outlined the responsibility of captaining a West Indian team on tour in England. 'West Indians in England, bus drivers, guys who work on the Underground, some of them don't have a great life. Maybe their cricket team can give them a little bit of pride. When they're talking with English fellas they can say: Yeah, but did you see what we did to you at Lord's?'

I began comprehensive school in 1976 and gradually evolved into a reliable, if not always flamboyant, opening batsman. It was a month after the West Indies had beaten England 3–0 in that year's test series. The outstanding highlights were Viv Richards scoring 291 runs, Michael Holding taking 14 wickets, and the West Indies amassing 687 in the first innings at the Oval, which was parched and bare of grass due to that year's drought.

At school it always seemed as if cricket was a game struggling to maintain its respect among my peers. Football was considered to be the only sport worth paying any serious attention to. Only a handful of my peers at school were willing to indulge in any serious conversation about cricket. I was always particularly disappointed when I attempted to initiate cricket conversation with other kids of Caribbean descent. I always failed miserably with my efforts, as they thought it was weird to consider cricket a topic of meaningful conversation. Cricket was viewed as a game for the older generation. A 'West Indian grandad's game', dull and associated with rum-sipping, stout-drinking, calypso and dominoes.

Playing competitive cricket for a south London comprehensive school was also fraught with considerable difficulties. We had no playing fields surrounding the school. For games lessons and competitive cricket games against local schools we had to hire a pitch in a local public park or get bussed to hired pitches in the south London suburbs or leafy north Surrey.

We always seemed to be the poor relations against schools we competed against. Our kitbag looked like a collection of equipment purchased at a church-hall jumble sale, in comparison to the pristine equipment being paraded by our opponents from the more suburban south London and north Surrey. Our Inner London Black/White/Asian cross-section of team members were always envious of our well-heeled, well-scrubbed and better-prepared north Surrey opposition. Their teams always wore immaculate whites, while we dressed in a roughly assembled array of cream, light-brown, beige and yellow.

Victory was always sweeter against these sides. After a particularly narrow victory against a north Surrey team in Cheam, all our players invaded the playing area to celebrate with the batsmen who had struck the winning runs. The Cheam school was furious about the way we behaved, and our overenthusiasm was punished. Our PE teacher/make-shift cricket coach was put under intense pressure to concede the game, due to our unreasonable behaviour.

I continued to ply my trade as an opening batsman for school teams throughout the years, until the end of my period as a sixth-former. My Stuart Surridge bat was kept in good order; I continued scanning the sports shops in Croydon for a pair of Tony Grieg-style SP batting gloves (left-handed). I played West Indies v. England games with my mate Nick and West Indies v. Pakistan matches with my mate Shakil in their back gardens.

The West Indies cricket team under the leadership of Clive Lloyd grew from strength to strength, and the 1980 series with England was, for me, a defining moment as an observer of West Indies cricket. The 1980 England v. West Indies match at the Oval, London, is where I first witnessed how powerful the feeling of victory against England at cricket could be. It seemed the ideal occasion for the thousands of West Indian supporters around me to let off steam, express a sense of collectiveness and re-create that particular West Indian way of watching and appreciating cricket, in deepest south London.

Used beer cans were bashed together to create a rhythmic noise. Records deriding England's South African born captain Tony Grieg were being played by mini-sound systems. Chicken, rice, salad, beer and rum were being consumed. Abuse and banter were exchanged between West Indian and English supporters, and the regional, political and cultural differences between Bajans, Jamaicans, Trinidadians and Guyanese were temporarily put on hold.

Before the West Indies began beating England regularly, and before there was a large West Indian population in Britain, West Indian cricket was often damned with faint praise. Fallibility made West Indian cricketers 'uninhibited' and 'colourful'. By the time I began to watch cricket on a regular basis, and particularly with Clive Lloyd as captain up to the mid-80s, carefree amateurism was replaced by hardened professionalism.

It seemed to symbolize a 'coming of age' of Caribbean sporting competitiveness. West Indian national self-assertion on the cricket field also increased the self-esteem of British-based West Indians and their descendants.

However, supporting West Indian cricket could be a lonely job in years to come. While the first generation of Caribbean migrants to Britain pass away, and their descendants turn to football or American sports, I can imagine the horror of an England v. West Indies match in twenty or thirty years' time, with very few West Indian supporters in the stands. Ticket prices for test matches are becoming prohibitively expensive, and those for the first three days of a five-day test match are difficult to obtain. Virtually all seats for these matches are now booked months in advance.

The music, revelry, banter, flags and special atmosphere brought to English cricket grounds during the 70s and 80s, which increased in volume with West Indian successes on the field, was thwarted by the cricket authorities. By the end of the 80s, drums, whistles, flags, bells and flaxons were taboo.

As a result, during the 1988 and 1991 West Indies tours, Black spectators were notable by their absence at grounds in London and Birmingham where they had previously turned up in larger numbers. The lack of atmosphere was also noticed by my England-cricket-supporting friends who longed for the 'carnival atmosphere' now absent from these grounds.

Contrast this with the scenes witnessed during the 1997/1998 England cricket tour to the Caribbean. Thousands of English supporters joined in with the passion, revelry, music, drinking and crowd participation during all of the test matches and were welcomed by the vast majority of West Indian supporters and cricketing authorities. During the test match in Barbados there appeared to be more English Union Jack-clad cricket spectators than Bajan supporters in the ground.

Appreciating West Indian cricket is rooted in the sporting choices I made as a young boy in the 70s, which have stuck with me through adulthood. I still support Leeds United Football Club despite having grown up in London; England in international football; and Wales at Rugby Union despite having no Welsh heritage. I supported Belgium in *It's a Knockout* on television because I liked their yellow outfits!

Those emotional moments, epic performances, that particular Caribbean way of playing and appreciating the game, memories of a childhood supporting West-Indian cricket, and the voices of John Arlott, Jim Laker and Peter West will always propel me to the Oval, Lord's or Old Trafford. Meanwhile, despite the efforts of some cricket counties to encourage Black youth to get involved in the game, and Black players, including Dean Headley, Mark Butcher and Alex Tudor being regularly selected by England, my peers and descendants increasingly seek their sporting spills, thrills and the scent of millions in football and American sports.

In 1950 the West Indies beat England at Lord's for the first time. Caribbean people in Britain and all over the world celebrated. This year sees the fiftieth anniversary of that famous victory which inspired Lord Beginner, a calypsonian who was at the game, to compose the calypso classic: 'Cricket, Lovely Cricket'.

AMANI NAPHTALI

Afrikan Holistic Theatre: Towards a Cultural Revolution

A paper written on the growth and evolution of a holistic Afrikan art practice within the context of the British Black Theatre Industry. A practice that looks at the central relationships and universal oneness of Afrikan art forms, whether performance, healing or social, and how this informs and is part of the totality of one's life and cultural perspective. In short the interrelationship of all things

   – Amani Naphtali, Writer/Director

The growth of non-naturalistic art forms under their many headings, such as Performance Art, Combined Arts and Live Art, has led to a revolution in performance style and format. The compartmentalization hitherto practised within the Western art world and theatres favoured a naturalistic form and acted for a long time as a stranglehold on creativity. Afrikan artists played a pivotal role within this art revolution, but with the demise of many pioneering companies in the late eighties and early nineties, the contribution of the Afrikan form became marginalized in terms of the wider society's lack of cultural recognition. Afrikan players and performers year after year laid the foundation stones of many of the styles that now proliferate in the art worlds of Great Britain, Europe and elsewhere. They had to fight, piecing together the threads of our history with words, song and dance. Many of them were not given the respect and acclaim which they truly deserved. Their collective works, handed down to them through ancestral memory, formed the root which later flowered into the diversity and multiplicity of Afrikan cultural art that is open to the Black artist today, and, we the people of the diaspora, owe them all a debt of gratitude.

The ancestors know who you are, what you were and did. Respect to all the ritual artists, art history will not forget your contribution to culture and ultimately to life itself.

From Actor to Artist, towards a Holistic Afrikan Theatre

For many years cultural-specific groups, such as the Afrikan-Caribbean community, ones that exist within England's diverse, multiracial society, have found it hard to gain specific experience of their artistic heritage. Within established art-training institutions only small gestures towards culturally specific programming were ever attempted. The Black actor, left to swim nationless, was destined never to be given the chance of training in the specific art forms of Afrika or even those of the Afrikan diaspora. We thus had a Black Theatre that was sometimes out of cultural context with its own people's artistic dynamism. The music in the street was sweeter than that in the theatre, the dancing and style of the street was cooler and more sophisticated than that presented in a theatre production.

Black Skin White Masks

This situation ultimately led to some problems of communication and identification within our community, since the form of presentation adopted by most actors was predominantly naturalistic and Western in style. We had a theatrical situation of what Frantz Fanon aptly called 'Black Skin, White Masks' or, more to the point, 'Black Actor, White Theatre'. This cultural anomaly could not sustain itself for long, or contain the explosion of art forms and fusion of styles that continually arose from the grass roots; like the Sankofa bird, this led the way forward while looking backward into our history. The realization came that an artistic return to the styles and genres of Afrika's civilizations, matched and fused with the dynamism of contemporary culture, would result in a powerful cultural aesthetic.

An Afrikan Genre

The search for an Afrikan Holistic Theatre became the principal aim of many artists of the diaspora: the exploration, research and presentation of ancient art forms from a contemporary perspective; the freedom and fusion of performance styles, drama, dance, music, the spoken and written word, poetry, song, visual arts and new media; challenging the mind, voice, soul and spirit of Afrikan Artists, and enabling them to place themselves within a fresh, new and empowering context. This nurtured the further development of a new Afrikan Art vibe, as demonstrated through the renaissance of the holistic methodology, with archaic genres alerting the mind and body to the pulse of art from the heart, awakening the inner drum towards tangible vibrations. It enables the release of rhythm, stimulates the imagination, and supports the process towards an analytical critical opinion.

Emphasis on the preparation of the body as a performing tool shifted focus to the exploration of the individual's capacity for emotive and dynamic forms of culturally based expressive art, bringing the artists face to face with a variety of forms, with the ancient traditions of our ancestors, whose legacy can be found in most contemporary art, from ritual to rap, Afrikan dance to hip-hop. The artists explore form and style, getting in touch with the inner creative self, leading towards internal understanding, a personal methodology, and feeding into and enhancing their external performance and so, the relationship with the audience.

Generic Application

Afrikan holistic art has a community-wide generic application and should not be reserved as the sole property of so-called professional artists. Art workshops should be open to the general public to provide a platform to explore and present the artistic traditions of Afrika and other indigenous peoples. Inspiration is the key to developing a fuller understanding of the creative process across the performing arts spectrum. Therefore, within the developing ethos of Afrikan holism, art for life's sake is a fundamental principle underpinning the work, with the emphasis on the understanding that the artist exists within every individual, a process of synthesizing or fusing various creative and healing art disciplines. The separation between Actor, Dancer, Singer and Poet will be broken down, allowing each element to flow freely in and out of the others, thus allowing the individual progressively to find the other art forms within themselves – the search for the eternal artist, the creative spirit of cultural expression.

The Healing of the Nation

Afrikan holistic art contains certain central elements that set it apart as a priceless community resource with many contemporary applications as a cultural tool. For example, the holistic fusion of the healing and performance arts, for so long an endemic aspect of our culture but often seen as primitive by Western academia, now forms the basis of dance therapy, drama therapy, chant and musical healing. Afrikan holistic art can play a well-needed role within the area of psychological or spiritual trauma/ Black mental health. These treatments are socially necessary; one just has to look at the growth of the alternative-healthcare industry to realize that there is scope for viable, economically sound practices that, if utilized, can be a healing balm to many of our people's ills.

Things have a way of coming around, but we have to make sure that as Afrikans, we are not the last people to catch on to the value of what has historically always belonged to our race. Let's not miss our own cultural gravy-train.

The Politics of Change, towards the African Cultural Renaissance

The British art establishment is now faced with a dilemma. If it does not address the racial inequalities endemic within British industry, then the imbalances within arts provision due to years of underfunding will continue, thus undermining any hope of national cohesion. When one looks at what has been done over the last fifteen years literally to dismantle the Afrikan performance arts industry, it becomes clear that the destructive attacks and lack of resources which have typified our relationship with art agencies is due to the fact that Black people's culture is not respected to the same degree as other, European cultures. That is not to say that our arts are not fully utilized, even usurped, by the vivacious British cultural appetite, as it consumes our culture in an attempt to form the fundamental building blocks of the post-2000 cosmo-Britannia super-cool.

It has to be made clear that it is not only the police force that has within its structures practices which prove detrimental to Afrikan peoples. We find it harder to get funding, yet we are supposed to be a priority group; when we actually do get arts funding, the venues seem to have little or no understanding of what our people actually want and often refuse our community performance groups access to their hallowed stages. Maybe that's the problem in a nutshell, maybe they don't want Afrikan Arts to flourish at all. That is to say, venues up and down Britain seem to want to dictate our agenda or to have one of their own. Even when a successful show emerges from the ranks, it then has to convince élitist theatres of its worth and, finally, to ride the abuses of an oftentimes sarcastic and patronizing art press. All this social warfare and miscarriage of justice takes place under the official banner of equal opportunity and multicultural provision.

Afrikan peoples, however, have the right to represent their culture as a specific, rather than as a blurred part of Britain's multicultural monovision. Otherwise, this will ultimately lead to watered-down versions of minority cultures, bowing to and being absorbed by the dominant culture, blindly singing 'Viva Cosmopolita'. So what has to be done now is to establish how our communities can take control of the provision and visibility of Afrikan theatrical performance, and to decide whether or not we continue to allow political lip-service to be paid to our artists and their work. Especially in the light of the post-Stephen Lawrence-affair atmosphere and the supposed guilt and reflection of the British state and cultural industries.

We must always remember that when it comes to art, our culture doesn't have to sit passively behind anyone else's, least of all that of the West, whose culture we have played such an active part in creating. Whether in song, dance, poetry, drama, painting or sculpture, Afrikans can hold their own in the world, have contributed much and continue to contribute to the history, evolution and continuation of world art.

So we are talking about money, finance, the economic means by which power can be wrested back from the dominant culture in order that we ultimately gain control of our own artistic destiny. If we want Afrikan Arts to be respected, then that same respect must start at home, the support for our arts must first come from within our own communities. If we want schools of learning and venues that understand and truly cater for our needs, then we will have to open them ourselves, run them ourselves and finance them ourselves – it is as simple as that. What's the matter, do we somehow feel that it is an impossibility for Black peoples to muster the unity of action to work towards projects that reflect our cultural aspirations? As Billie Holiday aptly put it, 'God bless the child that's got its own.'

Yours in Art,
Amani Naphtali

YVONNE ST HILL

Reclaiming Home

Childhood Views

I sat suspended in time and space in the tiny plane, enveloped by massive, white clouds etched against bright blue, mesmerized by the great rivers snaking their way through the lush, vibrant rainforest below. It was a big moment for me. At last, I was going to see Guyana's famous Kaieteur Falls – the world's highest single-drop waterfall. This trip triggered memories of other journeys, many years ago, into the vast greenness of Guyana's spectacular interior. And it triggered reflections on my entire life.

I'd done it in reverse. In 1961, when so many were leaving the Caribbean to go to England, my family left, shortly after my birth in London. My father, a Barbadian, had been offered a job in what was British Guiana at that time. He was very excited about returning to contribute to his region.

So in many ways, I grew up as a real Caribbean and South American child, thriving in the rich, warm, tropical environment of this spacious, beautiful and remarkable country. I loved the wildness, vibrancy and lifeforce of the huge, powerful South American continent; swimming in ice-cold creeks, fishing in wide, brown rivers. Each tree, bird and flower was a miracle created just for me. I was fascinated by the amazing mixture of races, culture and religion.

But England still remained home. For I'd been born there. And 'Nana', my mother's White English mother, was there. She adored me and I adored her. So in many ways, I felt like a foreigner just passing through Guyana.

When I was four my family returned to England on long leave. I was thrilled. Being with my grandmother was the major highlight. It was great to have aunts, uncles and cousins. I was amazed by the diversity of food and things to do. Watching television and feeding the pigeons in St James's park were special treats. For me, England was a huge playground to be enjoyed.

Then, when I was eight we went back to England again for a year, while my dad extended his studies. I was more aware of my environment now. My relationship with my grandmother was maturing. She always spoke about her late African husband and other Black people in such respectful and positive terms that I learned so much from her about being extremely proud to be Black.

I was better able to appreciate the parks, museums and places of historic interest. My sister and I enjoyed the fact that in England we were doing things in class that we'd done a couple of years ago in Guyana. It gave me some much-welcome time to relax. I liked the more interactive teaching style and the many choices of craft and sports.

I first became aware of race issues at school. Over the years, Guyana has had very difficult race relations between people of African and Indian descent. However, somehow this had never touched me personally. I'd had lots of friends of African, Indian, European and Chinese heritage. For me and my circle of friends there had never been a distinction. We played together – that was it. But in England my sister and I were the only Black children in our school. We were different and always stood out – the centre of attention. A few children called us 'Cocoa Beans', asked us if we had tails tucked up under our skirts and if we lived in the tree-tops. However, this didn't really bother me. I felt sorry for them. Generally, I was very happy at school and felt welcomed by most people. But I had now lost my innocence.

When I was almost thirteen, we left Guyana and moved to Barbados, my father's country. Over the next decade and a half we continued to visit England for short holiday periods. Going to England continued to be a treat. I always looked forward to spending time with my relatives and friends as well as the wide spectrum of activities which England had to offer.

Adult Experiences

A sudden air pocket shook me out of my deep thoughts. My mind jolted back to the present. Misty blue-grey mountains loomed on the horizon. The land below was no longer flat but was starting to rise and fall. I stretched and settled back down to my day-dreaming.

My relationship with England changed considerably as I matured. In my early thirties I'd decided that it was time to live in England, as an adult and professional. Over the years, I'd developed a thriving sustainable development consulting practice and had worked throughout the Caribbean. But now I was really thrilled about the prospect of expanding my horizons personally and professionally and learning exciting, new things.

But it turned out to be a very difficult time for me. The lessons I learned were not the ones I'd wanted or expected. Instead of getting a lot of guidance, it felt like I was often the one explaining how to upgrade systems and programmes and how to mobilize resources. In the Caribbean we have to learn quickly how to create a lot with very little, to be competent in many different areas without much direction. So my professional experience in England didn't stretch me in the way I'd expected. I felt disappointed and let down.

Things were even harder on a personal level. I finally started to understand the real implications of Great Britain's colonial past. I realized that at some level so much of what was around me had been built on resources taken from Africa, Asia or the Caribbean. I also started realizing how 'Eurocentric' the popular world-view was, and how often science and technology are seen as 'quick-fix' solutions, whereas true spirituality and healing are marginalized. I recognized that the rich, complex and diverse world-views from ancient Africa and Asia, which tend to integrate science with spirituality, had been dismissed. The vision that I'd held for many years of England as my home was shattered. This was incredibly painful, and I felt ashamed of the part of me which was European.

Finally, it was this pain which led me to search for a new way of thinking, living and being. I went back to Barbados and retrained in healing and personal empowerment, studied African drumming and learned more about the world-views of different cultures. I also started my own 'journey back to my soul' and to write about my experiences. I learned to merge and integrate the many different components of myself – the sustainable development planner, the healer and the writer. I was able to claim all of the different aspects of my ancestry and history – the African, European and Caribbean.

In 1998 I returned to Britain. I was more grounded and balanced than I had been the last time – five years before. I was clearer about how I needed to live my life and what experiences I needed to create in order to grow. I understood that it was my responsibility to set things up in such a way that they worked for me and not to expect others to do this. I was now a multifaceted human being with a broad range of personal and professional interests and I was able to really enjoy sharing with different 'communities'. So, with this mind-set, I was able to fully embrace the land of my birth once again.

It became possible for me to recognize and celebrate some positive things which had been with me for many years, but which I hadn't had the clarity to see before: the fact that over the years England had become a useful springboard into the Continent, and hence I had been able to travel there extensively; that my mother's lifelong friendship with White British families has always kept a door open into an experience of England that might otherwise not have been as accessible to me; that I boldly go anywhere that interests me, even if I'm the only Black person there.

I also received a beautiful and unexpected gift. I had been dreading going back to England because 'Nana' had died a few years earlier. I'd expected it to be really traumatic to get off the plane and not go straight over to see her. But somehow, I could sense her soul wherever I went. This helped to make Britain 'safe' to me in a way that it had never been before. My White grandmother helped me further to claim and celebrate being Black British.

Final Reflections

My experience as a Black British person is perhaps a little unusual. For most of my life I have lived in the Caribbean, visiting England only for relatively short periods. Even more unusual is that it was my White grandmother who initially helped to set the stage for me to have a tremendous sense of self-worth as a Black person – and who helped to make England home for me.

I also think my Caribbean grounding has given me a lot of self-esteem as a Black person. Growing up, seeing Black people running countries which have equal votes in the international arena to the Western 'giants' and being called from an early age to make a very real contribution to young Black economies is very, very empowering. These experiences have proved to be extremely beneficial to me whenever I'm in Britain.

Suddenly, everyone in the plane gasped. I was brought back to the present. The incredible waterfall was in the distance. A gigantic column of golden water and white spray against striking green. A sight of grace and great beauty. A wave of tremendous gratitude washed over me. I was so grateful that I had been raised in a context where I could claim this great land of Guyana, the tiny island paradise, Barbados and the historic and diverse land of Britain all as home.

OLA OPESAN

The Proliferation of African Businesses in the UK: Will Africans be the New Asians of UK Business?

This essay is an attempt to examine some of the key factors that have brought about the rise in the number of UK businesses owned by Africans, and especially those businesses owned by West Africans. Although it is an introductory essay, there is still the need to search beyond observational and anecdotal evidence gathered via informal interviews and to garner empirical proof that there has indeed been an increase in such businesses. Should this increase in African businesses in the UK be ascertained, a hypothetical model for analysing African businesses will be introduced to aid further research into this emerging area of the UK economy, which has until now received little attention.

Introduction

In 1990 it was observed that there was only one prominent consumer-focused business owned by an African in the E13-postcode area. Popularly known as Mama Ghana's place, this business was located on Green Street, opposite West Ham FC. It sold food produce such as yams, plantain and okra as its main source of revenue. The 1991 census recorded 11,882 Black African citizens living within Newham, compared to Newham council's 1999 estimate of 20,565 (i.e., 5.6 per cent of 212,170 in 1991 and 9 per cent of 228,500 in 1999). Today, the number of African-owned businesses, on or off the two main streets that pass through the E13 area (Barking Road and Green Street), exceed thirty in number. Types of business present in this location include hair-dressing salons, food/stationery stores, restaurants, specialist video retailers, a vehicle-repair centre, a charity shop and a number of outlets which specialize in serving this niche market.

The Rise of Black Businesses

In 1990, when Dayo Johnson and George Noah of Phone News International published the first edition of *The Green Book*, there were approximately thirty listed Nigerian businesses. Two years later when this was revised there were over fifty entries. In 1999 a number of Black-business directories and magazines were launched. The *UK Black Links Business Directory*, published by UK Black Links (UKBL) in April 1999, is 'dedicated to promoting London's 19,000 Black businesses, which caters for a Black community that spends in excess of £10 billion annually'. Its predecessor, *The Black Pages*, was 'released in the early 90s', but has not been updated since. However, in March 1999, the AD4ALL (business directory) was introduced as 'a promotional listing of businesses set up and managed by Blacks and other ethnic minority groups in the UK'. One of its founding directors, Olu Adekunle, estimated there to be over 5,000 Black businesses (inclusive of 1,000 Nigerian businesses) in London alone, despite a significant percentage of such businesses failing to survive the first year. Another directory, the annual *African and Afro-Caribbean Business Directory*, is currently in its fifth edition.

In addition to business directories a quarterly magazine entitled *Black Business & Culture* was established in 1997. The ninth issue of this magazine went on general release in the second quarter of 1999.

Despite this proliferation of publications, few publishers are confident enough to estimate or state the number of Black businesses or, in particular, the number of African businesses, they believe trade in the UK. Nevertheless, 'following the release of a government White Paper entitled "Our Competitive Future", a small business survey has been launched in London to identify and address the lack of accurate statistics about Nigerian and African businesses in the UK.'[1]

Factors Contributing to the Establishment of African-Owned Businesses in the UK

'The history of Africans in Britain can be traced back to the Roman period, but currently documentary evidence suggests that it is only from the sixteenth century onwards that Africans from the western part of the continent regularly visited or resided in Britain.'[2] The author of the above quote goes on to state that 'West African students, especially prior to the 1940s, comprised one of the most important sections of Britain's Black population.' The majority of the African students who arrived in the UK in the early 1900s, through to the 1980s soon returned to their respective countries after their period of study. Not until the late 80s and early 90s did African students and economic migrants begin to regard the UK as their 'home'. The incidence of this mind-set increased among Africans in direct proportion to the rise in despotic and incompetent leaders in their respective countries. Only at this juncture did many Africans begin to invest in UK-based businesses, unlike previous generations whose investments had been limited to securing predominantly residential property. This recent development, of Africans settling in Britain, has had a twofold effect on African businesses. Firstly, the increase in the population of Africans in the UK (219,555 Black Africans in 1991 compared to the summer 1997–spring 1998 Great Britain average of 351,000 Black Africans estimated by the ONS (Office of National Statistics)), has created the opportunity for more niche retailers to satisfy the increased demand for African goods. Secondly, having given up the transient lifestyle of previous generations, many Africans developed the confidence, found the time and gained specific (UK) experience to establish and nurture UK-based businesses. In fact, a fair percentage of African businesses in the UK have been established by second- and third-generation Africans.

In addition to there being more Africans settling in the UK, the level of education achieved among this group is almost certainly another key factor that has led to an increase in the number of UK-based African businesses. As stated above, many Africans arrived, initially, to study (and that includes many Africans of dual nationality). Again, several of the economic migrants were able to successfully process visa papers in the first place only because they belonged to a profession. Considering that many accountants, lawyers, doctors and other professionals have to undergo further exams and years of retraining in order to be certified and be able to practise in the UK, a reduction in visa applications from such professionals might have been expected. Instead, history records that the opposite happened – mainly due to the rate of pay (coupled with the increasingly favourable exchange rate) and standard of living in the UK, which proved too enticing to ignore or to allow mere strictures on the free movement of trade to become an insurmountable barrier. No doubt this pool of knowledge has stood African businesses in good stead during the conceptualization and establishment of UK-based businesses.

Obviously, there is a need to determine how the state of the general UK economy has impacted on African businesses over the last decade. More specifically, it would be helpful to determine whether a relationship exists between levels of unemployment and business start-up rates? On this particular issue there appear to be two schools of thought. One viewpoint, backed by Mohan Luthra, the author of several publications in the area of Black and minority studies in the UK, asserts that, 'generally it appears there is little relationship between unemployment and self-employment when we analyse the data (Labour Force Survey, OPCS, January 1984–87 averages) across ethnic groups', though he later modifies the above stance by paradoxically suggesting that 'there may be a converse relationship i.e. when unemployment is low then self-employment goes up as people feel confident to take on the risk of establishing businesses, particularly in the case of ethnic minority business'.[3] On the other hand, Nana A. Bambara-Abban vII, in his paper produced for the Education Development Services of the University of East London, states that, 'With the increase in unemployment in the 1980s many members of ethnic minorities found themselves unemployed and many were "forced" into self-employment.'[4] It appears that further, specific and up-to-date research is needed to resolve this issue. However, on the issue of government attempts to influence the economy and hence business start-up and success rates, both writers concur that government enterprise schemes, such as the Enterprise Allowance Scheme, Single Regeneration Budget and Youth Training – not having been targeted specifically at Black or ethnic minorities nor implemented by agencies proportionally staffed by people from these communities – have not been able significantly to increase African-owned businesses in the UK.

Another likely factor in the increase in African businesses in the UK, which the author strongly shares, is the theory of Africans being natural traders. Unlike in the UK, where secondary employment is usually formalized and known as part-time work, in several West African cities it is most common for government workers, teachers and even those in the professions to have a 'side trade' or, if you prefer, 'PP' (private practice). Several West Africans will be able to identify an aunt who may be a teacher but sells clothes to her friends and colleagues for an extra source of income or an uncle who is a doctor but runs a fleet of public-transport vehicles to supplement his state salary. This need for supplementary income, probably fuelled in part by the pressure of some African societies place on their citizens to 'build a house' (or remain a nonentity), has no doubt allowed a number of Africans to set up businesses with the knowledge and experience accrued by helping their parents in their 'side trade' or 'private practice'. In a similar vein, Mohan Luthra purports that Asian and African communities possess what he calls a 'pre-capitalist business background', which aids business formation in the UK – a 'patriarchal capitalist society'.

Although there may be other reasons which have ensured the increase of UK-based African businesses, the above covers most of the key factors. Nevertheless, one last factor that is vital to consider is access to banking facilities for Africans in the UK. Most African readers will probably have a horror story or two concerning the initial attempts of friends or family to open a personal current account. Going by this anecdotal evidence – that a number of banks (especially in the 80s and early 90s) appeared reluctant to open personal accounts to Africans – what chance was there of an African opening a business account or, more importantly, securing loan facilities or other financial support? Some would say little; however, the present reality seems to offer a different perspective. Bunmi Jenyo, CEO of the SAB group of companies, disclosed that not only had his bank, NatWest, encouraged and aided himself and other African entrepreneurs in their respective businesses but that by 1997 his relationship with his bank had developed to the stage whereby NatWest was enthusiastic to join the African Business Partners forum and go as far as being a sponsor to its annual African Business Executive Awards Night.

At present there appears to be little research available which gauges how African entrepreneurs have fared in accessing banking facilities. Although Dr Sam Egharevba, whose doctoral thesis centred on ethnic-minority businesses in London, is certain that the dominance of Asian businesses in the UK was greatly helped by their founders securing financial support from the now defunct BCCI (Bank of Credit and Commerce).

Important criteria for accessing loan facilities as a business are the entrepreneur's collateral and business viability. N. A. Bambara-Abban vii states that as 'large institutions (banks) have virtually no experience of ethnic minority businesses, they may rely on "race-based stereotypes"'. Nevertheless, he concludes 'Fortunately for this group of migrants (Africans), due to their level of education and attitude to racism and business, many were able to access funds from banks . . .'[5] Traditionally, many entrepreneurs have started a new business venture by providing property as collateral and, as previously stated, since Africans have started to settle permanently in the UK, many more have become home-owners than prior generations – with properties of increasingly higher value. This increase of collateral among Africans in the UK is a major plus factor when it comes to securing loan facilities from banks or other institutions.

An African Business Model for the UK

African business has passed through a number of distinct phases during its development in the UK. The four phases suggested below inform the model's categorization. The model itself is an attempt to establish a framework whereby future researchers and writers in this area can make vital references and links between disparate African businesses in the UK. Types of business, such as retail, service, manufacture, etc., would have been one method of classification, but this method does not distinguish sufficiently between African businesses, since many are retail but may incorporate manufacturing and/or service elements. Geographic areas of concentration of African businesses (for example, Peckham, Brixton, Dalston) could have been another method on which to base a model.

However, this classification tends to acknowledge only businesses with a shopfront and not office- or home-based businesses. Therefore, the following model has the distinct advantage of being able to view African businesses in the UK individually and comparatively. Nevertheless, it must be noted that the following groupings, while being fairly distinct, are not mutually exclusive.

First generation

Those referred to as first-generation African businesses are enterprises which were established to cater mainly for a 'niche market' or specific community. Although these types of business were some of the first to be established, the start up of such businesses is ongoing wherever large concentrations of Africans appear. Businesses that come into this category include ventures such as the *Trumpet* (a newspaper that started off by supplying news, monthly, to Nigerians, before widening its appeal to Africans in general), the African Video Centre (wholesaler and retailer of Black video- and audiotapes) and Club Afrique, an East London club-restaurant.

Second generation

Businesses in this category are characterized by qualified professionals who relish the thought of being their own boss, or who, still wishing to practise their trade, are 'forced' to find gainful employment by establishing a business in which they can utilize their training, i.e. accountants, GPs, solicitors, barristers, etc. Many of these businesses are operated from home or from small offices, although some, such as Ned Nwoko's law firm, based on the prestigious Gray's Inn Road, can afford more sumptuous surroundings. Included in this category are organizations such as Chakatcha, which teach and perform African dance, and photographers / videographers, who record special occasions. Although the businesses in this category are available to the wider UK community, most were established to serve, and still service, a client base dominated by their fellow nationals or Africans in general.

Third generation

These are businesses established by entrepreneurs who are specifically motivated by profit. Yes, profit is the aim of all business ventures, but unlike the owners of first- or second-generation businesses, entrepreneurs behind third-generation companies establish or develop ventures which appeal to the community at large in order to maximize profit. Catering for a national or African niche or practising their profession does not form a secondary objective. For example, the SAB group of companies has an MOT division which provides a service available to all car owners in its catchment area. Also, Obatala Arts, a London establishment where students with learning difficulties, or the unemployed, can train in IT, media and visual arts, is another organization in which the majority of clients are from the wider community.

Given that the terms 'first generation', 'second generation' and 'third generation' can easily be misconstrued to suggest businesses set up by first-generation Africans, second-generation Africans, etc., it must be made clear that the titling refers not to generations of Africans but to the developmental phases that African businesses have passed through in the UK. So, it is interesting to note that a business such as Hackney Radiator Repairs, established over thirty years ago as Stamford Hill Radiator Repairs by Mr George (soon after arriving from his native Sierra Leone), is an example of a business that falls within the third-generation category rather than the first, since his venture targets all motorists within the local area.

The many Africans establishing security firms also fall into this category rather than the first because few trained or studied security as a profession, and most establishments that can afford security personnel are businesses outside the African community.

Future generation

At present, the majority of African businesses are run by owner/managers, i.e. the owner is heavily involved in the day-to-day running of the business. Future-generation African businesses will be owned by entrepreneurs versed in project viability who will be willing either to provide financial resources to or start up a business for competent management. Some of these businesses will simply be seen as having African sleeping-partners, shareholders or venture capitalists but many will be backed by entrepreneurs in the mould of Richard Branson or Anita Roddick. And it is this type of business, which draws on a diverse client base, that will bring African businesses to a par with the Asian business community – which congregates in and dominates several UK areas due to intra- and inter-company trading and credit arrangements.

Conclusion

Despite the limited research into African businesses in the UK there is substantial evidence that points to a dramatic increase in the number of such businesses. Should this trend continue, within the next decade the African business community will be as well respected, and carry as much clout as their Asian counterparts. Tony Blair's attendance at a dinner organized by the Asian business community in the run-up to the 1997 General Election was well publicized. However, last year he courteously declined an invitation from the African Business Partners to grace their Awards Night. Should African businesses continue to impact on the UK economy at its current rate, then surely this snub will be reversed in the near future. In fact, African Business Partners expect Tony Blair to lobby for an invite to their Awards Night before his tenure expires. That is, as long as the African business community remains focused, and does not permit a little success to breed complacency for, in the words of Bunmi Jenyo, 'Success is a journey, not a destination.'

Notes

1. F. Macaulay, p. 6, *Trumpet*, May 1999
2. Hakim Adi, p. 2, *West Africans in Britain 1900–1960*, Lawrence & Wishart, 1998
3. M. Luthra, p. 367, *Britain's Black Population* (Social Change, Public Policy and Agenda), Arena, 1997

4. N. A. Bambara-Abban VII, p. 2, 'Research into the development needs of Black businesses and organizations in the UK', University of East London, 2000

5. Ibid., p. 3

TREVA ETIENNE

Colouring the Face of British Film and Television

Historical Context (Film and Television)

Black people have been living and working in Britain since at least the early sixteenth century. Stephen Bourne's research states that 'images of Black people in British cinema can be traced back to its beginnings when, in 1896, Lumière's Cinématographe released *The Wandering Negro Minstrels*', and that 'there has been a Black presence on British television since the BBC launched its services in 1936'.

The achievements of Black artists are charted through the century; the silent film era in the memoirs of Black stage and screen star Paul Robeson; in the 1950s with Black film actors like Earl Cameron, Errol John and Gordon Heath and ground-breaking BBC dramas like *Othello* (1959) and the pioneering drama-documentary *A Man from the Sun* (1956). ATV also produced quality drama, such as Ted Willis's *Hot Summer Night* (1959) and *The Big Pride* (1961). There were popular performers like Trinidadian singer/actor Edric O. Connor (a forgotten TV star of early post-war BBC) and entertainer Winifred Atwell, who, at the height of her popularity in the 1950s had her own series on BBC and ITV.

The necessity of preserving the history of British popular culture in film and television is essential for archive purposes, yet the Black contribution to this formative era seeks urgent recognition, for it is still marginalized, undervalued and poorly understood. Compared to Black America's visible published histories and documentation, the considerable difference in the respective histories is not widely realized. Film stars like Sidney Poitier had already established a Black presence in Hollywood – but on television in 1950s America the racist cartoonish caricatures of *Amos and Andy* were the norm. These only disappeared, according to Stephen Bourne's research, in the 1960s, 'to make way for the – then – near-visionary integrated casting of series like *Star Trek* and *I-Spy*' and that by contrast, 'British television after starting out with a very real – if casual and inconsistent – progressiveness, allowed it all to be almost completely eradicated in the late 1960s', to the extent that, aside from the ghetto of pop music, viewers believed that Black actors emerged on British TV with the 1970s sitcom *Love Thy Neighbour*.

The British Film Industry is remarkable for its lack of racial diversity. It still reflects a predominantly Anglo-Saxon world. The current minorities who reside as citizens of Britain are taxpayers, contributors to the lottery, the BBC licence fee and eligible to vote. Britain's Black and Asian population contributed approximately £238 million in licence fees in 1999 (figure based on the number of households shown in the census). They were rewarded with fewer than twenty hours of television, mainly on BBC2. They also make up a significant percentage of our domestic cinema-going audience. Yet the fact remains that in the closing years of the millennium no Black/minority British cinema has yet been established.

Current Context (Film and Television)

The Film Policy Review Group report states that 'members from ethnic minorities are seriously under-represented.' Clearly, research would show that once training has been completed, the number of unemployed trained professionals merely adds to the existing list of filmmakers who have been trained but they find little in the way of employment. These are the issues minority filmmakers want discussed if the industry is really to maximize its creative potential. Even then, it has to create a level playing-field for ethnic-minority filmmakers to enter the frame. The massive international success of *The Full Monty*, for example, a film which came from an idea brought to a producer by a Black filmmaker, Paul Bucknor, demonstrates how our creative input can help revitalize the British film industry.

The recent success of films like *The Full Monty* and *Secrets and Lies* shows that the British film industry appears to be recognizing the importance of ethnic inclusiveness. In time, and given the opportunity, there will be a new breed of British writers, directors and box-office stars. Steven Spielberg snapped up Black British actor Razaaq Adoti for *Amistad*, Anthony Mingh-ella cast British Asian actor Naveen Andrews in *The English Patient*, Mike

Nichols cast Olivier Award-winner Adrian Lester in *Primary Colours*, and in 1997 Marianne Jean-Baptist received a Best Supporting Actress BAFTA and Oscar nomination for her performance in Mike Leigh's *Secrets and Lies*. These faces have the potential to open a movie domestically or abroad doing what England expects – patriotically to 'fly the flag' – as Black stars from the industries of music (Mel B., M-People, Eternal, Desiree) and sport (Lennox Lewis, Paul Ince, Linford Christie) successfully do. In sport, Manchester United, the richest football club in the nation, uses two star strikers, Dwight Yorke and Andy Cole, to enhance their chances of winning the league and to generate commercial box-office.

Two years after receiving her prestigious nominations for *Secrets and Lies* and being snubbed by not having been invited to the 'Best of British' boat party at Cannes, whatever happened to Marianne Jean-Baptiste? And Gordon Warnecke of *My Beautiful Laundrette*? The film careers of Daniel Day Lewis and Marianne's nominated contemporaries, Emily Watson and Kate Winslet, are evident, yet we are still to see either Gordon or Marianne's talents projected in another British film. Is the old saying – 'White actors have careers; Black actors get jobs' – still relevant?

Hollywood

Hollywood has benefited from revenue generated by its ethnic filmmakers (i.e., American Jews, Italians, Irish, African-American and American-Hispanics). The financial rewards from minority non-star movie hits such as *Boyz N the Hood* clearly reflect this. This film grossed over US$50 million at the US box office and had 11,954 admissions on 23 screens in Paris on 28 August 1991: on its opening day, *Boyz* set new records as the largest Black-themed film opening in Paris, beating the previous record, set by Spike Lee's *Jungle Fever* (5,111 admissions) and *New Jack City* (3,600 admissions). In 1995 *Waiting to Exhale*, starring Whitney Houston, eclipsed the success of *Boyz* grossing US$70 million to become the USA's twenty-seventh biggest box-office draw of the year.

Through innovative film marketing and distribution strategies generating multiple-income streams from TV, home-video sales, merchandising, music soundtracks and publishing, these new culturally aware all-American filmmakers are producing movies that sell all over the world. Global audiences are quick to learn, cross over, integrate and be entertained. After all, a good film is a good film, in any language, in any territory. So why do we in Britain refuse to see the potential growing in our city of London, the gateway to Europe and currently the 'coolest' city in the world?

Training

The classic institutional response to ethnic minorities in film has been to set up more training courses, based on the understanding that there is no visible ethnic talent and that therefore this talent needs to be trained. But this is a false premiss. Since the 1950s, and significantly since the 1980s, there have been minority filmmakers trained inside the Skillset schemes, film schools, broadcasters who have funded courses and other institutions, and many through the early workshops initiated by Channel 4. Remi Adefarisin started as a BBC cameraman in the 80s and is now one of the top cinematographers in the country, having worked on *The English Patient* and *Truly, Madly, Deeply*.

Britain has experienced ethnic filmmakers who are writing, producing and directing films (shorts, mainly), recruiting the support of Shepperton, Twickenham and Pinewood studios, Goldcrest Post-Production, Fugi Films, Panavision, Lee Lighting, Rank Labs, Arion and Telecine. All this industry support proves that it is understood that there is a lack of financial support for the ethnic film industry and that there are interested parties who want to encourage new talent. It is the search for finance that is always the challenge. These filmmakers are pushing the boundaries with fresh images in mainstream stories, in their aim to develop and introduce the untapped market of alternative British talent to the world stage.

New training and development initiatives will not eradicate the suspicion of the British Black/minority filmmaker, who perceives the British film industry to have been cancerous with institutionalized racism and suppressed with fear, miseducation and ignorance since before the Second World War. Writers should be able to feel confident going into the system and not be pre-empted by fear of the same regime of confused questions and queries which undoubtedly rejects their scripts through lack of understanding and cultural education. However, the industry can provide a climate in which both long-term political and social action begin to build a more tolerant and confident British film industry. The recruitment of a culturally diverse workforce will contribute to the creation of a dynamic and innovative film industry relevant to the needs of the twenty-first century.

Marketing and Distribution

A substantial P&A (Print & Advertising) budget and access to a major distribution network is a factor crucial to the success of any film. How significant then, that a low-budget Black film, *Dancehall Queen* (Island Digital Media – a division of Island Records), shot on DVC for $500,000/£0.3m) with no star names, and released as a straight-to-video project, was subsequently blown up to 16 mm, shown, on a limited number of screens, and grossed £98,808, nearly as much as the widely released commercial film with top Hollywood star Joe Pesci *8 Heads in a Duffel Bag* (£130,888). *Dancehall Queen* earned more than Kevin Spacey's critically acclaimed directorial début *Albino Alligator* (£59,854), and more than Rik Mayall's *Bring Me the Head of Mavis Davis* (£63,956). *Dancehall Queen* continues to do brisk business in the US and will probably do well in Southern Africa, Asia (particularly Japan) and the Caribbean. *Smilila's Feeling for Snow*, starring Julia Ormond, a British Hollywood actress, grossed £103,321, less than *Booty Call*, a Black film shown in a limited number of venues and grossed £154,757.

Both Black and White British audiences are more likely to watch a film by or starring an African-American than a film starring many of the best-known British actors. Wesley Snipes and Samuel L. Jackson induced more British audiences to see their films last year than home-grown directors Mike Leigh and Ken Loach or actors like Robert Carlyle or Helena Bonham Carter. In 1998's UK top-box-office chart, Eddie Murphy's *Dr Dolittle* ranked at number two, grossing more than 007's *Tomorrow Never Dies*. Wesley Snipes's *Spawn* made more money at the box office than Brad Pitt's *Seven Years in Tibet* and Lisa Kudrow's *Romy & Michele's*

High School Reunion, despite the much larger P&A budgets of those two films. Black director F. Gary Gray's *Set It Off* did better box office than Kevin Costner's blockbuster *The Postman*, and more people turned out to watch Michael Jordan, a basketball player, in *Space Jam*, which grossed £11,227,704, than the much-hyped British movie *Shooting Fish*, which grossed £4,023,825.

Ayoka Chenzira's *Alma's Rainbow*, produced independently for US$500,000, with no star names, made the top forty of the Billboard's home-video charts. At number thirty-nine, it was placed between Morgan Freeman's *Kiss the Girls* and John Travolta and Nicolas Cage's *Face Off*. Samuel L. Jackson's production of *Eve's Bayou* directed by Kasi Lemmons, also made it on to Billboard – making history: two African-American directors in these charts. TriMark Pictures invested US$8 million to promote *Eve's Bayou*, twice the film's budget, ensuring 659 US screens and a wide mainstream theatrical release beyond that of any other film by a Black female director in Hollywood's one-hundred-year history. *Alma's Rainbow* was released in 1993, a time when existing alternative distribution outlets were closing, but rose above these odds. The Billboard video charts show that there is potential for financial returns in other markets for indie film.

In the same way, films made about the British urban experience appeal to new audiences of White and Black, for whom urban culture is a real-life experience. The African/Caribbean/Asian experience is potentially commercial, particularly in the US, where African-Americans presently represent 35 per cent of the American film market and 15 per cent of the world market. British African/Caribbean/Asian films have the potential to exploit this market, as well as others of significance in Southern Africa, Australia, Asia and Europe.

The Red Dwarf *Phenomenon*

Red Dwarf is BBC2's longest-running and highest-rating sitcom, with an audience of over 8 million people and eight series to its credit (it was BBC2's number-one show in 1997). These statistics are even more impressive in that the show is multiracial, with half the lead characters being Black

British. The series has won numerous awards, including an international Emmy award in the Popular Art category and a British Comedy Award Best Sitcom, and it was voted favourite TV programme by *NME* readers. Recent audience-composition figures show that *Red Dwarf* appeals to all ages/racial backgrounds, and the split between male and female fans to be fifty-fifty. Viewers aged between four and twenty-four constitute 40 per cent of the audience, another 40 per cent are aged between twenty-four and forty-four, and the remaining 20 per cent even includes a number of people over sixty-five.

Video sales of *Red Dwarf* in the UK exceed £2.5 million. 'Smegs Up' sold over 260,000, and its sequel 'Smeg's Out', released in November 1995, sold 125,000 units in six weeks. All the *Red Dwarf* titles feature in the Gallup Top 125 bestsellers, with series one dominating the video chart and holding the number-one slot in the summer of 1994 and third and fourth positions in the BBC's own all-time bestselling-title list. The *Red Dwarf* videos have won eight awards from the British Video Association. There are four bestselling novels, merchandising deals under negotiation with the USA, Japan and Australia. *Red Dwarf* clothing sells more than 1 million items per year through HMV, Virgin Megastores, Forbidden Planet and mail order. Worldwide sales include Australia on BBC and UKTV(cable), Belgium, Canada, Croatia, Denmark, Eire, France, and French satellite. The shows are remastered and purchased by Hong Kong, Israel, Namibia, New Zealand, Norway, Poland, Spain, Thailand, Russia, Malaysia, Czechoslovakia, Slovenia and Sweden. Japan's NHK terrestrial channel purchased fifty-two shows. *Red Dwarf* is now available in 55 per cent of American homes through PBS stations. *Red Dwarf The Movie* is in development, with feature-film deals being offered from the UK, the USA, Australia and Japan. This is all proof that a good idea that integrates multiracial images in a mainstream project can demonstrate commercial revenue. Yet why in the advance mailshot publicity for its 1999 spring programming did the BBC use only the two White lead actors and neither of the Black actors?

Conclusion

As history has proved, a discretionary DO NOTHING policy will not ensure fairness or an accurate view of contemporary England, and it is important that Britain gets it right. The present government cannot want to invest in a film industry that denies the country's artistic, creative and cultural resources, offering only a distorted perspective of Britain. If it continues to act in denial by either consciously or subconsciously promoting a policy of IF YOU ARE NOT THERE YOU DON'T EXIST, this is tantamount to saying that, as you are not visible, there is no need to give you visibility on screen. This can only instil more long-term problems politically, socially and economically. It is Britain's responsibility to build a confident future generation. Film and television are essential in enriching the perspective of the dominant host group. There are areas of British life that are intrinsically Black/minority and should have the same appeal as any cultural group, so that it is inclusive, not exclusive. Established White talented British producers and companies have been integrated into circles that provide funding and support. We can already conclude that minority filmmakers are at a disadvantage in achieving success without the Department of Culture, Media and Sport (DCMS) and others committed to inclusion on all industry levels. Even if investment is found for films made by ethnic minorities, there is currently no infrastructure to distribute and market British cultural films. The feeling is that institutionalized racism exists and that the doors have been closed before they even start to open.

Fifty years ago the culture of pre-war British films (early comedies like the *Carry On* series) sold a menu of traditional fish and chips, steak-and-kidney pie and Yorkshire pudding. Now, postwar British culture can boast an international menu of *new* traditional British culture including Chinese, India, Thai, Greek, Italian, Japanese, African and Caribbean. As these minority cultures enrich the diet of British society, can we not imagine for a moment how these cultures can enrich and colour the face of British film in the new millennium, offering the world an enviable variety of diversity and choice.

Research Sources

Black in the British Frame: Black People in British Film and Television 1896–1996 by Bourne, Stephen, London: Cassell, 1998

Black Edwardians: Black People in Britain 1901–1914 by Green, Jeffrey, London: Frank Cass Publications, 1998

Black Filmmaker, Vol. 1, Issues 2, 3 & 4, by Adebowale-Bellos, Linda and Shabazz, Menelik (March, June & September 1999)

Stories

RAY SHELL

Sister Girl

Sister Girl was in a hurry. A huge hurry. She was in such a rush she hadn't even kissed Ahmed goodbye, she knew he would hold that against her . . . later.

She tore down Brick Lane, like the loose cannon her friends always accused her of being, hair, scarf, headphones flying in all directions.

Due at the Hot Box, in Brixton at 7:30 p.m. to audition for a chirp job they had going, she was running . . . in Adidas sneakers . . . a little late, it was now 7:27.

Her mobile was dead, so Sister Girl couldn't buzz Ms Thing (aka Carrie), her pianist, to warn the ivory tinkler of her dis-position; earlier that day, the evil One-2-Oners, had chopped her. A cheque she had sent them, the week before, for £496.32 had bounced all the way back to Stringfellow's, where she had been working, briefly, as a lap dancer, until she took a leave of absence to have THE OP. Sister Girl, still too sore to dance, was mired in the poorhouse, desperately needing a coin infusion, so this audition was heaven sent, which was why she was flying down the street like a hyped Bat Girl, black silks flapping in the air.

'Come the fuck on!!!'

Sitting on a bench at Aldgate East Underground station, she applied her make-up, while gently encouraging the unpredictable District liner, that would take her to Victoria, to step up its pace; she had to get to the club before 8:15 or she wouldn't get seen. Teasing out her bushy, black, Egyptian man-trap eyelashes she remembered the conversation she was having with Ahmed just before Ms Thing called to tell her to: 'get your ass down to the Hot Box immediamente!!!'

Encircling the lips that Ahmed said looked like Pamela Anderson's, with Iman's Black Cherry stick, Sister Girl sighed; she was worried about Ahmed as well as the train that was still nowhere in sight. There was nothing she could do about the slow-ass train and less she could do with the gorgeous-ass Ahmed who was even more luscious than her favourite pop star, Lyndon David 'horny' Hall.

Ahmed, a fervently macho twenty-two-year-old, was getting more than a teensy-weensy bit frustrated.

'. . . If I can't have it properly . . . then you'll have to jet . . .'

Ahmed had shouted those words at the back of her £10 auburn weave, as she dashed out of his flat above a Brick Lane spice shop. Sister Girl was well pleased that her Brooklyn homegirl's telephone call had saved her from a confrontation she was ill prepared for; she couldn't give Ahmed what he wanted until downthere was healed, and she had no idea how long that would take.

'Finally!!!'

The District liner lurched into the station belching electric sparks.

A fat Scotsman, dressed in a dirty kilt, Special Brew in hand, serenaded Sister Girl as she tried to push past him into the train.

'Do you mind???!!!'

The fat Scot wouldn't move out of the doorway.

'No lass . . . not if you don't!'

He bowed low before her, almost falling out of the train.

'Move, man!!! . . . the door's about to shut!!!'

Sister Girl jumped between the closing doors, knocking the tipsy Scot against the side of the train.

'Feisty! Feisty! I love a feisty lass!'

'If you only knew . . .'

Sister Girl muttered under her breath as she settled into a seat as far away from the enamoured kilt as possible.

She clicked a pirated Brandy into her liberated mini disc; she had asked to see it at one of those serial stereo shops on Tottenham Court Road, the salesman had gone to answer the phone and never came back, so Sister Girl scarpered out the door, mini disc in hand. She loved her mini disc, it was hot; it gave wicked, thumping bass as did her beloved Ahmed.

He and Sister Girl had not yet consummated their tryst, but she could tell in the fire of his French kisses and in the force of his wide wedge, lodged up against her bandaged coochie, threatening to break through his red silk Calvins in her cotton wrap, that Ahmed's furious Peter was a real womb beater. She shivered in anticipation as she refused the Albanian mother, begging with three children under the age of two strapped to the miserable-looking woman's back, breast and thigh. The tied-up, fat, listless children, who didn't look an inch hungry as described on the mumbling refugee woman's calling card, made Sister Girl think of the many children she wished she could have with Ahmed. He had already mentioned marriage, wanted to take her to meet his family two nights before . . . the Spice kid was serious . . . he knew what he wanted and Sister Girl knew that she could never be what he really, really wanted . . . not really. Four times a day . . . sometimes five . . . as Sister Girl knelt between his full, lean thighs, pleasuring him the only way she could . . . at the moment . . . he questioned her intensely, as if in a trance, his voice rising as his passion raged out in force, stinging her hard at the back of her pumped-up throat.

'. . . virgin? . . . are you a virgin? . . . are you a virgin . . . ARE YOU A VIRGIN?????'

Sister Girl was never virgin; there were a lot of things Sister Girl wasn't, none of which she could tell Ahmed, who didn't strike her as an Equal Opportunity employer.

Ahmed, a Christian refugee, was now a born again Koranic, Ahmed was hyper-Ital, Ahmed was God selective.

'Gotta leave that man . . . he'd kill me clean if he really knew . . .'

Sister Girl didn't MIND THE GAP, nearly losing her stiletto-heeled foot, running off the District liner to the Victoria liner, Brixton-bound train . . . ten minutes . . . she would be on the train, it was 8:05 . . .

Worried, angry looks greeted her as she entered the Victoria liner headed to Salvation Town, the magnificent Brixton, London's own Harlem UK. Sister Girl glanced at the travellers packing out the train . . . suddenly feeling uneasy, which confused her. The Blacks dominating the hot moving box seemed angry, dangerously so. The White gruppies . . . many of them youngish, moneyish thirtysomethings . . . looked distinctly worried . . . frightened even. Sister Girl gripped the overhead rail tightly, trying to steady her nerves, trying to fan away an eerie wave of *Déjà Vu* . . .

The collective mood of the moving hot box appeared to Sister Girl to mirror certain moments in Global Black History . . . the day after the first showing of Alex Haley's discredited *Roots*, the evening of the OJ murder-trial verdict . . . the day after Stephen Lawrence was killed . . . the evening of the McPherson report . . . she had lived this Black anger . . . she had clocked this White fear.

'What's happened?'

Sister Girl let the old dear in her bright African gear sit down in the only available lottery seat.

'There's been a bomb . . . near Brixton station.'

Sister Girl could see in the brown old woman's angry, worried eyes, the beloved faces of the ancient one's entire generation and her wonder of their safety.

'A BOMB????!!!!'

Sister Girl repeated the information too loudly as the train stumbled into Brixton; her mind flew to Ms Thing, her Sister-In-Crime-Home-Girl was in Brixton in a subterranean dancehall across the street from the Tube . . . she had to get to a phone.

'Shit!!!'

A gate across the escalator prevented passengers from going upstairs to the station entrance; shouting faces . . . worried eyes . . . crying arms . . . weary backs . . . frightened minds . . . milling aimlessly into each other . . . one disturbing question on the lips of an outraged collective mouth.

'WHO DID IT!!!!!????'

Sister Girl turned to her left, trying to find another route to the surface or a phone . . . running instead into the arms of a commotion at the edge of the platform.

'Trains are not meant to be stopping here!!!'

A Black platform conductor was yelling at an Asian train driver as he tried to herd the erupting passengers to the parallel platform, where another Victoria liner waited to ferry them back to Victoria, or anywhere else except Brixton where thirty-nine shocked, bloody, nail-riddled bodies counted themselves blessed.

Sister Girl jumped on the Victoria liner scurrying back to the Safe City where dangerous Bogey Bombers rarely ever preyed . . . she prayed, as sweat streaked her Iman mask, that Ms Thing was all right; she had not invited her favourite ivory-tinkler to accompany her to Lon-don Eng-lund to be killed by vicious, swirling, bingo-bombers.

'Hel . . . lo . . . ?'

Ms Thing sounded . . . wounded.

'You all right?!!!!'

'Girl . . . where is . . . you???'

'ARE YOU ALL RIGHT!!!!!'

'Don't you scream at me you late heifer!!!! I'm the one who should be screaming!!!! Can't even turn up to an audition . . . girl . . . you are sad!!!!'

'I COULDN'T GET NEAR THE PLACE!!! THERE WAS A BOMB!!!!'

'What . . . ???'

Sister Girl put the phone down.

Ms Thing was fine. That was all she wanted to know.

Later, as she glided out of the curry house, situated a bit further down from Ahmed's flat, a veil of calm descended over Sister Girl's mind . . . for the first time that day. She was bringing dinner back to her man . . . her Ahmed . . . who had clutched her up in his arms as soon as she stepped, shaking, through the door . . . her Ahmed . . . who had kissed her all over and gently held her in his arms, trembling.

'I thought I had lost you . . .'

He had never said that before.

It would be so difficult to leave Ahmed but . . . who knows . . . maybe they could work it out . . . it was tricky . . . but love could conquer all . . . even gender ambiguities . . .

'I'll tell him over the phone . . . that way if he freaks . . . he can't mash me up . . .'

Sister Girl thought this to herself as she stood before the steps leading to the top-floor love-nest; she sighed, then turned to look out the door to the building directly opposite, marked 'Police Station'. She shuddered briefly, thinking of the tele-film showing the burning, smoking, bewildered Brixton; she had watched this laying in the comfort of Ahmed's strong arms.

Before turning to float upstairs, on the wings of desire, to share an aromatic, incense-lit curry dinner with her lover man, she blew a kiss to Brick Lane Police Station. For the first time in her life, Sister Girl felt so, soooooo, safe knowing that Babylon was right across the road.

RONNIE MCGRATH

The Day Before That One, Too

Mr Frank Scribble could not go on anymore. Those bastards that threw the acid in his face were locked up for good, but they sure as hell could not restore his sight. It was a bleak day. Rain had fallen for a week now, and with no eyes to see, all he could do was think. Think about all the things he would never again be able to see. Like, for instance, his typewriter, and the words on a page. He was the best short-story writer in the country, and there was even talk of making one of his collections into a film. Sure, it could still go ahead, for the work was already complete. But what was the point of all that? he thought. That is, if one was unable to see the damn thing come to life.

Yeah, those bastards did a real good job on him all right. Frank felt his way towards the window and stood looking through the glass in the manner of someone whose attention had been caught by something. Some cars rumbled by and he stood there counting them. One, two, three . . . Oh, fuck this bastard world, he cursed.

'Frank! Did you call?'

It was Meg, his wife. She was in the kitchen preparing his kidney beans and rice. He loved those beans, and he loved his rice, especially the way Meg cooked it. God bless that woman, he thought. So loyal, so very loyal. Then he was struck with melancholy again and began to feel sorry for himself.

'Honey, did you call?' Meg repeated. Her voice held a placid tone and was full of concern for him.

'No, baby, I didn't!'

He could hear her rattling some pans, then he heard the tap go on and the water oozing out of the nozzle. The food smelt good, and this lifted his spirits momentarily. He began muttering to himself again. To think that all those amateur bastard writers with their amateur bastard shit were going to pollute the world with their second-rate crap. He was the best and they knew it.

'Honey, what did you say?'

'Nothing, dear, I'm just talking to myself!'

The sound of a bus intruded his thoughts, and he listened until it could no longer be heard. He felt his way to his chair and then slumped in it like a dead weight.

Yeah, without sight his life was not worth living any more. He had once thought about putting his stories on tape and then having Meg type them out on the typewriter but, hell, it wasn't the same. He liked the look of the words on the page. He liked to see the shape of his story. Most writers didn't even realize that a story had a shape. That a story had spirit. That to bring a story into the world was like watching the birth of a child. All they wanted was to be in print. To see some third-rate shit in some third-rate book sitting atop some third-rate shelf. If only he could have his sight back. Even if it were only for a day, he would show those bastards what writing was really about. He would take the form to its limit: write a piece, beginning middle and end, in just ten lines. It was something he'd been meaning to do for a long time. But now this, this world of darkness. He edged his way to the lip of the chair and called to Meg.

'What is it dear, what is it? Are you all right?'

'Yes, I'm all right, dear. Just come here and sit yourself down, will you?'

'But the food, it will burn.'

'Forget the food, I have something important to tell you.'

Meg grabbed hold of her apron and wiped her hands dry. She then walked into the room, drew up a chair and sat in front of Frank. She blinked, knotted her fingers, and waited for him to say what was on his mind.

'Now listen to me, dear. You've been a good wife. I mean, a man could not ask for a much better woman than yourself.'

Meg listened with intent but grew quickly impatient. 'Honey, what's your point, the food . . .'

'Will you just forget about the damn food for a moment, this is very important!'

She felt a slight unease at the tone of his voice and sunk into the chair obediently.

'Now, listen to me, Meg, I want to set you free.'

'For God's sake, honey, we've been through this before.'

'I mean it this time. A woman like you deserves to be with a real man.'

'Stop it, honey! Stop it! Why do you torture yourself?'

'You still have your looks and fifty is not that old.'

'Stop it! I'll have no more of this talk, you hear me? I love you, Frank, I love you!'

With that, she stormed out of the room and went back to the kitchen. He looked searchingly with his ears and he heard some tears. That damn woman, why the hell does she never listen to a word I say? he thought to himself. Then he fell into another bout of melancholy, and this time he thought about putting a gun to his head and taking his own life. But then the traffic began to rumble outside and he couldn't help but count the cars that drifted by. Just like he'd done yesterday – and the day before that – and the day before that one, too.

MAUREEN ROBERTS

Uncle Pete

He died, finally, he died. His family were happy at last. It was only a few months ago that he had run out into the street half naked, shouting, 'They going kill me. They want me money. They going kill me.'

After staying out all night he would come home, bringing the stench of rum, beer and cigarettes from the pubs he had sat in all day. He would drag into the house trophies from this life outside of the family. One night he brought branches from a tree. Huge branches which he had dragged through the street and forced through the front door. Pulling them in with dog's mess, dead leaves, a bird's nest. He dragged it through the hallway, through to the kitchen, out to the back garden and tried to set it alight.

'Jumbies,' he shouted, 'jumby everywhere. They trying to do me. All 'a them dealing, but me, going fix that.' Rushing back into the house, he tried to find newspapers to get the fire going. He rampaged through the kitchen, flinging open cupboards, pulling plastic bags out of their hiding-places. Tossing everything aside that got in his way. He found no newspapers, so he moved back into the house and into the living room. There would be newspapers somewhere in there. Framed pictures, glass ornaments, crocheted doilies were flung about the room. He was pulling the cushions from the big settee when the feeling took him. He unzipped his trousers and urinated over the furniture. This was nothing new. He had been relieving himself wherever he felt like it for a while now. The carpet on the stairs and passageway had been pulled up. Discarded long ago because he urinated and defecated on it.

> Abide with me fast falls the eventide;
> The darkness deepens; Lord, with me abide;
> When other Helpers fail, and comforts flee,
> Help of the helpless, O abide with me!

The sound of the hymn brought me back to the graveside. Reminded me that I was here to mourn. A few, brief hours snatched from my office. The heels of my black court shoes were sinking in the mud.

I looked down and immediately found myself back in the surgery. It had only been a few months ago. I had rushed there straight from work. Cold, damp, my body weakened by flu. It was the last time that I would see Uncle Pete alive.

He sat scrunched up in a chair, like a dog-eared Sunday magazine. He was wearing a thick, grey-black wool coat. Like all those people who live on the streets his hands moved constantly, nervously. He was rummaging through a clear plastic bag filled with bottles of pills. No one sat next to him. We had all instinctively moved to the other side of the waiting room, away from his smell and his dirt. The scent of his urine flooded the air around him. Some inconsequential minutiae made me suspect that I knew him, had seen him before. Some half-remembered shape of jaw or space between eyelid and brow.

'Uncle Pete, is it you? Is it you, Uncle Pete?'

Reluctantly I crossed the divide that separated us. Repelled by instinct, forced by duty and respect. I was afraid. I might have been walking towards some demented stranger who would not know me. He might embarrass or threaten me. I might be made to look foolish.

Someone in this condition could never be a relative. These were the people you walked around or stepped over in the streets. You did not meet their eyes because in that exchange you would understand the loss of dreams. He could not be related to me because then I could become as he was now.

'Momo, is you?' The eyes did not look at me. Explored instead the hem of my coat, the plainness of my black shoes.

'Yes, Uncle Pete, is me.'

'You awright, Momo?' We talked in short sentences held together by long silences. It was a conversation of sorts. I told him about my travels, my work, my flu. He never held my gaze but occasionally glanced briefly at me. Through his eyes I caught the depth of pain that stretched far, far within. Feared reaching down and finding the naked child, the boy, and the man whom he had buried.

The receptionist asked me to go through and sit outside the doctor's door. I said my goodbyes and left him, almost with relief. In a state of shock I drifted through the heavy glass doors. When had this man been transformed from someone who was young, strong and alive to a body that was dying?

It was the smell of urine that told me he had entered this second waiting area. Helped by the receptionist, he shuffled through the doorway. Unkempt, unwashed, he sat on a chair next to me. I looked up and smiled.

'You seeing Dr Kapoor, too?' he asked.

'Yes, all the family still with the same doctor.'

'You know, Momo, I not feeling so good. You can lend me some money to take a bus home?'

He begged without shame, the lie flowing as easily as the rum that would slide down his throat. I gave him all the change I had on me, knowing full well that the bus he needed to take was alcohol. Small, neat glasses of white rum were the only thing that could kill the longing for home.

> Swift to its close ebbs out life's little day;
> Earth's joys grow dim, its glories pass away;
> Change and decay in all around I see:
> O thou who changest not, abide with me!

I look down again to where he is lying inside his coffin. This time it is my eyes which cannot meet his; explore instead the hem of my coat, my shoes.

'Uncle Pete, is it you? Is it you, Uncle Pete?' I whisper.

> I need thy presence every passing hour:
> What but thy grace can foil the tempter's power?
> Who like thyself my guide and stay can be?
> Through cloud and sunshine, O abide with me!

'I have to go soon, Uncle Pete. I can't stay long. I have to go back to work. I came to see you one last time, but I'll have to go soon.'

We did not stay with him for long. After the wreaths were laid family and friends turned their backs once more and walked away. I left him, too, just as I had that day at the surgery. Left him encased in darkness, under the cold earth of a foreign country. There would be no going back home for him. No long, hot days sitting on a veranda entertaining friends. No purchasing fish by the bay. No chopping coconuts to drink the sweet water. No catching manicou at night. No drinking sweet cocoa tea while eating bakes and saltfish on a Sunday morning. No breadnuts, no yam, no mangoes, no moonlight walks with a warm breeze blowing on his back. Home was now a wooden box being covered with earth. His sons, his brothers, his friends, had all taken turns, to shovel earth on to his coffin. Burying for ever his hopes and dreams. Burying his desire to 'make some money and go back home'. Five years, that had always been the plan. 'We'll stay in England for five years.'

> Hold thou thy word before my closing eyes;
> Shine through the gloom, and point me to the skies:
> Heaven's morning breaks, and earth's vain shadows flee
> In life, in death, O Lord, abide with me.

They sang. We sang. I left him. I had to go back to work. This time I could not even give him a little change, 'for bus fare'.

'Momo, is you?'

'Yes, Uncle Pete, is me.'

BRENDA EMMANUS

Train Games

It was late afternoon, the train was only half full. A middle-aged man wearing thick framed glasses sat in her view on the opposite side of the carriage. Two seats in front, his half-bald head was buried deep in a paperback. Squinting at the pages, he used his heavy square hand to push his frames securely on to his nose, and extended his arm to clasp his coffee without even moving his eyes from the page. This amused Maya. Her attention was then stolen by the frustrated voices of two young children in the block of seats directly in front of her, interrogating their mother about when they would reach their destination. In an irritated fashion, the woman attempted to pacify them with a Thomas the Tank Engine story. She attempted in vain.

Maya felt a sense of increasing discomfort. She became aware of a glare from the passenger sitting in the seat parallel. He was staring at her, scrutinizing the mass of corkscrew curls that crowned her head, and her toned, androgynous body, wrapped in a modern slip dress. She switched her head right and watched him instinctively reach for his newspaper. She responded impulsively with a flirtatious smile, which she retracted like a rubber band when returned with his blank expression. 'What's his game?' she thought.

With her head now forward she watched him out of the corner of her eye, riffling his paper, oblivious to the fact that a couple of the sheets had slipped through his fingers and landed clumsily on the passenger table. She had become his view now, the stranger familiarizing himself with her through indiscreet stares up and down her nervous torso. Maya shuffled uncomfortably in her chair, adjusting her satin dress with her baby-soft hands, flattening the folds of fabric that had gathered around her stomach.

'Tickets, please!' The inspector clumped his way towards her. Maya seized the opportunity to grab a glance at the voyeur while handing the inspector her ticket. Something triggered her pleasure zones. The stranger was her kind of handsome. His build appeared firm and athletic, his clothes stylish, not flashy. More creative than corporate. 'Thanks, lovely lady!' smiled the lanky inspector, handing her back her ticket. His nicotine-stained teeth were parted by a small gap, enhancing his geeky appearance. 'Ooh, that's nice!'

'Pardon?' The inspector's comment had thrown her.

'Your necklace. It's gorgeous. My wife Lil has something similar, got it from her mother. Yours is probably one of those designer jobs, though, isn't it?'

Maya was unsure whether his comment on her pendant was an insult or flattery. Perhaps he had mistaken her Nefertiti for Queen Victoria? She thanked him all the same. While he clipped a hole into the stranger's ticket she stole a second glance. Their eyes locked into a temporary freeze. His stare was confident, his mouth slightly open as his tongue massaged his teeth, as if searching for food stuck between the cavities of his molars. He looked away, tapping his lean fingers on the table-top to the undisclosed tune playing in his head.

The 3.25 from Shrewsbury to London gathered load. A trio of businessmen returning from an early meeting negotiated themselves into their seats, briefcases and mobile phones in tow. Rucksacked students juggled cartons of drinks and sandwiches along the aisle, while a group of eager pensioners sat divulging their life stories in loud conversation. The seats around Maya and her anonymous companion remained empty. Was it their vibes that discouraged others, or was this fate? She folded and unfolded her horsy legs and peered out the window in an effort to distract herself. The journey saw scenes change like seasons. The sun was now piercing through the glass, causing her to squint. She closed her eyes and raised her head to feel its warm embrace, but the subtle heat enervated her senses and brought her only momentary comfort; and the presence of this sandy-skinned stranger watching her with undefined intention made her increasingly self-conscious.

'What's his flipping problem?' she quizzed silently. 'Like I haven't seen him gawking!' She felt both anxiety and anticipation. A smile knocked hard at the door of her mouth, but she refused to let it in. Another split-second glance was enough to register him in 'The Crumpet Zone' as she and her friends called it. Most men assigned there were those in their fantasies: actors, musicians and sportsmen. Boyfriends were expelled once they'd messed up. She wished he would talk to her so she could conclude how she felt and discover who he was.

Maya peered at the window, hoping to catch his reflection in the glass. The brilliant light and dark shadows caused by the trees and buildings formed a blurred image; no assistance to her growing curiosity. 'He's either really cool . . . or a pervert!' she thought. 'Maybe he's just shy? Perhaps I should make the move. He looks my type . . .' She stopped her thoughts in their tracks. 'Her type' had never been that good for her. They liked women, instead of *a* woman, football instead of films, and lounging with the lads instead of lovemaking. Fucking, yes, but never preceded by steamy sessions of foreplay in a country cottage or hotel suite – more often on a sofa during her favourite film or in the back of a car, like teenagers whose parents were always indoors. She was yet to meet a man who would release her sexual fantasies like lava from a volcano. Until that moment, her fantasies would remain just that.

She pushed her curls back against the foam seat and tilted her head to look out of the window once more. She observed the further evidence of spring. The carpets of green fields were embroidered with blossom-filled trees. Cows sauntered aimlessly, and tractors ploughed through maize fields like slaves through cotton plantations. These train rides home after filming always stimulated thoughts of a rural lifestyle. She imagined herself married to a devoted man, with two kids and a cottage near the lakes. A life more green than grey. But this was more a Caucasian reality than a Black woman's. Maya knew she was an urban chick at heart.

She had lived in Brixton for over eight years, a fact that her counsellor mother and lawyer father never appreciated. She loved their four-bedroomed semi in Croydon but, for her, it lacked the soul of sw2. She could get into the centre of town in thirty minutes, and her best friend, her only true, non-media-related friend Steph, lived five minutes away. They ate chicken yakisoba at Fujiyama's, saw indie films at the Ritzy and spent many girly, giggly nights downing too many pink pussy cocktails in the Satay Bar.

Her thoughts crashed back to the present with a jolt of the train and the sound of a newspaper sliding across the table, away from this mysterious, goateed Black man now stretching his leg across the chair and on to the fatigued carpet of the aisle. As he gripped the head of the empty chair beside Maya for support, her body stiffened. Her eyes followed his frame as it moved towards the toilet and buffet cars. He strode with slow wide steps, almost gliding past the other passengers who were too preoccupied with their own activities to watch him. Maya was attracted to him more now she had a clear rear view. Long legs, tight buttocks, what was he trying to do to her? She shifted in her chair when she felt a tingling between her legs. 'Shit!' She sighed, unsure whether it was from relief that he had walked off or disappointment that he'd said nothing to her. 'Am I really that desperate?'

She waited for his return, resting her chin on her fist. Other passengers had joined the train but not their carriage. Gradually Maya became aware of the muffled ringing of a mobile phone. She checked her own. The luminous green light was dull and the panel smiled back at her. It was not hers. She quickly realized that the repetitive ring cried from the inside of the leather rucksack on his vacant seat.

'Should I answer it?' she asked herself, looking around at the remaining passengers in the carriage, who were oblivious or uninterested. 'No, I'll just tell him when he comes back.' She had found a reason to talk to him. She stared at the bag intensely, as if casting a spell. The ringing stopped. Looking up, she noticed him returning through the automatic doors. His hands were empty.

'He was gone long enough. He must have been having a shit or checking his face in the mirror!' She chuckled to herself. Maya tried to imagine which option it had been as he slipped back into his seat without acknowledging her. She snatched a quick front view, which reinforced his magnetism. Her self-esteem sank like a stone in water. She felt like a puppy in a shop-window. 'Maybe he's gay?' she thought.

In her frustration she tried to switch off. She closed her eyes and imagined him vividly in her mind, where she held more control over him. Instantly she saw him stooped over a toilet bowl, trousers down below his knees and face screwed tight in an attempt to relieve himself. This was not how she wished to experience this cool and silent stranger. Maya took control of her day-dream.

This time he stood, strong legs astride, facing the toilet bowl with his manhood in his left hand to assist its aim. Staring into the mirror above the seat he took his free hand and gently stroked down his face, from the peak of his high cheekbones down towards his chin, flipping his face from left to right, checking for evidence of shadow and stubble. Shaking the remaining drips away from his tool he slowly dragged his Calvin Klein boxer shorts over his peachy buttocks.

Four days of demanding work colleagues and late nights were starting to take their toll. Maya's eyelids grew heavy. She fought back a yawn, stretching her mouth like a cow chewing grass, and then surrendered once more to her day-dream. The soft rumbling of the train underneath her seat, coupled with her vivid thoughts of the actions of this stranger, made her moist and warm. She wrapped herself in a blanket of pleasure caused by his inactive presence on the train and his image in her head. Reality and fantasy soon faded to black.

'Ladies and gentlemen, we have arrived at Euston. Please take all your personal belongings with you . . .'

The announcement woke Maya. She flicked her head like a chicken to establish her whereabouts, shook her body back to consciousness and, embarrassed, wiped the dribble from the corner of her mouth. Even before grabbing her bag she looked across for the object of her desire, but he had gone.

Dozily she collected her thoughts, then her belongings from the table and the shelf above her seat. Annoyed with herself for not having taken the initiative and missing an opportunity, she felt a fiery rebellion rush through her as she decided to be a rubbish junkie and leave her half-drunk Diet Coke and her newspaper on the table. In her rush to leave the now empty carriage and return to her batchelorette flat, she failed to notice the torn piece of reporter's pad with the hurriedly scrawled name, number and 'Call me' which her bag swiped clumsily to the floor.

CATHERINE R. JOHNSON

Scary

I had a handful of Jamie Andrew's hair in my hand. It felt slippy and shone like syrup. I turned my hand and wound the hair around so that the skin on his face pulled his eyes into slits. He made a thin hurting sound.

'Never' – I twisted his hair – 'never' – I twisted some more – 'Do that to me again! OK?'

He made a bubbling noise like Sarah's guinea-pig. I didn't know if that meant he was sorry or not, so I looked into his screwed-up face. 'Say you're sorry!'

'Will not!' That just tipped me, I can tell you. I brought my knee up hard to his privates and watched him fold in half and yell for his mammy. His face went red and tears started. I should have run then. I already felt much better. This was one cure that worked.

'It's fair now, Jamie,' I said.

He was still doubled up. I rubbed his back. 'OK? All right?' He looked up at me, his eyes like little chips of watery-blue sky. I wanted to tell him that how he looked now, face all down and red and that, he'd made me feel the same and worse. He never understood at all. He just thought I wanted to beat him up.

'I'll get my brother on to you, Serena!' But he said it in a high-pitched little-kid's voice, so I wasn't scared.

'No returns, Jamie. It's over. OK?' I said it slow. 'Everyone agreed, Sarah, and Orla, and everyone.' I put ma hand out. 'Quits?'

But Jamie Andrew was mewling and mewling, and I can see he's not having it.

The door of the house banged, and Jamie Andrew's mother was putting out the washing on the rotary dryer. I saw Jamie's eyes flick over to her, and I know he's going to start up the bawling loud, so I run. All the way up the Brecks and over Ward Hill to the observatory.

I ran and ran until I almost fell through the door into the ringing room. Les was ringing gulls, kittiwakes and petrels, holding them careful with their wings folded down. He stroked them sometimes to calm them, tiny, gentle touches just under their beaks or on the top of their heads. Love, it looked like.

They're strange, gulls. Their beaks are bright yellow, straight from a paint pot, but their feathers are that shade of grey you can never get – however hard you try to mix up the right colour.

So Les takes one look at me, puffing fit to burst and with my jacket all pulled around, and I can tell he knows something's up. 'Serena!' He says it sad like he's upset, not cross. 'Don't even tell me, I just don't want to know.' His voice is soft, so the kittiwake trembling in his big hands doesn't have a heart attack. 'You should have been back half an hour ago, did you not see the plane? Lyn's got a roomful of new visitors and she needs all the help she can get.'

I pull ma wellies off and sneak into the big room. Lyn's explaining to the visitors about the island, about the catering and about how there's absolutely no smoking in the bedrooms. There's loads of them 'cause of some Russian warbler that's warbled off course and sighted at Vaasetter last week. It was in the mainland papers and everything, and Les has been out every day in a little hide he's made, watching for it. Then I hear Lyn.

'. . . And over there is Serena, our daughter.' Twenty pairs of eyes goggle at me like I'm the Russian warbler, poor wee bird.

The English need an excuse to goggle, usually the first time they catch sight of me they do daft cartoon double takes, then they just stare out of the corner of their eyes. You can see them at dinner, their tiny birder brains going click, click, click, is she her daughter then? And if that's the mother then he's never the father.

The Americans, and we get a few, not just for the birds but for the woollies – they buy them even though they're all machine-made nowadays; I've seen Sarah's mother make a couple by hand, but she never sells those. Anyway, the Americans always come right out with it in their best TV voices: 'And where did you blow in from, honey?' Like I was a fulmar crashed into Ward Hill and not able to get up and fly off. At least if I was a fulmar I could sick up over them if they got too close.

I slope off to the kitchen where Astrid, who does cooking and meteorology, is chopping leeks.

'Did you get him then? That nasty boy?'

She's all right, Astrid, she talks in that swooping Norwegian way and she's the prettiest girl on the island. Jamie Andrew's big brother probably dreams about her even when he's away at school in Lerwick.

'Well, I hope it's over and you can get back to normal now. He is just one stupid boy. And, anyway, who can say where people should be or not be?' She sliced the air with the kitchen knife. 'I mean, should I be here or only in Trondheim?' Her blonde eyebrows arch up into two rainbow shapes.

I open ma mouth to tell her that it wasn't me that started it, but Astrid would call that whinging, so I shut it quick.

Lyn comes swinging into the kitchen. 'You'll never guess,' she says.

From the look on her face I'd say a Russian warbler has just warbled into the front room, perched on the bookcase and posed for the visitors.

'Serena!' She grabs my shoulders and steers me back into the big room. Most of the visitors are away to their bedrooms, but there's a woman in the big armchair, reading a book on her lap. She looks at me, and I look at her. 'Serena,' Lyn says, 'this is Dr Natalie Boyce.'

Dr Natalie Boyce's eyes smile hello and flick back to Lyn. They smile at me again, and I can just tell she's thinking the same way as me. Ma face is burning and hers is too, I know. Lyn is not embarrassed at all. She's warbling on and on about how Dr Boyce is a naturalist – 'Isn't that right?' – and how she works in London studying feeding patterns of small migrating birds.

Dr Boyce is grinning at me, but I know she's laughing at Lyn, being so Lyn-y. Lyn just doesn't get it at all. Anyway, Dr Natalie Boyce puts out her dark chocolate hand for me to shake.

I feel her hand warm and soft. I can't ever remember shaking a darker hand than mine. Three whole shades darker, I reckon she is. Smooth and slightly sheeny. Makes me look yellowy – ill like when Sarah's baby sister had the jaundice. The traders that come, the Pakis – Lyn tells me off for calling them that, but it's what I get called too, in Lerwick – they're the same colour as me. But they're only here twice a year. Of course I've seen other black people. On *Blue Peter*, in *EastEnders*, that Fiona from *Coronation Street* – but she left. And Scary, of course.

Dr Natalie Boyce speaks. 'Hi,' she says, just like that.

'Hi,' I say back.

Lyn's face looks like it's ready to spilt in two, she's smiling so hard. 'Maybe Serena here can show you round the island.' She pauses, almost worried. 'That is, Dr Boyce, if you don't mind.'

I look at Lyn; she is so embarrassing, it's such a set-up. But Dr Natalie Boyce is cool, she's got to have a wash first, she says.

I take her out on Bu'ness at first, as far away from the crofts as possible. The wind's pretty hard and Dr Natalie Boyce – 'Call me Natalie' – is nearly blown over. I show her where the gulls nest and where the boat was wrecked three years ago. We walk along the bay in North Quay, and she says to me after a while, 'So, Serena, what's it like up here?'

I shrug. I mean, this is the whole of ma world. This is ma island. Everyone knows me, sees me coming. But I like that. You know. And I say nothing. I walk her over to Les's second hide. He'd near enough kill me if I took her over Vaasetter. We sit in the dark, looking out of a little oblong of light. And Dr Boyce is in heaven. Her binoculars glued to her face.

So I'm back to thinking about Jamie Andrew.

They had me pinned on this flat rock on the beach at the South Harbour. David and Jamie Andrew and Orla, although she said she was just going along with it. We'd done the Spice Girls at school, Sarah was Sporty, Orla was Baby and Katie was Posh. I had no choice. I was Scary. Obviously.

They held me down on this rock. Jamie Andrew had the laundry-marker but I'm not stupid and I wouldn't open ma mouth, not for anything. They wanted to do a dot on ma tongue – 'Just a wee one, Serena, it'll look dead cool' – but I said no.

So Jamie Andrew was getting cross; he was the manager, he said. But he just liked winding me up. I was staring up at the sky, clouds all whipping past, opening tiny flashes of blue. Lapis lazuli like in ancient Egypt. Always, always, before that I'd been the witch, the troll under the bridge, the yellow Power Ranger. I never complained. Easier not to. But I hate the Spice Girls. Les always makes me listen to the Upsetters. Says it's ma cultural heritage.

Then Jamie Andrew puts his knee on ma front and puts his face this close to mine. And I can see the marker in his hand. TOXIC, it said. Toxic, I think.

So I had to get him back.

Meanwhile, in the real, outside world, Dr Natalie Boyce has put down her binoculars and is writing something in her notebook. She has long fingernails, well longer than Lyn's, and she looks at me and says, just like all the others, 'Where are you from then, originally?'

I look at her sad. 'Round here,' I say, 'these parts,' and walk slowly back to the observatory.

HOPE MASSIAH

MOT Time

The house always reminded her of her parents' old house – pebble-dash, plastic tubs of pink geraniums, and nylon curtains frothing at the front windows. All that was missing were her mother's glass animals lining the window-sill. Jenny rang the door-bell and waited, cheque-book and pen in hand, thinking about what she could say to get away this time. She took a deep breath as the door opened.

'Hello, hello.'

He stood holding the front door, shading his eyes. He was totally grey now, hair so white that it made his face look darker and made his colours appear reversed, like a negative.

Jenny took a step towards him. 'How's it going, Dad?'

'Good, good. How's things?' He wore a short-sleeved checked shirt, clean, faded jeans and new-looking trainers.

'Fine. Fine,' she replied. 'I have to collect Omar soon, so . . .'

She hoped that, as usual, he would separate her car keys from the pile on the table next to him, give her the MOT certificate, tell her the cost and let her go. He sniffed, the sharp intake that preceded most of his sentences.

'You could come in for a minute. Get a cold drink or something. Annette's grandmother is here from Barbados.'

'Ahhm, well.' She had to think quickly. 'The babysitter, she has to go . . .'

But he had turned and was walking into the gloom of the house. She followed him. He was limping, she noticed. That was new. He didn't seem to be in pain but limped easily and comfortably. She wondered whether it was just age.

He had been retired for four years but kept busy preparing cars for MOT and doing minor repairs. At any given time a third of the cars parked in the short cul-de-sac were ones he was working on.

'Pamela still got the Jetta?' he asked over his shoulder.

'No. Andrew gave her a new car, for her birthday' – she paused – 'last week.'

Her father looked puzzled. 'It was her birthday? I always get her and Angela mix up. Pamela is . . . July, Angela is . . .'

'November.'

'And you is August. You will be thirty . . . ?'

'One.'

'That's right, that's right.' He brightened. 'What he get her?'

'Oh, a BMW.'

He stopped and turned expectantly. 'Seven series?'

She had no idea. 'Yes.'

'Uhmm.' He nodded and stretched out his bottom lip appreciatively, then turned and continued walking through the hallway.

'Seven series. But parts is expensive. Tell her I know somebody who can get parts, not cheap, but not too dear.' He hesitated. 'But she won't . . .'

For a moment Jenny thought he was going to acknowledge his lack of contact with her sisters.

'But she won't be needing parts for a long while,' he said wistfully. 'That's the beauty of German engineering. Right, here we are.'

They had walked through a cramped galley-kitchen to the back garden. A small woman, with skin like a well-used paper-bag, sat on a chair in the middle of a postage-stamp lawn, frowning at nothing in particular. To her right, an adolescent boy bounced a basketball on the strip of crazing paving that separated the lawn from the flower-bed. Behind him, a younger girl tussled with a twisted garden-hose. Annette stood on the patio, hand on plump hip, turning meat on a tripod barbecue.

Jenny had first heard of Annette on her trips home from university. To Mummy and her friends, Annette was 'that poor girl, jus' up from Barbados, man lef' she, struggling with two li'l babies.' Her mother always ended with 'Of course my girls is different, I train them to be independent, high-fliers.' Jenny hadn't seen Annette as a person, more as an object lesson of how her mother did not want her to turn out. Then, three years ago, her father had moved in with Annette.

Jenny smiled briefly at Annette and turned to the garden, looking with interest at the hollyhocks, roses and delphiniums. In the bed at the back she could make out rhubarb, tomatoes, and the pink heads of spring onions.

'I see you noticing the garden. Nothing to do with me.'

Her father used the same dismissive tone that he had used when he argued with her mother. He would end their rows with a scathing put-down and retire to the front room to play his Owen Grey record. Over the years it became scratched, but he never replaced it. Instead the needle would crash into the middle of the record, splitting the silence left by the row, giving the words extra spite: *The more she get, the more she want, woman a grumble.*

'It's Annette,' he continued. 'Green fingers. Anything she put her hand on.'

Annette, beaming, turned sausages and chicken drumsticks. The smell of the meat made Jenny's mouth water, but she tried to ignore it. Annette looked like she was putting on weight, Jenny thought with satisfaction, the flowery tent-dress couldn't hide it.

She reminded Jenny of all the single mothers at Omar's school: standing around their buggies all day, smoking and gossiping, getting fatter. That wasn't how she had been brought up. Her husband Carl had left her when Omar was a baby, but she had found a babysitter, gone back to work, taken her banking exams, even got a promotion. Her son had just started school – well dressed, well adjusted, reading and counting. And she hadn't let herself go.

Annette, though, looked positively frumpy. This made it possible for Jenny to be sociable, ask about the garden, accept some food.

'You haven't met my trildren' – Annette still had a heavy Barbadian accent – 'Mark, Michelle, cumma.'

Mark, a burly boy and Michelle, shorter, and with the same glasses and pinned-back hair as her mother, walked towards Jenny.

Her father stepped between them, and said 'Mark, Michelle. This is Jenny. My youngest daughter.'

He encompassed the children with one arm and rested the other tentatively on Jenny's back. The boy gave an unintelligible teenage grunt, and the girl said a shy hello.

Jenny smiled hello, stepped away from her father's touch, and said brightly, 'So, Dad, what's the damage this time?'

He frowned slightly. 'Well' – he gave the children a slight squeeze and let them go, but his eyes followed them as they moved awkwardly away – 'for argument's sake, let's call it a hundred and twenty. There was the MOT, and the back light, and I did all the points and the plugs, and one of your linings was about this thick.' He held his thumb and forefinger a few millimetres apart.

'Gosh. Really?' She had no idea what a lining was or how thick it was supposed to be. Her father always told her what was wrong with the car, and she found that she got away quicker if she didn't ask any questions. She balanced her cheque-book on her bag and wrote out the cheque.

'Oh, I din' even give you a drink,' Annette exclaimed. 'Michelle, get Jenny a drink and, Granny' – she turned to the woman on the lawn – 'you want a drink?' She then turned to Jenny and whispered, 'Granny is staying with me till December. You know.'

Jenny smiled and nodded, hoping her lack of interest didn't show. Granny, who had been staring into the distance, tilted her small head in a bird-like gesture and said, 'I could drink a little pop.' She then leaned forward, looking at Jenny for the first time, and said, 'She de lawyer?'

'No,' Jenny's father replied. 'Dah is Angela, the middle girl. Jenny is a bank manager. First black woman in the south-east.'

The older woman peered at Jenny a moment longer, then sank back into the moulded-plastic chair.

Jenny felt a prickle in her chest. She saw Mummy sitting in a chair in the emptied living-room of their old house. She had looked as old as this woman. Her body still filled the seat but her face had collapsed – skin drooping and grey, eyes lifeless, mouth hanging slack. The three sisters, shocked at the sight of their normally opinionated mother, had fussed and fluttered around her like noisy pigeons, packing, organizing, telling Mummy she was right to sell, right to get away from Daddy and *her*, better off staying with Pamela. Throughout, their mother had sat silent, pulling a tissue apart with a hand that, overnight, had frozen into a bony claw.

Pamela and Angela had broken all contact with their father. Jenny told her sisters, and herself, that she only saw him because she could not afford a proper mechanic. Although the sisters were adamant that they did not want to see him, they cross-questioned Jenny after each visit and speculated about why he never rang them. Pamela insisted that he was 'too shame' to contact them, while Angela usually concluded that he didn't care about any of them.

The girl Michelle gave Jenny a frosted tumbler containing a fizzy yellow drink and walked carefully to her great-grandmother with the other glass. A breeze picked up, making the trees rustle and the rhubarb leaves wave like enormous, friendly hands. The old lady sipped her drink and smacked her lips. The children squabbled over the hose. Annette and Jenny's father examined a rose-bush. Jenny stood alone, watching them and wondering, for the first time, why she came.

Her father noticed the children fighting and walked swiftly, in spite of his limp, towards them. Jenny, remembering his response to the sisters' arguments, drew in her breath. He snatched the hose from the siblings but playfully punched the boy's chest and patted the girl. Jenny's chest felt tight. Annette and her father walked to her, both still beaming. She put her glass down and held out the cheque to her father.

'Right. I got your papers in the house somewhere. Stay and talk to Annette,' he said, as she made to follow him. Jenny felt as if someone with metal fingers was squeezing her chest.

'I need to go to the toilet.'

She was relieved at how normal she sounded. She followed Annette's directions and ran up the stairs, trying to ignore the pictures lining the wall, but one, of her father and the boy at Disneyland, caught her eye. They were on the top of a roller-coaster with their hands in the air. Her dad was wearing a floral shirt and a straw hat. She tried to remember her father playing with her or Pamela or Angela but failed. Jenny stumbled up the rest of the stairs, breathing heavily. She did not have a single memory of fatherly tenderness, as a child or as an adult.

The day Carl left her she had rung home wanting Mummy, but only her father was there. He came to collect her, and Jenny had cried noisy desolate tears, all the way from Tottenham to Streatham. He had said nothing, made no attempt to comfort her. Just driven her home and excused himself as soon as she started to tell Mummy what had happened.

Jenny washed her face in the pink and green bathroom and hurried back downstairs, determined to leave. She heard Annette's voice as she reached the back door.

'Wul-law, my ankles swelling up already.'

Annette was bending over, holding the sides of her stomach, and Jenny could see a distinct bulge. She suddenly saw that it was only Annette's stomach which was fatter.

Annette looked up at her. 'Twins. Did your Daddy say?'

Jenny's jaw dropped, no words, no thoughts came into her head. Her mouth hung open.

Annette looked puzzled, then turned to Jenny's father. 'Victor, you 'in tell her. You said. He said . . .' Her eyes pleaded.

Jenny's chest felt as if it was going to explode and she felt an urge to put her head back and howl. Victor avoided their eyes and frowned at the floor. He sniffed distinctly. 'She knows now.'

'Dad, my keys. Can I have my keys?' They were all looking at her, even Granny. She realized that she was shouting. Not waiting for him to respond, she turned and walked through the house to the front garden.

Jenny stood cradling her bag to her chest as her father backed the car out of the garage. The red Golf gleamed, shiny as lipstick. He got out of the car and gave it a final wipe with his chamois leather.

'I kep' it in the garage. These trees,' he pointed, 'they drop a sap. Would mess it up.'

He had taken off his shirt, and salt and pepper hairs sprang jauntily from the top of his white vest. In spite of the grey and the wrinkles in his face, he looked sprightly. He walked round to the passenger side and got in. She got into the driver side and stared ahead as he repeated details of the car's workings. At last he finished, patting the dashboard with a 'These is good little cars.'

'OK, Dad, thanks, see you next time.' She snaked her fingers towards the keys on the dashboard.

'Yes. As I said, I'll keep an eye out for a new carburettor.' He folded the MOT certificate into a concertina. His gold ring gleamed against fingers blackened by a lifetime's car grease.

She knew what was going to happen next: He would bid her a cheery goodbye with a few more car-maintenance tips and a kiss that would leave a cold patch on her cheek. She would drive home and ring her sisters to try to make sense of it all. Next year would be the same. He was nearly seventy now; how many more years of silence did they have?

'Dad, why do you still wear your wedding ring?' The words surprised Jenny almost as much as him. Her father looked at the ring as if noticing it for the first time.

'Well. I still married. I mean . . . just because . . .'

'But you left, you left Mummy.' Jenny stumbled over her words.

Her father shifted, rubbed his legs and sniffed twice. 'Hmmh. Well. Things wasn't always how they seem.' His voice sounded rusty.

Jenny listened, watching a boy and a girl, teenagers, on the street in front of them.

'I mean . . . dah is the trouble.' He spoke more confidently now. 'People think they know, but you can't always judge a book by its cover.'

The boy, small and wiry, kept pushing the girl into the road, then saving her. The girl squealed on cue.

Jenny tried again. 'But did you ever . . . why did you marry Mummy?'

'Your mother . . . She was the only girl in Bayfield who . . . who could drive a car.'

The girl, lanky, with heavy gold earrings, turned on the boy and gave him a strong push that ended in a hug, then they ran giggling into one of the houses.

'She was big, a tomboy . . . and she could drive a car. You girls take after her.' He gave a concluding sniff. The street was empty now, just two rows of houses staring each other down. 'Oh, well.' He rubbed his legs again, but didn't move.

Jenny could make out the distant tiny screams of children in the gardens behind the houses. What he said made no sense. She had asked the wrong questions and used up all her energy in the asking. She turned to receive his kiss and saw the raisin on his shoulder: A mole the exact size, shape and texture of a raisin. She suddenly saw herself climbing up into his chair and playing with the raisin while he read the paper. She saw herself squishing it, trying to pull it off.

'Pull it off. Eat it,' he would say.

She would try and try, and end up howling in frustration. Then he would laugh at her and say 'Hush' sternly, pick her up and pretend to throw her away.

And as she flew screeching through the air, her fear and rage and frustration would meet and coalesce into something as pure as joy. And he would put her down and she would tug and tug at his scratchy navy-blue leg and he would shout, 'Move' and try to shake her off, but gently.

Jenny looked down at the floor so he could not see her crying. All the juice boxes, sweet wrappers and crisp packets were gone, and she could smell Shake 'n' Vac.

She realized that he was waiting. Waiting for her to say something, to mention the coming children. She couldn't. 'Bye, Dad.'

Out of the side of her eye she saw him deflate, then make an effort to draw himself up. 'Good. Good.'

Jenny couldn't look at him. She opened her mouth. Nothing happened. The last time she had been in a car with her father was the day Carl left her. He had been silent then, as she was silent now. For the first time she wondered whether his silence was like hers, due not to a lack of interest but to feelings clumping and sticking and refusing to separate themselves into words. He had, though, immediately left what he had been doing and driven across London to take her home, to someone who could talk to her and comfort her. She opened her mouth again. 'So, she is pregnant.' That was all she could manage.

He shifted. 'Well, it was Annette, I had my time. If it was down to me . . .' He shrugged dismissively but could not hide his pride. 'She wanted to. She still young. So . . .' He shrugged as the words petered out.

Jenny reached out awkwardly and rested her hand on his shoulder. Just for a second. She felt the raisin on his shoulder. It was smaller and firmer, more like a currant, but it still felt real.

CHRIS ABANI

Becoming Abigail

She thought it might rain but so far it had not. A slight breeze ruffled the trees but it was not cold. Not really. She suddenly wished she had seen a London fog, the kind she had read about. A decent respectable fog that masked a fleeing Jack the Ripper or hid Moriarty from Sherlock's chase. With a sigh she stopped walking. She was here.

The sphinxes faced the wrong way, gazing inward contemplatively at Cleopatra's Needle rather than outwards, protectively. But Queen Victoria had ruled against the expense of correcting the mistake. She stood gazing out at the dark, cold presence of the Thames, wondering what had happened to its spirit. Was it still alive and looking after the city that had flourished on its banks for so long, or lost in the antiquity of Rome and Normandy? When exactly had the Celts lost their fire, to become this insipid race? Breaking open a packet of cigarettes, she fumbled clumsily to light one. She did not smoke. With her first ever drag she imagined she could see them, the sad lonely souls who had come here, to the Needle, to do it. Suddenly afraid, she smothered a sob, choking on the harshness of the tobacco, eyes tearing.

She had taken and been taken by many men in her short lifetime, none of whom had really seen her. Noticed anything about her. Like the fact that she wore bronze lipstick. Or had a beautiful smile that was punctuated perfectly by dimples. That she plaited her hair herself, into tight cornrows. Or that her light complexion was a throwback from that time a Portuguese sailor had raped her great-grandmother. None of them noticed the gentle shadow her breasts cast on her triceps as she reached on tiptoe for the relief of a stretch. Nor did they know she had cracked her left molar falling out of a mango tree like a common urchin, or that her father beat her for the shame and fear of it until the lushness of mangoes stolen and eaten behind sacks of rice in the storeroom brought a near-sexual release. Most just smelt the odour of lust she seemed to give off. From then on they were too busy moaning sweatily over her or trying to get her to let them. But he saw these things immediately. That was how she remembered it anyway. Even before she undressed, he had divined her truth through the thin fabric of her dress, the tattoos that were burnt deep, yet remained invisible to most. He traced their outlines on her skin with sensitive fingers. Loving her all night with the gentle brush of a butterfly. Sketching her into being. Unfurling before his rain, her petals kissed his sun, winding-vine-hope. And their joining was a sweat-tear-pouring calypso, whimpering, screaming and hollering their souls home, to the accompaniment of bedspring-steel-drums. Other men she had known just wanted to empty their lives into her. Dominating. Selfish. He was tender, giving, gentle, loving.

She had been ten when her first, fifteen-year-old cousin Edwin swapped her cherry for a bag of sweets. Its pound-weight of caramel and treacle promise the full measure of his guilt. Then, while stroking her hair tenderly, he whispered softly that he would kill her if she told anyone. Not that she would. Her father was till lost in his grief for her mother, who had died bringing her into the world. There was no one else to tell.

Unfortunately, she grew up looking like her mother. So much so that her dad never called her by her name. He called her Abigail. Her mother's name. Not that she was surprised. She had been a ghost all her life. Invisible. No one saw her. When people looked at her, they saw her mother. Abigail Tansi. Woman. Wife. Lover. Warrior. Suffragette. The first woman to run for public office in the entire region. Everyone talked of her. Spoke of her fearlessness in confronting the men in her community in the fight for women's rights. It was said that when she heard tell of a wife-beater, she would call round and calmly and politely explain that if he did not change his ways she would cut off his penis. There was a quiet power to her that always left these men breathless and secretly reformed.

All her knowledge of her mother was based around the single faded photograph in the black frame in the living room and the stories she heard. From strangers, family and especially her father. She would seek out anyone who had known Abigail and offer to trade a chore for an anecdote. At first she was trying to reclaim her mother. Re-create her memory, make it concrete, physical. Fashioning a new persona that was self-sustaining: parent and child. But this was not entirely true, because when in a dream she saw her mother's ghost, in yellowed-lace wedding dress, coming for her, arms outstretched, she fled in terror. Waking with a scream, she realized that she did not want her mother back, she wanted to *be* her mother. So she collected vignettes about Abigail. Hoarding them gently until late at night, when all was silent apart from the occasional call of a night bird and dogs baying longing at the moon, she would unwrap them in her mind and feast, gorging herself. Sated, she traced their outlines on her skin with soft fingers, burning them in with the heat of her loss, tattooing them with a need as desperate as it was confused. Sewing a new skin, a new being, becoming Abigail.

The cigarette burnt her finger as it smoked down to the filter. With a yelp she threw it into the river, following its glowing path, imagining she heard the hiss of its extinction as it hit the thick blackness of the water. Sucking her finger, she watched a train rumble across a bridge, spanning the water in flickering lights from the coaches. Fumbling about in her bag, she pulled out her purse. Opening it, she stroked the faces of the two men she loved. Her father, obsidian almost, scowling at the world. Derek, white, smiling as the sun wrinkled the corners of his eyes.

'I am sorry,' she muttered repeatedly, the sound a mantra to soothe her.

None of this would have happened if she had not let Peter talk her father into letting her come to London with him. He was married to her elder cousin, Mary. She had been a bridesmaid at their wedding. Still a child at twelve, although her bosom was a mature swell. Later, at the reception, Peter had cornered her in the bathroom. Surprised at her fearlessness he kissed her, finger exploring her treacled centre. They were interrupted. Panting, he returned to the reception, the scent on his finger driving him to distraction. He had left for London with Mary shortly after. That was three years ago. He returned once a year but, being away at boarding school, she always missed him. He usually took one of his or Mary's younger relatives back to London. 'But my father needs me,' she had argued then, not wanting to go when he told her he had come for her on Mary's request. 'Besides, will it not get crowded with the other relatives you've taken to live with you already?' Mary needed her, he explained. All the other kids he had taken back had fallen in with bad crowds and run away.

It was getting chilly and she wished she were wearing more than a light denim shirt. No point in catching a cold as well, she thought, sniffling unconsciously. She remembered reading in a *Reader's Digest* somewhere that all aeroplane landings are controlled crashes. She wished the plane bringing her and Peter to London that day had crashed. Her father had been only too willing to let him take her, believing that her life would be better. That London would provide access to a higher standard of education and living. She felt his sacrifice, knowing that he was fighting his heart, the urge to beg her to stay. But there was also a fear in him. Perhaps he thought he might blur the lines of vision between seeing her as his wife and seeing his wife.

The fighting had begun from the first night they arrived. Abigail could not imagine why Mary would let Peter hit her like that and not fight back. She stood on the threshold, unsure what to do but knowing she had to do something. Their shouting had woken her from sleep. She crept out of bed, tiptoeing past the two other teenagers she shared her room with. Although she knew them by face and name from back home, she had never spoken to them until now. She thought it odd that they slept all day and then left home in the early evening, not returning until the very early hours of the morning. Peter and Mary never reprimanded them for this. If anything, they encouraged them. She did not understand it at all, but then to be fair, she had been there only a few days. Her attention returned to the fight. They seemed to be arguing about her. From what she could gather, Mary did not want her there, which she found strange, as they were really close. The crack of Peter's backhand across Mary's face decided it for her. Abigail flew at him, gouging a deep furrow under his eye. He shouted and kicked wildly. One of the kicks knocked her clear across the room. He snarled at her and stomped off. Mary sobbed and just kept repeating one line, over and over as she cradled her.

'You should not have done that. Shouldn't have.'

A week later she found out why. He burst into her bedroom one night. She was half asleep and started up as though a nightmare were following her into the waking world. Two men stood in the door-way, the hall light fuzzing them into dark-haloed shapes. From the feral breathing and almost soundless smirk, she could tell that one of the shapes was Peter. The other was a mystery to her.

'Peter?' she ventured, pushing the bedclothes aside and making to get up.

But it was the other figure that approached her.

'Hello, little girl,' the voice husked.

'Who are you?' she demanded.

'You do not need to know that, little girl,' the man said. He was now standing in front of her. Menacing. She tried to retreat under the bedclothes, but he pulled them away. She scuttled back but he grabbed her and pushed his weight on to her. She fought him, shouting, calling for Mary. The man was like an incubus, the weight of his lust crushing her, melting her limbs to jelly. The more she fought, the heavier he got. 'Yes, little girl,' he grunted. 'I like it when you fight.'

'Mary!' she screamed, finally finding her voice.

Mary appeared at the open door of the bedroom. Tears washed foundation from her face in brown streaks. They locked eyes; Mary's pleading with hers as she stepped back, gently closing the door behind her. Peter smiled triumphantly, and turning to the man, he chanted, 'Do her, do her hard.' The weight on top of her stirred excitedly and she closed her eyes to the searing shame of his penetration. And all the fight just went out of her. It did not last long and, from her prone position, she saw the man get dressed, count out some money and hand it to Peter before leaving. She did not fight when Peter mounted her next. Now she knew why the others were out so late. What they did for a living. It continued nightly the same way, except the incubi were different – and the acts. Oral. Vaginal. Anal. Hers. Theirs. It was all so confusing and days blurred into weeks and into months. Until one night, unable to stand it any more, she screamed, invoking the spirit of Abigail, and with her teeth, tore off her rapist's penis. In the ensuing panic, she ran out, half naked, severed penis still clutched in her hand until a passing police car picked her up. Derek was the social worker who came for her the next morning.

She had found it hard to believe that this short, balding man could help her in any way. But there was a kindness about him. Quiet, warm, reassuring. At first she would not open up to him. The police search of hospitals had so far failed to turn up anyone with a missing penis. Weeks passed, and Derek visited her every day in the correctional facility where she was being held. She knew it was his job, but with time she liked to pretend that he was her friend and that he came to see her because he wanted to. Cared. Truth was they did become friends, developing a deep rapport. Gradually she had opened up to him, told him a little about her life. He tried to put the puzzle together. Mother died during childbirth. Child probably abused by successive male relatives. Ran away from home one night clutching that terrible legacy. Not uncommon. But no matter how hard he pressed, the memory of Mary's eyes at the door on the first night of her rape kept her from telling him or the police about Peter. Derek's colleagues recommended psychiatric treatment in a confined facility, but he fought them. He did not believe her crazy. Meanwhile, the search for her parents turned up nothing. It was as though they did not exist.

The sound of laughter carried clear across the water and she interrupted her brooding to see a brightly lit party-yacht sail past. It was colder now, and the water darker and meaner, and she longed for some warmth. A passing policeman stopped and watched her for a few minutes.

'Are you all right, miss?!' he called.

Startled, she dropped the cigarette she was lighting as she turned. Picking it up she nodded. He hesitated, but something about the sphinxes chilled him and he moved on.

Suddenly realizing that she could not live without him, she ran away from the foster-home Derek had arranged, turning up on his doorstep. He looked up from his report and glanced at his watch. It was late, and he was not expecting anyone. Getting up, he walked down the hall and peered through the spy-hole. She stood shivering on the stoop.

'Abigail?!' he exclaimed, opening the door.

She collapsed melodramatically into his arms, and he had to carry her inside. She was shivering so hard her teeth were chattering. He could not understand why, it was a warm night. The cold seemed to come from within her. He waited until she was sipping from a mug of hot chocolate before he pressed her for answers. There were no problems at the foster-home, she said. It was just that she missed him. He explained that theirs was, and had to remain, a professional relationship. But even as he said it he was fighting his urges and feelings for her. Then she broke down and sobbed out the entire story, about her mother, her dad, cousin Edwin, all the other boys after that, and finally Peter and cousin Mary. Her pain was heart-rending, and he was hugging her, soothing her. That was when he loved her. That night. And she was hooked, coming back again and again over the following weeks. The scent of them together was intoxicating, driving them both closer to the edge of danger, inflecting their lovemaking with the deliciousness of fear.

The new cigarette had also burnt out. She sat on the back of the sphinx and watched the traffic wink past. She wondered what they would make of her, perched up there, riding the sphinx. Pulling a compact out of her bag, she adjusted her lipstick. One last cigarette, she thought. Not that it mattered at this point.

Trust was something she was not very hot on. The only people she did trust were Derek and her father. So when her foster-mother confronted her, demanding to know who she was sneaking out to sleep with, her first instinct was to lie. But some note of concern in her foster-mother's voice, or some deep ancient yearning for a mother, made her speak about her and Derek. Even before she had finished her first sentence she could tell from her foster-mother's face that something was wrong.

The reprisals were swift. Derek was fired from his job and was facing charges of abuse of a minor. Nothing she did helped. Her impassioned denials, her claims to have fabricated the story, her letter saying it was her fault, that she had raped Derek. Nothing helped. Forbidden to see or speak to him, she could only watch, heart on fire, as his disgrace was finalized publicly.

Now, here she was, trying to find the strength to do this last thing to save him. She felt sure that if she went away, everything would blow over and life could return to normal for him. Maybe even her dad could get over the loss of Abigail if she was not around. She had never meant to hurt either of them. She sucked heavily on the cigarette, coughing through the harsh tobacco, tears stinging her eyes. The coughing fit caused her to drop her bag and it fell at the foot of the needle, contents spilt: a compact, lipstick, some tissues and a purse. She looked down at it, then at the cigarette. A tug sounded its foghorn and the wind picked up. With a sigh she flicked the stub at the darkness and followed it, her body hardly making a splash.

Memoirs

JOANNA TRAYNOR

The Child Has Come Home

To cut a really long story dead short, I'll just say that my dad didn't hang around after I was born. Nearly forty years later I embarked on what promised to be a long and hopeless search for him, knowing only his name and his situation at the time of my conception. I found him quite quickly, though, surfing the Net in my bedroom. Well, I found an estranged wife of his who put me directly in contact with various relatives in England. A couple of weeks later, off I went to London to meet my Nigerian great-aunt, who was over on a visit. She'd raised my father as her own after my grandmother died. I was curious and apprehensive, prepared to be delighted and disappointed all at once. The meeting went well. Although I'd been prepared to unpack some of the mixed-race baggage I'd been carrying around all my life, it remained largely undisturbed.

Baggage? I'm of mixed-race blood in a mixed-race marriage with a mixed-race man who only caught my attention because he was, at the time, sporting a serious tan. I knew he'd lighten up, and I half-feared we would too, but twelve years later his bite just got harder. We got on. He's a Plymouth man who spent his childhood roaming parks and woods. He spent his summers jumping into the sea blindfold from high dive boards down the Hoe. He had attitude and more seaside than he knew what to do with. As a young man, he left home to travel the world – well, Asia and Africa mostly. Twelve years later he returned and met me. He's down-to-earth Plymouth, a rugged man, a gentleman with a sense of adventure. Righteous in his own style. Straight out of a Hardy novel if you will. His mother is White South African of French extraction and his father, a White Protestant Yorkshire man. He likes to call himself half-African but I won't let him. My father is Black African and my mother, a Lancashire lass, daughter of Irish Catholic immigrants. I like to call myself half-Irish but Robbie won't let me. Genetically, we're exact opposites. The African War of Apartheid, the English War of the Roses and the Irish War of Forever are mixed in our blood, past and present. We're mixed race, mixed up and mad for each other.

Having Black African blood puts a different and, in this country of Whites, darker light on matters of genealogy. A visibly mixed-race couple who share the same culture but not the same skin tone remains a more remarkable and 'open to controversy' phenomenon than an invisibly mixed-race couple who are culturally worlds apart. Robbie and I were both born and raised in Britain, but because I'm Black, I'm different. All my life there's been a nagging need for me to be different. I talk White, dress White, drink eat and play White, but I'm Black. Perhaps it was a need to fill this cultural gap that drove me to find my father.

A few weeks after meeting my great-aunt, I received a call from a cousin telling me that the 'The King' was in town and wanted me to call him. This impressed me, but don't get me wrong. Right up until I discovered my father was a chief, I, like the White man, could accept sovereignty only as a national institution, the lead position of power open to only one man, regardless of the tribal diversity within the nation. I'd met too many African princes to take them very seriously. But now I knew that my dad was a chief, perhaps the cultural hierarchies of West African society needed a somewhat closer inspection. And by now, of course, I understood completely why I'd never been able to look up at the Queen and take her for my leader.

The King was in town and he was asking for me.

The King had brought a letter from my father and wanted me in London to collect it personally. The following Saturday I arrived at a house in Surrey Docks and was met at the door by the King's daughter. She showed me into a lounge full of sound system, television and posh sofas.

After twenty minutes, the King himself appeared, in a big white nightie. He was wide faced, with a menacing grin and serious voice. The pictures on the walls were of him in full regalia wielding a golden stick. We shook hands, sat and talked about my father, his chief status, the district where he lived, the function of the King, the culture, the religion, the rest of the family. He handed me the letter from my father and we talked about my impending trip to Nigeria to meet him.

Then two men arrived, in short-sleeved shirts, jangling keys, looking for all the world like a couple of taxi drivers. To honour their King they sank to the floor and prostrated themselves before him, in full prone position, waiting for a bishop-like tap on the head before rising again. The King could expect no such respect from me. Not in Surrey Docks anyway.

The men set about the drinks cabinet. It was eleven o'clock in the morning. I was given a kola nut to chew on, which is something like chewing a pencil – not the end of a pencil, the whole thing, the wood, the lead, the lot. Gagging on this taste, I watched as the King poured gin all over the carpet, chanting and wailing as he poured. His elderly wife started her own chanting then, and the men, who had now formed us all into a circle, joined in. They were chanting for some time, and between chants they took sips of gin from a small clear glass. On my arrival, the King had warned me that that particular day was a special date in the Muslim calendar, and so I assumed the ritual to be some Africanized Muslim prayer to Allah with alcohol thrown in. At last it was my turn for the gin. I knocked it back and said thanks. And then the King took my hand.

'Omobowale, you belong to us now. You are in the palm of our hand. How do you like your new name?'

'Sorry?'

'Your African name. Omobowale. It means "the child has come home."'

'Oh I like it,' I said. 'I like it very much.'

I tried to repeat it but couldn't, so I wrote it down and said it back to myself a few times. The more I said, the more I liked it.

On the train going home, I repeated again and again, 'Omobowale. Omobowale.' It sounded like a secret.

'Robbie,' I said, the minute I was through the door. He was in working jeans. He'd mowed the lawn and was feeding the dogs, looking up at me, tired, worn out. 'Omobowale,' I said. 'What do you think? Omobowale. "The child has come home." Do you like it?'

'Eh?'

'Omobowale. My African name. You say it.'

'What was it again? Say it again.'

'Omobowale. You say it.'

'Moby meebee.'

'No. O-mo-bo-wallay.'

'Mowallybe.' His face was crinkled up with the trying, the concentration.

'No, Robbie. You're not listenin', are yer? O-mo-bo-wallay.' He was washing his hands now. He turned to check my eyes, to see how serious I was. Deadly serious. 'Come on, for Christ's sake. It's not that difficult. Omobowale.'

'Leave it out. Yer name's Joanna.'

'O-MO-BO-WALE.' I was shouting now.

'OMOBYWALE,' he shouted back.

'At last,' I said. 'I think the least you can do is learn how to say it.' He was in a mood now, though.

I calmed him. We talked. Ate. Laughed. About half an hour later:

'What's my name?'

'Wallybally mojo.'

JUDITH LEWIS

Hey, English!

As a next-generation Bajan I had aspired to all the things my parents
expected in order to make way in a society that did not consider me
English. These aspirations had left me with an identity crisis which was
not resolved simply by convincing myself that I could assume a West
Indian identity. I had struggled with being English, my parents considered
me English, but society considered me Black, a paradox. I felt that an
overdue holiday would either crystallize this disparity or cause some
radical change in the way I perceived myself. I was off to the land of my
forebears in search of clarity.

I planned to visit 'Little England' in early October when the weather
would be cooler. The greyness of London was many miles away as we
rocked to the rhythm of a sudden burst of turbulence, heading for Grantley
Adams airport. Arriving by cheap-and-cheerful charter flight was not
exactly the grand entrance I had envisaged. Did flying fish really fly or
was I a victim of folklore? What was the female equivalent of a bulla?
While pondering these thoughts, the pilot announced that the temperature
was 79°. I was momentarily reminded of a conversation with colleagues
back at the office as to whether I would be *naturally* acclimatized by
virtue of my parentage. I lied to save face. I *knew* that the heat was going
to be a problem.

After the usual saga of falling overhead luggage, and those keen to be
met by even keener relatives, I descended from the bowels of the aeroplane
like a disorientated refugee. A sheet of sweat covered me – perhaps my
younger brother's suggestion of not wearing industrial-strength denim
had been more accurate than I imagined. Adopting contrived posturing
to cover my embarrassment, I was amazed to overhear a local woman
comment on how cool it seemed as she buttoned her jacket. I was
pleasantly surprised by the number of people who bade me good afternoon
in the short walk over to my relatives.

On route to my holiday residence I marvelled at the people my cousin
was hailing. Horn-tooting appeared to replace the traditional signalling

of 'Hello', 'After you' and 'Thanks'. It reminded me that I had *arrived* in my home from home, the land of my father and forefathers. A place where Black people made the rules and stretched them with an assured ease. Streets devoid of pavements, a place where sugarcane danced freely in the breeze. I assumed my Bajan identity with a proud smile.

On arriving in Black Rock, I recognized Auntie Clotelle's chattel house from a photograph she had recently sent, describing her house as above the rum shop and just below the blue house with the black-bellied sheep. Being a true creature-comfort woman, I hoped the house had all the mod cons I was used to at home. I was shown to my room and promptly indulged in a catnap.

Some hours later, I was woken by the smell of my national dish, flying fish and cou cou. I was grateful that I had reacquainted myself with cou cou a few days before leaving London, as looking as though I was tasting it for the first time would simply not do. Even more pressing was how to avoid the glass of mauby which was mocking me from a large jug at the head of the table. It was difficult to comprehend why it was so popular. I admired the way my family indulged as though it were some coveted elixir. I knew that my expression would belie the bitterness of the beverage, so I opted for good old tapwater. After Uncle Sylvan had said an extended grace, thanking God for my safe arrival, we started dinner. The remainder of the meal was spent *catching up*.

Awoken by the sun the following morning, I was surprised to discover that it was only 5.30. I felt triumphant that I had finally fallen into a deep trance in defiance of the vociferous crickets harmonizing on the verandah. My nostrils were tantalized by the wondrous aroma of bakes. Although a traditional Cornflakes type of girl, my parents had from an early age let us in on the wonders of bakes. They held an esteemed position, up there with corned beef and rice as a diet that had sustained many powerful Bajan notaries in their youth.

I took a long cold shower, planning my strategy for the day. This was followed by a hearty breakfast of bakes, eggs and Milo. The eggs melted so seductively on my tongue, I had to ask Auntie where she purchased such delicious eggs. She pointed to Gladys, the fowl who appeared to be relaxing by the fence. I looked at the remainder of the scrambled eggs and suddenly lost my appetite. There was something un-Sainsbury's about devouring her eggs, reducing her simply to a link in the food chain. Although my parents had recounted stories about how the guests at their wedding feasted on fowl killed just days before, I still had a problem with treating these animals as pet one minute and then slaughtering them the next. Perhaps I was too Westernized for my own good. The English fondness for pets was not something West Indians could associate with. I excused myself from the table and got ready for my first adventure.

Feeling brave, I rode the ZR bus into town. The journey was hot and sticky, and the upbeat driver seemed blissfully unaware of how full his minibus really was. He stopped time and again to pick up more passengers. My mind wondered to the *Guinness Book of Records* and how many people could fit into a ZR bus. I needed to relax and simply enjoy the pace of life. I was not on London Transport, and comparisons were pointless. The minibus pulled into Bridgetown, and everyone descended, wishing the driver a fond farewell and promising to catch him on the homeward journey.

I enjoyed the mystique of hiding behind my sunglasses and hoped that I did not look conspicuous. The wolf whistle took me by surprise. I tried not to acknowledge it until someone shouted out 'Hey, English!' Instinctively, I turned around to confront the person who would dare insinuate that I even looked foreign. There, leaning against a wall, selling snow cones, was the culprit. He casually strolled towards me, smiling broadly, as I retreated in the opposite direction. 'Me like you English, you have a nice bumper, wait up, nuh,' he shouted.

Once I reached the next corner I stopped to compose myself. Looking around, I realized that I was in Trafalgar Square and that Nelson had witnessed my lack of composure. Ascertaining directions to Cave Shepherd, I headed off in search of a refreshing cup of tea and some duty-free shopping.

Arriving back home, the early evening was hot and muggy. My cousin had decided to take me to St Lawrence Gap, to a place called the Ship Inn. She said it was an English pub and a group called FX would be playing. I had visions of 'Mine's a half' or 'Whose round is it?' She assured me that FX was one of the best soca bands of the island. Somehow, soca and pubs were incongruous. It was like Krosfyah meets 'Mine's a half of John Smith'. More alarming was the terror that suddenly struck me. I really could not dance, a fact I had managed to keep to myself until now by mastering the two-step. To be more accurate, I could not 'wuk up'. My hips and waist failed to cooperate with my desire to look as though I fully appreciated the rhythm of soca music. Everything about my conservative English upbringing would not allow my bottom to appreciate what I was trying to achieve in wanting it to rotate in that unaccustomed way. Practise, there was time to practise. I fell back on the bed, looking to God for guidance and for my hips to relax, relate and release. The smile on my face was broad, as I realized that I was enjoying the start of my journey home from home.

HENRY BONSU

A Brixton Tale

Not so long ago they would have stood together as soldiers, united in the struggle against the common enemy of racism. The younger man would give way to the elder in respect of earlier battles fought on his behalf. The older man would nod benevolently at the youth, hoping he would find an easier path yet stay true to the legacy. But something had changed. There they were, two powerful Brothas, ready to wage internecine war in the spiritual home of the Black community; not over a high crime or misdemeanour, but because the junior had barred the senior from entering a nightclub.

It was one of those pumping Friday nights when Brixton exerts a gravitational force not just on the cream of London's youth but also on its flotsam and jetsam. From hustlers loitering by the Tube to Black cats cruising in their GTIs; from tourists mesmerized by the tide of Black humanity to funky White gays queuing for the Fridge nightclub, nobody could resist the energy of the community. The President of South Africa himself, had recently been drawn to sw9 and said, 'It is literally the fulfilment of a dream that I have been able to visit this place.'

With its new multimillion-pound cinema, with its bars and rising property prices, the local development agency could now boast that Brixton, site of three 'uprisings' and so long the symbol of Black urban pain, was finally booming.

While this Notting Hill-style gentrification did little for the dispossessed, it at least provided people like me with an alternative to the West End. I always ended up in the Fridge Bar (an offshoot of the neighbouring club), which bemused some of my White friends. Why, they asked, did I limit myself to just one venue when there were at least half a dozen in Brixton? Unknown to them, like many Brothas and Sistas, I was operating an ethical social policy. Since the demise of the Brixton Brasserie, the Fridge Bar was the only late spot where you could hear good R'n'B tunes and see a healthy number of Black people. Apart from the Satay Bar, which did play soul music but closed early, everywhere else served up food or 'dance' music to a clientele so White we may as well have been in Surrey. It was evidence that for all the talk of multiculturalism, beyond personal or professional relationships between individuals, or special events like Carnival, Black and White were not genuinely at ease with each other.

Thus, when we arrived at the Fridge Bar, there were two queues – an official one to the left, made up primarily of grungy-looking Whites, and a more spontaneous one in front, composed of neatly dressed Blacks, who had no intention of humbling themselves. While the beat from downstairs pounded our ears, we hovered on the outskirts of this disorder, hoping to be selected for special treatment by the all-Black door crew. Unsurprisingly, those on the left were beckoned first, giving rise to mutterings that in the new Brixton, where money was the only god, Black bouncers were being employed to keep the Brothas out.

Then he appeared, the man they call the Angel of Brixton. Tall and proud, with thick grey beard and heavy muscles, in his uniform of broad leather hat and full-length smock he cut a commanding figure – an elder in his fifties, for whom the adage 'Black Don't Crack' was surely invented. As always, his leather-gloved hands clutched a large wooden staff – which almost certainly qualified as an offensive weapon but gave him the air of a latter-day Moses, desperate for a flock to lead.

I wasn't sure what he had contributed to the struggle, but from his age and bearing, I assumed he had seen active Panther duty in the sixties or seventies and acknowledged him solemnly. When he registered the Brothas' grievance outside the bar, his eyes lit up in anticipation of a fresh cause. Moses strode purposefully to the entrance, as though it were a Red Sea about to part for him. However, this was not the stuff of ancient bibles but a tale of modern Brixton. His path was blocked by the arm of a Man in Black who looked like the human equivalent of a Canadian grizzly. The elder looked outraged.

'Excuse me, I'd like to go inside,' he said.

'Sorry, you can't come in,' came the curt reply.

'Why not? Why can those (White) people go in, and these people have to wait here? What you're doing is wrong.'

The doorman could have referred to Moses's age or his dress sense but chose to hold his fire. The two men squared up to each other, like cagey nuclear powers, aware that if the button were pressed, the damage would be collateral. The Black bystanders looked on dumbfounded, while the Whites pretended not to notice. Moses's eyes searched mine for support, but I avoided his gaze, aware that the doorman might notice the treachery. Then the prophet pulled out his trump card.

'What is it about me that you don't like? Is it my clothes? Is it my staff? Is it too African for you? Does it embarrass you, seeing your heritage? People like me fought for years in this community to make it possible for you to open this club, and now you won't let me enter!'

Finally, the bouncer snapped. 'I don't know who you are or what you've done. I couldn't give a shit. I employ over a hundred people in this community, and it's all licensed by the council, so if you want to complain you can go to them, but you're not getting in here.'

Moses paused, realizing he was not part of this equation. He had won, but alas was beaten. I, the respectful draft dodger, nodded as he went on his way, tapping to the beat from downstairs, as I waited for the bouncer to make me one of the chosen few.

STELLA AHMADOU

Fragmentation

The other day, a friend asked me where my mum lived, and I said, 'Oh, in America.'

'Hmm,' she said. 'So far away? And you struggling with three children? Why don't you go to her? It will help you a lot.'

I did not discard the thought but held it tight. Don't get me wrong, I love my husband, but it's nice to have someone to help care for the children. How much support can a man give?

The same friend asked where my brothers were. I said, 'One used to live in Nigeria, but is now with my mother in the States, and the other lives here.'

'It's not that I think that a husband is not enough,' she replied, 'but sometimes it's good to have one of yours. You know what I mean?'

I nodded reluctantly. Why should I tell her that I have not seen my brother in a year? That I am more in contact with my family abroad than my family here. Why should I tell her how lonely it sometimes feels not to have the whole of my family together? How different it is back home, where, no matter how hard the political or financial situation, there is family.

In the West, we are fragmented. Divided. Split. Phonecalls cannot make up for the distance. It saddens me. Once, I was very close to both my brothers. What can you say when your relatives, so far away, ask how you are? If you say 'Not too good,' will they cross the distance to help salve your misery? So all I say is, 'All is well.' Perhaps it's so for other people. Is it because we are adults now? Gone our different ways? Will this happen to my sons? It's hard to tell. I am trying to forge closeness between them. I hope it works out for them in the future when I am no longer here.

Recently, I tried to link up again with my brother here. When I saw him, I realized that he had taken our state of isolation too far. In a warped corner of his mind, he had decided to cut all links with friends and family. He'd always threatened to do this in the past but I never believed him.

I always felt that even if you did not have family around, friends could be your family. I created a little family of friends that he shared when we lived together, and I was his guardian. He basked in their attention. But when it came time to grow up, he felt the only way to do so was by cutting all associations. Can we humans survive total isolation? I do not think so. People have been known to isolate themselves for religious purposes. My brother told me he wanted to go to Tibet. He wanted to be a Buddhist. He wanted to seek peace in his mind. In his quest he somehow lost the will to care for himself. I shall try to help him regain it. He was never meant for isolation. Perhaps he cannot cope with fragmentation.

There is something crucial here that I have not mentioned. It is the importance of environment. We have changed our country of domicile and it has affected our mental state. Other Black people were born and bred here, and they might also have this empty feeling, yet see it as part of them. It should not be. It's not the way we should be, but it's the way we are now. I am taking care of my emptiness by attending a spiritual church. I am making God a central focus in my life. I enjoy watching some of the matrons of my church pray and try to reach out to our spirit and to God. I get to that plane sometimes and I feel blessed. Other times I am so scared that everything seems dark and everywhere scary.

I now crave a change of environment. I will possibly do it. I want to live in a place where there is warmth and light. Perhaps the warmth will penetrate my inner frozen darkness and thaw it. Perhaps I will lose that fear. My family melts most of it away, but it comes back. I want it to be gone for ever. I want laughter in my soul. If and when I achieve this, I shall let you know.

HEATHER IMANI

Rude Boyz Don't Win

I have been to one live football match in my life. On 21 June 1998, I went to Paris, the Parc des Princes stadium, to watch a World Cup fixture: Jamaica – a.k.a. 'The Reggae Boyz' – versus Argentina.

The single coach on this jovial, boozy trip set off from Kensal Rise, north-west London, and was filled with the RJS firm (a promotions company incorporating a sound system) and selected extended family. Nearly half the passengers were women and children, caught up with the men in the euphoria of our team of part-time and borrowed players making it to the final stage of the World Cup competition. Our driver, a Scot, stuck his flag next to the Jamaican one we fixed to his windscreen. His affinity to us was returned: two rank outsider teams with over-hopeful fans. His flag remained.

For once, a coachload of Black people was waved through immigration. Despite our passports, the French didn't regard us as English, so we escaped the hooligan tarring-brush. Still, we had to wear that other stereotype when we aren't seen as troublemakers; we brought a carnival atmosphere to the World Cup. But what the hell: the sun was out, the sky blue, so we parked the coach and descended, regaled in team shirts, Jamaica baseball caps, flags, badges, wristbands. Tooting horns and trilling whistles, we started to street-party like minor-league Brazil supporters.

We followed the trail of yellow, green and black, and the sky-blue and white stripes of Argentina shirts. Bright-faced children bounded about, beside themselves with excitement. Faces were painted, hair was spray-dyed, flags worn as capes or wrappers or tops. Sweat. Singing. Breathless anticipation. Cafés and bistros sold us beer and water. Seasoned or thrifty drinkers had their own bottles or hip flasks; brandy was the drink of choice. An impromptu sound system was set up on the roadside from the back of a battered van with UK licence plates; an impromptu barbecue too, set up near by, produced from the back of a sparkling estate car, also with UK licence plates. A woman started to jerk chicken on the barbecue. The sound system fired off its one track over and over: 'Rude Bwoy

Don't Fear'. The jamming crowd fully understood the reference to Jamaica's David facing an Argentine Goliath. Streams of sky-blue and white flowed in amongst our sea of yellow, green and black, ready to jam with us to outernational reggae, a universal language.

Then police intervened. They apprehended the jerk-chicken woman and the sound-system man. The crowd jeered. The police relented. Music was restored. The crowd cheered. The party began again. Girls and boys resumed their wild competitions to be the most outrageous dancer, or to bellow the lyrics over the music loudest of all, or both. Everybody, adult and child alike, was high on the sun, the music, the intensity of the occasion. Nobody seemed to mind the one tune endlessly rewound-and-come-again – except members of the firm. So RJS took over the music. Hands aloft, they paid homage to the blast of dancehall superbass and whipped up the crowd at the same time. The mash-up speaker – it sounded like just the one – could barely cope as RJS's reggae boyz drew the last decibel of spitting, buzzing bass from each track they played. When they selected 'Heads High', the tune of that summer, a chorus of 'Wh-ee-eel!' and 'Blow-blow-blow!' thundered from the sweaty, tipsy crowd in recognition; sweaty, bedraggled children screeched and stamped their delight. Even the Argentinians went wild – and they had probably never even heard the record before.

Then it was time to go in. Time to cross the road and leave behind those without tickets for the match. They numbered many. It was like crossing the Red Sea. My mouth felt dry, my legs weak. I was going to the Promised Land. I had bought the last available ticket from RJS on impulse and I was leaving behind my closest girlfriend. She told me she didn't mind; she would head for Galeries Lafayette or Printemps, the department stores in the centre of Paris, and do some shopping while the match was on. After all, she had no interest in football. Now she stood, wrong side of the Red Sea, no ticket to the Promised Land, looking at me. I felt like the traitor she clearly saw in me. Three Mr Fix-Its worked on getting her a ticket from someone who knew someone they knew – that kind of vibe. But now, the bell had tolled and the mobiles hadn't . . .

We neared the entrance to the stadium, my friend tagging along, in denial. Then our favourite Mr Fix-It came through. He met a spar of his with a spare ticket. We didn't care about this stranger's brethren, who hadn't turned up (yet). We didn't care if he would be slaughtered later.

'Him late,' explained the spar. 'You no hear 'bout Black Man Time?'

'But *I* want to see Jamaica,' said my friend, wailing.

'Yuh brethren a form fool,' said Mr Fix-It. 'Ah noh Black Man Time, him *naa* reach. Come-come-come, sell her the ticket.'

So ticket and money – less than we'd paid for ours – were exchanged, and my friend skipped through the turnstiles, beaming. She may have had no interest in football but, right then, it became a matter of life and death.

Inside the stadium, the stream of sky-blue and white had become an ocean. Yellow, green and black shirts were reduced to small pools. Jamaica supporters sat in small pockets in the Argentinian section – and the Argentinian section was the whole stadium. We blew our horns and whistles, we hollered and stamped and danced when the stadium's system boomed out reggae tracks to introduce our players. But the rush of noise from Argentina's fans when they cheered the salsa tracks played and sang their football chants went straight through my heart. It was so loud, it was like a roaring silence. And it was then I had a realization.

This was not the Promised Land at all. We were in the lion's den. We had no football chants, no football songs for Jamaica. To my shame, I knew only two lines of Jamaica's national anthem – two more than most people around me. Only one of our party, a thirteen-year-old boy, knew every word. He sang with such passion, clusters of supporters on both sides turned to watch, amused by or proud of his solitary defiance.

At kick-off, our only hope was that our team of Jamaican Davids had not forgotten their slingshots for the Argentine Goliath. They had. Early on, a Jamaican player was sent off for an innocuous foul, and the team of ten men battled vainly against one of the favourites to lift the cup. Jamaica got pasted: five goals to nil.

Still, we refused to hang our heads. After the match, we spilled out on to the streets to shake hands and pose for photographs with Argentina's jubilant fans. They wanted to swap congratulations, and also badges, hats, flags, team shirts: anything to remind them of the day the Reggae Boyz challenged them – and lost. Along with a couple of Argentinian football chants, I learned *suerte*: good luck. '*Suerte, Jamaica, suerte!*' they had called to us as we partied before the match and as we made our way into the stadium. Now ours had run out, and we wished it back to them for the next round.

Memories of Millfield

I was not intelligent enough to go to university – this according to Mr Richardson, career counsellor at Millfield School. I'd been assigned to him for a thirty-minute assessment of my academic future. He was an English-literature teacher, not mine, but I tended to listen to those who knew about books.

I murmured a thank-you as I left his office, then made a detour for the common rooms where I telephoned my mother, howling. She was in London at the time and had enough time to give me my life history:

'Look here, you're the smartest child I know, though you never did listen. So why are you listening to this silly man, telling you you're not intelligent enough to go to university? Your father went to Oxford University. Balliol College. Politics, philosophy and economics. Never forget that!'

My mother would never use the word 'racist'. If you offended her, you were 'silly', and if she upbraided me that day it was justifiable. She was paying for my attendance at this, the most expensive boarding-school in Great Britain, so referenced in the *Guinness Book of Records* that year. Now I was using the same toilets as people I would later recognize in magazines, on billboards, on screen, and would never be impressed by them for that reason.

My friends at school were the sort who wore anoraks, loathed their anoraks and their middle-class parents for buying them anoraks in the first place. They were also the sort who wanted to study English literature, as I did, so we later got together to share our assessments.

'Can't you study something other than English?' Julie asked.

Richardson thought she ought to apply to Cambridge.

'Like what?' I asked. Um, she didn't know. What about political science? Or anthropology?

'Aw, she's not that thick,' Karen said.

I stopped speaking to my friends for a while, because they could not see the one reason Mr Richardson had for making such an assessment of my intelligence. Julie had copied my essays in the past. Verbatim. I had to remind her to make changes so she wouldn't get me in trouble. Karen was mindful enough to ask what-d'you-get? what-d'you-get? after every test. How could they suddenly doubt my ability?

Perhaps it was they who were the less intelligent ones. I remembered how they rarely came to my support when they should have – when one girl poked fun of Black people's lips; when another did impressions of Chicken George from *Roots*, and I eventually became angry with Chicken George himself for being so lowly and cheerful; when our drama teacher (and I never once laughed at that woman for having body odour) accused me of being a bad sport after I refused to sing 'Bingo Bango Bongo, we belong back in the jungle' in a school play.

I try not to remember my Millfield years. They were embarrassing years, no other reason: dry skin, chapped lips, flares and an afro. Spots on my forehead because my hormones were conspiring against me even as I ended my teens. It was the late seventies, and I was shadow-dancing to 'I Will Survive' during school dances and lapping up the usual praise for being able to move in rhythm. 'Nights in White Satin' would come on, and that would be the end of that. The good would be giving themselves tongue-lashings, the bad would be doing whatever it was the bad were doing those days, I never knew – I must have been the 'ugly'?

Of course it could have been worse. I could have been a gymnast, like the four in my house who got up early in the morning and, to top that, ate salads for supper; no socializing; no breasts. But damned if I forget that Richardson man. Or the boy who wanted to slap hands whenever he saw me. The girl who thought I ought to model, naked in a cage, like Grace Jones. And I certainly will never forget that one Nigerian boy who swore he would never date Black girls because we had greasy hair and flat noses. I wish that I could, because there is something truly pathetic about not being able to let go of school grudges. But if racism is a learned behaviour, then the reaction to racism is also learned, and that always starts with remembering.

I remember hot-faced indignation, getting prickly armpits from irritation. I remember choosing to ignore my offenders, so they wouldn't have the satisfaction of knowing how hurt I was, giving myself stomach cramps. For nothing.

I did attend university. I graduated with a 2:1 in business and accounting and became a chartered accountant. Later I would escape unemployment in the early nineties by emigrating to the US. It was here that I discovered English literature again, through reading the works of African-Americans. I would begin to write about my own life, including my four years at Millfield, and come to understand that, as a writer, I should see no difference between a person who would make me doubt the power of my mind, and a person who would hang me from a tree.

Mr Richardson may have believed his assessment was correct. I would also like to think that, had I been more outspoken, my experience with him might have been different. I only know that no one needs to be told they are racist; you tell them for your sake not theirs. And if people are smart enough to employ malice, they are usually smart enough to hide it. So, these days I allow myself the luxury of doubting a person's intentions, but I don't doubt that they are as intelligent as I am – once they begin to act silly.

Train

When I was no more than three years old, my father told me, my sister and my next-age-up brother that a train ran through our loft. He had climbed a ladder to get to the loft, and we had stood at the foot of that ladder, mouths open. I seem to remember my mother's voice in the distance, calling to us from downstairs, but my sister may dispute this remembrance. What I do know is that on another occasion I asked him about the runaway train in our loft. I recall his back and his gait as he walked away from me. We were on the first split-level landing, upstairs in our terraced, brown-bricked house in east London. He walked towards the back bedroom, and I trotted behind him. I can't remember my exact words, now, more so his back, which seemed very high and broad and rigid. He didn't look behind me as he spoke back, saying, 'What train?', then kissed his teeth. Just his back and gait answered my question. Because they were part of his lie.

I know as little about my father as I do about the reproductive processes of a bumble-bee. The latter I had been taught during my secondary education in a school with its perceived reputation falling about its ears; its White male charges, if a certain way inclined, wore steel-capped boots and bovver jackets. Their Black counterparts seemed to hunch together in Gabiccis and tight Farrah trousers, their hair shouting. The girls looked on. Teachers walked in wide circles around the boys' toxicity, saving their voices for the restrained, the children who had no choice but to learn from the politics of the classroom rather than what were the streets of east London twenty years ago. And they told us of the bumble-bee and its queen, the industriousness of the male and the quiet, swollen hunger of its mistress. As with much that was learnt, we held on to snatches of facts rather than all the intricacies, and what I can remember now of the subject is minimal at best. Although, knowing me, I was one of the ones to ask questions, yet the answers would barely stay with me unless written down in the textbook marked 'Biology'. And so the answers to the questions about my father have touched me momentarily, but left as easily as they were delivered.

I know that he was born in St Andrew, Barbados – Chalky Mount to be exact. I can tell you this because I have had to repeat this fact to a number of people, for a variety of reasons. Also because I visited the area of his childhood when I was fourteen years old. Every other body appeared to be called by my name. None of them was able to sustain my gaze for more than a second.

I know that he was one year younger than my mother, and that they had married in England – the picture with the robed, White vicar and heavy wooden church door told me more than any words had – and I know that their married life had been acrimonious long before the final split. This much I do now know.

I also know that he is a Virgo man who, according to close relatives, was mild-mannered and dutiful; one of my aunts is fond of recalling the fact that she had visited our east London home to find him cleaning the floor by hand. Reputedly, a good man.

Yet I do recall him holding a knife, and my mother bleeding. Maybe I should be more clear on this; I remember the blood on my mother's hands and her crying, and his eyes and mouth moving and the police sirens sounding and the blue lights poking through the front bedroom window. I must have been on level one of the three steps that divided upstairs from downstairs, because, at three years old, there is no way I could have seen over the banister to recall what I saw. Yet I remember.

I know that I would like to ask my father a number of questions, and that I don't know how I would ever have the right opportunity to meet with him and speak to him. I have an irrational belief that I wouldn't know what to say but suspect that words would flow more easily than would be expected. He would be the embodiment of a lie to me, of course. He had lied to me and my siblings to save us from a perceived harm, yet hadn't had the patience, or the courage, to let the lie live like a legend or die a hero's death by his own hand. Instead, with his back to me, my father had told me that he no longer belonged to me, and that, all along, he was his own person, to do with as he willed.

IONIE RICHARDS

Nine Nights

'Your father is dead.'

The words didn't touch me. They came at me in determined strides, and I slipped my wiry waist past the pain. My skinny legs moved swift and I escaped round the corner of the door. I smiled. It didn't get me then. In the church, strangers fussed, and I felt special as I stood watching from my safe vantage point. I saw mourners reel and sob as though testing their throats for song. I, untroubled, soared with the tune of the organ, singing my blessings wholeheartedly. As we stood around the grave, the words came at me again. I could see the sympathy in people's eyes as they nodded and repeated: 'Your father is dead – poor child.'

The cold biting wind snatched away their speech and saved me. I hid behind my mother's coat and the words bounced off my pretty yellow taffeta Sunday-best dress like a great Gary Sobers save, and my heart cheered for it could not slip through. I waited patiently, silently eager to return home.

I stood on the front step and pressed the door, but they kept coming in. Anonymous hands patting my head, moving me aside, tutting with words that floated out of reach. I moved more determined, with my foot against the entrance, to hold back the flow I could not understand. Oblivious to my ejection they came, and soon the house was filled to bursting with the throng of people.

The transformation was immediate. The instructions came quick and fast, disconnected from arms and limbs, just voices that fired off each task.

'Carlene, fetch more sandwiches.'

'Carlene, cut up more bun and cheese.'

'Carlene, wash more glasses.'

'Help hand out the curry goat and rice.'

The self-satisfied merry-makers ate and drank until those too full to stand now wedged themselves on seats, on stools, on the edge of beds, untidying the house.

Expelled from the bedroom I spied through a crack in the door. The smell of incense and fragrance oils mingled with the smells of spices converging from the kitchen. A small group of adults had gathered in the room with Mum centre stage. Six women and a preacher surrounded her. They prayed and sang words of no comfort, littered with stories of ghosts and misery.

'Don't sleep in this position.'

'Put garlic against your door.'

'Sleep with the lights on.'

'Spread salt in the four corners of the room.'

'Don't sleep alone.'

The preacher was laying hands. He pulled Mum down to a murky place that must have been salvation. I wondered why it had to be found on the floor.

The candles flickered, and illuminated spirits rose up on the walls of the bedroom, bobbing and moving excitedly.

I knew then that the preacher in his smart grey suit was none other than an obeah man in disguise. I had heard stories in the past and did not believe. On that night I knew that he was real. I trembled in fear, knowing that angry spirits were coming to get me because I would not cry. I ran from the landing, chased by the sound of the chanting and the shrieks from the women inside the room. The rhythm of drums grew louder and louder in my ears, and my head swelled to burst. At a safe distance I stopped and listened, but all I heard was the fast furious beating of my heart.

I watched as the last revellers departed, leaving behind a newfound silence that weaved amongst the debris and trappings of a party. Mum slowly climbed the stairs to retire to her bedroom. I wondered whether the words of the obeah man, the omen of the women, the fear of everyone, was drumming in her head, for the lights remained shining. Captive, I waited for tomorrow, for the ordeal to continue the next day, and the next.

I watched as each day my protector, my safe anchorage, changed into a subdued, bent and troubled woman. Her eyes were glassy, not from her usual rich and comforting laughter, but from a silence unfamiliar to my ears. She shuffled from room to room as though searching, and I followed clinging, trying to recapture the world I had before.

There was no sanctuary, as the dominoes slapped hard against scratched wood on the dining-table, drowning out the purpose of the occasion. Tuneless sounds whined out from the gramophone. The deep bass boomed and quivered as Millie's high shrill voice talked of her Lollipop. I watched couples spin and contort their sweaty bodies. The women towered above their partners with their beehive hairstyles and angry stiletto shoes, puckering the lino flooring which would never recover from their mass punishment. I knew I would never again be able to feel the smooth, polished surface when I slid along the hallway in my socks. My runway now held no joy.

I watched the men in their two-tone suits closely, to see if I could identify which ones had strawberry-, blackcurrant-, or lime-green-flavoured heads. My attempts failed as the strong smell of alcohol overpowered me. I backed away, repulsed, taking refuge in the folds of my memory.

The fetch and carry became part of my routine, and nine days and nine nights seemed like an eternity. No one said 'I am sorry your father is dead' any more.

For the message had soaked my flesh when I was not looking, and I was left dripping with my sorrow.

DEBORAH VAUGHAN

Lady-in-Waiting

Take up the White Man's burden
Send forth the best ye breed
Go, bind your sons to exile
To serve your captives' need
To wait, in heavy harness,
On fluttered folk and wild
Your new-caught, sullen peoples,
Half devil and half child
   – 'White Man's Burden', Rudyard Kipling, 1899

I am a lady-in-waiting at the Royal Palace of Westminster. I daily negotiate an existence within the belly of the beast. I walk taller to be above condescensions. I am the first to acknowledge, ignore or look away. My speech is precise but subtextually layered. That is how I maintain my power in a place where power is everything. Each day I embrace history in this institution which gave birth to the Abolition of Slavery Act, 1834 – but not before slavery had become legally, economically, physically and morally untenable. I am reminded of the slave uprisings in Barbados (1816), Demarara (1823) and Jamaica (1831, 1832). I know that I am an African in every land, because my prominent forehead graces the faces which are the toast of Somalia and my cheekbones are meticulously sculpted in West Africa. My lips are full because they are opium. Mine is the face that bridges the gap. And any issue in relation to my skin tone has originated not within me but within an 'other'.

Within and beyond this legislative enclave, my tan skin is a spit in a sea of whiteness. I know that light is within me, but I let others persist with the misconception that night is no longer ephemeral and begins at me.

Courtiers abound, and here, as everywhere, you will find Black people who fear the repercussions of defining, through association, their Afric-anness. Some will exclude you because they dread losing the coveted role of Black protagonist in a colour-coded drama. And too many will succumb to the worst in their nature and behave like crabs in a basket. And there are those who excuse, yet still employ, their Moorish complexions to improve their status. And more than a few use their skin as ladders to White endorsement and acceptability. And amongst us there are people who are gatekeepers, whose delight it is to keep us out. They have a nigger reflex in a mainstream context. And that is how they achieve charcoal success.

Within and without parliamentary society, misogyny is rife, as is racism. And within, as without, the dominant voice is White and male; the interlude is White and female – and blonde. I implore that I too am a genteel woman. But during the power play, which usually ensues, I recognize that I am more. I am an opinicus.

I and another gentlewoman (who will remain nameless to protect her innocence) walk through the hallowed corridors of democracy. Head-wrapped, her complexion as dark as her iris, she becomes the feature and I, lighter, and to the European eye further from Africa, become the sequel. We immediately and dramatically prepare ourselves to show our photographic passes. Preparation is better than compulsion. It is vital that we create sisterhood and act in unison, thus declaring that we are the revolutionary other. We do not work in the kitchens or wait at tables to rescue plates and cutlery. We do not push industrial Hoovers along lanes of carpet. In the midst of egalitarianism Black presence and purpose is deemed peripheral and merely tolerated if it is subordinate. We have to endure White slights and Black backbites. So she and I must remember that we eat plantain. And our hips militate towards an individual peace and collective destination. We are not ashamed because we did not beg-beg the job. Or know someone who knew someone. We did not entertain the thought of letting our families do the work that nature had divined our brains to do.

Racism is an insidious motif in our multicultural fabric, a delicate pattern absorbed in the global mural. Sadly, melanin remains the sin, and humanity loses so that world markets win. In the metropolis, the vivid becomes pastel as ethnicity mutates. But these scenes remain part of an essentially urban landscape. In Great Britain, when the *Empire Windrush* landed, the empowered and the powerless welcomed Caribbean industry but feared miscegenation. Yet one half-century later the mixed-race revolution is celebrated and heralded as an indication of indigenous tolerance. But assimilation is not integration. And integration cannot begin and end at the hips; it is the union of liberated minds and uncensored lips. Therefore, whether Black or White, every impulse and development must be scrutinized to ensure that it is organic and not designed.

In Parliament, the House of the White Man's Burden, the progenitor of colonialism, this court of elected kings and queens, an elaborately ornate symbol of multiple and interwoven histories, we could address our minds to matters of import. There are many questions. But maybe the first question should be, why are African and Caribbean leaders manufactured in the West and not organically grown? The second, why is it that a writer who dares question or criticize the status quo is censored or killed or, worse still, unpublished. And a battle-weary voice may ask why reparations for Africa are such a contentious issue when it is African society which provided the model for the British aristocracy. And African toil that created the wealth to fund Britain's industrial revolution. And it is the African who died fighting in wars, as far back as AD 200, against someone else's enemy. After centuries of being disappeared in Europe, it is the African that undertook the final passage to return and resuscitate an ailing empire.

I know who I am and I understand what I believe. So I will leave others to wonder if I am a lady-in-waiting or a courtesan.

CRUSADERS

Poetry

UJU ASIKA

Said the Moose

The following poem is based on a true story. In 1988 a moose in Vermont fell
in love with a local cow. The cow, of course, ignored him. This, perhaps, is
his song.

If I could only moo and you would listen
I would sing you love songs that would churn your heart.
We would walk with our tails laced
and touch noses like old fools.

I dream of pastures
where the greener grass is always on our side;
of days spent slipping daisies behind your ears
and flicking flies from your hide with my tongue.

But when I wake there is always someone staring,
pointing a beak or hoof in ridicule.

One afternoon, I made a pattern in the meadow
then shyly offered you my heart of grass.
The other cattle sniggered, you turned away
and my heart drooped.

I spent mournful hours
berating my reflection in a bucket:
My antlers are crooked,
my face is much too long, I thought
and hung my head.

Now I keep my distance.
I watch you as you wander out to graze,
I wait for you beside the gate
as the sun thins and spreads to a wavering line.

The bull flares his nostrils in disgust.
Silly moose
you'll be waiting for her until the cows come home,
he snorts and scuffs his hooves.
I stand my ground.

I may not be smart or handsome
but I have the strength of five reindeer
and the patience of an ox.

Besides, I know you watch me watching you.
Sometimes you swish your tail more than you should.
There are secrets between us that you dare not whisper
Even to the hay.

I have loved you since December.
It is June.
And still I cannot tell you why I feel this way
or why all tracks I follow lead to you.
What do I know of chemistry?

Although you have offered me nothing but disdain,
although you have given me nothing but dappled dreams
I wait for you.
Who says we have more to lose than a dish and a spoon?

I have heard stranger stories than my own.
Believe me,
when you jump over the moon again
I will be waiting on the other side
strong enough to catch you if you fall.

SALENA `SALIVA´ GODDEN

Clipped and Caged

And so,
Because some place,
Somewhere,
At sometime,
Somebody,
Told him,
He could not fly,
He never tried.
He had huge,
And beautiful,
Brown and white wings,
That is true.
He was also a bird.
But because somebody,
Somewhere,
Decided at some point,
To discourage and dismiss his potential power of flight,
he never sought to regain it,
Never truly believing he could fly in the first place.
Therefore,
he was never unhappy that he could,
Or could not fly.
He went about his life as normal.
He was bullied at school for having a large nose,
Which was of course a beak.
One day,
He got a job in an egg factory,
He got a girlfriend,
Together,
They got a flat,
And lived.

One day,
He even forgot he had wings,
Forever and ever,
Amen.

CYNTHIA HAMILTON

Ambrosia (Fodder of the Gods)

It's said that creamed rice is holy cuisine,
Porridge too lumpy, and custard too plain
Stir, stir it in the pastel-blue tureen.

Though mortals often use the dish to wean,
Could this be clearly looked on as profane?
It's said that creamed rice is *holy* cuisine.

The gods may choose to never eat their greens,
They think creamed rice has greater gifts to gain,
Stir, stir it in the pastel-blue tureen.

They rarely seem to like a change of scene,
Mere mortals find they only can explain;
'It's said that creamed rice is holy cuisine.'

A holy inclination seems to lean,
Toward a meal that's easy to sustain,
Stir, stir it in the pastel-blue tureen.

Though Gods usurp the milk and rice and cream,
We mortals find it fatal to complain,
It's said that creamed rice is holy cuisine,
Stir, stir it in the pastel-blue tureen.

Parody of Dylan Thomas's 'Do Not Go Gentle into that Good Night'

Gluttony (One of Seven Deadly Sins)

Is gluttony a deadly sin
Or is it just a way
To cultivate a double chin
In which to catch your gravy in
And make a foul display?

Could it be food is just the height
Of ecstasy to you?
That's why you burp and slurp and bite
And quite incite your appetite
Without attempts to chew.

If breakfast, lunch and dinnertime
Appear to be the same,
Would this explain the reason why
Your meals are massive when you dine
Regardless of the name?

The food you pile upon your plate
In stunning quantities,
Is always in a fatty state
And almost seems to tempt the fate
Of countless maladies.

You start the day with food upon
A mind with greed in store.
We don't know where you get it from
And question the phenomenon
Of where you put it all.

You fill your mouth with anything
That cares to fit the shape,
And won't think twice of cramming in
Or beating, forcing, ramming in
The bits that might escape!

You fear you may be overweight?
We hear you now confess.
A smaller cup? A smaller plate?
The answer's clear for Heaven's sake!
Why not try eating less?

Rhyme scheme taken from Lewis Carroll's 'Phantasmagoria'

NOLAN WEEKES

The Same Ol'

I'm using the same ol' pen
on the same ol' paper
to express the same ol' ability in poetry

Mainly about the same ol' things
that occur in the same ol' and new
generations

Like the same ol' problems
that are resolved by the same ol' solutions
that are later forgotten
causing the same ol' repetition
called stress!

That are resolved by the same ol' solutions
that are later forgotten
causing the same ol' repetition
called depression

That are later forgotten
causing the same ol' repetition
called confusion

So you can see
it's the same ol', same ol'

The same ol' lives we're living
are lived for the same ol' reasons

The same ol' wants and fads
dictated the same new trends
there's no end!

How I envy newly born babies
who learn new things
like crawling, eating, speaking
then learn the skill of understanding
then realize all the new things
are in fact the same ol' things
that everybody else is doing

So as you can see
it's the same ol, same ol'

It's the same ol' moi
and the same ol' them

It's the same ol' birds
flying in the same ol' beautiful skies
The same ol' drunk with the same ol' vin rouge
It's the same ol' poem
with the same ol' start, middle
and possibly the same ol' ending.

But then again
maybe I should end with something new
like

I remember being in bed after sex
and thinking
the same ol' me
with the same ol' ways

But I now know the same ol' continuation
of the same ol' issues
develops the same new me
mentally

'llows me to see the same ol' relationships taunted by the same ol'
breakups followed by the same new lover for the same new sex,
leading to that same ol' line,

'I think she's the one.'

4 weeks later,

The same ol' change of mind.

'We don't really have anything in common.'

So you can see,
It's the same ol', same ol'

How I envy innovators and inventors
for the same ol' ideas
that nobody else thought to do.

MALIKA BOOKER

For Clara

You are Victorian Myth
Stories circle your village with exploits
how you beat three boys at once
throwing sand in their eyes
the time you climbed two chairs
to take food Grandma placed beyond reach
and fell to the hard floor still chewing fast fast
to avoid detection nursing a broken hand

The 1959 voyage to London
dad saw twenty-two inch waist
buxom hips olive eyes
there was
love and marriage
love and patients
love and parties

Now I watch you for signs of the old
or was it young you
I sit at family gatherings as elders
send children back and forth to fetch and carry
aunties watch pots of chicken
and salt fish smells fill the house
long sermons bless the food with grace
and grumbles

I sit outside circles of old uncles
with children's high-pitched screams and casualty yells
as background sounds listening to patriarchs
rumbling wisdom drunk on rum
look at their gold toothed smiles

as wedding bands wave in dramatic talk
to receive sprigs of truth
about the girl you once were
this seems another time
before me
before marriage
before mother
she was Clara

I love the one I know
I can read her like Braille
as I am her seed dropped
watered tended and bloomed

I ask you about her and through your silence
mouth locked shut I create you
seeing a young woman
signs of age thickening her waist
walking the streets of dreary London
eyes blinking fat lines of tears
hands doubled over her stomach
moaning for God's help with her rent

She wraps a thicker layer
binding her heart as yet another lover leaves
then sits alone under winter skies
screaming at the world
the house noise for company in a red carpeted
room as Bosnian Rwandan British news images
flicker in colour on her screen

Wait   this is not about you but my quest
a woman grappling with the hourglass of age
counting my time to motherhood
questioning your journey

And we sit today as mother and daughter
our roles have left us
we sit as two women.

ASHA BANJOKO

Would you . . . ?

If I sat in a corner rocking backwards and forwards violently
would you disown me?
If I ran across a busy main road stark-naked
would you be disgusted with me?
If I heard voices in my head every time I closed my eyes
would you be scared of me?
If I sat in a room alone and talked to myself like it was OK
would you think I was freaky?
If I wore a long white flowing gown with a cross around my neck
would you believe in me?
If I lay face down in a coffin
would you pay your respects to me?
If I passed every one of my GCSEs with an A or an A+
would you be proud of me?

I thought so!

The Sea

Every evening at 7 o'clock he meets her
His cold dark body engulfs
Her long attractive stretch
His body has changed from
The diluted pale turquoise
To the concentrated midnight-blue
By 11 o'clock the next morning
He is barely tickling her fingertips
But she waits patiently
For him to return again.

KOYE OYEDEJI

Twenty-One Tears for Years

The Crow said she loved me
But she doesn't
The Crow said she was mine
But she wasn't.

There's an art in the way she eats her carrion
The way she picks my flesh, the way she carries on.
I saw her at club Windrush, crows free before eleven
She was working low profile a nest to rest in south London
A heaven scent that disguised pheromones from hell uptown.

I said, 'Not tonight I'm washing my wings,' with fear.
She spoke of how we ravens have picked at her worms for years.
She said, 'I'm fresh.
It's our turn.
We're all that.
And then some.'
I never knew you birds could shed crocodile tears.
There was no one there to wipe my tears.
There was no one there concerned with calming my fears.

There are twenty-one tears, for each year that I've longed to say my
    part
Yet they couldn't take my words without breaking my heart
Now I know I have to go back to start, as
Simple words become my complex art.

The Crow said she loved me
But she doesn't
The Crow said she was mine
But she wasn't

Even after the Swan called you a slag you took him back
Even after I hear he told your mother you took crack.
Now you threaten me on the phone with your caws and croaks
I almost choke on humour, what the fuck?
I'm disposed of in a quest for security then you tell me it's rotten luck?

All of a sudden you're a comedian, the joker's wild.

Deception at the hands of your glossy black plumage,
I was the best thing that never happened to you in the midst of
carnage
You said, 'You're fresh.
It's your turn.
I've been hurt.
Now you burn.'
I never knew I could shed tears and remain centre stage.
There was no one there to wipe my tears.
There was no one that was concerned with calming my fears.

For twenty-one years through fears this life's become a curse
Let me say my verse before I take my hearse
Let me play this game, this game that hurts
I've got to break your heart before you break mine first.

I'm all used up, the material items you seek easily blend
Like the trips to the pond with the swans on the weekend.
I watch us do it again, come again then back again
Still I sit and wonder why we piss in our own pen
When we could just as easily leave the fluid with them.

Once again the Crow kills the Raven, as it did yesterday
Still those that'll love me tomorrow will say it doesn't have to be that
way
And those that claim they love me today are simply lying, that's their
way.

What's done is done let it all go to hell, to rot, to decay
It would be a sort of heaven for me to see that this is also how you'll
    pay.

'Cause you tried to make me sit an exam in which grade 'F' stood for
    faggot.

The Crow said she'd never betray me
But she lied
The Crow said she'd always be there for me
But now she hides.

The Crow said she loved me
But she doesn't
The Crow said she was mine
But she wasn't.

DENRELE OGUNWA

April

April showers
wet a poet's tongue
verse is reborn . . .

April winds
caress my naked breast
run lover's fingers
through my hair
kiss my brow, my lips
with soft showers

April rain
brings memories
pungent, smoky
like a rain-doused fire
each raindrop
echoes
the tranquil teardrops inside

April winds
blew soft petals
from a premature bloom
scattered dreams
drift and fade
in deference to awakening day

The wind is me
the wet is me
I am wet and windy
I am April

Denrele Ogunwa

April winds
coax the sleeping tendrils
of a poet's mind
make it a whisper . . .

CHARMION TOGBA

Slaughterhouse

One then two then three then four
Soon there will be no more cattle
Left grazing in the fields

Sort of suicidal
They came running
To the slaughterhouse

In their minds
They're as fat
As they will ever get

A confused herd
Running into each other
Making desperate shrilly noises

With no plans to abort this
Infested with madness
Trampling upon fallen carcasses

It might be me
But I don't intend to auction my body

The slaughter continues
Whilst I stay low
In a pitch-black ditch

I'm on the outside looking in
Observing all these things
Only to find myself suddenly drawn in

I'm now on the inside next in line
To face the slaughterhouse
My number's up, it's my time

A last look reveals
Darkness engulfs me
The thud from the earth
Confirms the slaughterhouse has got me.

LEONI ATKINS

The Diva

The Diva has many definitions. But is easily recognizable.
Full of attitude, strength and positivity.
Back in the day, when there was no such label
Auntie, Aunt Jemima, and Mammy were all we were named,
The names not defining their affectionate sound.
Drawn, suckled, sucked, beaten, maimed, and blamed for all that was
    wrong.
The Diva feels hurt but tries to go on.

Symbols of sexuality. The Diva. With her full brown lips and ample
    round figure, the
Bane of her life.
Everyman loves it, except it seems, her own. Betrayed.
As he crosses the line to the other side.
She tries to be PC, but deep down inside,
The Diva feels passed over and cast aside.
The Diva feels hurt but tries to go on.

The present parallel to the past.
She looks for inspiration in her revolutionary own.
Ida, Zora, and Rosa who fought the first fight and cast the first stone.
Today we sill strive to make things better,
But the past still hurts and with no full guarantees.
The Diva feels hurt but tries to go on.

The Diva approaches the future finally recognized as a 'strong black
    woman'.
But with her hallmarked strength, The Diva feels left behind and
    forgotten.
Still she remains strong, if not, failure is imminent, so The Diva
    remains silent.
The Diva feels trapped, but tries to go on.

From the old school Motown Diana, Martha and our own Gladys
   Knight.
The Diva feels hope and picks up the fight.
With refreshed vigour, she starts to answer back, to those who
Dare call her 'bitch', 'ho' and other names to pull her back down.
Hurt maybe, as these names escape from the other half's mouths,
The Diva starts to wonder . . . have they forgotten us too?

The future approaching fast. From Oprah to Toni to McMillan and
   Walker.
The New Generation of musical and literary Divas.
From Li'l Kim to Left Eye and just call her 'Miss Jackson'
The Diva starts to realize that things must change.
For my, your, and our daughter's future as well, we need to let go
Of the silent barriers that prevent us from knowing what we could
   know.

And so The Diva carries on.
She'll carry the torch into the next millennium.
To teach us what she has learnt.
The Diva is enlightened and long may she keep on keepin' on.

RAYMOND ENISUOH

Unforgotten Promises

A bloodline much thicker than water,
links me to you my ancestors.
As you gaze down upon me,
from the pinnacle of my family tree,
guiding me away from racism
and pitfalls;
leading me safely to my destiny.
Never forgetting your vows
of freedom or death
I am a piece of history,
representing you in this day.
Still hearing your laughter,
still tasting the bitterness of your tears.
I acknowledge the legacy
you have left
by remaining steadfast,
in these rainy days of exile.

Reflections of Hate

Stony stares my frequent greeting,
I know the ritual well.
Violent eyes cut the silence,
feelings too confused to tell.
Vulnerability mixed with suspicion,
flavour these glares from my own race.
A hostility now mirrored,
by the frown upon my face.

A Caribbean Sojourn

(Dedicated to the pioneer West-Indian immigrants)

The lingering stench
of black unemployment,
and chronic underachievement,
clouds those bright, sunny memories
of mangoes and sugar cane.
Now that we know for sure,
the wind no longer rushes
in our direction.

NATALIE STEWART

Mrs Platonic

I hear voices at times,
Friendly whispered acknowledgments of my personality assets.
She's so safe man!
They wake me from my sleep at times.
They're never screaming,
Just consistent friendly whispered acknowledgments of my personality
    assets.
One ah da mans dem!
The same whispers that lead me to believe that I will never be more
    than a
Best Friend, Bredrin, Sistren, Idren, Mrs Platonic,
Are the same spoken excuses used when I attempt to change that.
Something whispered in my ear, assuring me that the eyes that met
    mine and the smile
From over the road, were merely a polite gesture that if captioned,
    would say
'Morning', rather than 'dam you look fine.'
The same words, were spoken over the phone after two months of
    dating as my hopes for
The ideal man declines the offer for the leading role,
Preferring to be the supporting actor cast as 'the best friend'.
Another best friend.
Another, almost strong man, willing to play safety.
Just stay safe with me.
This means, you can still sample my cooking. My door is always open.
I am the wife of fifteen or more men and I have eight long
    engagements.
No marriage has or will ever be consummated. No, I'm Mrs Platonic.
Besides in their eyes I am beyond needing. I am Bionic. Superwoman.
   Above woman.
Above emotion.

Still I hear the friendly whispered acknowledgment of my personality
    assets.

She's so clued up.

My plight blurs and I have the strangest problem. I do some things too
    well, or is this

Just my way of explaining my pain?

I cook, I listen, I laugh, I reason. I am counsellor and adviser. I am
    concerned, giving,

caring, and sharing.

I am Mother.

I am Sister.

I am Best-friend

I am Mrs Platonic.

And I hear voices.

Friendly whispered acknowledgments of my personality assets.

There just aren't any women like you out there.

I am . . .

Mrs Platonic.

02:14 a.m. Sunday 21 February

R. AKUTU

Question to MOBO (97)

Don't you ever want to lock all the doors
Close all the windows
Turn up the TV
But lock that establishment outside?

Not because you hate
But you need it not to invade your space
Your little time for pride

Don't you ever want to lock yourself in
With your brothers and sisters
Beautiful spirits
Inhaling the aroma
Which is unexplainably but brilliantly us?

To feel your heart explode
Into a thousand coloured spiralling fireworks
As our spirits leap up to embrace the aura
the joy of you, me, we

To climax in the meeting of our true souls
And sigh that peace-filled sigh

Don't you ever feel like that?

Silence
No reply?

It must be me then,
A solitary firework watching in the hope, we might fly.

Schizoid Zoo

Yap, just another day at the schizoid zoo
Come on, come all let's join the queue
Of slowly awakening
And mentally conforming
And darning straitjackets that abide by their rules
So just shuffle along to their jungle tune

Just another day at the schizoid zoo
Come on, leave your otherside at home to stew
It won't fit in
You don't make the rules
It's hard enough your pigments so shady
And those breasts you're carrying will make you askew
As you shuffle along to their jungle tune

And if you should dare to wonder
About seemingly innocent smiles
That exude pink spiked opinions
Or even condescension that shine in eyes
Or words that rob you blind of confidence
I'm telling you girl it's all in your mind
Just shuffle
Just shuffle
And lose yourself inside the tune.

Yap, just another day at the schizoid zoo
Come on, come all and join the queue
Of mental confusion
And pivoting psyches
And struggling insides
And doubting judgement
And gagging the self, the culture, the you
As you shuffle along to that jungle tune.

bLACKmALE

Eyesee3 (IC3)

30 April 1997:

You chat more shit
than the Tories – 'CONSERVE YA IFS! –
Seat ya butts!
& check ya maybes!'
The 1st of May – be 97 reasons
NOT to be
'cos in the run-up you're shady
cause focused eyes to blur vision like hazy,
but
I don't follow no particular party
'cos Tony Blair –
you're a lay bore
or raving mad like dem loonies
'Cha! 'Dem foolie!'
Mama tell me
to sing
not follow no false king
Paddy Ashdown? run London?
You're ALL taking Libs
telling fibs
with your politricks
Democratic? – don't care 4 my demographics
you'd all sell souls to gain votes in my demographic
that's why my demos are graphic
with inclination to switch
throw brick
break down concrete bricks

while middle men with classy homes
groan & throw fits
making laws
while ignorant about my situation,
shady business just to gain profit
I profess
do me right
then I won't chat no mess
try to shut my trap
when I chat 'bout da cess
arrest my development
inhibit but won't exhibit the speech of people everyday
you inhibit but won't exhibit the speech of people everyday

Election Day – May One 1997:

Blue?
Yellow?
Red?
It's ALL Grey – which way??
U see
I need the deal *real*
to know your politricks
on the intricate
so you urban heads with law degrees
got knowledge too precious to lose it –
DON'T ABUSE THE SHIT!
I know I'm ignorant to the politic specific
but the bigger scheme of things
got me open like Pacific
& the feeling's horrific
some shit so important
& me bordering on mythic!
But it's gonna take a mystic

with millions to hold me back
I decipher these poster campaigns
dem Yellow bellies
with their Red tears
cha!
It's all Blue murder!
To fool the voter
plastic smiles swivel around drivel
instil false hopes on a rota
dead-end quotas,
we just want to know
so?
Fuck the colours!
show ya true shades
'cos the 1st of May, be our 1st deadline to the last days
to the end of all this
for lack of a better tact –
cack!
Either way
that's fact

Eyesee3
split-tooth smile,
grinning,
garmed up in grey suits
2 many pinstripes
regimented
silver metal jail bars
pin-striped lines
which mirror deep scars
got too many of me
looking for Southern Comfort
a life of fast cars
in the arms
of girls that make West Indians shout 'Cor blimey!'

Eyesee3
stiff neck
tight shoulder
clenched-arse politricktion slimy,
got too many of me
praising Mr Crimy
Miss Grimy
& dissing Mr Irie, Ms Fiery
why we??
I guess skin-teet' smile
clammy handshake
while when backs turn
fingers morph into rakes
masking hate
bringing fate,
buying the 24 crate
packaged in brown, green & clear bottles
'Recyclable!'
so use quick-speed

May Two – New Age:

May 2000
May 2 fingers protrude up! . . .
& stick down my throat
still feeling sickly!
Wha' gwan happen to my unborn pickney?
Unseen wifey?
It's likely
shit will go down swiftly
wipe beaded sweat from brow
wail 'Crikey!'
so to stay alive
keep afloat
I pen words with wit like Mikey,
keep raw & real to self like Mr CE,
& in crowds

use elbows with Zulu pace like Gizmo,
& stay true to bLACKmALE
'cos eyesee
if we . . .
poll with a tick
& keep the polls moving on tricks
politricks reform to politics
& tricktions get turfed
when we get our ticks on!

It's a shame
this year legitimate
but didn't play the game
register the claim
no hope,
so didn't share the vote
& I limited my scope
so no voice
when chest is starved of oxygen
from poxy gents
but like double M
return with the stance of a mack
next time
when I & I and me
& 1 million masterstrokes of the pen
come again plus a friend
claim spots tick a box
then join the dots
make it hot . . .

Now Eyesee3
starched shirted trench-coats tremble
upper constituents shiver and tremble
cause elegant but evasive public speakers
to babble & scatter
mumbled words of non-wisdom

& all that shit with dem
& behind every parliament man
is a vex-faced cow
wondering 'what will they do now??'
and will these 'ghetto youth' go . . .
'BANG!!'

R a SAMUEL

Paris Romance

We were together once,
back when her life was nothing but an intention.

You see hers is a life of incubation,
she needs twenty-four hour TLC,
then after a lifetime of devotion
and dedication
quintessential
for a sturdy foundation.
On occasion I speak
with a kick she responds,
I'm like 'look quick,' in anticipation
of a future celebration.
Maybe a joint contribution to the
generation of the new nation.

But it was what my mind heard
what my ears couldn't hear
nor could my eyes see
that's what was destined to hurt me.
Throughout that time I waited to see
her, the voice kept on telling me it wouldn't be, couldn't be.
Eye says further adventures awaited me
I said, 'if you're true let it be'
whilst wondering is this prophecy
or simply Hyper stress getting to me.

Then came the anticlimax right on the sly,
before I get to say hello
I'm press-ganged
into saying goodbye.

You were born only to die.
I'd asked how and why.
It's arguable that you were sent to
open my eye.
The one that cannot cry.

GEMMA WEEKES

YOU-And-
-me.

my WHOLE life HAS BEEN
DADANDHISWIFE
MUMANDHERHUSBAND-AND-
HERLIFE-AND-MYTWO
BROTHERS-AND-MY
FRIENDSANDTHEIRLOVERS-
AND-MYAUNTANDUNCLE-
AND-MYGRANDMOTHERAND
GRANDFATHER-AND-
MYBROTHERANDHIS
GIRL-AND-EVERYONEANDTHEIRWORLD-
AND-EVERYONE/ELSE/WITH
THEIREVERYONE/ELSE-AND
THEIREVERYTHING/ELSE-AND-

-me.

so it can't be.

YOU-AND-YOURLIFE-
AND-YOURDREAMS-AND-
NIGHTMARES-AND-
YOURFAMILYANDFRIENDS-AND-
YOURFUTUREANDFEARS-
AND-YOURMIND-AND-YOUR
SOUL-AND-YOURDOS-AND-
YOURDON'TS-AND-
YOURMEMORIESANDGOALS-
AND-YOURNEEDS-AND-
YOURWANTS-AND-YOURCANS-

AND-YOUR
CAN'TS-AND-YOUR
BLOODY/DAMN/FUCKING—
YOU/YOU/YOU/YOU
YOU/YOU/YOU
-AND-

me.
like a

flea.

Fragments

I do not remember the violence
Of the broken glass –
Just splinters that litter the red
Carpet with tears, painfully shed.
You broke us. The past
In parts like Mum's best china.
All now is silence.

Fragmented. Shards slit
Your tired face. I was too young
To understand – yet understood
You had split yourself. I knew you would
Not harm me. Your head hung
Between your hands – folded, resigned.
Your cheeks glittered.

Still. You sit on the bottom step
in the daggers of shattered window –
shattered cup – shattered doorframe –
Collapsed inwards, bleeding shame
into the carpet for a dark stain to grow.
I had to leave you behind
To grow outside. Still you kept
Me in parts.
In parts.

ROGER ROBINSON

On being asked to write a poem
about the murder of Ibrahim Sey

Well here it is   take it,
while you're here
you might as well take this
one I wrote for Joy Gardner,
about police
sealing her life
with masking tape
cursing them
with the breaths
she didn't know
would be her last.

Here   take this one
for Wayne Douglas
whose punctured head
dripped liked an egg timer.
The echo of his voice
in the cell
the only answer
to his screams for help.

Or have this one
I wrote about Blair Peach,
or about Marlon Downes,
or Cynthia Groce,

For what good are they
what's their use other
than to use them as paper
to wipe away blood

or to soak up tears
of grieving families.
Here have them all,
no ink scribbled on paper
gave their heart one extra drumbeat
or one extra tide of breath
surging from their lungs,

and until poems
can bring back these lives
they're worth nothing,
nothing at all.

Essays

GEMMA WEEKES

Divided We Fall?

The small kitchen hissed with the aroma of frying food as my friend cracked another egg into the pan. With a hand balanced on one slim hip and the other controlling a plastic spatula, she shot a disappointed glare at me.

'Girl, you seriously need to stop being so naïve!'

I threw an *I-don't-give-a-shit-what-you-say* look at her, nostrils flared, eyebrows a vision of arched nonchalance. Still though, I didn't immediately go off at her in indignant self-defence. I wondered, *'Is she right about me?'* squinting into my friend's attractive features. There was always a confident set to her jaw, something of the free spirit in her smile. Yet I saw the bitterness and insecurity of her difficult life in both, and so much *anger* burning deep in her brown eyes. She was still so young and, just like me, too young for such negative certainties. The acrid smell of burning stung my nostrils, alerting me to the fact that the eggs had burnt before they were even cooked.

An acidic scent. It made my eyes sting.

I hadn't seen Michelle in ages, so I'd taken a chance and come over to visit, even though she wasn't on the phone. After the prerequisite hugs, screams of 'How are you DOING!' and 'You are looking GOOD these days, girl!' came the anticipated . . .

'So what's up with that guy you introduced me to the last time I saw you?'

With that slightly queasy eagerness we have when talking about the person that seems to . . . breathe life into living . . . I began to tell her about Shawn. Tentatively. Braced for her inevitable cynicism. I told her that we were still together, and intended to keep it that way. She asked me more of those predictable questions between girls, giggled and teased through my toned-down version of the juicy 'details'. We filled the small kitchen with secrets and noisy laughter.

Somehow it made me feel like a liar to trivialize the whole thing so much, though – even through the hilarity. I struggled to tell her more than the material and physical info she was angling for. I revealed how natural it seemed for us to be together, how much we had in common and how determined we were to keep this thing going. Her next question sliced through my softly spoken confidences like an arctic breeze through humid summer air.

'So. When's he going back to the States?'

I paused, knowing that she would never understand. I mean, *shit*, I had barely accepted it myself. I couldn't believe he was leaving.

'Next month,' I said shortly. We'd met only two months before, in February.

She looked puzzled. 'Bloody 'ell! Already? So when's he coming back? What, in September?'

'Um . . . No. His scholarship is over.' I grimaced down at my folded hands. 'He's going back to school in New York.'

She gave me the look that always conveys doubt concerning my mental health. 'Do you really believe this shit is gonna last?'

'Yes.'

'You're really gonna stay with him till you finish uni, in TWO YEARS? You're gonna stay faithful? I mean coz, if he's all the way in New York, you . . .'

'Yes to both questions, girl!'

'Come on! You really believe he's gonna do the same for you, all the way across the bloody Atlantic? You just gonna waste all you *raatid* time and have nothing to show for it!'

'I trust Shawn!'

That was the Last Straw.

To trust a man? That was like trusting the British weather. It was her first commandment never to commit such a heinous crime. And a Black man at that? That was beyond stupid and right on into the realm of insanity. *Never Trusteth a Man, For All Men upon the Earth are Dogs.*

So she told me I was naïve, and her hand flew from her hip in a gesture icy with dismissal.

Usually, I would have just given up and changed the subject, because Michelle had been through too much crap to change her mind now. But this time I was more than a little pissed off at her readiness to mistake my optimism for stupidity. '*Just coz* she *don't have a man!*' Besides, I'd been thinking a lot about the situation between British Black men and women for a while. I was secretly hurting at how few Black couples I'd seen together; it seemed like all the brothers were rushing to acquire a White partner and less dark-and-nappy babies. I mean, love is love – but it wasn't just love at work here, inferiority complexes and ingested lies definitely had their share of the statistics. The truth is, I felt angry, helpless, disappointed and, most of all, betrayed. But it had recently occurred to me that maybe the sisters had a part to play in this frightening scenario. And, sadly, it was often ones like Michelle, no matter how justified their prejudice was.

Right then, I argued back at her on a personal level, why *I* was right about him, why *I* was prepared to invest in the relationship, why that didn't make *me* some kind of idiot.

Since then, though, I have realized that it is *not* personal but a problem of epidemic proportions, a problem that took a trip to the US for me to pinpoint.

That same summer I left for a three-month work and travel programme in the said country, and discovered an entirely different type of relationship between Black men and women. Namely, one *exists*. They have problems, no doubt, but African-Americans realize that it is a relationship worth preserving. In the UK, however, that sense of connection and intimacy is rapidly degenerating.

While reading one popular book by a Black British writer, I identified one of the main stereotypes which is contributing to that degeneration. One portion reads: 'It seemed as though White men knew what they were doing when it came to love and women. Black men didn't have a clue – except for sex.'[1] This sort of writing is by no means rare in Black British fiction; it's the norm. These ideas are ingested and stored in the minds of women and young girls who feel they have something to prove. Black men are allegedly worthless ('except for sex') and often treated as such by British Black women.

In Britain, a brother often cannot even approach a Black woman and ask the time without her blasting him out of the water. 'Do I know you?' she says with a snarl and a twist of her neck. A request to dance from a brother could be met by a string of four-letter words. Often, young women feel pressured by their friends to display a certain attitude. In a conversation I recently had with a girlfriend, she revealed that her friends tell her she's 'too open and friendly with guys'. It seems obvious that to a great extent Black women feel obligated to fulfil the stereotype of being 'tough' and having 'attitude', to counteract the negative image of Black men. This concern is poignantly expressed in *From the Mouths of Men* by Alwin Peter.[2]

In this book Black men's views on Black women and relationships are examined. When they are asked what they dislike about Black women, the biggest consensus is 'Black women who prejudge and assume the worst about Black men.' One man from the sample comments that 'Black women . . . have a negative stereotypical opinion of Black men . . . often that negativity is based on hearsay, myth, lies and general bullshit.'[3] They simply want to be given a fair chance.

To test out these views further, I recently questioned a group of young men from Birmingham, Manchester and London I met at a barbecue. Their ages ranged from late teens to mid-twenties. When asked what traits they usually associated with the Black woman, they were understandably nervous about making such a generalization. However, I managed to extract a few comments and found that several came up time after time (along with the obvious ones about physique!). Black women have *attitude*. Black women *don't take shit*. Black women are *strong*. We sisters feel like this is who we're meant to be, and this is not in and of itself a bad thing, but there are no prizes for being unapproachable! Independence means being able to have your own aspirations, opinions and plans for life. It does not mean that you have to ignore and belittle the other half of the Black race. As one gentleman commented in *From the Mouths of Men*, 'we are stronger together than apart.'[4]

OK, I know you girls are already a little steamed at what I've had to say. To be fair, Black men often do a lot to justify tough treatment. There are, no doubt, reasons for the hard glint in Michele's brown eyes. Many of our men are watless, dishonest, unambitious, promiscuous, shallow losers with no direction in life. As a sister, I know well how frustrating it is to see so many Black guys who are not willing to make something out of themselves, who are stuck in a rut, who have ten kids by eight different 'babymudders'. And of course – to me the worst hurt – the Black men who are now too good for us sisters. After we've taken shit for centuries, and needed every ounce of toughness and attitude for us to make it, many Black men now think it's fine to impose eurocentric ideals of femininity on us, when that's never been a part of our culture! Why should we have to change now? It's true. But a lot of these attitudes, and misunderstandings and destructive stereotypes are a result of the media and our inability to detect the cancer that is destroying us as a community, as two beautiful sides of the same coin.

Another important aspect of the healing process is that we *allow ourselves to have high expectations*. What a man will do is largely a reflection of what we expect (and demand) of him. If you have confidence in a child's intelligence and expect him to do well (treating him in this manner), he usually will. In the same way, if you expect a child to play up and do badly at school (and it does show), he'll fulfil that prophecy. Many of us don't *expect* Black men to make a commitment, do something with his life, be a good father, treat us with respect. This compromises his self-esteem. He resents us because our low opinion burns him like an abandoned hot comb left on the fire! Raise your expectations and demands on his morality, make him feel that he is worthy of your confidence and belief.

These low expectations and opinions reflect on to the next generation. When a Black woman with these ideas has a son, he grows up feeling that he is destined to be worth nothing more than the size of his organ and the price of his car. Don't ever think that a child can't sense these things, because he can. AND IT HURTS. We are creating a new generation of Black girls who think that Black men are worthless and a new generation of Black men who believe them. All you have to do is look at damaging cultural myths such as 'good hair' and 'fair skin' to see how easily complexes are passed on. The fragility of the relationship between Black men and women in this country is only one symptom of much wider, deeper social problems.

Stateside, I felt as though there was a Black *community*. I felt a real sense of connection amongst people of colour – a nod on the street, a smile exchanged on the subway, even just an acknowledging glance.

In Britain, however, many of us do not feel the need to make our presence known. This is made evident at events such as the march for Black men that took place in '98. First of all, there was a very low turn-out.

To add insult to injury, my brother, who attended the said event, was outraged to see a popular, prominent Black British celebrity walk straight past it like it was doo-doo under his shoe. Few Black celebrities use their status to say anything about the Afro-Caribbean experience in Britain and instead prefer to remain culturally unthreatening. We would rather bash each other about the shortcomings of the opposite sex.

But there is a contradiction inherent in this way of thinking. Namely, how can we feel this way about our brothers and sisters without those prejudices reflecting on to ourselves? How can we have a lack of respect for Black women without it tainting that which we have for sisters, mothers and daughters? How can we fail to respect Black men without it weakening our love for brothers, fathers – our *sons*? Simple. It can't be done. The cycle of self-hate continues. There is enough hype in the media about how useless Black men are. It's all been said – too much. This one is for sisters like myself who have had enough of the 'blame game'. This isn't the way to deal with the pain of that brother who hurt you when you were seventeen, or the Dad who wasn't around when you were growing up. Be discerning, learn to dissect what you're looking at. Don't reject brothers for the sake of it because they will *simply stop asking*. A walk through central London will quickly reveal that more than a few already have. Next time, just smile and give a brother the time, nuh girl! If someone wants to dance or asks you to give them your number, do so or not, but be polite and have some class. You can be firm without being rude – don't reduce him to rubble! Believe me, you'll feel better about yourself and so will he. It's our responsibility to create a better spiritual climate for the Black children who will follow us. We can't move on as individuals until we learn to love ourselves as a community, learn to value ourselves despite all the negative images that are reflected back at us in society.

Before my visit to America, I felt that there was something wrong with Black male/female relations in Britain, but I couldn't pinpoint it. It was all I'd ever known or experienced. It is a very deep-rooted problem, borne of misrepresentation, misunderstanding, miseducation and – most particular to Black Britain – an unwillingness to face our problems. The disturbing rise of Black-on-Black violence testifies to the fact that we need actively to improve the way we treat, raise and represent young Black men in every capacity. And who could be more powerful than us? The mothers, wives, sisters, girlfriends, grandmothers, aunts? We need to dig deep and give them the positive reflection they can't get from the rest of society. I feel as if my eyes have been opened. I hope I've done the same for you.

Black women – please – learn to trust again. Black men – please – be worthy of it.

Amen.

Notes

1. Williams, Marcia, *Flex*, The X Press, London, 1997, p. 59
2. Peter, Alwin, *From the Mouths of Men*, Inglis Publications, London, 1998
3. Ibid., p. 19
4. Ibid.

KEVIN LE GENDRE

Father of Freeform: Joe Harriott, Man and Music. A Personal Take

I remember 1998 as a year of broken light on shapeless shadows, a year when things were not just unclear, they were out of synch – almost like a musical score in which the horns and strings are running at the wrong tempos. For Britain's Black community the Stephen Lawrence affair, dragging into its fifth year of tortuous inconclusion, became a leitmotif of tuneless second-class citizenship.

Yet in the midst of all this anguish the Windrush celebrations took place. Books, TV programmes and gala performances all marked fifty years of the Caribbean presence in the UK. Pioneers from sport and education such as Arthur Wharton, Britain's first Black footballer, and E. R. Brathwaite, trail-blazing teacher and author of *To Sir with Love*, were duly honoured. However, some people, important cultural figures in immigrant experience, were overlooked.

The name Joe Harriott means little to most Black Britons. This is both poignant and ironic, considering that Harriott was one of the greatest jazz musicians the UK has ever known and that 1998 was the twenty-fifth anniversary of his death.

Born into poverty in Kingston, Jamaica, in 1928, Joe Harriott was brought up at the famous Alpha orphanage in Kingston. Run by strict nuns, Alpha became an unofficial music academy of the highest order in the forties, producing some of the most important names in Jamaican musical history, such as Tommy McCook and Don Drummond, both of whom became members of the legendary group the Skatalites.

An outstanding musician from the age of eight, Harriott excelled on clarinet, baritone and alto sax. After leaving Alpha he played in Jamaican big bands such as Ossie da Costa's, coming to London with him in 1951.

Harriott made an immediate impact upon his arrival. Playing at London venues like the Studio Club, his virtuosity quickly brought him to the attention of both the music press and fellow musicians. In 1953 he put his own group together – a racially integrated one which featured the excellent

St Vincent-born trumpeter Shake Keane alongside British musicians, such as the brilliant drummer Phil Seamen. Harriott toured nationally and further increased his profile.

The early fifties was an exciting time in jazz. In the States, bebop, the frenetic, rhythmically complex style that had challenged the swing idiom of the previous decade, was giving way to the nuances of modern jazz.

Charlie Parker, the man who had led the bebop revolution in the forties, was in the twilight years of his life, and new stars like Miles Davis, John Coltrane and Ornette Coleman were making themselves heard. Harriott had absorbed Parker's innovations but quickly established his own musical identity, his own voice.

'He had his own particular style,' says Coleridge Goode, a Jamaican bassist who played with the biggest names in European jazz, Stéphane Grappelli and Django Reinhardt, before joining Harriott's quintet. 'He used the music of the times but he gave it his own inflections. He was very forceful, very decisive in his playing.'

Michael Garrick, a pianist whose trio shared the bill with Harriott's quintet at the Marquee club in the days when it was a jazz not a rock venue, had this to say about Harriott's writing: 'Joe's compositions, like "Coda", "Abstract" or "Beams", these are unique in music, not just jazz. They have a lot of humour as well as a thrusting jazz quality.'

So much for Harriott the musician, what of the man? 'He was very bright, very argumentative,' recalls Garrick, who would later record a series of jazz and poetry albums with Harriott and writers like Laurie Lee. 'He could either be seriously argumentative or have great fun with it. He had an excellent way of twisting words.' Harriott had all the prerequisites of a star; charisma, buoyancy and talent.

In 1960 he confirmed his originality in startling fashion with the album *Freeform*, most of which was written from a hospital bed after he contracted tuberculosis. This was a work which was starkly avant garde and moved away from set harmonic sequences. It came at a time when jazz was in a state of flux – new standards were being set.

The previous year, Miles Davis had explored the possibilities of modal composition on *Kind of Blue*, John Coltrane had given the tenor sax a new emotional intensity with *Giant Steps*, and Ornette Coleman had shocked the jazz establishment with *The Shape of Jazz to Come*, a record which also emphasized abstraction, albeit in a very different way to Harriott's.

Despite the image that jazz had as a music of free expression, it was shot through with divisions and factions. Traditionalists and modernists didn't mix. Harriott's music was problematic in that it didn't fall into any neat compartments. Not everybody dug it, as Coleridge Goode recalls. 'A lot of the musicians would scoff at what we were doing, they just didn't understand, because the accepted form of jazz in those days was four beats to the bar. Joe had a concept of breaking things up and not playing in a strict tempo. He wanted the music to convey specific feelings, to paint pictures with sound.'

The mid-sixties saw Harriott break more new ground with Calcutta-born John Mayer, a symphonic composer who won a scholarship to study at the Royal Academy in London. Arriving in England in 1952, he worked regularly with classical musicians, then in the sixties he met Dennis Preston, a producer for EMI who suggested that Mayer's quintet collaborate with Harriott's to develop a fusion of Indian ragas and jazz. 'Joe was the best. The parallel between his ideas and mine were perfect,' says Mayer. 'Joe was a pioneer in putting forward his freeform jazz. That's the reason why he tackled the indo-jazz fusions so well – because he had already broken away from the structure of the chord sequence.'

Using layers and layers of counterpoint to replace the harmony which is non-existent in Indian music, Mayer wrote complex parts that Harriott caught on to instantly. 'He could understand the raga, whatever he played . . . although it was jazz, the sound, the essence of the raga came out. He was tuned into what I was doing.' With the chemistry between them well established, Mayer subsequently geared his writing to the idiosyncrasies of Harriott and his excellent pianist Pat Smythe.

What was Harriott like to work with? 'Bloody difficult!' laughs Mayer. 'He was sometimes very stubborn. He would argue with everybody. We argued about everything, crazy things, sometimes musical things, then how should we go on the bloody coach to a gig. He was difficult.' The affection in Mayer's voice suggests that Harriott had considerable charm underneath the feistiness.

Released in 1967, *Indo-Jazz Fusions* received great critical acclaim, and its impact on both jazz and rock was huge. In the mid-sixties Indian music was a source of inspiration to anyone from John Coltrane to George Harrison, both of whom met the great sitarist Ravi Shankar a couple of years before he took the Woodstock flower-children to a natural high.

The popular ideal of the day was one of mixing Eastern and Western musical styles; Harriott and Mayer were among the first to do it. And among the first to use the term 'fusion', which would become an important subgenre in jazz in the seventies.

Despite these credits, the name Joe Harriott remains a relatively obscure one outside jazz. The average layperson will name Ronnie Scott or maybe Johnny Dankworth and Tubby Hayes as the heroes of British jazz. Why wasn't Harriott a bigger star? Everything suggested that he would be.

He won polls in the British music paper *Melody Maker*, he was the first British jazz musician to win a five-star rating from the highly influential American magazine *Downbeat*, he recorded for Columbia records, one of the biggest labels in the music business.

For all his talent, Harriott was never as visible as he should have been. Take that in both the figurative and the literal sense. When jazz hit television in the sixties, the BBC broadcast *Jazz 625* from Ronnie Scott's club, and visiting Americans were given top billing. But some Brits also bolstered their profiles – Ronnie Scott, Cleo Laine and Johnny Dankworth were marketed as jazz stars. Harriott, a Jamaican with an uncompromising character, wasn't.

'He was very fiercely proud. He wouldn't play the sort of hanging-in game. He wouldn't hang around at Ronnie Scott's to be seen,' explains Michael Garrick. 'He thought himself above all that, so he didn't make any effort to become one of the lads, and that's very important in British jazz, and he just didn't go for that. You're either in with the crowd or you're not. He was never in with the crowd.'

While African-American musicians were treated like stars, Caribbean players with British citizenship were a different proposition. 'If you were John Coltrane it was "oh, you must be marvellous, you're an American jazz player, you must be great!"' explains John Mayer. 'Joe was just as good as, but he came from the colonies. In those days the Caribbean and India still were considered British, we'd just got our independence, in a way it was too soon for us to just be . . . ourselves.'

Had Harriott been African-American as opposed to African-Caribbean, things would have been different. In fact, he surely would have improved his career prospects had he chosen to relocate to the States. But he never went to America, despite many offers from people, such as the great bassist Charles Mingus.

A mistake, some would say, but let's not forget that the mid-sixties was a time of high tension in American race relations, and that many Black American jazz musicians had emigrated to Europe to escape discrimination. When told that he had more chance of finding equality in Europe, Harriott's reply was trenchant. 'Why should I want to be equal, when I'm clearly superior?'

Harriott had a flat in Clifton Hill, St John's Wood, for most of his life. 'He lived very simply,' recalls Sharon Atkin, his common-law wife. 'There was a record player and records in his flat – mostly Charlie Parker, and some Sonny Stitt. He had one photograph in his whole flat, and that was of Charlie Parker. He liked to play bar billiards in the Clifton pub, next door to where he lived.

'He'd go in there and play piano because they had a room with a fire and an upright piano. So sometimes I'd drag him in there and make him play.' He was fond of a drink and was also known to be a gambling man.

In the early seventies his career declined. Demoralized and in poor health from years of smoking heavily despite his chest problem, he left London to tour the country. He was due to play in Southampton when he fell ill. He was hospitalized in October 1972; the diagnosis was advanced cancer of the spine. 2 January 1973 was the day the saxophonist drew his last breath.

Had Joe Harriott lived through the seventies he may have enjoyed a resurgence, given the popularity of 'fusion' music which he had helped to usher in. Or he may have changed direction altogether. His erstwhile collaborator John Mayer went on to write arrangements for progressive-rock gods Emerson, Lake and Palmer.

Indo-Jazz Fusions is available again now, twenty-five years after Harriott's death. One can only wonder why it's taken so long for such a recognized classic to be reissued, when so much sixties jazz has been regularly repackaged for a good decade now. The thorny question of Harriott's 'invisibility' again comes to the surface.

In the mid-eighties, when Courtney Pine, a Jamaican-descended sax-ophonist, emerged as an exciting new voice in British jazz, he frequently dropped Joe Harriott's name as an influence, yet nobody pushed for the late Jamaican's classic albums to be repromoted. Harriott still remained largely 'invisible'.

With hindsight, it's clear that the music industry never really appreci-ated his brilliance. In many ways Joe Harriott was before his time, part of a generation of Caribbean musicians for whom Britain simply wasn't ready.

Had he made music in the late seventies or early eighties, his career would have coincided with the emergence of a more distinct Black British identity, and he may have found receptive audiences and record companies. Instead he was caught in a post-Empire no-man's land that inevitably destined him for obscurity.

Yet what does that all mean in the millennium, almost three decades after Joe Harriott's death? Are Black British musicians still destined for 'invisibility' or have they moved on to a higher plane of self-realization?

The failure to recognize Joe Harriott as a great player in his lifetime is perhaps less significant than the denial of his right to be part of the British jazz establishment. Perhaps the most pernicious side-effect of Harriott's invisibility has been the distancing of the Black British com-munity from jazz music itself.

The lack of venues, the conspicuous absence of Black British jazz musicians in the Black British press, as well as in national newspapers, the stigma of exclusivity which clings to a music which is already perceived to be difficult – all of these factors have conspired to anchor jazz in a territory which appears alien to many second-generation Caribbeans, some of whom don't even think about jazz in terms of Black music.

The point is that Joe Harriott, along with the likes of Lord Shorty, Ernest Ranglin, Miles Davis, Bob Marley and Curtis Mayfield, belongs to the universal spectrum of Black music, one which is built on pluralities. Singular pluralities.

Harriott sounded different to English players because he'd soaked up ska and mento in his youth, as well as having attuned himself to the harmonic and rhythmic innovations of Charlie Parker – he was a superlat-ive example of the uniqueness born of the artistic cross-pollinations of the Black diaspora. His voice was that of an African-Caribbean channelled through an African-American artform – jazz.

Caribbean jazz history, from the solid bedrock of local players such as Ernest Ranglin and Tommy McCook through to expatriates such as Harriott, Coleridge Goode and Shake Keane, is a rich one, but it has always had to wrestle with the demon of poor documentation.

Over time the name Joe Harriott has lost currency in jazz music. People are quick to equate his name with the album *Indo-Jazz Fusions*, but I wonder whether that plays into stereotypes about exotic music. *Indo-Jazz Fusions* is often held up as his masterwork, yet the music was mostly scored, not improvised, and improvisation was Harriott's forte.

The overemphasis on this particular recording may also stem from the current vogue for Indian music, which again does not highlight Harriott's greatness as a jazz musician. *Abstract* and *Freeform* do that – but how often do we hear them on the radio? How often do we hear them on Black radio?

As the years have passed, the stories of his drinking, gambling and womanizing have all conspired to push Harriott's musical achievements into the background. What we have is the romanticism of the doomed talent, the straitjacket of the fallen hero – this has become a convenient vault to which the whole Joe Harriott legend can be consigned.

It's important that this doesn't happen, because Joe Harriott's story is of tremendous relevance to second-generation Black Britons, whether they think they like jazz or not. Musicians such as Harriott, Goode and Keane brought to British jazz a stance, spirit and attitude that are redolent of the Caribbean. The touches of irreverence, of impishness, of fantasy, stem from a distinct artistic heritage. It's really part of the same energy that inspires a man to turn a discarded oil-drum into an alto, tenor or soprano steel-pan.

When I listen to the Harriott composition 'Modal' and hear Shake Keane tapping on a glass in the opening bars, I hear a touch of 'home'. I see my father in a dimly lit front room in darkest, deepest Kent – smile on face, glass in hand. I hear a rhythmic finger doubling a calypso beat on crystal bacardi. And my mind overflows with the shuffling high notes of pan and jazz.

In fact, I must sit my father down with a rum 'n' coke and play him some Joe Harriott. He'll ask me who he was. I'll tell him that he was a saxophonist from Jamaica, not Trinidad. And to avert a long, fiendish kissing of the teeth, I'll quote an English musician, talking about Joe Harriott's brilliance. 'In the time that's elapsed it's become clearer and clearer to me that he really was a very great saxophonist,' comments Michael Garrick. 'I have some recordings of him in people's front rooms, just blowing on standards, and I play them to people on summer jazz courses that I teach as a blindfold test, and they're all astounded, they all say, well, it must be someone who's as good as Charlie Parker. "Of course it is," I say – "it's Joe Harriott." '

MAHLETE-TSIGÉ GETACHEW

Enter the Professionals

England changed us. With each generation we became taller and more inclined to speak back to our parents. However, one thing that hasn't changed – but desperately needs to – is the Black obsession with profession and qualification. You know what I'm talking about. Think back to Parent-Teacher evenings at school, and the chances are that your memories will not be too different to mine: smug prefects offering you watery squash; you deviously trying to steer your parents away from the teacher for whom you haven't done any homework since early October; intently peering at friends and their parents ahead of you in the queue to work out what sort of mood the headmaster is in.

My PT evenings were always remarkably colourful events. Sometimes, I suspected the staff were even more afraid of my parents than I was. Mum and Dad mistakenly thought these nights were an excuse to give their natural militancy free reign, never mind the casualties. They didn't have patience for history and geography and regarded the art, drama and music departments with as much mistrust as they, in turn, regarded my parents. They were polite to my head of year – just about – but didn't understand why my school reports included sections on things like 'personal behaviour', 'attitude in class' or, worst of all, '*self-expression and development*'. They would descend on the maths and science teachers like avenging angels of education, ballpoints ready to take obsessive notes about marking schemes, syllabi and attainment levels. I grew to fear these comments. They would invariably be read aloud to me every time I failed to get an A for an assignment, like some ritual of penance and punishment (and I was penitent; those notes were *punishment*).

I was too young to understand why it was important that I do well at school, but I have since 'seen the light'. Oh yes. And although I, like all Black people everywhere, am a Believer, I am too British ever to reach the fanatical determination sometimes seen in those older than me, or those who are my age but aren't third-generation immigrants and still have that zeal and unremitting fear of unemployment. I mean, Africans and profession – this is *heavy stuff*. It scares me, the way it stretches across the continent and has a hierarchy as meticulous and symbolic as anything religion has to offer. The Holy Trinity of Doctor-Lawyer-Engineer, attended by the accountants and teachers, radiant and orderly as the ranks of cherubim and seraphim. The unemployed, burning in hell, clutching their income-support claims and begging to be readmitted into the sacrosanct realm as mature students. Of course, like all the best religions, the key elements of it exist in most cultures. The Indians have got it pretty bad, too, as have the normally nonchalant Mediterraneans. Check into any NHS hospital and the chances are you'll be seen by an Asian consultant. Scroll down the register of candidates for an accountancy exam and the majority of names will not have austere Anglo-Saxon cadences.

If asked why they push their children so hard to do so well and in such restricted fields of achievement, then African parents will usually claim they do it out of anxiety for their children's financial futures (and their own, since the impoverished culture of tending parents in darker years is still very present). I can respect and appreciate their anxiety, but I do not see how their concern for a secure financial future can override their concern for emotional and mental well-being. (You try working at a subject you don't like for years and see how emotionally and mentally wholesome you are left feeling.) Equally, I do not see how what should only be mere *concern* for our financial future can be allowed to translate into parents more or less dictating the terms in which we are educated. It seems to me that in most cases they are unfairly wielding the axe of parental authority, 'For your own good' – a prerogative that exists in Old Africa and is strangely out of place in choice-and-Oprah Britain.

There is, of course, a not-so-secret secret agenda behind parental encouragement that you pursue the sciences and generally work obsessively hard at school. This is the desire to brag about their child to colleagues, friends, family back home, people on the bus . . . Doctor-Lawyer-Engineer are internationally recognized as awesomely challenging qualifications to achieve and professions that pay well. What they say is, 'My daughter is a lawyer.' What they project is, 'My daughter is clever and rich.' Take the joke about the Jewish mum running along a beach shouting, 'Help, my son the doctor is drowning.' Her inordinate pride –

greater than her anxiety – is supposed to be amusing. But you try being brought up as that son and see if you find the joke funny. I can laugh at it now, but the first time I heard it I was, quite frankly, dismayed. Laugh? I nearly *cried*.

University life is difficult enough (disregarding the unpleasant phenomena of puberty and poverty), and when you're doing a demanding subject that you don't even like, it can be truly hellish. I still shudder when I think back to those misbegotten hours I spent doing A-level chemistry. I'd sit in the classroom, swaying in a trance of insipidity and boredom, too afraid to snap out of my stupor in case the depression overwhelmed me. Valencies. Electron spheres. Titration. Not only did I not care (I could not bring myself even to pretend that I cared), but I actively hated chemistry with an unequalled passion; more than I hated sprouts, or injustice, or the Nazis. Damn, did I hate chemistry.

Of course, the hours I spent weeping and sweating over homework were bad enough, but at the back of my mind was a secret terror that I would somehow be forced to carry on studying it at university. I was stuck between a Scylla and Charybdis of working really hard and still *doing badly* (thus inspiring pity and contempt in my parents' contemporaries and relatives here and in Ethiopia) or, equally unappealing, working really hard and then *doing well* (thus providing them with an excuse to push me to study yet more chemistry). Laugh? I nearly *cried*.

As far as I can tell, it doesn't matter how hard you work, there is going to be someone on your course who can work at least as hard as you and, moreover, either has natural talent or passion for the subject. You try to explain to the acolytes and high priests in the Church of Profession how very miserable you are, or how ill-suited you are to the course, and at best they will listen politely and look a little bewildered. They might understand that you are unhappy, perhaps even sympathize with you. But you must stick with it. You must persevere. After all, they managed, didn't they? And things were much harder Back Home. And they are not feeding you and paying your upkeep for you to qualify as a *pop star*.

But, equally, it seems to me that it is dangerous to disregard the creative arts. They serve a purpose more functional than cathartic, and more universal than merely unique. Plato said that creative arts teach us everything we know, and their impact can never be overstated. Why else is propaganda so pernicious and advertising so lucrative? The Americans are keen proponents of self-expression and development – they invented it, didn't they? – and the rest of the world can laugh all it likes, but ultimately it is American TV, music, lifestyle, fashion and culture that we meekly assimilate without giving the matter a second thought. My uncle often sits around bitterly complaining that English people are unnecessarily ubiquitous given their relative absence of contribution to science and technology; he doesn't seem to see the connection between a pervading awareness of British culture and a high proportion of Britons being permitted – indeed encouraged – to pursue interests in the creative arts instead of being channelled immediately into medicine, business, law or engineering at the first indication of academic talent.

Introducing yourself to people as a 'performance artist' might not have much clout with folks here (and even less kudos with the family Back Home), but for as long as TV and radio are dominated by Caucasians, then how can we possibly expect other cultures to receive widespread acknowledgement? Even less obvious disciplines like geography and history need Black and Asian representation, otherwise atlases and the history of the world will always be eurocentric, with Africa and Asia hovering on the peripheries despite their substantial bulk. One reason why American culture is so internationally dominant and why English is so widely spoken is because of the volume of writers and broadcasters that this relatively small nation has produced and the amount of investment the government is prepared to put into communication media.

It is certainly time for the old order to pass away, and although we will always need doctors, lawyers and engineers, we also need artists to interpret the world. People may claim that academically and vocationally the arts are an easy option, but they can be just as rigorous as professional exams. If anything, they can be more daunting, because of the complete absence of guidance you receive. At least professionals can look forward to hefty wage packets when they've survived the nightmare of *vivas* and re-sits; artists are meant to be content with the obscure sense of self-gratification they receive which, nice though it is, isn't always sufficiently inspiring to make you soldier on in the face of scepticism, mockery and overdue rent. Give artists recognition as professionals; they deserve it.

ANDREA ENISUOH

They Think We Don't Care

When was the last time you went on an anti-racist demonstration? Go on, think about it. Think long and hard and see if you can remember. Perhaps you were at one of the demonstrations organized after the nail-bombings in April 1999. Or were you at the protests outside the Stephen Lawrence inquiry when the racist thugs were supposed to give evidence?

The sad truth of the matter is that most of you weren't at either. When it comes to demonstrating, against racism or anything else, Black people don't exactly rush out in their droves, do they? Well, that's the common perception anyway. Demonstrating: marching and all that kind of thing – well, Black British people aren't really into that.

And it's a perception that, whether true or untrue, makes me mad. Why? Because they think we don't care. By 'they', I mean the establishment – the 'powers that be' or whatever you want to call them. The people who make the racist laws, who control the racist police and, in effect, control our lives. And if they think we don't care, they'll think that they can get away with it.

And it makes me mad because I'm sick of people marching in our name. I'm sick of turning up to demonstrations about issues that primarily affect my people – racist attacks, racist murders or even racist immigration laws – and being met by a sea of White faces. Don't get me wrong, of course White people should be demonstrating against these things, the same people that are attacking us will probably turn on them next, but if I hear that slightly desperate-sounding 'Black and White – unite and fight' chant coming out of the mouths of majority White demonstrators one more time, I'll crack up.

Do you remember the nail-bombings? I do, vividly. First it was Brixton, the following weekend it was Brick Lane. It looked like any Black area anywhere could be next. And I remember how we all started to feel: apprehensive, scared even – let's face it, nobody really wanted to go shopping in a Black area for a few weekends after that. I also remember talking to a good friend about it. 'What can we do?' she asked. 'How can we stop it happening again?' I answered like a shot; I had after all been thinking about it all night. 'What we need is a demonstration,' I declared. 'Something that shows the strength of the community. Something that shows that we're not isolated.' And you know what? My friend looked at me as if I had proposed that we hold a party on the moon. 'I'm not being funny,' she replied, 'but what would that do?' And I suppose, in reality, that's the problem. If you don't feel that it can achieve anything, if you don't think that it will make one jot of difference whether you're out there on the streets or not, then what's the point?

There have been exceptions though, times when we've felt so angry, so hard done by as a race, that we've taken to the streets in droves. Look at the uprisings of the mid-1980s, when in Brixton, Toxteth, Moss Side and Bristol St Paul's, Black people took to the streets in anger. They were events that shook the country – and terrified the establishment. In fact, it terrified it so much that they felt that they had to do 'something'. So, on a very small, inadequate level, they put a bit of money into our communities. They built a few high-profile community centres and gave a few of us jobs within the race-relations industry. Small gains, but something. Now, if they were prepared to do that after what they considered a riot, imagine what we could win as a cohesive force.

There are always people around trying to organize our communities. There are the well-meaning left-wing anti-racist groups, whose life-mission it is to get Blacks and Whites to unite and fight. Then there are a whole number of self-appointed Black leaders whose mission seems to be to get quotes on behalf of the Black community into the press. But if either section wants to get Blacks out on to the streets in large numbers, then they'll have to learn a few things. To the anti-racist groups (and I say this as someone who has worked with such groups for over fifteen years): we're not cannonfodder that you can wheel out any time it suits you to take on the establishment. The issue of racism is too important to us for that. Be genuine, do the groundwork and don't just sail into our communities at the merest hint of trouble – then sail back out leaving us to pick up the pieces. Black and White *can* unite, but Black people don't like to feel used. I'm not saying that all White-led anti-racist groups do this. Some have a brilliant, long-standing record of doing work and gaining respect in Black communities. But many don't – they've exploited us. And if there's one thing Black people have, it's long memories.

And those supposed Black leaders would do well to remember that also. We may be more inclined to turn out when our own people are organizing the protests, but unless there is a coherent strategy, a long-term strategy of what they aim to achieve – and it better be more than a few column inches in the *Voice* – then they'll find we get sick of their photo opportunities very quickly.

In 1993, after the murder of Stephen Lawrence, make no mistake about it, Black people wanted to do something. Well, those that knew about it did anyway. Yet it took years for the national press to pick up on the Lawrence story in any big way. Like Rolan Adams and other victims of racist murders around that time, it seemed at first that Stephen's murder would pass virtually unnoticed. Maybe because it was one racist murder too many, or maybe it was because Black people thought that this time they could actually achieve something – whatever the reason – this time we turned out in force.

It was a demonstration called by, amongst others, the Black community group, Panther UK. The aim was to force the closure of the fascist British National Party's HQ (which they claimed was merely a bookshop) in Welling, Kent. This bookshop had become the focal point for racists and fascists in south-east London, where there had been a massive increase in racial attacks and murders. Over 50,000 predominantly Black people turned out on the demonstration on 16 October 1993. Angry, because yet another young Black man had lost his life and certain that this time something had to be done, Black people marched on Welling.

Unsurprisingly, the police did not let any of the demonstrators near the BNP headquarters – they were there to protect it! Over £1 million of taxpayers' money was spent on drafting in 7,000 policemen to do exactly that. Police fought running battles with the demonstrators. Many arrests and cracked skulls later, the demonstration dissipated. Although it had been a tremendous show of strength by the Black community, that night it was portrayed on television as nothing more than a riot. Images flashed across TV screens of young Black men's heads streaming with blood and demonstrators in full-on clashes with the police – hardly pictures that would encourage Black families watching at home to go on the next demonstration.

This brings to light another issue that often discourages Black people from demonstrating: the police. On most demonstrations there are complaints of police brutality. Trade unionists have experienced it for decades. Animal-rights protesters, environmentalists, all have a story to tell about strong-arm tactics by the police. Even human-rights demonstrators protesting against the visiting Chinese Premier Zhu Rongji experienced the heavy-handed tactics of the police in 1999. And if the police are prepared to use strong-arm tactics against those groups, imagine what they're prepared to do to us.

So taking to the streets can be dangerous. True. But is that really a good enough reason for us not to fight for our rights? I don't think so. But that's just one of many excuses I've heard given as a reason why my brothers and sisters won't be marching with me. 'It's not a Black thing' is another. 'It's just not something that Black people have ever really done,' others have told me. Well, those people should check their history books. Even recent history tells a different story. In 1977 it was young Blacks who turned out in force to take on the fascists who marched through Lewisham. While others were Rocking against Racism with the Anti-Nazi League, Black people were literally taking on the enemy.

In fact, in the 1970s there were an untold number of Black-led demonstrations. Not just against the fascists either, but on a number of issues. A major issue was the way that Black children were being treated in schools. These were the days when labels like 'educationally subnormal' were given out to Black children like sweeties. Black mothers, some working two or three low-paid jobs at a time, still found the time to organize protests. Small and localized protests, most of them may have been – but the point is that many Black people went out on a limb to coordinate them. So don't tell me that demonstrations aren't a Black thing.

Many young Blacks in Britain look to America for a lead on almost everything: music, fashion, sports. When the Nation of Islam led the Million Man March in October 1995, it caught the imagination of thousands here in Britain. It was an inspiration, but seemingly not one to be replicated in Britain. On the third anniversary of the Million Man March, the UK Nation of Islam planned their own Ten Thousand Man March. But even with the support of Operation Black Vote and the Society of Black

Lawyers, this was to be a pale imitation of the original. While police and press claims of only 2,000 attending are laughable, the size and impact of the march was nothing like the US version. Black politicians were noticeably absent from the event. While in America a whole range of politicians demanded to speak, here, few even bothered to send messages of support. But let's face it, we cannot mirror the experience of African-Americans – there's not enough of us here for a start.

But even if we can't become their mirror image (and why should we?), we can learn from their experiences and build on them. Please don't tell me that all those Malcolm X caps and T-shirts really were nothing more than a fashion statement.

They think we don't care, but how could we not? Our children are being failed by the education system. Young brothers are being attacked and murdered by racists. And the police? Their institutionalized racism means that we are seven times more likely to be stopped and searched than Whites, our women make up 20 per cent of the prison population, the men 12 per cent. One quarter of Blacks say that they have been racially abused or threatened in the past twelve months.

They think we don't care, but how would we not? When we think that we'll be effective and able to influence change, we'll be marching in our thousands. When an organization comes about that truly reflects what we feel and what we want, we'll come out in droves. Personally, I can't wait till then, so I'll carry on marching. I'll be marching for Stephen Lawrence, for Joy Gardner, for Michael Mensen and all other victims of the racist society that we live in.

What will you be doing?

Stories

KOYE OYEDEJI

Home: The Place Where You Belong (Memoirs of a Modern-Day Slave)

1.

I don't like it when I'm sober and my eyes are open, I can see things. I can see the truth. The drugs don't work any more.

There'll be victory when the bouncers stop thinking that they are the law.

I walk down Leicester Square on a Wednesday night and watch them push my people into line like they're chattel, cattle, and in many ways I guess we are cows, British beef. Yes, I have a beef with these bouncers, regardless of their colour they colour me troublemaker because of my colour. What annoys me even more is the fact that we don't accept that we are guilty of what they accuse us of. I approached a young guy in the queue; you see, he looked to be no more than sixteen, wearing jeans that had every colour of the rainbow on them. But they were designer's, a statement, so I am supposed to excuse them. But that's always the way, though, isn't it? We dismiss the eyesores. We ravens, we spread our black wings and somehow find it difficult to get our feet off the ground.

'Listen,' I said, 'Why are you here?'

Confused, he looked both ways, wondering who it was I was talking to.

'I'm talking to you,' I said.

'What's up, bruv?'

'Bruv? Do I look like a brother? My brother's no monkey, my brother's a raven.'

'What's that?' he said, stepping forward, acting like he didn't hear me.

'You heard.'

'Naah-naah,' he said, shaking his head, 'I don't understand what you're saying.'

'What's happenin'?' said his companion, a light-skinned boy who looked a little older, his face covered in zits. He talks like he's Don Juan, pushing his face forward with confidence when he should be hiding that shit at home.

I said, 'I remember when we would spend our pocket money on Bazooka Joe bubble gum and collect the small comic strips that were wrapped around them. Now it seems we need something more, leather jackets, mobile phones, fast cars . . . intelligence.' I turned and walked off towards Piccadilly, half-expecting them to stab me in my back.

Why not? They did it four hundred years ago and if you look carefully enough, you'll see that nothing much has changed.

'And this also has been one of the darkest places on the earth.'
'Something you can set up, and bow down before, and offer a sacrifice to.'

2.

I set myself up for a challenge every Friday at 3 p.m., in room 31, Venison House. It's where I go to meet my counsellor. He's late today, ten minutes past. I sit at his table, doodling on his pad as I stare at the empty seat across from me. I was going to tell him about my encounter with the youths yesterday and how ashamed they made me feel about myself.

Now he's making me feel ashamed of myself waiting around like this. That's when I really start to think carefully about a few things. It's him that claims I need someone to talk to, it's him that I pay substantial amounts of money to hear my problems. I don't even call them problems, he does.

So let me get this straight: in not so many words but rather hints, he tells me I've got problems, I pay him and he's happy.

Who have I been kidding?

I leave a note next to my doodle telling him that I shan't be coming back.

Ever.

I shant be coming back ever.
Nicky M.

3.

I stare at my reflection in the mirror and watch the steam rise up around me. It blurs my face, and I could easily stop it from doing so, you know. All I need do is turn the tap off, but I must confess how much I hate the way I look. I pick up the soap, but it can't clean where I'm dirty. When I was a child I used to try so hard to scrub myself clean; that was until my foster-mother told me it was my skin and I should be proud of it. I asked her why my friends at school called it dirt. She said they know no better.

They know no better is what I used to believe.

I study my body in the mirror with much scrutiny; it doesn't even hold up to its expected attributes: a flat arse, one breast bigger than the other but both virtually non-existent. I like the thin waist though, and I can finally see the rib cage; I am losing weight, but I suppose it doesn't matter any more. By the end of the night I shall be dead. Gassed, I will be lying on top of my bed with my picture of my foster-parents tilting on my chest. I wonder who will find my body and what they will make of it.

I tiptoe over the cold lino and make my way to the kitchen, turn the hobs on, turn the grill on, turn the oven on.

The phone rings and I let the answering-machine get it.

'Hello, Nicky, Nicky, it's me. I got your message, Nicky, and I think that we should discuss the matter. If you still feel that you don't want to continue your

sessions after that, then that's fine. With regard to me not turning up, I believe there was some confusion as to when your next session was. I expected you today, as always on a Friday morning.'

I went over to the calendar. Shit, he was right as well. I had arrived a whole day early, further proof that I was losing my head. I turned the gas off, slipped on my tracksuit, trainers, brushed my hair and took a quick hit on the little cocaine I had left. It is last meal-time. Last rites.

4.

He leaned back in his seat. He has plenty to say, but he's waiting for me to speak, it's the same old counsellor's trick. I've been to see so many of them, though, I'm used to what they expect, and I often prefer to go against the grain, it's so much more interesting. I started doodling on his Post-It notes in silence. I can't speak first. I shan't speak first. I won't speak first.

'You're fired,' I said.

He came forward in his chair, much too calmly for my liking. 'And why is that, Nicky?'

'Because I no longer need your services.'

'And why is that, Nicky?'

'Because it's not paying off.'

'And why is that, Nicky?'

I shrugged my shoulders. 'I dunno, maybe there just isn't any way to help my problem.'

'So you confess that there is a problem.'

'I never ever said there wasn't one.'

'So tell me about how you feel.'

'So that you can get one last pay cheque out of me? I don't think so.'

He put his notepad in his drawer and removed his glasses; he looked real cute without them, and I found him attractive, which was unusual because I never really went for Asian guys. No, let me confess the truth: I never really went for any guy other than the White guy. I knew no better. And only now that I've reached the end I feel ashamed of myself. I never really knew what it was like to be a Black woman.

'As it's your final session, I'm here to listen as a friend,' he said. 'I don't want any money, you can leave when you feel like it.'

'Really?'

'Yes.'

'Truthfully?'

'Yes.'

'You'll listen?'

'No.'

'I'm sorry?'

'I won't listen, I'll hear what you're saying.'

He leaned over and looked at my latest work of art on his Post-It note. He looked disappointed. I guess he should be, he has never really known how I feel, not until now, that is, not until it is too late. 'It's all to do with identity, I suppose. How many sessions have we had? Six? Seven? I wasn't going to tell you that I grew up with White foster-parents in Sheffield, but what does it matter now?'

'And why didn't you want to tell me this?'

'It would've been too easy to say that because I was the only Black child for miles I was bound to feel isolated.'

'It would?'

'Yes, because ever since I arrived in London I've felt worse. We have no culture, what we do is either adopt the culture that surrounds us or we try to imitate the culture of our own people back home but contradict ourselves by trying to Westernize it.'

'You feel it is not possible to live like our people?'

'Not if we were born here and have lived here all our lives.'

'But how does that affect you directly?'

'Home is the place where you belong.'

'Yes, and?'

'Where is my home? It's not as if I could go back to Africa and fit in, is it?'

He smiled. 'Perhaps in time you could. But have you considered that here may be your home?'

'Yes, I ask myself that sometimes, and when I enter certain hairdresser's and see the way they look at me or when I apply for jobs and listen to the "reasons" why my application failed, my question is always answered.'

5.

I turned the gas taps on as I got undressed, making sure that all the windows were shut tightly. I picked up the framed photo of my foster-parents. They tried their best, I suppose. They were in their late sixties when I was six; by the time I turned fifteen I knew I'd be alone in adulthood. They tried, I suppose, tried to live, tried to make me live. A graceful failure.

Why do the bouncers think that they are the law?

No matter what the season is, it is always cold outside.

The club I wish to enter has a short queue outside, a club for those who have no home to go to.

Heaven is a YMCA.

Tonight I'll have a chocolate dinner and think about all the bitter-sweet things people said about me:

'*The seedless grape.*'

'*New season brand.*'

'*South African.*'

'*Picked to be eaten.*'

Tonight I'll take my heart to bed. A little voice says, '*Wouldn't you rather sleep alone instead?*'

I said, 'You sound like a real poet to me.'

'But didn't they tell you poetry is dead?'
I'm not mad, I'm just alone without a real home.

6.

As I lie on the bed with the picture on my chest I begin to dream. As always I dream of a raven. It's in flight and has nowhere to land because the earth is covered in water, dirty water, polluted water that has contaminated animals, crows, magpies, lying dead, floating on the surface. It travels for a while before finally spotting some dry land, the top of a mountain on which a swan lies with broken wings resting against the branch of an olive tree. The raven decides to land and begins to nurse the swan's wounds, and in return the swan shares its food. This goes on for many days and nights until one day a dove flies by and circles them for a while before landing on what looks like a solitary island surrounded by water. Moving quickly, it picks a leaf from the branch and takes off again. The raven looks at the swan, asking itself whether it should stay or follow the dove towards the rainbow. It decides to follow, knowing that the swan will have to stay behind, as it has not recovered.

There is a smile on the wind, the trees dance; a *tempus machina* is coming.

I have often asked myself if I was the raven or the swan, now I know that it no longer matters.

7.

I'll sleep and hopefully it'll be comfortably.
I hope the gas will consume me easily.

Follow me towards the rainbow.

ALLISTER HARRY

The Headmaster's Office

Toussaint was transfixed by the brass sign. It clamped his feet to the floorboards and stirred his buried memories. He felt the erased black letters weakened its impact, somehow the gaps undermined the sign's authority, yet the heavy pine door remained imposing. He'd expected it to be bigger – gigantic – as he'd remembered and imagined, but the door seemed to have shrunk. Perhaps he was right to come back.

Toussaint yawned. He'd forgotten how the heat in the basement hit you like a lullaby. He knocked on the door, hesitantly, yet the sign smacked the dusty floorboards and polluted the silence. If only he'd been better in the slips. (Their old PE teacher, he couldn't remember his name – only that he was bow-legged – had been right: he couldn't catch a cold.) The clatter ran along the sullen corridor, laughing like children, gleefully beckoning The Head. Toussaint froze. He couldn't turn back now.

Edward Peter Roper had been appointed headmaster of St John's Boys' School in 1974. The first thing he did was call an impromptu meeting with his new deputy and the caretaker Jeff. It took an hour to find him. Jeff was notoriously difficult to locate, but he was easy to recognize: he was never seen out of his huge brown caretaker's coat. From a distance, he resembled a child expected to grow into it.

The Head believed his predecessor's office was inadequate 'for my expansive collection of first editions', so called the meeting to discuss alternatives. Jeff saw an opportunity to justify his position. To his knowledge, the biggest available room was on the lower ground floor – next to his utility room. It had been empty for years, and would be no trouble for him to renovate. He flicked his mousy hair from his face and waited for a response.

What Jeff called his utility room was little more than a cupboard. It overflowed with the useless junk he believed a quality caretaker always kept 'just in case'. As he was rarely found taking care of anything at St John's, the teachers could only imagine the scenario he inferred.

'Basically, I could have it shipshape in a few weeks. Depends if you don't mind being down there on yer tod.' He looked squarely at The Head with staring hazel eyes.

The Head smiled, with undisguised insincerity. 'It's imperative that you complete this task to the zenith of your ability . . . as the new headmaster I'll be looking to make some, er – adjustments – around here shortly.'

Although The Head's veiled threat was clearly directed at Jeff, the deputy was sure he saw The Head's granite eyes flit in *his* direction as he mangled language in that unique fashion. Once Jeff was dismissed, The Head confessed that as long as his first editions received a decent home he didn't care if he ended up in the laundry. In fact, he quite welcomed the exclusivity of his new location. But his deputy wasn't listening. He was thinking about that look.

Toussaint stared at the looming door; The Head hadn't heard the racket. He noticed the pine had lost its smooth gloss. A lick of varnish wouldn't hurt. When he was a boarder in the eighties he used to imagine that door was a rootless tree-trunk. Fourteen years on, he still feared it would topple and that no one would hear him scream. You're an adult now, he reminded himself, and carefully replaced the sign. But he couldn't go through with it, the clamour somehow punctured his confidence. He decided to return another time, when he'd figured out what he needed to say.

Shola would know, she was never short for words. He'd always thought it was because she was a journalist. The first time he had set eyes on Shola he hadn't been able to ignore her delicate, curvy body. He came to view it as compensation for putting up with her tough head. He wasn't surprised when she gave him the ultimatum. He'd always known she would – once she found out. Still, he wasn't ready for it when it came.

'What I'm trying to say, baby, is it's time you decided what you want . . . from us. I'm tired of being locked out. I've tried giving you space, but I can't love a stranger any more. Two years we've been together. Two years. And you won't even talk about the nightmares. Now you're taking liberties, sleeping with – with SOME FUCKING WHORE! . . . look, you're destroying us both.' She stopped abruptly; it was her final word. Then she added quietly, 'You know how I feel about you, T, but I won't let you drag me down just because you're weak.'

She wanted me to change. Change! Like a man can change overnight. Just because she's been reading some fucked-up books. I wanted to tell her she needed to make some changes, too. I wanted to say, you're not perfect, you're not perfect, you're holding me back. I wanted to kiss her, caress her, tease her about her short, defiantly natural hair. And suggest we make love. Instead I punched her. Clean in the face.

Toussaint turned and crept towards the stairs. The heavy ceiling pressed down on him. He had to get out, but he couldn't leave. He'd banished the only person he had ever really allowed himself to trust. He blamed The Head. Maybe he *was* looking for someone to blame again – anyone; after all, The Head hadn't punched Shola. But he also knew that nineteen years ago The Head had begun slowly to pick away at his life. He'd been asking himself 'why me?' ever since he could remember and imagine.

I only hit her once. I've never hit her before. I've never punched any woman before. I didn't realize I was the type. I wished I could take it back as soon as it landed. I was right all along, I didn't deserve her. But I'd still betrayed her.

It's just . . . when I heard the determination in her voice. It scared me. It really scared me, and I exploded. I always thought I would be the one to split up with her. I stared at her shrunken shivering body, wishing she would hold me, need me. But she looked up as if I was a stranger, an intruder in her home. Inside my skin I cried. I cried like some little girl. But no one could hear my tears.

Once the new office was ready, The Head asked Jeff to help him procure a decent bookcase for his 206 first editions. Jeff was only too happy to oblige, and confessed to being a bit of an expert in the area of bookcases. Before his promotion the only place The Head could keep most of his books had been in the loft at home. His wife, a natural browser, had discovered many of them for him. She would have been felicitous about his promotion. Constance was the only person who really knew how much the position meant to him. Since she had passed on (he couldn't bring himself to say 'died') he hadn't ventured back into the loft. It had been only six weeks since she asked him to put some of her old paintings up there. A week later she was gone – her heart. What with the new bookcase, he supposed he'd have to go up there now.

Once the bookcase was installed, The Head asked Jeff to change the office door from glass to wood. He didn't wish to be distracted every time Jeff ambled past. By this point Jeff was considering taking a sickie or killing The Head. Since the big meeting Jeff had been spotted with uncharacteristic regularity around the school. He promised himself that in the future he would not be as forthcoming with his janitorial knowledge.

Toussaint stood at the door. He couldn't go back to sleepwalking through life, hoping he'd given his nightmares the slip. For too long he'd felt like a ghost lugging around its own carcass. But it was too late to leave now; behind that door was his life. He held the sign with his left hand and hammered on the door with the free one.

'ENTER!'

He felt the command in his stomach. The voice was gruff, not deep, a tenor that wished it was a bass. In Toussaint's head that pitch was the strangled siren of evil. The air smelled of ancient books. He suddenly realized it must have been there all the time. The mustiness made him think of the teachers at St John's, they wrung every drop of horror out of The Head's location.

YOU BOYS. Pay attention! You don't want me to send you down to the basement.

Toussaint opened the door. It squealed gently and a warm gust of linseed oil rushed his nostrils. Toussaint recognized him immediately, even though The Head's ruddy dome was bowed. He sat behind his chaotic desk, engrossed in the *Telegraph*, oblivious to the fact he now had company. Toussaint eyed his solid arms. He was still bull-shaped, ready to burst out of his crumpled white shirt and black tie. Toussaint edged forward, fumbled in his mind for the right words. The wooden cabinet, stuffed with silver sports trophies, sagged on the wall to his right. He'd always imagined them as gloomy pigeons. The black-and-white photo of The Head, captain of Exeter University's rugby team, hung near the birds; his dishevelled blond hair threatened to upstage the side. On Toussaint's left the prodigious bookcase lingered along the wall. It always struck him as a waste of space – it had only ever been half-full.

'Can I assist you?'

Toussaint stopped dead in his tracks. He was startled more by the indifference in The Head's voice than the voice itself. The Head didn't wrench his nose from his newspaper. Suddenly the room began to murmur, then hum. Toussaint recognized the tune: the echo of a thousand silent screams. It was his own voice.

'It's T-T-Toussaint, sir – I m-m-mean M-Mr Roper,' he blurted. For once he didn't care about his stutter. He concentrated on walking; he was so tired. The Head looked up, squinted at the Black man lurching towards him, took off his glasses, held them like sweaty plimsolls and craned his bull neck to get a better look. Toussaint was stunned by how old he looked. Surely that wilting face couldn't belong to that taut, cruel body? Time had scrawled its signature on every corner of his face, his pale blue eyes were sealed with anguish.

The Head couldn't believe what he beheld. A pang of fear, tinged with pleasure, tossed and turned in his heart and left as quickly as it came. He'd never expected to see those full lips again, that illuminating face that seemed to offer hope, the stubborn nose that braced brown velvet eyes; he was taller, perhaps slimmer in the face, but it was definitely him. Toussaint Muir.

'I don't recollect you.' Just as The Head averted his eyes and turned back to his newspaper, Toussaint glimpsed the smirk threatening his mouth. Then the past erupted in his chest. He felt himself lunge at The Head. His head was spinning. No. It was the room, the room was spinning. He was standing still.

Suddenly the cricket bat leaped in front of his eyes. It leaned menacingly against the bookcase, a sleeping tiger glistening in its new coat of linseed oil. A deep fracture flashed through its heart like a lightning scar. Then it stirred from its slumber and growled, *'I'm here. I'm here.'* The bat began to throb, Toussaint's head was throbbing, *then I heard it chuckle, A CRICKET BAT WAS LAUGHING AT ME! It was cackling. I was cracking up, he was calling me weak, he was screaming: you're weak, you're weak; I'm weak, I'm worthless, he's hitting me, striking me, striking me, striking me, won't stop, when will it stop, please sir, stop! I can't feel – I can't feel – my bottom, I won't cry, the pain, this time I'm going to die, I won't cry, this time, I'm going to die, why won't SOMEBODY save me? Jeff, someone, please knock on the door.*

Toussaint roared from the edge of his soul: 'D-D-DON'T FUCK WITH ME! WHY D-D-DID YOU DO IT? Why did you do it? Why me?' His chest heaved, and his hands were clenched as tight as a baby's. The head looked up.

'What are you babbling about?'

Toussaint was staggered by his tone.

What this insolent boy needs is a good hiding. Thinks he can just waltz in here and abuse me like I'm some peasant. After all these years the stuttering fool still has no regard for his superiors. Sometimes beating is the only language that little boys understand. It can't hurt, it didn't do me any harm. They'll all thank me for it one day.

All the ambitious young teachers are after my position. They think I don't know. But no one has the respect of the boys like I do. As Constance used to say – before she passed on – no one at St John's deserves to become headmaster more than me.

Toussaint didn't know when he picked it up but now he was gripping the bat like an axe over The Head. 'WHY ME?' he wailed through tearful eyes. 'It's b-because I'm b-b-black, isn't it?' He cocked the bat. 'ISN'T IT?' But deep down he didn't believe that. He believed it was because he was weak, and it showed in his eyes; all The Head had done was to see his essence.

The Head stared up at the heavy bat. His nightmare had come alive; one of his boys had returned to kill him.

Muir, did you know you were the bravest boy in the school? Despite your stammer, despite your colour, you always tried harder than everyone else. No matter how hard I thrashed you, you never cried. You were the only one who never cried. I was never that brave. But, like the others, I knew you would never tell.

'ANSWER ME!'

The Head replied by throwing his hands, dramatically, in front of his face. 'Please! Don't hurt me. I'm just an old man,' he cowered.

And Toussaint saw something he couldn't have imagined. It was fear flickering in The Head's grave eyes. He thought of Shola, how she looked through and beyond him. He realized The Head would never tell; it was his last vestige of power. Toussaint yanked the bat back and smashed it into The Head's desk. The Head whimpered, the bat smashed to pieces, spraying like a pile of autumn leaves kicked by the wind. Toussaint turned, walked slowly to the door and slammed it behind him. The Head smirked, with relief. As Toussaint flew up the stairs he heard the sign crash to the floor with a hollow thud.

Outside the school gates, in the dim sunlight, he scoured the street for a telephone booth. He needed to call Shola. He had a story she might be interested in. If she would listen. She would listen, he whispered, and picked up the receiver.

UCHENNA IZUNDU

It's a Hard-Knock Life

I've just learned that I'm even more African than my parents are. Up till now, I've always denied it.

Don't laugh, it's not funny.

Self-realization is a very scary thing indeed. I thought I was liberated, living in this multicultural London, and that it was my parents who needed to 'fix up and get with it'. But I've just had Nkem, my cousin, tell me to $!"* and die to my face. I was proper insulted. Koro-koro.

Is it because I've had bad experiences with relationships that I can't be happy for her?

I DON'T think so.

Yeah, I've been through bastards one, two, three and four, and all of them messed with my money and with my head. I'm persecuted in my own society with guys who do the run-around in *real style*. Take my *word* for it.

So, there are nice ones out there. Those of you who have them, good for you.

I'm jealous.

So what? I ain't denying it. When I too am in the land of milk and honey with fine man, then my tone will probably change, but at this moment I'm not, so there.

I'm all for watching interracial love on the TV screen, on the likes of Rikki and Jerry and what not. I was part of the crowd that would be, 'Nuh, man, that's out of order . . . Let them be . . . Love knows no colour, no boundaries . . . You can't help who you fall in love with . . . The kids will be enriched, having the best of both worlds . . .' Blah blah blah.

'All grammar,' my dad would say. Because when interracial love came knocking on my door, I just went 'Er no' and immediately slammed it shut.

Nkem, my cousin, is like the sister I never had and never wanted. Stunning, super-clever and popular. But I love her to bits, even though I was sick and tired of hearing comparisons being drawn between the pair of us by *mes parents*. If there's one thing African parents never learn while in this land of the living is that doing so, like, lowers one's self-esteem. It's amazing how the Western style of parenting just never penetrates.

This incident then just seems all the weirder, because it was only ten minutes prior to meeting Nkem at the library that I'd been chatting to Trisha, my best friend, about getting married and having babies and stuff. Anyhow, Nkem was lending me her notes to photocopy and all rushing-rushing me, saying how she had to go meet Paul.

'What's up with this Paul, man?' I was moaning. 'I never see you these days. Ain't you ever hear that men will always come and go but family stays around for ever?'

She laughed. 'Get a life and give me my notes.' Biting her lips and looking at her watch anxiously, she murmured, 'I don't want to be late.'

I looked at her closely. 'It's true, you know. You've never said much about him except that he's a friend of a friend and that he's safe.'

Nkem nodded vaguely, and the bright light of the humming machine distracted her for a second. Suddenly she became focused. 'Have you finished? Good,' she said, before I had a chance to talk, grabbing her sheets out of my hands.

'Is this the real deal?' I asked, panting. She was walking so fast, almost military-style, to go see her 'precious Paul'.

She paused. 'Why do you ask that?'

'Coz of the way you talk about him, and both of you are literally up each other's cracks, man. God knows, I never see you these days.'

'Sometimes you can be so coarse.'

I grinned. 'I try. So spill. I wanna hear all the nasty details.'

I was bitterly disappointed. All Nkem rewarded me with was a goofy, mysterious smile. 'I feel very strongly about him.'

'And? You've told me jack. What does that mean?'

'Precisely that,' she retorted. Glancing at her watch again, she squealed, 'Oh, darn, I'm going to be late!'

And with that she ran off into the sunset to spend quality time with her man.

The hall lights were off when I arrived home, and the whole place appeared to be deserted. It had been a hard day's work at the library. I'd intended to stay late and do some reading for tomorrow's criminology class but, of course, being sociable, talkative, popular and the like, I ended up cracking jokes with my brethren and checking some nice man left, right and centre who I had not seen before. My life is long, it's hard being me, what can I say?

Okonkwo, my younger brother, was in the kitchen making cereal, in other words 'dinner' for himself.

'Where's Mum and Dad?' I shouted, dumping my bag next to the staircase, which I knew annoyed the hell out of him, because I never carried it upstairs, as I couldn't be arsed. He was a neat freak.

'You missed some action,' he mumbled, Frosties in his mouth. 'Mum and Dad just jumped the car round to Ngozi's place. Ngozi's having babies, man.' Ngozi was Nkem's mum, and in any other household she must be addressed as 'Da Ngozi', as this is the respectful thing to do for someone older than you in Igbo culture, but she allowed it with us. I saw Ngozi as my older sister; she was pretty cool, easier to deal with than my own mum.

'Why, what happened?' I asked, switching on the kettle to make gari. Mum had left my share of the okro soup in the microwave. Okonkwo started sniggering. 'Nkem brought Paul home.'

'Yeah and?' Sometimes he could be sooo tiresome in relaying information.

'And he's white.'

I screamed.

It took me twenty minutes to make food which normally took two minutes, as I was in what they call 'deep shock'. Okonkwo thought the whole issue was pure joke. 'I dunno why you're so surprised,' he said, washing up his bowl immediately after eating. 'Nkem has problems, boy. I've always said she's white, and now she's with her own.'

'Shut up,' I snapped.

'It's true though,' he insisted. 'She listens to her whale music' – this is what he called Nkem's love for panpipe tunes – 'she can't dress, speaks like a dictionary, dances like a mark . . .' He shrugged. 'She needs to fix up, bwoy, fix up big-time. I've always said it, wigger in reverse.'

'What happened?' I asked desperately, trying to ignore his cussing, because I actually agreed with him, but I was also extremely protective of Nkem when Okonkwo went into one.

'Nkem said to Ngozi that she may possibly bring Paul, and Ngozi was all for it, really up to meeting him. Then Paul, blond hair, blue eyes, steps through the front door all holding Nkem's hand, and Ngozi and Uncle David' – this was Ngozi's husband, who insisted on being addressed formally – 'almost died there and then.' Okonkwo at this point bust up laughing. 'Then, once he's gone, Nkem chats fart about how she's in love and she wants to marry him coz they've been talking about it. Ngozi just got straight on the phone to Mum and Dad. They both splurted over there to see if the gal has gone mad.'

He began stacking the dishes. 'I've got to give it to her though. She's dread bringing home White man, saying she's gonna marry him.'

'She's serious?'

Okonkwo looked at me. 'When have you ever known Nkem to joke?'

'But this is like her first man! No wonder she never told me nothing! I tried milking her today for some info, and she was all there saying how she feels very strongly about him.' I swallowed some soup, feeling hurt that she hadn't confided in me. 'I don't even know what to say.'

At that moment the front door was unlocked and our parents came in, talking hurriedly in Igbo. I called greetings to them. Both were tall, stately people, well respected in the community. My friends were amazed at the beauty of my mum. She made a great effort to look good all the time.

'So what did Nkem say?' Okonkwo barked the minute mum came into the kitchen.

She sighed. 'Only God knows where we've gone wrong.' My father took out a couple of glasses and poured them both some drink.

'How's Ngozi?' I asked.

'Distraught. What else do you expect?' Dad answered.

'Is it that bad?'

'Nkem is wholly serious. She claims that she's in love and she'll marry Paul regardless of what any of us say.'

'I don't really get what the big deal is,' I said. *Ma bouche* had this bad habit of saying one thing while my heart is really thinking another.

'What's that supposed to mean? You were the one who screamed when I told you now,' Okonkwo snarled.

I gave him a cool, condescending look. 'That's because I was so shocked to hear first that she's talking about getting married and second because Paul is white.'

'You lie.'

'Whatever.'

'Can both of you shut up with your nonsense?' Mum snapped. She began pacing the kitchen anxiously. 'I don't understand. I just don't understand. We've really tried to practise our culture here for you so that you understand who you are and where you come from. When did white people ever become part of the picture?' She suddenly looked at me. 'I hope you have no intention of pulling this same kind of stupidity that Nkem is talking about and expecting all of us to tolerate it.'

'Oh, so for once Nkem's actually in the wrong. Wow, that sure makes a change!'

Dad kissed his teeth. Mum lectured. 'That's all you learn, disrespecting your elders and opening your mouth to talk anyhow. Try going back to Nigeria, let's see how far that attitude will take you. *I di iberibe*'; in other words, 'You stupid one': Igbo style, straight off the boat.

'Well, we're not in Nigeria now, Mum, are we? We're in London, different attitudes, different lifestyles. Nkem wants to shack up with some white man. She loves him, good for her. It's you lot that's making life difficult, not her!'

Okonkwo laughed as he made his exit. 'You're in for it now, boy.'

'Are any of our relations married to white people?' Dad asked. He always tried to take the rationalistic approach whereas mum and I went for blows.

'No.'

'Precisely. We believe in marrying amongst our own, and Ibos who don't, we look down on them. They haven't done themselves or their families justice. White people and us, we don't share the same culture, it's not workable, practical or viable. Just tell me how on earth Paul is going to feel comfortable or understand what is going on when we do things the traditional way.'

Sipping some of her juice, Mum said, 'The best bit of this entire farce is that Nkem believes that since Paul grew up in Nigeria while he was young, that suddenly makes things seem so much better.'

'Don't it? At least he has some idea where we're coming from.'

Dad sighed. 'When are you going to understand that we're not the same? They don't speak or think like us. Nkem is disgracing her parents – and the children, chi! They're going to be the most confused of all.'

'I don't believe that.' Dad also has this tendency to make sweeping generalizations, which really gets on my nerves. 'The way you're talking no one would guess that you've been living here for the past twenty years and that you see this kind of thing all the time.'

'And we see them break up all the time,' Mum murmured. 'There's statistics to prove it.' She put down her glass. 'Udo, I'm going to bed.'

I decided to try talking some sense to Nkem the moment Dad upped and went to bed too. I could *not* see the attraction. Yeah, so one can admire Brad Pitt and them from afar, but for me to get it on with one of them? Uh-uh, no sirree. I like my chocolate and I like it dark. I shuddered. Damn, how far had Nkem gone? She had never seemed too attracted to our own but I'd always thought that had been due to her never finding the right one. Okonkwo attributed it to the fact that their family had grown up in Edinburgh and the air up north had messed up Nkem's head severely.

'Ngozi?'

'Oh, hello!' She was breathless. 'I'm so happy that you called.' The explosion erupted. 'I hope that you're going to talk to your sister and get her to think aright.' My blood pressure is up. Nkem wants to destroy me! 'You speak to a child, they don't want to listen. Only God knows where she got this nonsense from.'

'I'll try.'

Nkem came to the phone several minutes later. Her greeting was tentative.

'Are you OK?' I asked.

'I've been better. Dad is refusing to talk to me, and every time I open my mouth Mum goes into a rant that never seems to stop.' She started sniffling. 'I never realized that it would be this hard. I thought . . . I thought . . . I just thought . . .'

'Hey, it's OK. They're hardcore Africans. What else do you expect?'

She giggled. 'Koro-koro. You always cheer me up. Thank goodness you support me.'

Silence.

'You do support me, don't you?'

Longer silence. 'Talk now, you're making me nervous.'

'Nkem, have you thought this through properly?'

'What kind of stupid question is that? Do I go around saying that I'm going to marry everyone these days?'

'No, but I don't think you know what you're doing. C'mon Nkem, White boy, Black girl. White boy, Black girl. T'ink about it and t'ink hard.'

'Your point being?'

'Didn't you hear me? He's White, you're Black. You're not the same. It's weird.'

'Do you say that when you see Black men and White girls together?'

That one I had to think about. I responded in the negative.

The next thing I heard was a tirade of abuse.

'You should be ashamed of yourself' was her ending note. 'You've grown up with White people, you adopt those parts of the culture that suit you and to hell with anything else. You know what's the worst? At least our parents say they're African and stick to it. You deny it when it suits you and fluctuate whenever you like because you have no clue whatsoever of who you are! It's the insecurity that makes you try to be even *more* African than them. It doesn't come over at all. You're a hypocrite, because then you try to dispute it!'

The line went dead.

Koro-koro.

AKINWALE OLADIMEJI

The Boy

The boy gazed at his aunt undressing in front of him as she did nearly every night. Her figure was Rubenesque, her skin purest ebony, dark as slick tar. Her breasts were upturned and medium sized, belly round with wide hips flowing into a big, round expanse of flesh, twin globules that Rodin would have liked to delineate. Her legs were chubby curvy baseball bats.

He was twelve. She was twenty-eight and not averse to exhibitionism. He learned that the first time he had wandered into the spare room she was using while on holiday at their home that hot summer. His parents had gone out, leaving them alone in the house. She had smiled at him on seeing him enter the room, thinking that this little handsome boy was once a curly haired beautiful baby she had cradled in her arms. She said that to him as she took off her top.

She is like the Venus of Syracuse, he thought as he studied her, remembering an image he had seen in an art book in the local library. She undressed so matter-of-factly, so methodically, that he knew she was not embarrassed by this invasion of her privacy. The memory of his aunt's nipples sticking out like little acorns and the curves of her luscious body filled his mind for days to come, till he picked up courage and wandered into her bedroom more often, after his parents went to bed.

The boy was first exposed to pornography at school – the back of his school at the end of a wintry day to be exact. There, he and a group of classmates had pored over a magazine that one of them, a ginger-haired, bespectacled boy, had stolen from his older brother's collection. Most of them had gaped as 'horny young girls get it in the ass' and 'willing wanton bitches suck cock' in adverts for adult movies. The older boys, who had seen things like this before, were cool, nonchalant. The boy's heart beat loudly, his breath came in jagged spurts, and when he looked at the erection in his underpants he noticed that it was bigger than anything he had ever experienced. He felt like running away from the others, so they would not notice his huge hard-on and make fun of him.

His name was Kehinde. It was a Yoruba name traditionally given to the youngest twin. The Yoruba believed that the second twin was actually the older twin, who had sent the first twin as a scout to survey the world. His older counterpart had evidently not liked what he'd seen, for he had died shortly after birth. At present Kehinde was an only child. He was a sweet boy, with bushy eyebrows and an otherwise feminine face.

Kenny, as his friends called him, was starting to notice the sexiness of his world, from the sex-saturated adverts in the media to the girls in his school with their svelte figures and their bags slung across shoulders and nestling next to budding breasts. In some cases the breasts were fully developed and ripe for suckling. Kenny often wondered when he would get his first taste of sex.

Lately, he had noticed that the new neighbours next door had a daughter a few years older than him. She excited his imagination in a way few women he knew did. She had a body of exquisite proportions, the voluptuousness of her entire build overwhelming him and delighting him with its wholesomeness. She was just like his aunt in that respect, content with her look, luxuriating in it as far as he could tell. She usually walked down the street swinging her hips and eliciting stares of admiration. She had a caramel-coloured complexion, jet-black hair and glowing black fires for eyes.

He often watched her walking past from his window and noticed her big backside in her favourite brown miniskirt as the sun shone and crystallized the contours of her curvaceous body. She was an aesthetically pleasing, awe-inspiring dish, hot and ready to be devoured. He chuckled as he thought of this analogy. *Like succulently juicy chicken.* He imagined the fresh-basted roast chicken his mother sometimes cooked on Sundays. Mouth-watering. So heady it filled the house with an aroma that sent him to the source of the smell time after time, till the cooking was done. He thought of the anticipation and then the realization of his desire when the meal was placed in front of him and wolfed down. And then the blissful contentment that followed as nature allowed digestion to take place. If that was what sex was like, then he was in for a heavenly experience when sampling it for the first time. His yearning grew even stronger.

It wasn't until a few days later that Kehinde noticed that his neighbour's room was adjacent to his. He could peek into her room and vice versa. He did this once in a while, but she usually turned the lights off before undressing for bed. Once or twice he would find her reading a book, unable to sleep. She would read until she was drowsy, then turn off the lights and undress in the safety of the darkness, her privacy safeguarded from onlookers. The boy was not sure what he was looking for but decided he would continue scrutinizing her sensual skinscape till he found it.

Months after the last voyeuristic session he happened to peer out of his window and look down at the street below, and noticed her lights were on. Quickly switching off his light, he tiptoed to the window and stared at her room. There she was again, reading one of her paperbacks, but this time she was not dressed in her nightgown. This time, she was wearing nothing. A satin halter-top draped horizontally across her secret smile was all that lay on her skin.

Kenny strained, as if trying to see each individual hair visible above the top, descending in a whimsical line to where the silky material of the top met and stopped further visual exploration. The girl's absent-minded caressing of the kisses of her woolly pubic hair drove the boy insane.

On the street, the lights from the other neighbours were off. Kehinde wondered if there were other peeping Toms gazing intently at this gorgeous spectacle like he was. He discarded the idea. *This is a private showing just for me*, he thought. Presently his neighbour got up. *She's going to turn off the lights and go to bed now. Probably touches herself in the dark like I do.* His dick went a notch higher as that thought whizzed through his mind like a silver bullet. At the same time his heart sank, as he realized he would not get to see this glorious woman pleasuring herself.

She walked to a wall at the end of the room. He looked at her wonderful posterior and gave thanks to the benign being who had deigned him fit to see this goddess in her most natural apparel. But she didn't reach for the switch. Instead she grabbed her hand mirror and took it to the bed with her. She then lay on the bed tenderly and spread her legs in a smooth languorous motion. The boy gaped as he caught sight of her gash. At that moment Kehinde didn't want anything more in life than to be in the bedroom stroking those pouting lips till she was sated and then begging him to undress.

She placed the mirror vertically between her legs and looked at her pussy for what seemed an eternity. Then, while holding on to it with one hand and still looking at herself in the mirror, she dipped one finger in her honeydew. As she rubbed back and forth, the boy clung on to the security bars on the window in his bedroom like an agitated crazed ape. The universe was still, watching this woman love herself. He was its eye.

That night, his own experience of solitary sex was his most lust-filled.

DIANA OMO EVANS

Journey Home

She was young and sweet
like the cocoa
her elders picked
under his forefather's whip.

What they noticed most were the insignificant things: the grace of sun heat resting inside their arms, the shadow of brown skin against green wet leaves. Dreaming. *Always dreaming,* their mother Anthea complained. Her large belly rested idly against the grubby kitchen unit, and she herself stood watching the two women, one foot balancing on tiptoe, her hair still rough and plaited from the night's insomnia. Dreaming. Her lips moving and words falling like she didn't know. Foreign words, Edo accents from home, 'nonsense', he always called it. Talking to yourself, he'd tell her in nonsensical drunken slithers, 'is 'he furz sign of mmmadnezz'. He'd shake a withered pink finger close to her eye and she'd lie seething on the edge of an explosion.

She could've killed him. Driven the rusty blade through his shirt, past the thick, hairy skin, through the ageing flesh which seemed to take on a dinosaur strength when he drank. Twist until there was only red, quiet and peace at last. Take her children home to the dusty ground and burning sun, trying hard not to remember how her own dreams had betrayed her. *The devil's country,* she muttered. *Evil spirits, let me be.* Her breathing had become tight, and she gasped softly, sipping milky tea to settle herself. Her slippers swished as she shuffled to the fridge to get the butter and tomatoes and carried them towards a table in the darkest corner of the room. His corner. Behind the door where he lurked through the black hours to confront his daughters when they came home late.

Kayla sat with Donna's head in her lap, watching her sister's long lashes glint in the sun. The warmth was bestowed by a lingering spring that showered and scorched capriciously. Beneath them the grassy earth was damp from the dawn's moisture. Kayla had a calming effect on

Donna, her 'lullaby voice' and 'soothing melancholy', Donna put it. The latter was the more lurid of the two, meeting confrontation and whispered praise every other step she took, often making Kayla feel like she had nothing to offer anyone, except her sister and mother, who had already crowned her oldest child heir to the domestic throne. She momentarily lifted and rotated her aching wrists, while Donna, thick brown knees pointing up at the breezy sky, carried on talking.

'Why does he have to do this? He's lucky, y'know, to have us. He doesn't realize he'd be nothing without us. I hate having to pretend things are fine all the time, when he's treating us all like shit.' For years Donna had wanted to leave home and get away from her father. She'd been saving all the money she earned from her job at the barber's where she spent three evenings a week after college and Saturdays, overlooking the male stares on her thighs and their thoughts inside her body. Almost seventeen, and she still didn't have enough to move out. Not that she'd leave without Kayla, who with her meek and sensible self seemed more ready to abide 'the ogre's' destructive ranting than resolve not to need him.

'He's just as abused as we are though,' said Kayla, aware of the forthcoming disagreement. 'He probably thinks the same thing about his mum. Last night when he was crying like that he looked so pathetic I just felt sorry for him.'

'How can you?' Donna retorted, lurching upwards so that the flat back of her uncombed hair made Kayla chuckle inside. 'He's a menace, even the neighbours are scared of him. And we have to live with him!'

They fell quiet as Donna sat right up and began picking bits of grass out of the ground. She couldn't understand her sister. What was it that made her so accepting of someone else's burdens? He was their father, yes, but abuse did not have to be passed down through generations like old clothes or bits of jewellery. Victims were responsible for themselves, just as her father was responsible for who he victimized with his own inner turmoil.

'It's your turn to do the stairs,' Kayla reminded Donna, always careful to carry out the tasks he set for them in angry times.

'I'll do it when I get back.'

'Where you going?'

'Just away, anywhere.'

'Don't be too long.' Kayla missed her sister when they were apart, especially at times like this.

'Come with me then.'

Donna knew she wouldn't. The women watched their mother wander out into the garden with a tray of food for them. Kayla thought she may have been crying, like she always did when her sorry husband had poked, harassed and shouted her down until 8 a.m., when he staggered off to work. The screams and high-pitched cries of the whole family bounced off the walls inside her mind. She remembered the blood dripping from her mother's mouth as he tried in vain to tug the passport from between her teeth. *I'm going. I'm going. I'm going home.* Their distraught mother had kept on shouting long after he finally ripped the papers from her, not wanting to remember that she couldn't really go anywhere. This was his house, his country, his world; they were fed by his money, clothed by him, all of them. She was his child as much as the girls were. Yet he knew nothing of who she was.

I'm going home.

She set the tray down, and Kayla reached up on to her feet to embrace her mother. She loved her White smile and soft skin, the coloured beads she wore and the way she took care of her hands, which always glowed, even when the snow fell. When they'd gone 'home' to Nigeria two years back, Kayla had been so proud of her. She walked strong, head high like an empress, shedding gifts and glory upon her admiring relatives. Kayla had watched her mother re-emerge, become joyful in the arms of her sister Rose. The two women had been entangled as children, so close they were, like twins. '*Ebava*', the elders called the two daughters as they stood hand in hand watching their mother's fingers weave thread into thread to make bright fabrics. Clammy nights would catch them giggling breathlessly to a perpetual stream of private jokes and innuendoes until their older brother would gruffly intervene. Rose had cried and cried at her sister's leaving. But their secret laughter never ceased to air their gloomy souls. And when Anthea came home, the two shrieked as one, stepping swiftly away to the space of light and life and love they owned.

Anthea's parents were strong figures in their community, her father's father a chief when he was alive. Their reactions to Anthea's inclination to marry a White man and inhabit the devil's own habitat frightened the stubborn young beauty. As far as she was concerned, she was the luckiest girl in the whole village to have been wooed and proposed to by a wealthy businessman from England, and under no circumstances would she decline the offer. Her parents blessed the union for the sake of her happiness, and Anthea became the first woman in the village to leave for White country with no chains on her feet. Times like this, when she came back, it was only her mother who sensed that Anthea's life was not as it should be. She had some inner curse etched beneath her skin that had not been there before. Mother would embrace mother, each one wishing she had never left her womb.

But they treated Kayla like a foreigner, disgusted with her for not being able to speak to them in Edo and outraged by her shaved head and unfeminine clothes. She could go nowhere alone and always having to wait for her cousin, Omo, in order to see or do anything was exasperating. Omo's friends eyed her with arrogant bemusement, whereas the girls who, perhaps, had she lived there, would've understood her better, exchanged quiet entertained looks when Kayla walked into a room behind him, in baggy trousers, no make-up, and a used jacket, looking so much like his sex. The adults simply and openly expressed their disapproval. A Western child should be grateful for her wealth and wear it for all to see. *She should be more like her mother. What is she teaching her?* Kayla had been glad when, six weeks later, they'd finally stepped back on to London streets. But even more grieved to see her mother shrink back into her old pink dressing-gown which kept her warm on cold, lonely days in the house that echoed so.

Donna was already shovelling omelette sandwiches and rice down her throat with a large spoon. The morning had faded now, and the day's chores loomed over their fleeting tranquillity. She hated it when Mum cried. It seemed to squash the juice from her heart. Kayla sat close to her mother, carefully placing her food in her mouth and occasionally taking a spoonful of the older woman's cornflour porridge. The sun beat hard now, and they could hear the sound of lunch-time traffic on the road on the other side of the house. Anthea took the letter, still unopened, from her pocket and gave it to Kayla to read to her. Moments later Kayla told her mother, 'It's from Rose.' Anthea's heart thumped and sent waves through her flesh. She looked at Kayla intensely, a frown of surprise and expectation straining her eyes in the bright light.

'My dear sister . . . we want you to come home . . . *Enene* is suffering again, and she might be ready to die. We don't know. She told me to tell you to come now. John said he will pay.'

Kayla opened another smaller envelope which had fallen out with the letter and found the ticket. Tomorrow afternoon from Heathrow.

Their mother's expression had changed to deep worry, tinged with slight and guilty joy. She wrapped the thick gown tighter around her and got up with the empty tray, jerking her head towards Kayla. This time she'd be going alone. Her brother was rich, almost as rich as her husband, and for him to send her just one ticket meant this was serious. When her mother fell ill like this, the family had to be together. For the first time since leaving Nigeria as a teenager twenty-five years ago, Anthea was alone. No White man's child no more. Kayla and Donna glanced at each other, also worried, not just for their grandmother but for their mother's intentions. They knew that any opportunity to return home was hope for her, and without them there she might not feel any immediate pull to come back to them, to him. They watched her stride sharply away to the back door and disappear in a heavy glimmer of pink through the kitchen door. Kayla ran inside the house after her mother to help her get things ready.

It was cooler now, as time crawled towards dusk and Donna let herself in through the front door. She'd heard the shouts even before she got to the front gate and nervous dismay began to reek havoc on her stomach. There he was again. Knuckles grey from ready fists, the lobster neck thickly bulging out of his white shirt. Anthea's suitcase was already packed and waiting in the hall-way for her departure the next day. Kayla stood at the top of the stairs as if struck by the devil's lightning. And Anthea. Anthea was the dark frame slumped over the bottom three steps. She was the red drops dripping from the reddened clothes. She was the head twisted at an odd angle to the rest of her. The passport lay just centimetres beyond her outstretched fingers.

*

His legs were rigid, his breath loud and short. 'You . . . belong . . . with me!'

She whispered, *Oddio . . . my name . . . my mother . . . I'm coming home.* And in another continent, a mother's womb opened to keep her child's spirit safe from harm.

IJEOMA INYAMA

Deeper Than Colour

God! Miss Halpern, our English teacher, is well renk! She reckons our class would be '*much more productive*' if we weren't sat with our friends. So she moves us about and makes us sit with people she *knows* we'd never sit with through choice. She's vex me *twice*, man! First of all, you don't expect to get treated like a first year when you're in the *fifth* year – I mean, her idea of a seating arrangement is well antiquated! And secondly, she's taken me from my spars, man! Ever since the second year, I've sat next to Heather Phillips, in front of Antoinette Varley and Takesha Brown. Now barely into the first term of the fifth and we get split up!

'Nadine Charles, I want you to sit next to John Danucci in front of my desk.'

Now she's vexed me four times, no, make that five. Sitting next to Danucci *and* in the front row. I can't believe it! Neither can the rest of the class. *Everyone* knows we're the worst pairing ever.

Let me explain some simple rudimentary classroom psychology, while I grab up my books and cuss my way down the aisle. See, I'm no roughneck, but I love my ragga and jungle . . . like the girls I go round with – Heather, Antoinette and Takesha. So naturally we get friendly with like-minded guys. Horace Batchelor's an example, 'Cept for Horace, the guys ain't true ragamuffins, but they do get a roughneck reputation 'cause they like ragga. Being Black helps. And if you can run the lyrics . . . well, you're talking god-like status.

But let me get back to Danucci. He hangs out with the 'trendies'. We call them the *Kiss FM posse*. They're into 'British soul' and buy their clothes from 'Hyper' – anything that's the latest t'ing. I mean, if it was thrashing two dustbin lids together, them lot'd be into that, no danger. So, us lot stick to ourselves, them lot do likewise – and never the twain shall meet stylee. I mean, if I went to some roughneck ragga sound dressed like them freaky deakies – some Barbarella meets and rough up Miss Marple kind of doo-lah I'd get nuff comments!

It must sound like something out of *West Side Story*, the Jets versus the Sharks. But it ain't. We don't have gang fights. Just a mutual under-standing that we don't have nothing to do with each other. And that's why me and Danucci are the worst pairing Miss Halpern could have made.

A ragga-loving, hardcore jungle *gyal* ain't got nothing decent to say to a trendy freaky deaky.

At morning break my situation is the focus of the playground discussion. Horace reckons that Miss Halpern needs '*hormone treatment*', or a good kick up the backside, or both, for what she's done. Then he hits on me!

'. . . and don't get no ideas!'

'Yeah, and I'm *really* your girlfriend, ain't I?' I snap. 'Besides, I couldn't go out with no freaky deakster. I'd be too shamed up to walk down the street with him!'

Horace has asked me out twice and twice I've turned him down. Truth is, I'd be too shamed up to walk down the street with *him*! I can't stand the way he's always got to have a comb in his miserable head – but does he ever use it? Now OK, I wouldn't get on the cover of *Black Hair & Beauty* (Takesha could easy), but I could sneak in between. So what makes a guy with no class, style, the personality of a crusty old pair of Y-fronts and looks that would make Godzilla a hunk think that I'd be interested in him? Try and explain that to Horace Batchelor. I've tried, but he won't listen. He reckons I'm the one for him. God knows why.

Two weeks and six English lessons have passed and I'm still sitting next to Danucci. I give him dirty looks, run down *Kiss FM* loud enough for him to hear and make sure my books cover at least half his desk. He ain't said a word to me. Maybe he's scared of Horace. But it really annoys me 'cause it's like I'm not there! He shares jokes and raves about the latest rare groove with his trendy pals – and they all sit around me, which I can't stand. And he exchanges loving glances with his girlfriend, Debra Haynes. She sits in the back row, two seats away from Heather. You've got to see this girl. She thinks she's *it*, her nose up in the air or looking down it at you. She's well facety! She thinks she's so hip in her clothes, but she always looks like she's wearing the clothes her grandmother gave her; which is probably the case.

Well, all that I can take. But then today Miss Halpern tells us she wants us to write a short story based on some aspect of our lives. Creative writing's got to be the thing I hate most. I get bored after writing one line! Anyway, she goes on and on about how she wants us to use '. . . *research as a means of getting information about your backgrounds* . . .' Which really means, bug your parents for the next seven days. I can't be bothered with all that. But Danucci and his crew think it's a great idea. Typical!

On our way home from school that afternoon, a crowd of us stopped by the newsagent's, ignoring the ten-foot-high sign that reads 'ONLY TWO KIDS AT A TIME'. And Danucci's in there with a couple of his trendy mates.

Hassle time!

Horace accidentally-on-purpose knocks into Danucci, whose nose is stuck in a music magazine. Danucci don't even glance up – Horace is well miffed. Then Takesha shoves me into Danucci and he almost drops the magazine. He glares at me. I'd never noticed his sparkling green eyes, his curly black eyelashes and . . .

'Nadine!'

My friends are all looking at me like I've grown a moustache or something. Danucci goes up to the counter with his mates to pay for the magazine. But not before giving me a look that could've had me ten foot under. For the first time I realize that he hates me as much as I hate him.

Talk about stress me out! I've got Miss Halpern on my back about that stupid short story I haven't written. Heather, Antoinette and Takesha on my back about fancying Danucci, and Horace on my back about going out with him. Well, before I crack up, I'm going to have one last go at getting some order into my life. '*Deal with each problem one at a time*' is my mum's favourite saying. First on my list is getting that story written.

Normally I never go near a library. Man, I break out in a cold sweat just thinking about one! But I force myself. The assignment's due in on Thursday and that's tomorrow! So in I go, on my own. I could've gone in with Antoinette and Takesha, as they love the library, but they'd already done their assignments. Heather *never* does assignments and she has the same aversion to libraries as I do – serious intellectual atmosphere, ughh!

I go straight upstairs to the study area. There are 'nuff kids in here, man! Swotting at the *beginning* of term? That's well sad, man! It's hunt for a seat time. I make my way past the tables. *No one was talking.* Can you believe that? Noses stuck in books. Disgusting! Ah-ha, a seat right by the window at the back. I could get away with eating my Mars bar without the crusty librarian seeing me. A freckle-faced, ginger-haired girl heads towards my seat. I throw myself into it. She gives me a filthy look and stomps off.

So I get out my exercise book and my Biros and take in the other kids around the table. Sangita, who's in the year below me; she lives in the library apparently. Tunde, a really quiet guy in my year – and the cleverest, Cheryl Watson, also in my year and a bookworm and . . . oh no! Danucci!

It's too late to move – there's nowhere else to sit. So I stay there silently cursing myself – 'til he looks up and sees me. (He'd had his head down in a computer book. That assignment's not due in 'til next month!) He kind of scowls at me, then returns to his book.

I can't concentrate on my story – it's that awkward. Ten minutes have gone by without us saying a word. This is driving me mad! I've got to say something!

'Look, I'm sorry about the other day in the newsagent's, but it weren't my fault.'

He looks at me, stunned, like he must've been preparing himself for aggro or something, particularly since none of his friends is around. But he still doesn't say anything.

'I said, I apologize. What d'you want, blood?' I hate being made to feel uncomfortable.

'Why?'

I can't work the boy out. 'Why what?'

'Why are you saying you're sorry when we both know you don't mean it?'

'Hey, you ain't in my head, so you don't know what's going on in there. But if you must know, I don't never say nothing that I don't mean. "*Better to offend than pretend*" is my motto.'

He folds his arms across his chest, looking triumphant. 'Not so hard without your mates, eh?'

'Neither are you.'

'I don't bother you, but you're *always* bothering me.'

A librarian near by tells us to be quiet, so we are for about half a minute. Then he goes: 'Is that your English assignment?'

I stop doodling on the page. 'Nah, I'm designing a hi-tech kitchen for my mum's birthday present.'

The librarian is glowering at us.

'So what's it going to be about?' Danucci asks.

'How the hell do I know?'

He's getting as narked as I am, and I feel my conscience prickling . . .

'I don't know what to write,' I whisper. 'I don't know *how* to write.'

'It's easy. Write about what you know.'

'Oh yeah? As easy as that? So what did you write about then.'

So Danucci tells me his short story. But he has to tell me outside 'cause we get kicked out.

Massimo, the guy in his story, is about eight or nine. He teases – no – bullies is more like it, his next-door neighbour's son Haresh, who's around two years younger. He'd call him 'paki' and stuff 'cause that's what all his friends at school did, bully Black and Asian kids. It was a mainly White school. Anyway, one day, Massimo's grandad Alfonso (I love the names) came to visit, overheard the name-calling and abuse and ordered Massimo inside. Alfonso told Massimo how hard it was for him being an Italian immigrant in the late thirties and forties because of Mussolini and that and also because he was well dark, being Sicilian. He told Massimo that he was shaming him by insulting Haresh. Massimo felt really bad because he loved his grandad (basically because he spoilt him rotten). Then Massimo ended up in a secondary school which was racially mixed and he had no problem forming friendships which rivalled the UN in their racial and cultural diversity.

'Our school's nothing like the UN.'

'So you guessed Massimo is based on me.'

'Just call me Einstein.'

He laughs.

'There's no way I could write like that.'

'Sure you can. Write about what you know.'

I look at him. 'I don't get it. Why are you helping me?'

He's about to answer when I spot my spars coming out of McDonald's. I freeze. Danucci sighs. 'You want me to disappear, right?'

They'll see us any time soon. So I goes, 'Well, you'd do the same.'

He's got that same look he had in the newsagent's. 'Would I?' And he crosses the street in a huff just as they spot me.

The past three days have been a bummer, an all-time low. Oh, I got my assignment done and handed it in on time, no worries there. Except that it's crap. No, it's my friends that have been stressing me out – big time – with the Danucci thing. They've been saying that I'll be trading in Redrat for Jamiroquai. Yesterday, Horace got me so vexed that I cussed him about his nappy-never-see-comb head. As for Danucci, he won't so much as look at me. Worst of all, that's what's bugging me the most! I know now why I hated him so much. I was *making* myself hate him because I knew I *liked* him. But now with him ignoring me I feel so depressed I can't eat or sleep let alone think properly.

Enough is enough! I'm going to sort this mess out. So I write him a note and pull it in his desk before English class. If he still wants to know, he'll meet me by the huts after class.

'Ain't you afraid to be seen in public with me?'

I shrug my shoulders. I know he's pleased I left him that note. His green eyes are twinkling like crazy.

'I want to apologize.'

'Like last time?'

'You're making this really difficult.'

He leans against the wall. 'Good. You really pissed me off the other day.'

'I know and I've been suffering since.'

'Friends giving you a hard time?'

'*You're* giving me a hard time.'

Silence. I count the stripes on my hi-tops; one, two, three . . .

'I've always liked you Nadine.' He says it so softly.

'I'd never have guessed.'

'And as you wrote me a note . . .'

'Yeah, I like you, too. I guess I was trying to hide it by giving you a hard time.'

He smiles at me. 'I ain't saying it's going to be easy if we're friendly-like, my friends'll give me a hard time, too, you know. But I would never cross the street if they saw me with you. It depends on how much you want to be part of the crowd.'

'I've been really miserable since that day, I feel like I'd be living a lie if I kept . . . you know, pretending.'

'Better to offend than pretend, right?'

'Is Debra Haynes your girlfriend?'

He shakes his head. 'Is Horace Batchelor your boyfriend?'

I roll my eyes.

Then he pulls me close to him and we kiss. Then he puts his arm around me as we head towards the playground, where everyone will see us! I ain't going to lie and say I feel a hundred per cent comfortable about it. But for my own peace of mind, I've got to give it a go. Especially since I've just written a short story about it. I mean, it's got to be a first in our school: a ragga-loving junglis girl going with a trendy freaky deak.

ANDREA ENISUOH

The Holiday

Natalie shook Davina roughly. 'Come on, wake up, you're not sleeping away our holiday.'

Davina reluctantly opened one eye and, groaning loudly, she turned over, her sheet still wrapped tightly around her. 'What time is it?' she croaked sleepily.

'It's eight o'clock and we've got our welcome meeting at ten. Before that we've got to shower and have breakfast – so get up!' She continued to shake her friend.

'All right, all right.' Davina sat up in the bed, her long blonde hair flying everywhere, a sulky impression on her sleepy face. 'We are meant to be on holiday, aren't we?'

Natalie sighed in exasperation, 'I'll use the bathroom first, shall I?'

Before Davina could answer she heard the bathroom door slam shut.

As Natalie showered, her mind raced over all the things she wanted to do while in Kenya. She hoped that Davina wasn't going to be too much of a bore. In an ideal world the girl wouldn't have been Natalie's choice for a holiday companion, not Africa anyway. Ibiza was more Davina's thing, sleeping all day, dancing and copping off all night. But when Natalie had won the holiday in a phone-in competition on Breeze FM, they'd informed her she had only a week before she had to travel. Of all the close friends that she'd rung, not one of them could get the time off work.

'M'dear, yuh joking?' Linda had laughed. 'Yuh 'tink that Mr Big-Shot Campbell will let me go gallivanting 'round Africa at a week's notice? Sorry, girl, that can't work.'

Even her sister had turned her down.

'Oh, come on, Diane,' she had pleaded, 'just think about it, me and you in Africa – the homeland. For two weeks we can leave dry London behind and mix with our peoples. I can't believe you're saying no.'

'You know I'd love to go,' Diane had replied. 'If there was any way I could, I'd be there. But, darling, this term is really important. If I'm going to pass this course then I need to get some good results. I can't afford to go anywhere.'

As a last resort Natalie had called her old schoolfriend Davina. She was all right really, quite a laugh usually, but she would never understand how important a trip to Africa was to Natalie. For Davina it was just another holiday, all the better as it was free. But, for Natalie, going to Africa was the most exciting thing she could ever do. Of course she'd been to Jamaica, loads of times, Mum and Dad made sure that the whole family went over regularly; for them it was important to keep in touch with home. But Africa – it was a dream come true for Natalie. She just wished that she could be with someone who'd appreciate it as much as she did.

At the welcome meeting they were greeted by a slim holiday rep with huge white teeth, brunette hair and a plastic smile. After distributing brightly coloured fruit-cocktails to all present she began the meeting. Her name was Helen, and she had a strong Liverpool accent. She told the twenty or so who were there that she had been in charge of Mombasa tours for this particular company for five years. 'And I can honestly say,' she gushed, 'that Kenya is the most beautiful place that I've ever been. Really, it's just too beautiful for words, it's an absolutely stunning place.' She then warned everyone not to venture too far from the hotel complex – unless of course it was to go on a tour organized by her company. 'The people here are very poor,' she said, her grin as wide as ever. 'They'll do almost anything to get money, so you have to be very careful. Even the little kids will try and con you.'

Natalie nudged Davina, her expression incredulous. 'Racist bitch,' she muttered.

'On top of that there have been a lot of violent political riots recently – though there is no need for alarm, and we still say that Kenya is a safe place to holiday. We do advise, though, that no party ventures out on their own.'

Jimmy needed to stretch his legs. He lifted himself from the splintered wooden bench and began to pace the length of the shelter. He was feeling impatient; he had been waiting here over an hour now. The hot sun bore down on him; even though he was used to the heat, sweat drenched the loose khaki shirt he was wearing. He was feeling thirsty. He glanced at his watch – already ten o'clock. The watch was quite an expensive one. A silver Sekonda, it had been one of last season's gifts; he vaguely remembered the tourist who had given it to him – an English gentleman by the name of Alistair.

Alistair had paid Jimmy over 1,000 shillings to be his guide around Mombasa for the week. He could obviously afford it; from what Jimmy could remember he had said he worked with computers. He was spending a week holidaying in Mombasa before he went off to Masai Mara on safari. So for a week Jimmy had been his guide. It had been easy money. Like most tourists, Alistair spent most of his time sunbathing by the hotel pool. Occasionally he would want to go into the city, to a craft market or on a nature trail, and it would be Jimmy's job to accompany him there and back. All he had to do was lead the way and shoo away the legions of street-traders and beggars who would inevitably descend on him. Easy money. The timing couldn't have been better, as his wife had just given birth to their first child, a daughter they named Wanjiru. Yes, last season had been a good one for Jimmy. Due to the riots there were fewer tourists in Kenya this year. That would mean that he would have to work extra hard to make money.

'Could you believe the way she was carrying on?' They were back in their bedroom, and Natalie was ranting to Davina, who was too busy deciding what to wear to listen properly. 'Don't do this, don't do that, is this a prison camp or what?'

'She may have a point,' muttered Davina, pulling on a pair of shorts she had bought for the holiday. 'God, my legs look white – I hope they tan quickly.'

'No, she hasn't got a point.' Natalie was still ranting. 'All they're bothered about is making money for their company. Well, I'm not staying stuck in this hotel when there's the whole of Mombasa to see. I think we should go and have a bit of a look round now. What do you think?'

The good thing about Davina was that she was easily led. 'Yeah, we could do that. As long as I get back this afternoon to do some serious sunbathing.' Davina slipped out of her shorts and into a sarong-style skirt. 'That's better. Shall we go now?'

Natalie smiled. Perhaps having Davina with her wasn't going to be as bad as she thought.

Out of the corner of his eye Jimmy saw the girls approaching. The Black girl caught his attention first. Tall, with glistening ebony skin, she wore a long blue sleeveless dress that was clearly well made. Probably one of those designer dresses that so many Westerners could afford. Red varnished toenails peeped out of her opened-toed, high-heeled shoes. Definitely a tourist, no local would wear such impractical footwear. His attention drifted to her friend. A White girl of about the same height; she wore similar attire but had a much lower-cut top. He laughed to himself. White women loved to show off their cleavage, even if they had nothing there.

'Jambo,' he called out, startling the White girl.

Natalie smiled broadly. 'Jambo,' she replied. Turning to her friend, she announced proudly, 'That's Swahili for "hello".'

This was going to be easy. Jimmy quickly rattled off a few phrases in Swahili, pausing only when Natalie held up her hand.

'I'm sorry,' she said. 'Do you speak English?'

'Ah, English!' Jimmy feigned surprise. 'I thought you were from Kenya.'

Natalie giggled but was clearly flattered. 'No, I'm from London, England. We're on holiday.'

'Welcome home,' Jimmy replied, before turning to Davina. 'And this is what they call an English rose?'

Davina smiled politely.

'This is my friend Davina, and I'm Natalie.'

'My name is Jimmy. How long have you been in Kenya?'

'Well, this is our first proper day. We arrived last night. We thought we'd come out and do a bit of exploring today.'

'And where are you staying?'

Davina looked at her friend in warning. Was she going to ignore everything the holiday rep had said?

'Malanga Hotel.'

Jimmy stepped back with a surprised look on his face. 'But that is where I work. Coincidence, eh?' He rattled off a story about being a nightporter and then quickly changed the subject. 'Kenya is a beautiful place. There is a lot to see. Nature, crafts, different races, everything in Kenya is beautiful. Why don't you let me show you around?'

'I don't think . . .' Davina was getting worried.

'Oh, that would be brilliant,' interrupted Natalie. 'The thing is that we don't have very much money.'

The charming smile never left his face, 'Ah money is not important, I already have a job. I show you Mombasa, and you tell me about England. I would like to go there one day, and I would like to hear all about it. Deal?'

Natalie looked to Davina for agreement. Davina shrugged, knowing that Natalie would do what she wanted anyway.

'Come,' said Jimmy, flagging down a rickety mini-van full of people. This, he informed them, was their bus. 'First I shall take you to the craft market.'

Davina and Natalie squeezed in between two other passengers in the back of the van. A man who seemed to be collecting fares thrust his hand out in front of them. Everyone else stared at them with amused looks on their faces.

'What are they staring at?' hissed Davina to Natalie.

'I don't know, maybe they've never seen a White girl before,' Natalie replied, scrambling in her bag for change. After about five minutes the van screeched to a halt to allow more passengers to board.

'For God's sake, there's no room for anyone else.' Davina was not enjoying the ride at all. 'I don't even think this van is roadworthy, you know.'

Eventually, it seemed they had reached their destination. Jimmy beckoned from the front of the van where he had placed himself. Clambering over the mainly male passengers, Davina and Natalie stepped out on to the road.

'I think before we go to the market I show you my village. OK?' Jimmy knew they would be shocked when he showed them the village. He'd seen it hundreds of times before; there would be shrieks and gasps when they saw how his people lived. Though he hated exposing his life in this way, he knew he had to do it. He decided that today he would lay it on extra thick; he had a feeling that the Black English girl would be particularly affected. They walked for about ten minutes before he turned off the main road. A few yards ahead the girls noticed a dilapidated hut with a crooked sign boasting 'drinks and food for sale' in red, gold and green lettering. This, the girls guessed, was the village.

Goats and fowl wandered freely, local children played, teased and chased them. Natalie seemed fascinated. Jimmy led her and Davina past many huts, most of which, he explained, were family homes. He told them how they were built out of basic materials and how one small hut often housed huge families. Then he led them to the village school. Though the school was shut for the holidays, he knew that even the state of the building would move them.

'This is our school,' he said, pointing at yet another small, ramshackle building. 'There is never enough of anything for the school. Everyone must bring their own chair to sit on.' He noticed Natalie shaking her head sadly. 'There is never enough of anything. Pens, paper, everyone must find their own to use. Maybe next time you come to Kenya you could bring pens and paper for our children?'

'Oh definitely,' the girls said in unison. Jimmy briefly showed them the village church. It was a large building, which, he explained, would be packed with almost every village inhabitant on Sundays.

'Now, I will take you to the craft market,' Jimmy said finally. Just as he was about to lead them out of the village, a tall thin man came running towards them, speaking rapidly in what the girls presumed was Swahili. Looking startled and upset, Jimmy turned to them. 'I'm sorry,' he said, 'I will have to leave you – I have had some very bad news.' He looked close to tears. 'My baby daughter, she is very ill. She has malaria, a very bad kind of malaria that attacks the spine. I'm afraid' – he paused to compose himself – 'I'm afraid that she may die.'

His friend touched his arm supportively and took over the story for him. 'You see, here we have to pay for everything, even hospitals. If the baby doesn't go to hospital she will surely die. But Jimmy cannot afford hospital costs.'

Natalie and even Davina were now close to tears. 'How much are the hospital costs?' Natalie asked gently.

Jimmy now rejoined the conversation. 'I don't know, perhaps 500 shillings.'

'You must let us help.'

Natalie looked to Davina for support. Davina, not even sure how much 500 shillings was, nodded her approval.

The money was handed over. Jimmy explained that he must get back to his family immediately and led the girls out of the village to the nearest main road to get a bus and find their own way back to their hotel. 'I am sorry that I could not be your guide,' he said.

'Forget that. We just hope that your daughter is all right,' replied Natalie.

'God willing she will be.' Jimmy kissed each girl on the cheek and left. Sauntering back to his home, Jimmy wondered at how gullible Westerners were. He thought of Natalie and laughed out loud. So desperate to be a real African, so desperate to fit in here. What ordinary African did he know who could hand over that kind of money without wincing. As he got closer to home, his train of thought was interrupted by his wife, who was running towards him.

'What is it?' he asked, realizing immediately that there was a problem.

'It's Wanjiru,' cried his wife hysterically. 'Our daughter has malaria.'

R. AKUTU

Counting Fruit

The kitchen holds its face in its hand, watching me dart from left, where
the chopping takes place, to right, where the cooker stands. She doesn't
watch over my shoulder or sing like she usually does but sits at the table
observing me as the stew begins to bubble and my eyes wonder on the
emergence of spring outside and note the need to cut the overgrown
grass in the garden. My brothers Ike and Chim can be heard from
the sitting room, debating the football match just finished. The phone
interrupts us. I pick up the extension from the counter beside the cooker
and hear his voice. It sounds clear and deep like cold bottled water from
the fridge. I am thirsty.

'Speaking.'

'I'm Anthony. Anthony Ikedi from New Jersey.'

I lose my thirst.

Auntie Bessie cornered me at the Onitsha women's dance last Saturday.
There I was, with Osadebe blaring in one ear, Auntie Bessie in the other
and me nodding my head like a fuzzy dog on a dashboard, the word 'yes'
coming out of my mouth before I realized what she was suggesting.
Trying to retract that yes was like trying to retract your finger from a
bread-slicer when it's already shredded.

'Are you still there?' he asks in his American-spiced accent.

'Yes, I am.'

'My sister told your aunt that I was looking for a wife . . .'

I cringed on the mention of wife.

'. . . They thought it would be a good idea if we got to know each
other,' he says.

I notice that he as a young voice, much younger than I was expecting.
I had visions of someone almost my father's age calling, but not so, not
so cute-sounding. Curiosity raises its head like a ten-month-old baby; it
matures, then bursts out like an adolescent schoolchild at dinner-time.
'How old are you?'

'What?' he asks.

'I said, how old are you?'

'You're direct. Thirty-eight,' he laughs.

I do the arithmetic, eight years' difference, borderline, I think. What the hell am I doing? Borderline for what? Just speak to him and get the hell off the phone.

'How old are you?' he asks back.

He catches me off guard, 'Thirty, thirty next month.'

'Your aunt tells me you're a doctor.'

'Yap.'

'Snap,' he says.

'What area?'

'Paediatrics,' he answers. 'And you?'

'Liver disease.'

'No kidding,' he says. 'That's my speciality, liver complaints in kids. Do you enjoy it?'

'Yes. Yes I do.'

And I think, this can't be happening, I'm talking to him, put the phone down. But instead I untangle the telephone wire, turn down the fire under the stew and join spirit kitchen at the table. My love for my work takes command of my tongue and matches the words out of barracks. I try to stop them but the troops just keep coming. His army joins mine in peace.

It's seven-thirty by the time I'm ready to put Sunday dinner on the table. There are five of us today; Dad, Ike, Felicia, Chim and myself. Mum is at her women's meeting, she won't be back till nine, and Janet, my older sister, isn't at home any more. She lives with her Caribbean boyfriend, Russell. Mum doesn't approve, of course, but none of us talk about it any more, it only leads to arguments.

I place the rice, stew, moi moi and plantain down on the dining table in the sitting room, then call everyone to dinner. We sit to eat; the bowls of food are passed round the table, dishes clink as spoons knock against the white ceramic dinner-plates.

'Who were you talking to in the kitchen?' asks Dad.

I stop the passage of rice and stew half-way between the plate and my mouth.

'Some man from America,' pipes in my little brother Chim.

I am mortified.

'What man?' Dad asks, probing further.

'The one Auntie Bessie gave Hope's number to,' answers Chim for me.

I want to throttle my noisy little brother; mostly I would like to know how he knows this information, but I see a look cross my father's face. He already knows. There's only one way he could know.

I feel my heart sink. My thirtieth birthday is fast approaching. You see, father has always been a modern man, my mother has always fought against this. He believes in love, not in arrangements like she does, but in my community to have two daughters over thirty and unmarried is a silent failure that pokes up like a pus-filled spot; no one mentions it, though this failure is ripe and you can bet there's a queue waiting to squeeze it.

'How did it go?' he asks.

'Fine, just fine,' I answer. 'Excuse me. I forgot the salt.'

I go to the kitchen and cry. Mum has won.

Anthony's letter arrived this morning; I feel the envelope in my left jean pocket. I sit outside in the garden with Janet. Having just cut the grass, the tangy smell of green tickles my nose, the shed sits quiet again in the far corner, and the wooden fences that partition us from our neighbours smile at the new sight of lawn. Mum and Dad are out visiting, the others are elsewhere in the house.

'He sent it,' I say to Janet.

'I don't believe you. Are you crazy?' says Janet. 'Some strange man calls you up from America . . .'

'He's not strange.'

'OK, some bushman calls you up because Auntie Bessie tells him to and you're talking to him.'

'He's not bush.'

'Well, he has to be if he has to get his sister to find him a woman . . .'

I've always been more traditional than Janet. It used to puzzle me why Mum's friends would speak English to Janet and Igbo to me, maybe it's because she sits like she doesn't quite belong, like a stray dog that's not sure if it should approach; I know they feel this and leave her alone.

When I was young I used to enjoy going with Mum to visit relatives when Dad was working late. Janet would always choose to stay at home with the younger ones. One day, Mum took me to a wake. It was like nothing I had ever seen before – the abundance of food, men taking pictures, women dancing with a framed picture, it seemed like a party to my eyes. But mostly I remember the songs they sang; they sounded so triumphant, I wished I understood more, belonged more. Mum gave birth to the other half of me that day.

'. . . And as for you, you must be desperate,' says Janet.

Maybe I am. I didn't think that at this age I would need to resort to this, I want to tell her how lonely I am and that I'm fed up of being jealous of her. She couldn't understand, of course. You see, Janet has never been alone.

She looks at me and relents. 'Let's have a look then,' she says.

I open the envelope tentatively and the photograph falls out into my hand. I don't want to look. Over these two months I have built a house around our conversations, furnished it and filled it with the children that come with my dreams. Its walls are flimsy on the air they are built on but, nevertheless, energy has been spent and I don't want the picture to fade away like a batik that's seen too much sunlight. We both look at it.

'What do you think?' I ask Janet.

'I don't know.'

'What do you think?' she asks back.

I look closely at the picture. It's dark in the background, like he's in a nightclub, and he's smiling, not a cute, sweet smile or a manly smile, quite plain – plain is better than ugly, but even ugly has the power to set off something inside.

'He's OK, isn't he, Janet, he's not ugly, is he? I mean, he's OK, he's not ugly, but he's not good-looking?'

'He looks a bit old,' says Janet.

'No, not too old. He sounds young, though. Besides, you can't tell from a picture, it's a bit too dark. Anyway, it's the man inside that counts, not his looks.' I say this to myself more than to Janet.

'If you ask me, dump him. He has to be a loser.'

'Not all of us can be like you, Janet.'

'What do you mean?'

'Never mind,' I say.

'No, say what's on your mind.'

'Leave me alone.'

'No, say what you want to say.'

'Leave me alone, Janet.'

'Say it.'

'Not everyone finds love your way, Janet. Sometimes you don't get that many options, sometimes you just don't get lucky.'

'What you talking about?'

'Look at me, Janet, look at me. I'm a thirty-year-old spinster and maybe, just maybe, this is the way it's gonna work for me.'

'What's wrong with you, have you lost it? You just haven't found the one for you yet, that's all.'

'Then why is it I'm the only one in this family who hasn't got someone? Even Chim's got a girlfriend.'

'Hope, you sound so childish. You know what your problem is, you always see what you want to see. Take a look around you. Do you think I'm having a great time, do you think Mum and Dad are having a great time . . . ?'

'What do you mean? What's wrong with Mum and Dad? What's wrong with them?'

'Nothing, you just get me wound up sometimes, and I just say things. All I mean is, you have this romantic notion in your head about everything, you've always been like that.'

'But you and Russell are so great together.'

'Most times it's bloody hard work. To tell you the truth, most times I wish I was like you. It's not that I don't love Russell, it's just that you don't have to compromise on what you want to do, you don't have all that extra baggage. I used to have so much fun looking for Mr Right it was great, all that flirting and being young.'

'I hear what you're saying, but I want what you have, what Mum and Dad have. I'm not getting any younger, and maybe this is the way it was meant for me.'

'Let's change the subject. This one's making me depressed,' says Janet.

We sit back in the deckchairs, the sun has cooled down, and a light breeze is beginning to stir. I look at my watch; Anthony is due to call, like he has most Sundays since the day he started.

I stand peering out of the second-floor window, waiting for Anthony's car. It is humid, and the sun beats down like a playground oppressor. I peel my dress away from my back, looking up and down the road. Britain is having one of its freak occurrences, a heatwave; there is no sign of him.

He called me two weeks ago saying he was coming to visit family here. So here I am, nervous and not really knowing what to expect but hoping against all hope that it will be all right. When we talk over the phone it's great, it's like talking to a good friend, we laugh and joke but, I don't know, will my house crumble?

A minute later he pulls up in a hired blue Cleo. I watch him get out and walk toward the front door. Christ, he's short.

The door-bell rings. I go down to answer it. I look through the spyglass. He's *damn* short.

I open the door, he walks in. Shit, he's about the same height as Chim when he was nine. His trousers are belted up under his armpits. Janet was right, he looks old. His hair is short, patted down into shape. His trousers are beige; this beige clashes with the lime of his shirt. As for his shoes, the patterned white-and-brown shoes – what can I say? I thank God my brothers are not in to see this. His appearance does not match his voice. I'm confused.

My Mum and Dad stand behind me. He nods his head and greets them, and I grab my coat. Dad begins to ask him who his father is, what village he comes from, what does his father do for a living? What district does he come from? I try to get him out before Dad can sit him down under the spotlight and interrogate him – and before my siblings return.

'So, which restaurant do you want to go to?' he asks, rubbing his chubby little hands, once we're out in the open.

'There's a local Indian place round the corner that's good,' I answer.

'Fine,' he says.

We get in the car and I direct him. We arrive at the restaurant, where the waiter shows us to a booth and hands us the menu.

Anthony looks around the booth. 'Everything here is so small,' he says.

I nod my head sweetly. There is a battle being fought inside me between the side that finds him physically repulsive and the side that found him mentally attractive. Four months of talking over the phone can't be all wrong. We got on so well. It is possible for attraction to grow, isn't it?

'That's what I love about America,' he says. 'There's nowhere like it.'

I nod sweetly, then stare at my menu.

'You can do anything you want there.'

I continue to nod sweetly.

'You just have to set your sights on what you want and you will do it.'

The battle between physical repulsion and mental attraction is now fifty-fifty.

'I got my citizenship last month.' He looks at me as if he is expecting a reaction.

'That's nice,' I say.

'Do you know how much I earn there as a doctor? There isn't any other country where you can earn as much.'

I don't respond. Physical repulsion is winning.

'Do you know, someone at your level could probably earn anything from £150,000 to £175,000? How much are you earning here, what, £10,000? £20,000?'

'Well, it's OK, but I much prefer working in London,' I reply.

'You have to be kidding, right? It's nice and all, but everything's just too small, it's like trying to squeeze yourself into a cup when you could have a king-sized tub.'

'Well, you of all people should know size isn't everything. Is it?'

He goes silent. I've done the worst thing a woman can do to a short man.

Physical repulsion has obviously won.

I am sitting in the dark in the kitchen listening to Mum and Dad arguing in mumbled tones. They don't know I've returned. I have images of the house I built, of him, and me, married and arguing just like them. I shudder at the thought. Mum and Dad are like a jigsaw puzzle, they fit. Marrying Anthony would be like taking a pillow and suffocating my babies. I start to cry because I want so much, I wish so much, I need it so much. I cry because I have this picture in my head of what it could be, and I want that picture, the picture that I created of Anthony and me in my head. Four months of hoping and believing have been blown away by an hour in his company.

I do what Dad taught me to do, I go to the fridge and take the bowl and start to fill it with fruit, one for my job, one for my health, another for my freedom and peace of mind, one for my sisters, and so on. I continue like this until I have filled the bowl with all the things I am grateful for and then I start to take out fruit for all the things I wish I had and put it on the table. There is only one fruit. I look at the bowl over-brimming with fruit and back at the one fruit on the table. One fruit, and that is only a fantasy, not like the reality of the fruit in the bowl. I laugh because I have so much, I laugh because I'm happy, I laugh because I am grateful to God.

Mum enters the room and turns on the light. 'What are you doing?'

'Counting fruit.'

She looks at me as if I've gone mad and decides not to ask any more questions; after all I am my father's daughter.

Memoirs

LEONE ROSS

Black Narcissus

I looked at the poster of Michael Jackson and sneered at my friend. We were both thirteen, hanging out in her bedroom in Jamaica, indulging in the usual preoccupations of girldom: boys, grades, music, gossip.

'I always thought that was a stupid idea,' I said, airily, pointing at Michael.

'What?' she said. She gazed up at Michael's café-au-lait features and the tiger he held to his breast. These, of course, were the days when Michael had a colour. Her pupils dilated. I could actually see them spreading across her eyes: tiny black balls of pleasure.

'Putting posters on your wall. I never liked anybody enough to be a fan,' I said.

I still remember those words because they were to come back to bite me on my proverbial ass. It wasn't Jackson who did it for me, or Grandmaster Flash's mischievous, pro-Black arrogance, or even the DeBarge brothers (and they wet a lot of knickers in those days!). For me, it was always Prince. Every bit of his doe-eyed, high-heel-booted androgyny.

Most of my friends don't believe it, but it was his song lyrics – not his eyes – that pulled me in. It was 1984 and I was nearly fifteen. From the first moment my then-boyfriend put him on the stereo, and I heard The Man crooning about wanting to be my lover, to be the only one that made him come . . . running, I was hooked. My boyfriend didn't get as much as a kiss that day. I just made him play me Prince's second album (the only one he owned) all afternoon while I sat on his bed, enthralled, asking: *who is this man?*

For a romantic teenage girl intrigued with the still-untasted proclivities of adult sexuality, Prince was the ultimate fantasy figure. He wasn't afraid to talk about sex, but his raw, uncompromising lyrics were undercut with mischief, a little-boy playfulness that hinted at mere voyeurism. He wasn't scary: his music, despite his bad-boy image, was about more than doing the nasty. It was about rejection, about longing, about first-date nerves, about emotion. Next to the inarticulate bravado of the boys around me, all lines and no substance, my fifteen-year-old virginal self fantasized about Prince, who would say pretty things, then take me to bed and do it . . . slowly.

And so the one-sided love affair began, no more extraordinary than the crush of any teenage girl but certainly interesting in its longevity. Prince sang his way through my life; he grew up alongside me. I wanted to be a writer, and the first piece I ever published, at fifteen, was in *Penthouse Forum*, an erotic fantasy starring Mr Nelson himself, who would have been only twenty-six at the time. *Penthouse* paid me $60 on a fuchsia-pink cheque, and I felt grown up.

It was Prince that I played when I was low, when a boy hurt me, when I wanted to be positive, when I wanted to feel strong and free. He sang his way through my exams and my tears, and he was always waiting for me at parties. I am sure that it is no coincidence that he was a fair-skinned brother, gazing down from my walls at my own fair skin in a country where I was affectionately teased as 'the White girl'. I am sure that it was no coincidence that his androgyny worked on my blood as I figured out and embraced my own bisexuality. For me, this pretty man was the ultimate looker, and I laughed privately when male friends called him a 'battyman' because he wore lace. I was already dismissive of gender roles, and he was the only man I saw playing with them. I am sure that it is no coincidence that I loved his roguish 'I-don't-give-a-damn-I'm-gonna-sing-about-oral-sex-and-masturbation-and-S&M-and-lesbianism-and-if-you-don't-like-it-you-can-step' attitude, growing up in a conservative country, where religion was the backbone of society and good girls didn't talk about it, even if they were doing it. I remember laughing my head off the year that Michael Jackson thanked 'the girls in the balcony' at the annual Grammys, all squeaky-voiced and fey. That was the same year Prince thanked *his* fans in a silky baritone that would have been respected by James Earl Jones and Barry White alike. By that time the posters had taken over my bedroom, and my mother was a little worried as I swanned around the house, Walkman on, singing 'When Doves Cry': 'Maybe I'm just like my *mother* – she's never satisfied.' I was his 'Darlin' Nikki', chuckling through his ode to female masturbation; in 1985 I wore a 'Raspberry Beret'; in 1986 I was careful to 'Kiss' only those men who acted 'their age, not their shoe size'; as AIDS became a household word by 1987, I rocked to *Sign o' the Times*; I wore yellow and black and my hair slicked back to celebrate *Lovesexy* in 1988. I took lovers who liked his music.

The posters followed me through university and were carefully packed when I left Jamaica for London to do my Masters degree. I was scared in the face of this emigration but comforted myself with the fact that my father had front-row Prince tickets waiting for me. I took the first man I ever lived with to the concert, and alarmed him when I refused to dance as mayhem swung around us. Dance? I was too busy drinking in Prince's face, yards away from me, humping the piano, sweet-talking his dancers, undressing the microphone. I only moved when he threw a bracelet out into the crowd and I threatened homicide on the heads of all the other girls who dived for it. I wore it once, then tucked it away, terrified that it would drop off one day and be gone for ever.

As real adulthood nipped at my heels, with its first job and the paying of rent, the obsession began to get embarrassing. I still played Prince on my Walkman at work when I was tired and the deadlines shook their fists at me, but I took the posters down after I coordinated a photoshoot in my house and the stills were rejected because Prince's face distracted the eye from our models (but of course! Who was more gorgeous than my baby?). I became a little tired of being the man's unofficial spokeswoman ('Why didn't he sing on the "We are the World" song?'; 'Why has he changed his name?'; 'Don't you think he's crazy/weird/ gay/sick/a terrible actor?'.) And of course, I had my own concerns: when his obsession with the scantily clad women on his stage strove against my feminist politics, I comforted myself that he mentioned big women in *Gett Off* and insisted on women of all sizes and ages being idolized in his first independently marketed video, *The Most Beautiful Girl in the World*. After all, in the highschool magazine that I'd edited, my profile had read: 'She loves Prince. We think she wants his wiry body which, despite years of exercising and dieting, she has been denied.'

Nevertheless, his politics seemed naïve. As gangsta rap made its name in the early 90s, the world was moving closer to the hard-core scream of disenfranchised Black youth. Prince's rainbow-tribe band and his 'get-your- kit-off-and-it'll-solve-all-your-problems' motto seemed very 80s. Sure, he sang about race and drugs and poverty occasionally, and I pointed out *Sign o' the Times, Ronnie Talk to Russia* and *Controversy* as cases in point, but it didn't seem enough.

As Prince's career moved from the heady days of *Purple Rain* to the critically lambasted *Graffiti Bridge*, it seemed less *de rigueur* to adore him. But I still did. He came to London every year around my birthday, and I bought tickets for each night and pretended it was only the two of us dancing. I remained in a six-month state of excitement the night I went to a Press party that he was supposed to attend, had just given up on finding him, then spotted him scurrying through a little hallway in the Limelight. We stared at each other for a few precious seconds, then he grinned and was gone. I screamed blood when I found out that he'd scooped six fans into his departing limo and taken them to McDonald's that very evening.

Ultimately, it was Prince who made me realize that dreams do come true, that if you want something very badly, it comes to you. The girl who never thought she'd see a Prince concert, living far away in Jamaica, and then saw one, the girl who never thought she'd look into Prince's face and then did, finally interviewed him. Oh yes, I did. 1 March 1995. I was doing a shift for a friend at a London newspaper, a shift I hadn't wanted to do, and the call came through. I hung up the phone on the actress I was interviewing and fled to Wembley, cursing the gods for the fact that I'd worn no make-up that day, but at the end of an hour Prince and I were laughing, gossiping and hugging. I was twenty-six years old, and for the first time in my life I believed there was a God who saw all things, believed all things and felt that it was quite appropriate for a little Jamaican girl to tell one of the pop icons of the twentieth century that stew peas, ackee and saltfish and a couple of fried dumplings would put some meat on his little-boy bones.

He was no disappointment either. He was funnier than I'd expected, more articulate than I'd expected. And I was reminded that he was – regardless of his personal obsession with spirituality-that-is-genitalia – a professional man knocking forty, a Black brother who got his first contract with Warner at seventeen, who defined a generation with his music, who accompanied many a young woman – and man – through the turbulence of adolescence. I wonder if anyone will ever research how many women lost their virginity to a well-placed Prince song on the stereo?

A year after the interview I named my first novel after some lyrics in a Prince song, but already the madness was waning. Two years after that I asked my publisher to remove any mention of The Artist Formerly Known As . . . from my professional biography (it read that I'd interviewed him). This was no longer a sign of adulthood, but the edges of yesterday, a stamp of girlhood.

The posters and the T-shirts and the press cuttings and even the bracelet now live in a dusty box in my cupboard. I am officially unobsessed and am no longer the first person at Our Price when a new CD hits the shelves. I haven't even trawled the Net for web pages on him (even though a little bird told me there are . . . hundreds). But any time I feel down, I take out the music and I listen again . . . and laugh, remembering the girl that I was. Remembering the woman Prince Roger Nelson has helped me to be: confident, sexual, in-yo-face, unashamed. Me.

KECHI NWAJIAKU

To Be or Not To Be Black British

In the beginning we lived in Scotland. It was only supposed to be for a short time, while daddy got his degrees and mummy got her nursing qualifications. We then tried to 'go home', back to Nigeria. With pomp and ceremony, kitchen cabinets, beds and wardrobes, we arrived on a big boat. But it wasn't much fun being Igbo in Lagos just after the Biafran war, especially if you were on the losing side and could speak only broken English with a Glaswegian twang.

> Oyinbo Pe-Pe
> Ifi Ifi Pe-Pe
> E go yellow mama

A hopscotch clapping song – kids in Lagos used to tease us with for being too 'White'.

We lasted a year. Mummy had had enough of not being able to get a job. So she packed her bags and her five kids and we all left, for England this time. Daddy followed later. Huddled together with our bundles of belongings, we arrived one cold night in Piccadilly Circus with its flashing lights and too many cars.

I was five when I started primary school and stopped talking. It was 1974. My Glaswegian accent was far too Scottish for east London's liking. It was bad enough that my sisters and I were Black, and that our hair was plaited with thread, like horns. I desperately wanted to blend and have hair that moved when I did. So I watched and listened and smiled and nodded or shook my head until I learned to speak cockney. For a while we spoke Scottish at home and cockney at school. But eventually cockney seeped through the nooks and crannies of our home. Like overgrown ivy, it took over everything.

'Haa-aa-llo-o, Daa-daay', soon became 'All righ', Dad,' as memories of Glasgow faded and Walthamstow's dulcet cockney tones took pride of place amongst latent Surulere smells. My father soon put a stop to it though. How a could a *Whole Accountant* allow his children to speak anything but 'the Queen's English'? Why else would he have refused to teach them Igbo? He wanted to make sure that their accents would never give them away. So 'All righ', Dad' became 'Good Evening, Daddy,' and we learned to speak with BBC voices and eventually settled down.

I'm sitting here in Senegal, thousands of miles from England, trying to remember what it feels like to be Black and British and wondering why it should make any difference at all to my life now. My brow begins to furrow and my laughter lines become fraught as the uneasiness creeps into the back of my neck. Escaping my Black Britishness was why I came here in the first place.

When people ask me where I'm from now, I say I'm Nigerian, adding as a deliberate afterthought that I've lived in England most of my life. This explains away my English accent and wards off the possibility of a backlash which comes with being Nigerian proper. Nigerian here is synonymous with drug dealer, '419er' (swindler) or prostitute.

Being Black doesn't mean much in Senegal, where the majority of the population is African. Although wealthy as individuals and as a group, White people (commonly known as Toubab) are a minority here and no longer have the political authority to Black-label anyone who is not White like themselves. Senegalese rarely describe themselves as Black, unless referring specifically to those amongst them who are quite literally black in skin colour.

Being Black in Britain often felt like being Black on someone else's terms. Black was not a language I spoke, or indeed a culture I understood or owned. Black was what I was called outside the warmth of my home. Inside, I was Nigerian, with a heavy dose of Roman Catholicism of the Irish variety. Although I couldn't speak a word of Igbo, I spoke English beautifully.

A Senegalese friend once asked me how he would recognize a Black person if he saw one in London. I stared at him quizzically, wondering whether this was a trick question. I immediately referred to colour, then began to lose myself as I struggled to describe attitude, culture, dress sense, music tastes and other variables which became meaningless as I went on.

'Are you Black then?' he asked.

Suddenly I wasn't sure any more. Maybe Black was just something other people said you were.

Being Black in Britain meant being of a social category, equivalent to or lower than working class. Racism perpetuated this myth, as do Black people themselves, in search of a collective identity. I could never fit into this category. I was Black, but very middle class, damn it! The product of a grammar school and university education, I spoke posh – 'as if I had something stuck up my nose'. I didn't have many Black friends, I didn't hang out in the right Black clubs, I couldn't street-wise my talk at a split second's notice. I just wasn't very 'down wit' it'.

What was worse was that, politically, I was really conscious and committed to the idea of being Black, acutely aware of 'institutionalized racism'. At work, where, apart from the receptionist, I was once again the only Black face, my presence served to ease guilty White consciences and I became a so-called spokesperson on Black issues.

Being Black in Britain was often a lonely experience.

Out of synch with my surroundings, sick and tired of feeling like an outsider in my own skin, I took off in search of a world where being Black was not something one had to prove but was a given. My six-year flirtation with Africa, where I now live, hasn't resolved all the tensions around Blackness. Questions of shifting identities, belonging and not belonging, are part of the tapestry of everyday life. Living in Senegal has sharpened my sense of just how much my Black British heritage has informed my view of the world. However, distancing myself from life in the British Isles has given me the space and freedom to feel at ease enough to review how I feel about this heritage, deciding what I take with me and what I simply leave behind.

SOL B. RIVER

Memories of Stillness

Memoirs – memories of what? All my days sometimes seem to be one, yesterday I was four, today I'm some other age. A thousand years is like a day in God's sight. Can a man write his memoirs whilst he is still in his twenties? Depends what he's got in his memory.

If I wrote everything I heard and saw, I would work even less than I do, so I'll keep this sporadic, simple and confused like my writing . . . and these few short words of memoirs should come from the feeling of whatever the moment was at the time. I'll attempt to speak about whatever influenced and drove me to the page. My writing has been described as disturbing and unsettling, but it's not that I ever meant it that way.

The truth is, I could say and I have said many things over the course of time. My notion was that Black and integrated theatre from casting to programming was taking its time. The truth was, that it was being held back and hacked at. I believed time was a second ago and that things could change over night. I still believe that.

I began writing in 1993. In 2000 I announced my retirement from solely writing two years ago. In 1994 I got one of my first real breaks and became Writer in Residence at the West Yorkshire Playhouse, a position I was glad to accept. Eighteen months later I left. I felt twice my age. I remember saying to my English teacher at the age of fifteen that some day I might write a book; she asked me to repeat myself and then she laughed. I remember the laugh . . . like you do. I left school with what you can call no prospects – except drama. I had decided that I would become an actor but was discouraged when I saw the parts on offer. My mother once called me a coward, and she was rarely wrong. Cowardice is something I considered long and hard . . . until I got over it. Just fear God.

I decided to take the long route and write scripts so that I could appear in them. But I discovered an agenda, it was an agenda that was to swallow me up, engulf me, entice me out of my bed in the middle of the night and force-feed me first thing in the morning. All I did was write about what I discovered until I could no longer pick up a pen. My major influences were from the 1970 Brazilian football team to Terence Trent D'Arby from Fred D'Aguiar to Jean-Luc Godard. Beckett has also been an inspiration. To date I have written thirteen plays and have begun to move into film direction, since that's where the larger audience lies. Theatre would sometimes have you travelling into oblivion until you met yourself coming back. I'm not sure what film will do to me yet. My aim was always to combine acting, writing and directing.

I should mention *Moor Masterpieces*, which was performed with Tyrone Huggins and Larrington Walker in 1994 at the West Yorkshire Playhouse. One of the most memorable things that happened during its run was my family turning up to see the first performance. After the show they seemed to spread themselves all over the theatre. I kept on having to ask where my mum or brother was, or where my sisters or my father had got to. They were talking, laughing; they, for that moment, belonged in that theatre, they had seen a play that said something about them and their lives. I remember being so very happy. Just for those moments my parents were proud of me. Since my mother could not be there when I graduated, the memory of *Moor Masterpieces* sticks out more than ever. My mother always used to give me this big kiss on the cheek and say, 'Well done, love.'

The enigmatic Jude Kelly, artistic director at the West Yorkshire Playhouse, created an opportunity for me which was closely followed by Yvonne Brewster, artistic director of Talawa Theatre Company. I remember writing *To Rahtid*, a twenty-minute piece which was eventually performed at the Young Vic Studio under Talawa's umbrella. It was performed by Angela Wynter. It was a pleasure to have Yvonne direct – and to have a director who knew how to get rid of a writer at the right time. I was glad to go. I'd been paid, and I was learning to let go of my work. It was around that time that I began to separate the art from the finance with a precision that caused someone to say, 'He's behaving too god-like.' The thing was, I learned how to negotiate for myself and distinguish the art from the contract. No agent at that time wanted to represent such Black British work. It's not easy negotiating on your own.

Have you ever dreamed you were in a dark tunnel and the route is only one-way? Have you ever lain so still that just the thought of moving your body is worth nothing. You're just still. Stillness is my main memory; at the moment my body is most quiet. I remember everything and feel nothing. Body wet with memory, saturated in disillusionment, wallowing in regret – in the pit of unhappiness. On my own.

I have heard of an artist's blue period; it always sounded amusing and pretentious. I like the colour blue. The philosophy of my writing was that there was an agenda and that agenda concerned the Black Diaspora in Britain. Once I had addressed this agenda within my work, the naïve idea was that we could all move on, playwright and audience. I did what I could, I do what I can. I discovered that art is a big place. I want to try another colour of mood.

I can't say writing has made me in any way happy, although it has earned me some respect I might not deserve. I'm still waiting to write that masterpiece, but even if I do, I don't expect to be congratulated to my face, because I'd be dead . . . I think that's the way it works.

I remember my mother saying not long before she escaped this world, she said that she wanted to travel on a train. I said, 'Mummy, you haven't been on a train?' She said, 'No, I'd like to go on a train.'

Let me count myself lucky then, because I have been allowed to do what I want, that I was nurtured the way I was. My writing put me in touch. I have been allowed so far to say what I feel and what I have learned, and despite this, that and the other, there is an energy to continue.

UJU ASIKA

Two-Tone Chameleon

Tell me about your schooldays, the best days of your life.

I remember this. The endless stretch of rippling wheat-fields and the unfamiliar stench of country air. September skies heavy with blue-grey clouds hanging low as my bottom lip. Fallen leaves trembling like small brown hands on the road ahead. The winding lane that goes on for ever although for ever is never long enough.

Our car pulls up outside the towering grey building. I open the door and place a size-three shoe print on the gravel with a desolate crunch. My brother and sister run ahead to join the throng of high-pitched voices and scampering feet. I glide along polished floors and hear the echo of my heartbeat in the hall. The slamming of a heavy door.

My parents are in the warm, carpeted study of the headmaster, drinking tea, eating chocolate Bourbons and discussing my fate. Outside I stand knee-high among strangers. The children around me seem twice my size. Boys and girls bounce holiday stories back and forth in front of the fireplace. Another newcomer, with sulky lips squashed between bright red cheeks, narrows his eyes at me and clutches his mother's hand.

Through tall, arched windows I watch a golden Labrador playing hide-and-seek with its own tail behind rhododendron bushes. There are acres of green as far as the horizon. Chestnut trees are shaking conkers to the ground. It is mango season back home. I imagine my cousins scraping bare brown legs to climb and steal their neighbour's fruit. Small pockets of loneliness form at the bottom of my stomach.

The supper bell rings. Children in striped dressing-gowns and furry slippers shuffle down to the pantry for their first meal away from home. I have no appetite. For seven days I will throw up at the taste of cold shepherd's pie, sour rhubarb-crumble, soggy bread-and-butter pudding. I would rather swallow tadpoles than toad-in-the-hole. I will grow sick with longing for the comforts of white rice and red stew, pounded yam dipped in egusi soup, fried plantain and black-eyed beans.

'*Bonjour, mademoiselle.*' I turn and bump into Madame Evans, formidable pince-nez and tight grey bun, who speaks to me in French. '*Comment t'appelles-tu?*' A smile freezes on my face and I nod stupidly like your typical foreigner. This is how the camera will capture my first school photograph: seven years old, head tilted slightly, Afro curls springing to attention, name-tags stitched the wrong way round on my navy cardigan and pleated skirt, and that light blue polyester polo-neck itching around my throat. '*Tu parles Français?*' My eyes strain towards the fire exits until she moves on to haunt another victim.

Climbing the wide front stairs, I find the bedrooms, following the clinical smells and names of English heroines: Pankhurst, Nightingale. I meet Alice, who will become my best friend. She is wearing pink flannel pyjamas and a pageboy haircut. One hand holds a stuffed elephant while the other is stretched out to welcome me.

I sit softly on the bed, noting how thin the covers are; noting that I have forgotten my duvet and I might freeze to death this night. This last thought cheers me up. My accent switches immediately, almost imperceptibly I blend. Two-tone chameleon.

Did I see them from the window or close up? My parents, waving, the car driving away, hardly any time to say goodbye and cry. Another door slams. Nigeria is already a memory, and my sister has been claimed by bigger, older friends. My brother will barely speak to me all term. I sleep on the bunk bed below Tamsin, and as she leans down to whisper good-night, her fine blonde hair is a brief curtain for the English moon. Something tugs and gently rips inside me. Tomorrow a White face will wake me up.

EVELYN GOODING

You Just Have to Get on with It

I left school at the age of sixteen, not really knowing what I wanted to do, so I went to college for a year and took my RSA stage 1 in clerical procedures. Then I decided that I definitely wanted a job. I was offered two and took the boring one because I thought it was stable. It was stable all right, stable and *dead* boring! After several other jobs I began to realize that something was missing, as I only ever enjoyed one job thoroughly, and that was working as an insurance retail sales clerk.

A few years later came the low point in my life that was to shake me up and make me realize what I really wanted. It happened when I was twenty-four and the mother of two boys, both under five. How disappointed I was with myself and my life – I felt that it was slipping away from me. I had two lovely, adorable children, but no sense of direction, no finance, no emotional stability – and a broken leg (caused by the father of my kids, so he wasn't there to support me). This was the worst time in my life. I spent six months at home, more or less housebound. I cried a lot, in pain, unhappiness and loneliness.

I really and truly could not see the light at the end of the tunnel. Horrible thoughts of permanent unemployment haunted me. I had to pull myself together, if only for the sake of the children. In the end, I did so with lots of support from family and friends. It was a long journey, and I never gave up, but I did despair and I did lose faith at times. But words of encouragement and support helped me through this long and difficult journey.

I started to think and plan on paper. What did I want to do? What would be the best route for me? What about the children? What about their needs? I decided that education was the way forward, and with two young children to support for the next eighteen or more years, financial stability was on my mind.

The thought of working with children appealed to me, but in what capacity? Eventually, I decided to apply for jobs working as a classroom assistant with primary-school children. I was soon offered a job in a nursery, then in a primary school, and after that in play centres and in a secondary school, working with children from all kinds of social and cultural backgrounds. I began to study part-time to teach primary-school children and to refresh my skills in maths, which I felt were very weak. I did this for a year and then enrolled on an access course in teaching, full-time. This presented a challenge for me, as the last time I had studied full-time was in 1986. It was now seven years later.

My eldest child had already started school and my youngest was attending the college crèche; everything was looking up. Studying was a financial strain though, as I had only income support to live on – but it was worth it.

During this period I built up my self-esteem and confidence and applied to university to do a primary-teaching course. I was offered a place. During my time at university, I found it difficult, as tutors and lecturers were neither clear nor supportive. I found myself doing re-sits, which did nothing to boost my confidence.

My strength, I found, was working with children in the classroom or in a play situation. However, on my last teaching practice I was told by the university that I had failed. I was devastated, largely because none of the tutors at the university had bothered to explain to me properly why they failed me. Even though I appealed, up to this day, no one has given me a good reason why I failed or gave me any advance notice, during my teaching practice, of any mistakes I was making.

Completing my two years of study, I gained a diploma in higher education. I managed to secure myself full-time employment within a local authority within six months of having been dropped from the teaching course. At present I have a new job with the same local authority, working as a family-link officer, with children, their parents and schools.

In the future I hope to finish my studies and earn a degree in education, social policy or in the social-work field. For the second time in my working life, I am content with my job, and I am making good progress. I work with families, and there are lots of training courses available via social services.

The main point to remember is that we all have dark periods in our lives, but they can become brighter and brighter until the light shines through. In the mean time, always have faith, because faith will get you through, with perseverance and determination.

MICHAEL HAMILTON

Run Reverend Run

It's raining heavily. I pull up outside the Camden Forum, London. Security takes a look at my photography equipment and, surprisingly, kindly lets me straight through.

'Yo, man, Run DMC been on for fifteen minutes.'

Enter, King of Rock is blasting at full decibels – one bungle a noise. A sea of Amorites (pale-skin people) are in the place, kitted out in black, skeleton skulls. Every motherfucker stinks of liquor, shit! What am I doing here? I thought this was a rap jam, didn't Run announce in the early nineties that he converted to Christianity, vice/versa Antichrist? When their only release I respect came out, 'What's It All About?', with a fly video. Hoping this was a start of a new era for them, promoting positive messages to the youth and known in the industry as fantastic live performers.

After ten minutes I had no doubt. They launched a full attack to completely blast off I man's eardrums. Making my way to the front to get some good photos, them brutes started jumping up and down like grasshoppers when the intro started for 'Walk This Way'.

Spilling beer, I quickly escaped to the corner front stage – 'Oh no, look pon them speaker box deh, come like a house.'

After Run tore the place down with 'Mary, Mary', he announced that he is now a minister, and his rhyming partner is also a convert. While he pledged his allegiance to Jesus Christ (yeah right) he's Raising Hell in the venue, and on Sunday he'll tell his congregation, 'Peace be with you.'

The only part of the concert that I smiled at was when the three sons of DMC came on stage and performed a basic freestyle.

After the concert Jam Master Jay was signing at the T-shirt stall. To my amazement security came up to me. 'Where's your press pass!'

'I don't have one,' I replied.

'You can't take no photos.'

While quickly calling for back-up I exited the scene. Of all the other professional photographers, security chose to pick on me.

I noticed everyone looking at me, thinking, 'What is this nigger doing in here?' The funny thing was all the blue-eyed nigger guards gave me that same cold stare. I had unsuccessfully tried to get a press pass four times.

Returning home, my head was banging. I was thrown completely off balance, feeling hyper, even though I hadn't slept for thirty-six hours, entering the kitchen humming 'The King of Rock' bass line, shit! Do you know that feeling when you're sitting at the traffic lights and out from nowhere this Spice Girl song enters your subconscious? Then you wonder to yourself 'Why am I singing this crap?' Hiphop is now controlled by demonic corporations; they have succeeded in bringing about a downward spiral in the youth world-wide. Once we had acts like the Last Poets, Sugar Hill Gang, Doug E. Fresh, Stetsasonic, Divine Stylistics, Kurtis Blow, Fab 5 Freddy, Eric B. & Rakim, plus the mighty Afrika Bambaata and the Soul Sonic Force. All this grew from the need of the oppressed Blacks/Latinos, who experienced racism, poverty, miseducation, homelessness and lack of knowledge of their identity and culture. It was a voice for the voiceless.

The majors started to introduce the heavy-metal aspect – remember when Grand Master Flash and Furious Five sold out to heavy metal? Then they introduced Run DMC, Beastie Boys, Onyx, House of Pain, Anthrax (which is a mental disease), Natas (which is Satan spelt backwards), Cypress Hill, Death Row and a whole host of others (for the deep info seek the books penned by Dr Malachi Z. York, the wisest man on the planet).

This resulted in making slang trendy, and bad posture, negative rap; they intended and succeeded in designing a new breed of degenerates. Look at the trend in the clothes – saggy pants, ripped jeans. Jamaican street-gangs had ripped their jeans or whatever when having clashes and would return with knife slashes or bullet holes in them. It became a trend. The wearing of trainers with no laces came about when bad boys went into the penitentiary and the warden would confiscate their shoelaces in case they hanged themselves.

Today they want our children to learn ebonics in school. The corporates have it in their music/movies etc. . . . What will happen when a youth can't get a job because he can't even spell, read or write properly?

Do you recognize the similarities between rap and heavy metal? Rap is the Black man's version. Remember the story of the Pied Piper, who led all the children astray, playing the flute? In this is a serious message. Run DMC also rapped about this; coincidence? No, we don't believe in coincidence. What does 'Run DMC' mean anyway? I don't know, so I will make something up. Well, 'Run' must be running as fast as he can from the truth, and 'DMC' must mean Devil's Mind Control.

Now I fully overstand why certain artists are always chanting down certain sucker MCs.

Rap music used positively is a powerful and popular form of music. As the pioneer Dizzy Gillespie said, 'There's gonna be a day when all Black music is fused together, and boy I know I'm gonna be around to see that day.' You were right, Dizzy, you passed on, after rap had its last positive cycle.

Rap music is just a product of our time, the synthetic music must be made in the best tradition of our culture. I ask myself, why don't my people listen to the great artists of our time?

KRS-ONE, CHANNEL LIVE, BLACK SHEEP, POOR RIGHTEOUS TEACHERS, GANG STAR, ICE CUBE, PUBLIC ENEMY, ROOTS, BUSH BABIES, JERU, SILENT ECLIPSE and ARRESTED DEVELOPMENT.

A human being can elevate him- or herself to a god on Earth, or a mere mortal, a brute.

Music should be a healing force that tunes us in with nature's look at our ancestors; they communicated with the power of the drum. The Nubian drum is synchronized to our heartbeat, perfect harmony with perfect sound vibration. Check this. Abdullah Ibrahim says, 'They call me a jazz musician, that's incorrect. (1) When you make the sound *oooh* you feel the vibration on your lips; (2) when you make the sound *aaahh* you feel the vibes in your heart; (3) when you make the sound *eeeee* you feel the vibration where? At the top of your head.' So we always knew we were sound scientists. Sound masters. As I heard a European so-called professor say on TV the other day, 'Where does sound go?' Listen to the sound of the steel pan, hear the note rise up and up, music is a key to the universe, it tunes us in, we should listen and learn how to play organic music made from nature's materials.

Yes, we are sound scientists.

Forward ever, backward never, in any endeavour, always stay clever, beware of false prophets in black leather.

PEACE OUT

RAFIEL SUNMONU

Living to be Me: Teenage Reflections

Wednesday 19 January 1983 at 3.25 a.m. I was 'born into the suburbs', as the Nike adverts would say. My mother was born and raised in London, while my father was born in Nigeria. I don't hear many family stories from either of them. I know that all my grandparents spent time studying in England in the sixties and then returned years later. Their stay in England was temporary; home always beckoned, even though they owned houses here. My existence, on the other hand, despite my African origins, lies within British culture. I sound British, and I am happy with whom I am. I do not carry the excess baggage that begs to know where I am from, and I am considered to be snobbish because I went to private school and have outgrown the people I used to play with at the weekends when we dug up worms. Some of those friends say that I am 'bigging up myself', but I just do not see the fun in hanging around telephone-boxes or loitering outside the local fast-food restaurants with nothing to do but collect unwanted labels from people who prejudge what we are doing.

My mother chose an infant school several miles from home for me because she thought it was good; the headteacher remembered her from when she was at primary school, which felt strange.

Her motto is 'Education, Education, Education', something passed down from her parents and theirs. But I wasn't pushed to excel to the extent that it would put me off, like some relatives were. Mum just gave me the confidence to believe that I could achieve. My secondary school, which I chose from the offers I had, suited me perfectly, and I thrived there.

I walked into a barber's shop in Brixton once, and the first thing the stylist said was, 'You're not from around here, are you?'

I sat down in the chair and started to reflect on what he was actually saying.

I resided in Kent and I was my parent's son, which is exactly what I told him. But taking out the flippant aspect of the conversation, I knew exactly what he meant. He could tell that I was not raised in a Black community. Yet unlike my mother, I do not feel the need to crave acceptance in the African world. I am like my father: I can identify with the land of my birth; there is no need to conjure up images of a distant land that I have visited only four times.

For me, there is nothing in between, nothing to make me feel not African enough. No cousins to tell me what I am missing, no parents to deliver the strong message of home.

I am the third generation, becoming removed from Mother Africa. Does that make me British? Yes, I do tick the 'Black British' box when asked questions about my origins, but if you ask me if I call myself British, that is another question for which I do not have an answer. I cannot confess to denying the African part of me, because I do not, but it is something I am not often called upon to think about. It is not a burning issue for me. I am more interested in how to achieve and how to be accepted on my own terms. I live in an area that is not reflective of myself. My parents say that means I have to work hard, focus on my goals and not let anybody deter me from getting where I want to be. I have lived outside London and in the same area all my life without, in a sense, actually being a part of it. Yet walking into that barber's, I felt that I had nothing in common with a Black British community and its stereotyped lifestyle either. I sometimes feel the odd one out for several reasons. Even though I have more or less internalized the norms of the people around me, colour stands before me, and maybe it always will.

Saying that, when I wake up in the morning, I don't scrutinize myself or recant a mantra, 'You are Black.' There is no need, as I know that it goes deeper than that. It is something that one is reminded of subtly all the time, and I learn by day and over the years just what it means. Yet I know that with my ebony skin, raven-coloured hair and a winning smile and personality, I can be nothing but proud of myself and who I am. *That* I know is unquestionable.

There are quite a lot of racist slurs painted in designer scrawl in the local alleyways and near the train station. I absorb the messages but discard what I perceive to be ignorance. It just serves to make me more determined to achieve because I take it that the artists will for ever be perfecting their mindless craft, spelling mistakes included, on somebody else's property. While they go shopping for paint, I'm busy plotting where I intend to be in the future.

I'm thinking of becoming a lawyer when I'm older, and even though it is a very competitive field, I can do it. I still remember when my mother and I saw a boy in his school uniform and she said, that's the school that you will be going to. It is a school that consistently reaches high standards in its GCSE results and is highly rated. That's where I'll be going for lower sixth.

I remember the time when a woman watched me go into the news-agent's on a school day. I wasn't in school uniform and she made a point of asking me if I was skipping school. I got a great deal of satisfaction telling her that I was on holiday early because I went to private school. From her face you could tell that she looked at me and saw made-up stories of who she thought I should be, not who I was.

In a sense, I am jealous of my younger brother, as he did not have to take any entrance examinations. Instead he plays sports 24/7 dividing his time between the local football team and a well-known athletics club. It seems unfair that as he approached the secondary-school stage he did not have to sit any exams. My parents' theory: he shouldn't be driven too hard before he is ready. In my reckoning, that was not the logic my grandparents would have invoked. Work would start immediately. If I had mentioned an interest in sport, there would have been a lecture. 'Sport! Which of your cousins waste their time playing sports? Did your uncle who is a doctor think of a sporting career? No. Your cousin who is a barrister? No. Shola who studied at Oxford? Indeed not. If I ever hear you mention it again, I'll help you break a world record in this house by running from me!'

As it is, my brother has the opportunity to do virtually what he feels like. Maybe I should wonder where I fit in, where I belong, but that's for the future. I am just Rafiel Sunmonu, the individual, and I'm concerned with holding on to the important key to what I believe is a prosperous and positive future.

JJ AMAWORO-WILSON

What I Found Amongst The Ruins

Imagine a man naked in the street in broad daylight, weeping as the sun wanes. Imagine him holding one framed photo and a brown-edged copy of the Koran, with his house behind him flattened into a pile of rubble.

Cairo, 1992. Being half-black, half-white, I was a token Egyptian. It was my second year there, teaching English to kids in a school in Giza. A glance out of my classroom window, and there were the pyramids. A moment of silence, and you could hear the bells of cows jangling beyond the playing fields, the Nile winding towards us.

It was a day like any other day: sunshine and calls to prayer, greasy felafel lining my stomach. I was taking a football session after lessons. I wanted to join in – I was twenty-two years old then – but I refereed instead while my Mohammeds and Ahmeds and Khaleds ran wild.

It happened with ten minutes to go: the ground shook. For a second we swayed, then all was normal again. I looked at the boys. Had anyone else noticed? They played on. At the final whistle I asked what it was.

'The soldier test bombs in the desert,' said Rami, a twelve-year-old, and I believed him.

We piled into the school buses waiting faithfully outside to take us home – some for the West, some for the East. I'd forgotten about the shaking of the ground, sitting there, my arse burning on the black plastic seat too long in the sun, with a pile of books in my satchel.

We followed the Nile, on a road lined with palm trees. We passed tourist hotels and fishermen. The buses were old and suspension-free and the roads older, so every bumped jagged your body. As we hit Sharia Giza, heading for central Cairo, the traffic thickened and smoke plumed from ancient exhausts.

An old dilemma – windows closed and sweat to a cinder or windows open and breathe carbon monoxide for an hour? As usual I breathed in fumes. It was a route I'd taken twice a day for a year. My eye was trained for all the oddities you could find and I'd seen a few in my time: a dead camel once lay on the main road for a full week; a lorry burning by the river bank just weeks before. But what I saw that day went beyond comparison, and it crept up on us slowly. There were people, too many people, sitting or standing, doing nothing. Along fusty Giza they sat on low walls, clutching things: children, chickens, pots and pans. Even the area of Zamalek, with its glitz and golden shoes in the shop windows, had too many people milling. Heading down Sahafayeen and Shobra, where families were squatting in the dust, this was where the truth dawned. We saw, behind them, their houses reduced to stone chips and yellow clouds in the air.

There was an eerie quiet. I saw just one man weeping and I heard no wails. The mosques pierced the sky, and the imams called the flock to prayer, as normal. It was the same but not the same. A shisha pipe with its glass caved in; a chair with a broken back; ornaments; porcelain dolls stupidly intact. The fellahin – the poor, who lived as they could, in ramshackle blocks and houses of shards and thatch – were hit the worst. The nation that built the pyramids also built its fellahin castles on sand. When the earthquake came those buildings toppled and crumbled like matchsticks. In the modernized areas, urban development had led to extra floors being added to already feebly made skyscrapers. When the earth shook, the towers came tumbling.

In the bus the children grew silent. The sun burned high, bathing Cairo in heat and light, and under it whole communities sat waiting. Waiting for what? For their homes to reconstitute themselves, for time to unwind or rewind, for the morning to come and be like any other morning? Where could the families hide themselves and their possessions now? Where do you go without walls, without roofs?

A boy called Badr, sitting in the seat behind, tapped my shoulder.

'Mr JJ,' he said, 'what is it?'

'An earthquake.'

He didn't understand.

'The ground breaks,' and I showed him with my hands.

'What happen the people?' he asked.

'Look around you.'

He was silent again.

One by one the kids were dropped off at their homes: smart, glowing blocks of flats, some with driveways and palm trees. Sometimes there would be a boab (a houseboy) watering the garden with a hose, his trouser-legs rolled up to his knees, waving in a greeting to the child as if nothing had happened that day.

I lived in Dokki, a moderately wealthy area, and I was the last off the bus, so I saw that none of the kids had gone home to rubble. My block, too, remained standing, damage free.

That evening I heard it all on the World Service. 5.6 on the Richter Scale. It sounds like nothing, but 5.6 will shred a hovel into kindling, rip the guts out of anything jerry-built. Extent of damage: unknown. Casualties: thousands. Foreign powers pledged their support and their technology. My round of phone calls began: checking on colleagues and friends and looking for more information.

Later that evening I went for a walk. I crossed the busy Dokki highway, past the Sheraton Hotel and over the first of the bridges that took you to Midan Tahrir, the hub of the city. I got on a bus, jammed to the rafters, cockerels under the seat, big-eyed children on knees, baskets of limes and cinnamon, and managed to squeeze in by a window. Life going on.

The bus was heading towards the City of the Dead, a suburb of tombs where the living cohabit with their ancestors, though it was not the destination but the journey that drew me there.

Peering into the darkness, I saw men and women retrieving things, starting again. A child was rolling a tyre along the road. Two brothers, maybe my age, were collecting planks of wood and laying them side by side. A girl hauled a bicycle from a mound of debris, its chassis twisted out of shape. I remember thinking that if she rode it, it would go in circles for ever.

They were off their knees, off the low stone walls, starting again under the gaze of Allah.

The following morning at 6.30 I got a call from the headmaster. They'd found a crack in the wall of the school. It would take a week to repair, maybe longer. It took a month.

Imagine a pile of stones and a patina of dust. Imagine the sun beating on your back and all around you laid waste by the shifting earth. Imagine your children in your arms and all you have – lying broken on the ground. Imagine digging in the remains with your bare hands and finding your roots and your strength. If I learned anything, it was that heroism is the ability to endure, to weep in public, stripped of all, and then to reclothe yourself, the ability to stand up and start again.

Half-black, half-white, I roam the world incognito. I have sat in a thousand cafés with their whirling fans, sweat-soaked walls, the smoke clouds of five continents ascending in their own heavenward meanders. I have listened to the click of dominoes, the low thunder of bombs, and the chatter of tongues alien to me. All of this pales in the memory when set next to that one tableau, beyond comparison: a line of families sitting still, flat earth behind them as wide and empty as the Nothing ahead. And all I know is this: when the earth shakes for me I will crouch in the rubble, look hard and dig deep. And maybe find my roots.

NYANTAH

The End

Before, when I was about to cry my fingers would tingle. I would always feel that tell-tale pinprick in my fingers before it reached my eyes. Now, I don't cry. I cried all the tears I had to cry when he left. I did nothing but cry; believe me, non-stop crying is exhausting. Crying is impractical – it makes your nose run, your eyes puffy, and it solves nothing. When I stopped crying I still had nothing. I had no real warning that it would end.

'What's wrong?' I asked.

He replied, 'It's nothing to do with you – it's something I've got to work out for myself.' That 'something' turned into 'I don't love you any more.' That turned into me throwing the ring that had been cut for my finger back at him.

I turned into an extra from an American soap. I remember standing against a wall for support, but my legs gave way and I slid down like a prisoner on the day of execution. His words hit me like bullets from a sawn-off shotgun – at close range – blowing a hole right through me.

'We never get to see each other any more,' he said. I was in my final year at university, project deadlines were looming, and all I needed was time to finish the work. I gave him the time when he was in the recording studio three days a week and the other nights he spent working. I would be graced with his presence four hours a week and I was supposed to be continuously supportive! Where was my support? I had to ask the age-old question: 'Is there anybody else?'

He said there wasn't, but the whole episode didn't make any sense. He chose to tell me all this on a day we had planned to spend together – quality time at last. I hadn't seen him in a week and was looking forward to seeing the man that I was going to spend the rest of my life with. Instead of seeing a film I saw my life as I knew it disappear. All the clichés about the world crumbling are right. I saw my perfect picture crumble. As it disappeared I felt my heart break. I remembered a phrase from a Spanish lesson I thought I'd long forgotten – '*Mi corazón es roto,*' 'My heart is broken.'

Over the next few weeks I tried to work out what had happened. We met and talked – in bed. I met someone else – something in me clicked when I met him, but it was the wrong time. My former love rang me and told me he was seeing somebody. She went to his university and was really nice – I told him I was happy he'd met someone. Conversation ended. An hour later the phone rang again – he needed to tell me that the person he was really seeing was someone who I knew and disliked. She lived ten minutes away from me, we'd gone to school and sixth form together, and I disliked her because I knew she had always wanted him. She was also White.

'She's not White, she's Mediterranean,' he would say.

I've never discovered exactly when he left my bed and entered hers. She'd waited four and a half years to get him. I have never had that degree of patience. Would I have hated them less if she had been Black?

My friends and I sat round a TV discussing my heartbreak, and we were like the women in *Jungle Fever* discussing this 'problem' in our community with Black men increasingly dating White women. It felt like there was definitely a fever going round, and I didn't have any intention of catching it.

I couldn't see it then, but his leaving was the best thing to happen to me. I've learned about the strength that was inside me all along, but I had to wait until the end to be able to access it. I become so entwined with another person that I lost myself. He was the first thing I thought about in the morning and the last thing at night. Now I have developed a life; I've made new friends, changed my appearance and started a career. I've evicted him from my life.

He was the wrong man for me, but in the dewy haze of first love I couldn't see clearly. I never want that pinprick feeling to come back to my fingers, or tears to leave their salty tracks in my make-up. I never want to see my perfect picture destroyed. I don't miss him, but I miss the situation – being wrapped in a cocoon of warmth and love and understanding. I miss having someone who was not only a lover but also a friend.

But *The End* helped me discover how to love myself.

Biographical Notes

CHRIS ABANI has a style of writing that has been described as Salman Rushdie meets Terry Pratchett on a hot day! His published novels include *Masters of the Board* (Delta, Nigeria, 1983) and *Sirocco* (Swan, Nigeria, 1987). His plays include *Room at the Top* (IBC TV, Nigeria, 1988) and *Song of a Broken Flute* (Uli, Nigeria, 1990) and his published poetry includes *Sundancer – Ten Poems* (Uli, Nigeria, 1990) and the collection *Kalakuta Republic* (Saqi Books, London, 2000). Several of his short stories and poems have appeared in anthologies such as *Burning Words, Flaming Images*, *em2* and *The Fire People*. Chris Abani divides his time between London and the US, plays saxophone and would like to know why kamikaze pilots wore crash-helmets!

PATIENCE AGBABI is an internationally celebrated poet committed to taking poetry into the twenty-first century. Three of her poems featured in Channel 4's *Litpop* series in 1998. Her first book was *R.A.W.* (Gecko Press, 1995), her second *Transformatrix* (Payback Press, 2000). In 1999 she was Selected Poet at the Poetry Café and Poet in Residence at Flamin' Eight, a tattoo and piercing studio in North London. She's currently working on her third collection.

STELLA AHMADOU has a BA in Linguistics and a Postgraduate Diploma in Information Technology. She has had many articles published in, among other publications, *West Africa*, *African Travel*, *African Concord* and other African-based publications. Her short stories have been published in several anthologies, including *Sojourners* and *Burning Words, Flaming Images*. She is working on the 'ultimate' crime fiction. Stella lives in London with her husband and three children.

R. AKUTU was born in the UK and started writing poems as a child. After finishing her BA and Masters in Engineering at the University of London, she progressed to writing short stories and magazine features. She has now completed her first novel and is in the process of writing her second. Asked why she writes, she says, 'Because I need to feed my soul and, like a photograph, words remain frozen in time, a testimony to who I might have been, even when I've changed or died.'

JJ AMAWORO-WILSON has worked in Egypt, Lesotho, Colombia and now London, where he teaches English as a foreign language (EFL). He has had plays performed in the UK and southern Africa and has contributed stories to various magazines and anthologies, including *Afrobeat* (Pulp Faction). He is currently writing an English-language textbook for Longman.

JOAN ANIM-ADDO was born in Grenada and lives in London. She currently divides her time between writing and lecturing. She is Chair of the Caribbean Women Writers' Alliance (CWWA) and edits the literary magazine *Mango Season*. Her plays, *At Gulley's Edge* and *Imoinda*, have both been showcased at the Oval House Theatre. Her publications include *Longest Journey: A History of Black Lewisham*; *Sugar, Spices and Human Cargo* and the new poetry collection, *Haunted By History*.

UJU ASIKA was born in Nigeria and raised mainly in the UK, but she still regards herself a true 'Naija' at heart. She is a freelance arts journalist, writing for *The Journal, New Nation, Touch* and *23:59*, among other publications. Some of her poetry is included in the anthology *Burning Words, Flaming Images* (Saks Publications). She believes in God, music, love, laughter and the healing powers of yam, plantain and beans with palm-oil stew.

LEONI ATKINS is eighteen years old, and lives in South-East London. She is studying for a BA in Media Studies at Westminster University. Her ambitions are to become the editor of a magazine and to create her own publishing company. In her spare time she likes to write articles and short stories, and she is currently researching ideas for a feature-film script.

SEFI ATTA was born in Lagos, Nigeria. She currently lives and works in the US. She has just completed her first novel.

COLIN BABB, 35, was born in East London. His parents are from Guyana and Barbados. After studying at the Polytechnic of Central London and the University of North London he worked as a journalist, language teacher, conference organizer, music promoter and librarian. He's now a Broadcast Assistant at BBC World Service. Apart from the West Indies cricket team, he is obsessed with Leeds United Football Club and the Welsh Rugby Union team.

ASHA BANJOKO is a poet and musician. In 1994 she won first prize in the Positive Images poetry competition sponsored by Nottingham County Council Library Service, and in 1995 she won joint second place in the same competition. In 1994 she also won recognition for her poem 'Racism' in a London poetry competition. She has performed her work at the Nottingham Playhouse, Wollaton Park Festival, Brewhouse Art Centre, the Royal Concert Hall and a host of community venues. Asha's hope for the future is to succeed with her writing and inspire other young people to put their thoughts and feelings down on paper.

PANYA BANJOKO a.k.a. STIKLA is a poet, story-teller and performance artist, currently studying for a Masters in Children's Literature at the University of Nottingham and writing her first novel, *Soul Sister*. She has been writing poetry since 1992 and performing since 1993. Her work is varied, focusing on love, and romance politricks and conflicts. 'My love for poetry is like sweet-smelling incense, affecting my sensibilities, energized by an inner sense to make sense of the nonsense.'

LINDA BELLOS was born in London in 1950, the daughter of a Nigerian father and a Polish/Jewish mother. She is a socialist and a lesbian feminist and a proud African woman who enjoys working alongside African men. She is amused to find that the British media cannot cope with any Black person who does not fit neatly into their pigeon-holes. 'Yes, I am quite "articulate" for a nigger!'

FLOELLA BENJAMIN is a broadcaster, independent producer, the author of more than twenty children's books and she has her own television company. Her children's production *Jamboree* is broadcast on ITV, and *Caribbean Light*, with Savoy chef Anton Edelmann, on Carlton. *Hullaballoo* has been sold to thirty countries and won the Parent's Choice Award in the USA for best children's video. She is Chair of the Women of the Year Lunch and Chair of Television BAFTA (British Academy of Film and Television Arts). She is also a member of both the board of governors for the National Film and Television School and the Stamp Advisory Committee, and Vice-President of NCH Action for Children.

bLACKmALE (Richard Mkloma) is inspired by life, personal experience and observations and presents RA: SCRIPT – Rhythm, Art, Poetry, Spirituality, Creativity, Reality, Innovation/Intensity, Positivity, Truth. He has performed at various venues in Europe, including the Jazz Café, Apples and Snakes, DJ Pogo's Lyrical Lounge in London and Calabash 98 in Amsterdam. He contributed tracks to the *Chocolate Art* EP and has performed in New York at the Nuyorican Poets' Café, where his performance was filmed for BET's Teen Summit, broadcast across America. Other TV appearances include Sky Digital's *Raw TV* and various programmes on Channel 4.

VALERIE BLOOM has performed her poetry extensively throughout Britain and the Caribbean. Her books for children include *Touch Mi, Tell Mi* (Bogle L'Ouverture, 1983, reprinted in 1990), *Duppy Jamboree* (Cambridge University Press, 1992), *Fruits* (Macmillan, 1997) and *Ackee, Breadfruit Callaloo* (Bogle L'Ouverture and Macmillan, Caribbean, 1999). Her selected spoken works, *Yuh Hear Bout?* (57 Productions, 1997), is available on audiotape. Forthcoming publications include *New Baby* (Macmillan) and *Selected Poems* (Macmillan).

HENRY BONSU was born in Manchester to Ghanaian parents in 1967 and became a journalist after taking a Modern Languages degree at Magdalen College, Oxford. He has worked on Radio 4's *Today* programme and BBC2's *Black Britain*. Now an award-winning writer and broadcaster, he has presented *Upfront* on GLR and *Word Up!* on Radio 5 *Live*. He writes regularly for national newspapers and the Black press. He is unmarried and lives in South London.

MALIKA BOOKER was born in England to parents of Guyanese and Grenadian descent and was brought up in Guyana. She has a degree in anthropology from Goldsmiths College in London. Her poetry has appeared in *The Fire People* (Payback Press, 1998) and *Bittersweet* (Women's Press, 1998), and she has been featured on the Tongue & Groove compilation *One Hell of a Storm*. She has performed her one-woman show *Absolution* at the Battersea Arts Centre in London and is currently working on a poetry collection.

BEN BOUSQUET is an African from the Caribbean, born in St Lucia. He served as a councillor in the Royal Borough of Kensington and Chelsea from 1978 to 1990, increasing his share of the vote at each election. He was selected as a parliamentary candidate in 1983, the only person in the Labour Party in the south of England to increase his majority that year. He was reselected in 1987, increasing his majority again, and taking Kensington from being a safe Tory seat to a winnable Labour one. Now he lives in the country, consults and appears occasionally on TV documentaries, lectures on Black history and is a consultant to the Imperial War Museum on the history of the West Indies during the First and Second World Wars. He is co-author of *West Indian Women in World War II*, and his next book is forthcoming from Lawrence and Wishart. He is also Chairman of the Association of Black Football Supporters and the cricket coach for County of Suffolk's under-twelves and under-thirteens teams.

JUDITH BRYAN grew up in London, of Jamaican and Guyanese parents. She trained as a social worker and spent many years in this profession. Her first novel, *Bernard and the Cloth Monkey*, won the 1997 SAGA Prize. In 1999 she was awarded a New London Writers Award by the London Arts Board and a K. Blundell Trust Award by the Society of Authors. She is currently working on her second novel.

JEAN BUFFONG was born in Grenada. She has lived in London for many years and is a successful writer. Her novels are *Jump up and Kiss Me,*

Snowflakes in the Sun and the much-acclaimed *Under the Silk Cotton Tree*. Her work can be found in numerous anthologies. Jean is the writer of the foreword of the British edition of *Sisterfire*, an anthology of African-American women's writing. She is a member of the Caribbean Women Writers Alliance and the Chairperson of the Ananse Society.

MARGARET BUSBY was born in Ghana and educated in Britain, earning an Honours English degree from London University. On graduating, she co-founded the publishing company Allison & Busby, of which she was Editorial Director until 1987. In recent years she has worked freelance as an editor, literary consultant, reviewer and broadcaster and has received several awards for her work. Her writing has appeared in many publications, and she compiled the acclaimed anthology *Daughters of Africa: An International Anthology of Words and Writing by Women of African Descent.*

FAUSTIN CHARLES was born in Trinidad and now lives in London. He is a poet, novelist and professional story-teller, and has toured Britain and the Continent. He is the author of the poetry books *The Expatriate, Crab Track* and *Days and Nights in the Magic Forest*, the novels *Signposts of the Jumbie* and *The Black Magic Man of Brixton*. His most recent publications are *The Selfish Crocodile* and *Once Upon an Animal*.

BECKY AYEBIA CLARKE (or Ayebia Ribeiro-Ayeh) was born and grew up in Ghana. She came to England at the age of sixteen and continued her studies, gaining a BA Honours degree in English Literature. She now works for a publishing company in the UK as Literature Submissions Editor. Her passion for African cultural history and thought and for Pan-Africanism has produced two children's books in Heinemann's Junior African Writers series. A third children's book is in the pipeline. She is a mother, a wife and an active campaigner for African literature which corrects European misconceptions and stereotypic images of Africans. She lives and works in Oxfordshire.

MERLE COLLINS is Grenadian. She is Professor of English and Comparative Literature at the University of Maryland where she teaches Caribbean literature and creative writing. A writer of poetry and fiction, her publications include *Because the Dawn Breaks* (London, Karia Press, 1984), *Rotten Pomerack* (London, Virago, 1992) and a selection of poetry on audiotape, *Butterfly* (London, 57 Productions, 1997). She is also the author of two novels, *Angel* (Women's Press, 1987) and *The Colour of Forgetting* (Virago, 1995).

DAVID DABYDEEN was born and raised in Guyana. He read English at Cambridge University and is Professor of Literature at the University of Warwick and Guyana's ambassador to UNESCO. He has published three collections of poetry, *Slave Song* (1984), *Coolie Odyssey* (1988) and *Turner* (1993); and four novels, *The Intended* (1991), *Disappearance* (1997), *The Counting House* (1996) and *A Harlot's Progress* (1999). He has also published two studies on the English artist William Hogarth, *Hogarth's Blacks: Images of Blacks in Eighteenth-Century English Art* (1985) and *Hogarth, Walpole and Commercial Britain* (1987). He has co-authored and edited *Early Black Writers in Britain* (1992), *A Reader's Guide to West Indian and Black British Literature* (1986), *The Black Presence in English Literature* (1985) and *Across the Dark Waters: Ethnicity and Indian Identity in the Caribbean* (1996). He has been awarded the Commonwealth Poetry Prize (1984), the Greater London Council Literature Prize (1985), and the Guyana Prize (1992).

MORGAN DALPHINIS was born in St Lucia, West Indies, and arrived in England aged eleven. He has published many articles and two books on Caribbean and African languages and on educational issues. He has taught in all education phases except primary and worked as a general, senior and chief inspector in London education authorities. He is currently Executive Manager, Academic Development, City College Birmingham. Morgan has a Ph.D. in Caribbean and African languages, an MBA, a BA in Linguistics and Hausa and a PGCE in ESOL and French.

FERDINAND DENNIS was born in Kingston, Jamaica, and came to Britain at the age of eight. He is a graduate of the University of Leicester and Birkbeck College (University of London). He has contributed to many newspapers and magazines, including *The Voice*, the *Guardian*, the *New Statesman* and *Granta*. His short stories have been broadcast on BBC

Radio 4, and published in *West Africa Magazine, Critical Quarterly* and *Kunapipi*. He is the author of two travel books, *Behind the Frontlines: Journey into Afro-Britain* (winner of the 1988 Martin Luther King Prize) and *Back to Africa* (1992). His novels are *The Sleepless Summer, The Last Blues Dance* and *Duppy Conqueror*. He lives in London.

BUCHI EMECHETA is an award-winning novelist and has published nineteen novels, including children's books, which have been translated into fourteen languages. She is a prolific essayist, and her essays have been published in many books and journals. She has also written plays for BBC and Granada television. In the eighties she was selected as one of the twenty Best British Young Writers. *The Bride Price* was chosen by the Library of Congress in the US as one of the best novels of the century. She has been a librarian, teacher and community worker and lectured in many universities around the globe. Buchi Emecheta has a street named after her in the London Borough of Lambeth. She is currently working on her latest novel, *The New Tribe*.

BRENDA EMMANUS has had a varied and impressive career in the media. Known nationally as a television presenter her work has included *The Clothes Show, Black Britain, Holiday* and the award-winning *This Morning*. Brenda is also an accomplished radio journalist who has worked for both the BBC and commercial stations. As a trained print journalist, she has contributed celebrity profiles, fashion, travel and topical features to a diverse range of publications, including the *Observer, The Voice* and *Pride*. Creative writing has always been a hobby she has wanted to take further. Brenda lives in South London. Her parents are from St Lucia.

ANDREA ENISUOH was born in Manchester to Nigerian and Jamaican parents. She holds a degree in Politics and Caribbean Studies from the University of North London and a postgraduate diploma in journalism. Highly commended in the 1999 New Journalist Awards, she now works as a freelance journalist. She has contributed to several publications, including *Hip-Hop Connection*, the *Evening Standard* and *New Nation*. Her short story, 'Courage' appears in the anthology *Playing Sidney Poitier and*

Other Stories. Andrea is currently working on her first novel, *A Foreign Constituency.*

RAYMOND ENISUOH was born of Nigerian and Jamaican parentage in Manchester in 1975. Aged twenty, he moved to London, attended Middlesex University and graduated with a BA Hons. in Third World Studies. As a writer and poet, influenced by African-American authors, he attempts to educate, inspire and uplift Black youth. Enisuoh has been published in *The New Nation*, *Alarm* and *Calabash* magazines. He is also a winner of the 1990 ACER young Black writer's competition. He is currently completing his first collection of poems, entitled *Chocolate Dreams*, and is also working on a novel entitled *Searching for Elijah.*

TREVA ETIENNE is an accomplished actor, producer and director. On television, he has played leading roles in dramas such as *London's Burning*, *Casualty* and *The Paradise Club*. On stage he has played the title role in *Macbeth* at the National Theatre and Claudio in *Measure for Measure* in Boston, USA. He has been writing and directing for the stage for fifteen years. He was assistant director on the popular TV series *The Real McCoy* in 1995, and in 1999 his short film *Driving Miss Crazy* was second-prize winner at the Acapulco Film Festival. He is on the Film Policy Review Group Action Committee to implement initiatives on developing the future of the British Film Industry.

DIANA OMO EVANS is a writer and journalist whose articles and poems have been published in *Pride*, *Touch*, *The Voice*, *2nd Generation*, and *Poetry Today* anthologies. She was previously Arts and Music Editor for *Pride* and was recently nominated Best Print Journalist in the Ethnic Minority Media Awards. She is half Nigerian and half English, twenty-seven years old, and currently lives and works in London as a freelance editor and writer.

BERNARDINE EVARISTO was born and raised in London. She is the author of a poetry book, *Island of Abraham*, and a verse novel, *Lara*, which won the Ethnic Minority Media Awards (EMMA) Best Novel Award in 1999. She tours worldwide and has held residencies in Zimbabwe and New

York. In 1999 she wrote the signature poem for HM Government's millennium brochure *A View from Britain*. She lives in Notting Hill, London.

VERNELLA FULLER was born in St Catherine, Jamaica. She was educated at Sussex University, the Institute of Education, London University and Goldsmiths College, London. She currently teaches part-time at the Institute of European Studies and is also doing a Ph.D., researching the achievement of Black pupils in schools. Vernella has written two novels to date, *Going Back Home* (1992) and *Unlike Normal Women* (Women's Press, 1995). She has also contributed to *Something to Savour* (Women's Press, 1996, Laurie Critchley and H. Windrath, eds.) and *Caribbean Women Writers: Fiction in English* (Macmillan, 1999, Mary Conde and Thorunn Lonsdale, eds.). She is currently working on another novel and a biography. Vernella has a fourteen-year-old daughter, Alisha Nadine.

MAHLETE-TSIGÉ GETACHEW is an Ethiopian undergraduate at Somerville College, Oxford, where she is reading Philosophy, Politics and Economics and has edited the University's *Alternative Prospectus*. She has no desire to be a doctor. Or a lawyer. Or an engineer.

SALENA 'SALIVA' GODDEN is known for taking poetry out of the classroom into club culture – making poetry to dance to. She is reputedly one of the most visceral, salacious and raw-gut talents around, and is a twenty-first-century visionary, with her company, Saltpetre, which records and produces definitive spoken-word collections, released on CD quarterly. She released *Egg Yolk Planet Fried*, her début album, in February 2000. She fears the Lord, makes excellent soup and bears an uncanny resemblance to rock guitarist Slash.

EVELYN GOODING was born in London in 1971 to Sierra Leonan parents. She is the mother of two children and has a Diploma in Education. She has worked with children in a variety of settings with different local authorities. In her spare time she likes to read literature and play netball. She would like to write about children, their education and home life, especially Black children, some time in the future.

BONNIE GREER was born in Chicago, Illinois, where she studied play-writing with David Mamet. She lived in New York City, where she worked as a playwright and dramaturge. She moved to London in 1986 and became a British citizen in 1997. As well as being an award-winning theatre and radio dramatist, she is a published novelist, short-story writer and broadcaster. Her second novel, *The Acrobat's Assistant,* will be published in 2001, and in 2000, *Riding the 9.03 – Short Stories and a Novella.* She is also writing a play based on her new novel. She is married and lives in London.

JANE GRELL was born and grew up on the island of Dominica. She has lived and worked as a teacher in Waltham Forest since 1976. She is a story-teller whose brand of story-telling – rhythm, games, poetry, song and story – is steeped in the rural African-Caribbean oral tradition. Her publications include *A New Life in Britain* and *Dominica,* and *A Small Caribbean Island.* Her work has been widely anthologized, and her latest publication, *Dr Knickerbocker and Other Poems,* is a core book in many primary schools.

CYNTHIA HAMILTON first began writing poetry at the age of seventeen. She began performing two years later in Liverpool while studying for her literature degree. Since then she has performed her poetry on radio and TV and has won several slams (becoming the UK Allcomers Slam Champion of 1996). She has also had two short stories published, and her poems have appeared in *Poetry Review* and the *Bloomsbury Book of Love Poems.* She lives in London, where she is a full-time bookseller, and performs as often as possible.

MICHAEL HAMILTON was born in 1971 in Shepherd's Bush, West London, and is a freelance media artist. He studied Film and Photography at Tower Hamlets College. His present work in progress is *84 Westbourne Road,* a short film he wrote, directed, produced and edited about youths and hostel-living.

ALLISTER HARRY was born in 1970 in Dagenham, Essex. He is a freelance journalist working in newspapers, magazines and television. He writes about arts and entertainment, and his features have appeared in the *Guardian*, the *Observer* and *GQ*. He was film editor and a columnist at *The Voice* and has researched and written for television. He also teaches journalism workshops and lectures on cinema. 'T E HEADMAS ERS OFF CE' is his first published piece of fiction.

CYRIL HUSBANDS is a story-teller, poet, song-writer and performer. His inspirations are his relationships with his son, partner, family and friends, his deeply held pan-African ideals, and his radical humanist politics. Cyril's preoccupations are relationships, politics, and telling stories about people who the mainstream ignores or marginalizes. Cyril aims to communicate in accessible, affecting and motivating ways, by seeking to find 'beauty in truth and truth in beauty'. He is currently working on a novel entitled *Schiz the Cat* and a collection of poetry and short stories entitled *Barefoot on Sacred Ground*.

HEATHER IMANI was born in London to Jamaican parents and is a writer of prose and poetry. Her short story 'Elenah's Telling' is published in the anthology *Playing Sidney Poitier and Other Stories* (SAKS Publications). She has also read her work at the Stoke Newington Arts Festival, Brent Black History Month and Brent Libraries Literature Month. Heather compiled and edited the publication *In Our Own Words: Memoirs of Caribbean Elders*, for a community reminiscence project.

IJEOMA INYAMA is a Londoner of Nigerian heritage. Her short story, 'Stephanie Brewster', was included in *School Tales* (Women's Press, 1990) and in 1997, the X Press published her first novel, *Sistas on a Vibe*, which was the winner of their X-Press Yourself competition. She is currently working on her second novel, *Strictly Roots*, for the X Press.

UCHENNA IZUNDU is twenty-one years old and of Nigerian origin, although she grew up in Scotland. She is currently studying law at King's College, London. Uchenna has enjoyed writing since she was knee-high, and her hobbies include reading, aerobics, acting, listening to music and seeing her friends, with whom she enjoys a good laugh! She is a published short-story writer and has written articles for the *Guardian* and *New Nation*. She hopes to become a journalist writing on social issues.

AMRYL JOHNSON was born in Trinidad and came to England aged eleven. Her education continued at Clark's Grammar School, London, and the University of Kent, where she gained an honours degree in English with African and Caribbean Studies. Her publications include *Long Road to Nowhere*, *Sequins for a Ragged Hem*, *Tread Carefully in Paradise* and *Calling*. Often anthologized in England, her poems have also been translated into French, German and Spanish. She lives in Coventry.

CATHERINE R. JOHNSON studied film at St Martin's School of Art. She has written six novels for young adults, including *Other Colours* (Women's Press), *Landlocked* (Pont) and *In Black and White* (OUP). Her short stories have been included in *Britpulp* (Sceptre) and *Allnighter* (Pulp Books), and broadcast on Radio 4.

LINTON KWESI JOHNSON was born in Clarendon, Jamaica, in 1952. He came to England in 1963. Johnson has published four collections of poetry and released twelve albums, and his work has been translated into Italian and German. He has toured all over the world with the Dennis Bovell Dub Band, as well as to give poetry readings. His twentieth-anniversary album *More Time* set 'If I woz a Tap-Natch Poet' to Johnson's unique brand of reggae music.

JACKIE KAY is an award-winning poet and novelist. She has had three collections of poetry published, including *The Adoption Papers*. Her latest poetry collection *Off Colour*, was shortlisted for the Poetry Society's T. S. Eliot prize in 1998. Her first novel, *Trumpet*, won the 1998 Guardian Fiction Prize and the Author's Club First Novel Award. 'Piano 4 p.m.' was commissioned by BBC Radio 4 as part of the Book of Hours for National Poetry Day.

FOWOKAN GEORGE KELLY was born in Kingston, Jamaica, in 1943. He describes himself as a visual griot, who records and expresses the essence of the individuals in his community along with their deeds through the medium of sculpture. He is also an occasional moulder and sculptor of words.

KEVIN LE GENDRE was born in England to Trinidadian parents. He studied French at the universities of Lancaster and Bristol and has lived and worked in France, Senegal and the Caribbean. As a journalist he writes predominantly about Black music and culture. Publications to which he regularly contributes include *Echoes*, *Jazzwise*, *The Journal*, *Independent on Sunday* and *Marie-Claire*. Kevin Le Gendre was born on the same day as Emperor Haile Selassie and his godson Delano Gournet-Moore.

JUDITH LEWIS was born in Hackney in 1962 to Bajan migrants. Her interest in writing started at the age of eleven and was fostered by her English teacher. Originally influenced by Thomas Hardy and Shakespeare, she discovered Derek Walcott, James Baldwin and Chinua Achebe, and then a plethora of Black literature. She has dual nationality and visits Barbados regularly.

JOHN LYONS is a Trinidadian poet and painter living in West Yorkshire. He has been twice winner of the Peterloo Poets Afro-Caribbean/Asian prize and was commended in the Poetry Society National Poetry Competition. His collections are *Lure of the Cascadura*, *Behind the Carnival* and *Sun Rises in the North*. His poems have also been widely anthologized, and he has performed both on radio and television. As a painter, he has exhibited nationally and internationally and has works in both public and private collections.

DR P. VINCENT MAGOMBE is a Ugandan writer, based in London, whose works include poetry, children's books, a theatre play entitled *The Fall and Trial of Idi Amin*, and a BBC radio play, *In the Shadow of the Russian Winter*. He is a co-ordinator of the African Literature Forum, as well as the Writers in Exile Programme of International PEN. He is also the Director of the media agency Africa Inform International and an expert analyst on African affairs for various UK TV and radio networks. He is currently a fellow of the George Bell Institute and a lecturer at the London City Literary Institute. He is the author of numerous Africa-related research materials.

E. A. MARKHAM was born in Montserrat in 1939 and completed his education in Britain, which has been his home since 1956. He has worked in the theatre as playwright and director, in the media and as a literary editor. His publications include a novel, *Marking Time*, six collections of poems, two of short stories and a travel book. He has edited a collection of Caribbean poetry, *Hinterland* (Bloodaxe, 1989), and *The Penguin Book of Caribbean Short Stories* (1996). Markham has worked in the universities of Humberside, Ulster and Newcastle and is now Professor of Creative Writing at Sheffield Hallam University. In 1997 he was awarded the Certificate of Honour by the Government of Montserrat.

HOPE MASSIAH was born in Barbados and brought up in south London. She is a writer, management consultant, trainer and researcher. Her poetry has been published in *Bittersweet, Contemporary Black Women's Poetry* (1998), and her stories appear in *Does Your Mama Know?, An Anthology of Black Lesbian Coming Out Stories* (1997), and as the title story in *Playing Sidney Poitier and Other Stories* (1999).

RONNIE MCGRATH is a founder member of the cultural group, London Afro-Blok, who represented Great Britain at the 1994 Commonwealth Games in Canada. In 1993 he was published and commended for his poetry by ACER (Afro-Caribbean Education and Resource Centre), who also published and awarded his writing first place in 1994. He has just completed his first novel, *Rice and Potato*, and an MA in Novel-Writing at Manchester University.

AMANI NAPHTALI is a writer, dramatist and ritual artist. He was a founder member of The Double Edge Theatre company and is now the director of a newly established theatre company, Creative Origins, and Director of the School of Afrikan Performance Media. He has recently completed two documentaries for Channel 4 television, one entitled *On A Northern Tip* and the other on the Black contribution to the Mersey Sound. His future plans include producing both theatre and film. 'Let my words sound.'

ROSALINE NWAGBOSO was born in 1948 in Zaria, Northern Nigeria, but came originally from Mbawsi, Abia State, Nigeria. She grew up in Northern Nigeria and studied with the Open University, where she obtained a degree in social sciences. She also holds a postgraduate diploma in librarianship. She has written and had published short stories, articles and book reviews and has written a book on African women in Britain. She is married with two children and works as a professional librarian. She also serves as a Justice of the Peace.

KECHI NWAJIAKU is a policy adviser for a British Aid Agency, presently living and working in Senegal, where she has been based for the last two years. She has written extensively on politics and social change in West Africa and is currently planning a doctoral thesis on politics in the Niger Delta of Nigeria. She also loves to sing jazz and blues and performs regularly with a Senegalese band.

NYANTAH is the pen name of a twenty-two-year-old London-based writer. She has written for *Calabash* and *Artrage*. Her parents are from Ghana and she currently works in public relations. She also enjoys writing poetry. She says, 'I wrote *The End* to help finally seal that chapter in my life. It's time to move on.'

DENRELE OGUNWA is British born, a Nigerian of Yoruba descent. She is a journalist, writer and poet, and her work has been published in various newspapers and magazines in the UK and Nigeria. She currently writes the popular arts column 'Artzone' for *New Nation*.

AKINWALE OLADIMEJI is a pudgy, anarchic product of a repressed childhood. No wonder his first tale to be published is about voyeurism. Living in south London, which he hates heartily, he is planning to keep writing till he becomes a Nobel Literature Prize winner – in the next two years. Failing that, he will apply his creative talents to boxing and have his brains beaten to a mush.

OLA OPESAN is the author of two books, *Another Lonely Londoner* (published under the pseudonym Gbenga Agbenugba) and *Many Rivers to Cross*. He has broadcast and published articles, short stories and poetry on BBC World Service and in *The Trumpet, Black Filmmaker* and other publications. Ola works as the editor of *Newsmakers* magazine and as a media consultant to the satellite channel AIT. He currently lives in London with his wife and two kids.

KOYE OYEDEJI: Do not judge me on the way that I speak or appreciate me for the things that they have permitted you to foresee. It's the way that I write that allows you to descry that my blood is not blue and my eyes are not green. The shadow of my body is the man that I am and that is the subconscious that controls our land. A shadow that only comes to light in certain conditions, conditioned are our words.

IONIE RICHARDS was born in Birmingham and is now based in London. She is a poet and writer and a founder member of a now-disbanded women's theatre group, Hucadzi, which wrote and performed plays tackling the issue of racism in education. These plays were the platform for her poems to be heard in the eighties. This anthology will be her first opportunity to publish her work. She is currently working on her first novel.

VANESSA RICHARDS is a Brixton-based and Vancouver-raised poet and has been a performing artist since 1982, and a writer since small days. She is also the Joint Artistic Director of Mannafest. The company is a leading Live Art conduit delivering exciting experiments in literature, music, poetry, DJ culture, visual art, new media and education. Most recently her work has appeared in: *The Fire People, Bittersweet, 360° – a Revolution of Black Poets* and *West Coast Line – North: New African Canadian Writing*.

SOL B. RIVER is a writer and director. His work to date includes *Identity, Dead Good Actor, Testosterone* (all 1993), *Moor Masterpieces* (1994, West Yorkshire Playhouse), *Ganga Psychosis, The Rat, Anaxos Gaspenster Lydora* (all 1995), *Mau Mau Manœuvres* (1996) and *To Rahtid* (Talawa Theatre Company, 1996). He wrote *The White Witch of Rose Hall* for the University of the West Indies fiftieth anniversary (1998) and other productions include *Unbroken* (Phoenix Dance Company, 1998) and *48–98* (Talawa Theatre

Company, 1998). His BBC Radio 4 writing credits include *March Against Fear* and *Making Waves*. He has directed *Brace Yourself* (1999), a documentary for Channel 4 with the RJC Dance Company and in the same year he directed the film *The Bitterest Pill*. Sol B. River's plays are published by Oberon Books.

MAUREEN ROBERTS is Grenadian and British. She grew up in London but has lived in Jamaica, America and the Cayman Islands. She taught English at Priory School in Jamaica and the Cayman Islands High School. She writes both prose and poetry. Her poems have appeared on walls (Poetry on Walls series), on London buses and in numerous anthologies. She is a member of Fishbone and Rhythm Writers writing groups. She has developed and managed theatre companies in England and the Cayman Islands. In Cayman she was a co-founder of the Cayman National Theatre Company, and her theatre company in England, ACT, has received substantial lottery funding. She also does community work with Sankofa Learning Centre and the Grenada St John's Library Project. She is operations manager of Ithaca College's London Centre.

ROGER ROBINSON is a poet and short-story writer. His poetry has appeared in anthologies such as *The Fire People*, and his short stories have been included in *Afrobeat* and the literary magazine *Gargoyle*. His first short-story collection will be published in 2000.

LEONE ROSS is a critically acclaimed writer. Her stories have been published in several anthologies. She has written two novels, *All the Blood is Red* (ARP, 1996), which was nominated for the 1997 Orange Prize, and *Orange Laughter* (ARP, 1999), reissued by Anchor Press and published in hardback in the US by Farrar, Straus and Giroux (autumn 2000). Leone was recently chosen to represent Britain at the Gothenberg Book Festival. She works as a creative-writing teacher and is presently writing her third novel.

JOY RUSSELL was born in Belize, raised in Canada and has lived in London for a number of years, where she works in television. Her work has appeared in various publications in the US and Canada, including *Don't*

Ask Me Why, An Anthology of Short Stories by Black Women and, most recently, in the UK anthology *The Fire People*.

R A SAMUEL has a City and Guilds qualification in Radio Journalism. He has worked at RTM radio, on the Sound Radio (RSL) and has taught radio journalism at Hackney Summer University. He writes book reviews for *Calabash* and was the guest editor for *Calabash* issue 6. In 1999, he was a winner in the Eastside Writer's Competition for novelists. He has just completed his first novel, *Hawk in the Air*.

RAY SHELL is a youngish American actor who studied play-writing and mass communications at Emerson College, graduating with a Bachelor of Fine Arts degree; he is also a member of Alpha-Phi-Alpha Fraternity. He has lived in Britain since the late seventies and has starred in numerous West End productions, such as *Miss Saigon* and *Starlight Express*. Ray also works in the music industry as a producer, voice therapist and creator of the TAIP program; his clients include Damage, Jamiroquois, Juliet Roberts and D'Influence. ICED is his first novel and he is currently working on a new novel, *Host*, and a musical, *White Folks*, which will be produced in 2000.

LABI SIFFRE is the author of three poetry books, *Nigger, Blood on the Page* and *Monument* and a play, *DeathWrite*. He is the composer and performer of the Ivor Novello award-winning hit song '(Something Inside) So Strong' and eight albums. Born in London, 25 June 1945, Labi Siffre is Gay, Black, 5 foot 10½ inches and likes a very dry vodka martini. He and his partner Peter have lived together for thirty-five years.

LEMN SISSAY is one of Britain's most popular performance poets. He recently published his latest poetry collection, *Morning Breaks in the Elevator* (Payback Press). He wrote '21st Century Poem' on the seminal dance album *Leftism* by Leftfield. His poems are laid into the streets of Manchester. He is recording an album for release in Germany and writing a children's book for Bloomsbury. His late father was a pilot for Ethiopian Airlines and his mother works for the UN in New York. He has also edited a definitive collection of new Black British poets, *The Fire People*.

DOROTHEA SMARTT is of Barbadian heritage. She was Brixton Market's first Poet in Residence, and an Institute of Contemporary Arts Attached Live Artist. She's contributed to *Bittersweet* (Women's Press, 1998), *The Fire People* (Payback Press, 1998), and *Mythic Women/Real Women* (Faber, 2000). Her Medusaplay Project, an ongoing live art work-in-progress premiered with Apples & Snakes for the 1998 British Festival of Visual Theatre. Awarded several commissions and bursaries, she's a member of Black Arts Alliance and an Afro-Style School 'graduate'. She lectures part-time at Birkbeck College, and is currently working on her first poetry collection.

NATALIE STEWART has been active on the performance-poetry circuit for the past year. She has had a massive impact on the for ever growing spoken-word scene and has had memorable performances at the Jazz Café, Black Pepper and Urban Griots. This young lady is the co-creator of 'Floetry', which has been described as an evolved form of poetry; she herself simply 'breaks it down' as *'poetic delivery with musical intent'*.

YVONNE ST HILL is a Barbadian/British writer, poet, holistic-lifestyles consultant and holistic-development planner. She has worked in sustainable development for eighteen years and promotes Holistic Development. She is also trained in healing and personal empowerment and has packaged her approaches into a Holistic Lifeways concept which she now integrates into mainstream development planning through her Holistic Lifeways for Holistic Development Programme. She writes widely on sustainability, healing and empowerment issues and also convenes workshops on these subjects. She has just completed her book, *Coming Into Wholeness: Planetary Transformation through Individual Healing.*

SUANDI is of Nigerian and British heritage, has been a performance poet since 1985 and in recent years has worked in Live Art. She tours nationally and internationally, and her last ICA commission, *The Story of M*, has received critical acclaim in both the UK and North America. Her work was recognized with an OBE in the Queen's 1999 New Year Honour's List following her Winston Churchill Fellowship in 1996. She is the cultural director of the voluntary organization Black Arts Alliance.

RAFIEL SUNMONU was born in 1983. He attended Darrick Wood junior school and gained a scholarship to Colfe's School, where he also won tennis colours and prizes for German. He is currently studying for his A levels, taking English, German, History and Japanese. Rafiel is a contributor to the publication *A Companion to Contemporary Black British Culture*, due to be published by Routledge in 2000. He has two brothers, Raman and Akeem.

VÉRONIQUE TADJO is a writer, illustrator and painter from Côte d'Ivoire. She earned her doctorate from the Sorbonne, Paris, in African-American literature and civilization. In 1983 she went to Howard University, Washington DC, on a Fulbright research scholarship, then returned to the University of Abidjan as a lecturer until 1993. She has written a collection of poems, *Laterite*, which won the literary prize of the Agence de Cooperation Culturelle et Technique, and three novels, *A Vol d'Oiseau*, *Le Royaume Aveugle* and *Champs de Bataille et d'Amour*. She has also written and illustrated several books for young people.

CHARMION TOGBA was born in 1978, in Liberia, West Africa, into a family of seven sisters and one brother. In 1991, civil war forced his family to flee to Sierra Leone. His mum and he soon left for England, where he now resides. He completed his secondary education at Brent Side High and began a musical career as a producer. He turned to writing and, while in juvenile detention, realized his ability. Now he works as a music producer, writer, scriptwriter and recording artist, amongst other business projects.

JOANNA TRAYNOR has published two novels, *Sister Josephine*, which won the SAGA Prize in 1996, and *Divine* (1998). In July 2000, her third novel, *Bitch Money*, is published by Bloomsbury. A former nurse and computer consultant, she works in the training industry as a press and PR manager, writing specialist articles on training and employment issues. She lives in Devon with her partner and two elderly dogs.

DEBORAH VAUGHAN is first-generation Caribbean British. She was born and raised in the Midlands. Her writing is a celebration and tribute to Caribbean people's *joie de vivre*, wit and tenacity. Her short play *Casualties* won a Soho Theatre prize and was staged in 1998. A law graduate, keen essayist and performer, she is completing her first novel and a book of short stories. She is Vice-Chair of the Caribbean Women Writers Alliance (WWA).

GEMMA WEEKES is twenty-one years old and is currently in her final year at Brunel University (studying English and film studies). Her interests include singing jazz, writing poetry, fiction, non-fiction and, eventually, drama. (She WILL write for food!) She used to include a boyfriend (easy come, easy go) in her life but now she fills up her empty days and nights with chocolate and poetry slams (sad, huh?). Anyway, she hopes to publish loads more stuff and be a total celebrity some day. Maybe even get a record deal . . . watch this space.

NOLAN WEEKES is a performance poet based in London. He is part of the collective 3 + 1.

MARIE GUISE WILLIAMS is a Mancunian who recently moved to London. Her repertoire includes poetry, fiction and creative-writing workshops. She has edited various publications and has featured in several collections, most recently *The Fire People, Healing Strategies for Women at War (seven black women poets)* and *Stranger at My Table*. In 1999 she received an Arts Council bursary towards her first novel, *Blood Orange*.

PATRICK WILMOT was born in Kingston, Jamaica, studied philosophy at Yale and Vanderbilt universities and he taught sociology at Ahmadu Bello University, Nigeria, for eighteen years. He has published books on sociology and political science, as well as a collection of poems, short stories and academic articles. Wilmot has been a columnist, political adviser, and reader for the African and Caribbean Writers series at Heinemann. He was one of the first victims of the Babangida-Abacha dictatorship in Nigeria, abducted from the street by security men and expelled in March 1988. He is married to Makki Saratu Wilmot.

SUSAN YEARWOOD lives in London and currently teaches part-time at the City Literary Institute and the East London Black Women's Organization.

She is also a Ph.D. student at Sheffield Hallam University, studying creative writing and is writing a thesis on looking at madness within Black literature. Susan reached second place in a national short-story competition. She has also published book and theatre reviews in national newspapers, magazines and newsletters. She has had a short story published in *Playing Sidney Poitier and Other Stories*, and articles on Alice Walker and African-American Culture in *Censorship: An International Encyclopedia*.

BENJAMIN ZEPHANIAH writes poetry which is strongly influenced by the music and poetry of Jamaica and street politics. He was the first person to record with The Wailers after the death of Bob Marley, in a musical tribute to Nelson Mandela, and since then has regularly worked with children in South African townships. In 1998 he was awarded an honorary doctorate by the University of North London. He works passionately and is patron for human, child and animal rights. He has published several poetry books for both adults and young people and recently published *Face*, his first novel for young people. He has also made musical recordings and written for stage, TV and radio.

PUBLISHER'S NOTE

After the advance payment for this book, to cover editors' and contributors' fees, has earned out against royalties, all future royalties will be divided equally between the following charities:

The Sickle Cell Society, 54 Station Road, London NW10 4UA

The African and Caribbean Finance Forum (Education), Lafone House, The Leather Market, Weston Street, London SE1 3HN